ALL FOR LOVE

All for Love

Rosie Boycott

Chatto & Windus

LONDON

Published in 1988 by
Chatto & Windus Limited
30 Bedford Square
London WC1B 3RP

A CIP catalogue record for this book is available from the British Library.
ISBN 0-7011 3071 7

Copyright © Rosie Boycott 1988

Typeset at The Spartan Press Ltd,
Lymington, Hants
Printed in Great Britain by
Redwood Burn Ltd,
Trowbridge, Wiltshire

For Daisy
and David

Prologue

Years later, Violet Harcourt could still remember every detail of the *Wilhelmina*'s limping escape from Singapore, and sometimes she would even dream about those days, so unlike any others in her life.

It had been her first experience of war, of seeing a close friend die violently, of risking violent death herself at every turn, of having no one – except herself – to depend on. And throughout there had been all those terrified children dependent on her.

She had come to see that the voyage had been a rite of passage, marking the time she had become fully her own person. Waking from one of the recurring *Wilhelmina* dreams she often found that she was smiling.

For though there were terrible memories, as often as not the dominant elements were not visual but the sound of a voice, the voice of the journalist, Tony Quigley. Quigley complaining about prickly heat or the way the chemicals in the fire-hoses had spoilt his expensive London shoes. Quigley revealing his – terrifyingly intimate – knowledge of her life. Quigley trying to make love to her.

'Come on, Vi,' he would say. 'This is the bedroom hour and I've found this very drinkable overproof rum. Let me lead you to my boudoir.'

'Sooner a goat than you. Sooner a hippo.'

He would give his ugly, exultant laugh.

'You don't mean it, Vi. We may be dead tomorrow. What a moment to get coy.'

At the time his smoker's drawl had enraged her. Later, she realised that he was trying to make things better the only way he knew – by playing with words and information like a juggler. He was trying to divert her attention, and his own probably, from fears that the spotter plane would return and from the horrors they had escaped in Singapore.

She noticed that he studiously avoided references to what had happened there, although on one occasion he fell into saying, with an odd mixture of sadness and a schoolboy's glee, 'You know we witnessed the end of the British Empire? Who'd have believed it?'

The light was quickly draining out of the sky, taking the dazzle off everything, dulling the aquamarine sea to a sullen copper. When all the light was gone they would be safe for another night. Perhaps.

She started to play his game of diversion back to him, like ping-pong.

'For God's sake, Quigley. You shouldn't be here at all. I almost died when I saw you scuttling up the gangway. It's like a black miracle.'

Delighted, he responded at once. 'I've told you Quigley's First Law? No aeroplane, lifeboat or newspaper is ever full. Room for one more, I always say.'

'Why does it have to be you?'

She was thinking of those left behind in the ruined city which the invaders would now be raping.

'The Almighty's preserved me to write your life-story.'

'God forbid.'

'Some women would be flattered. I see it as a drama of love and blackmail, power and persuasion in the highest places, leading to a government's fall, reverberations across the world, the loss of innocent lives . . .'

'Nothing innocent about your life.'

Again, the delighted, ugly laugh.

'I've not even mentioned the stolen love-letters, the jewels, the political intrigue. You're wonderful copy, Vi, always have been.'

'It sounds more like Wallis Simpson than me.'

She was trying to pass it off lightly but, none the less, the journalist's astonishing familiarity with the secret details of her life left her uneasy. How did he know all these things? What could his motives be?

The idea of Quigley's motives, like Quigley's ethics or Quigley's principles, amused her for a moment. Then she shuddered. Whatever the reason, he had given her an insight into what it feels to be hunted. I'm his prey, she thought, the target in his wretched sights. And all he does is make his jokes and string me along.

He was talking about the Duchess of Windsor, claiming that she was too withdrawn – and bony – to pass muster as a passionate heroine.

'You need a voluptuousness of spirit *and* body to play a part like that. Cleopatra had it, and you have it too.'

'*Quigley*. Your mind's gone. You sound like an alcoholic press agent from Hollywood.'

'They know nothing there about what I'm talking about,' he replied loftily. 'I'm talking about following your emotions wherever they lead. All for love – and bugger the consequences.'

Quigley always took everything too far, she thought. 'For God's sake shut up. I'm not just a cipher in one of your wretched stories.'

She saw his eyes sliding north-east, the direction from which the last plane had come. Secretly, he was probably as frightened as she was.

'Isn't it time we went to bed?'

'It will never be time.'

'OK.' He was entirely philosophic, admiring the label on the Tiger beer he was using as a thirst-quencher between slugs of rum. Perhaps he was simply very drunk. After a while he said, 'At least the sunset's crept up on us.'

For once he had used the wrong word. 'Crawled' would have been more like it. She had never before longed so much for the end of the day. The blood-red sun was finally sinking as if pulled on an invisible lanyard from below the horizon. Eventually, like a still ignited bomb, it spilled into the South China Sea. They watched the spectacle without speaking. With luck they were safe now till dawn.

Violet never became Quigley's lover, despite his constant invitations, but during the voyage she lost her antipathy to him, and was even grateful for his company when the children had been put to bed.

Waiting for the sunset became a nightly ritual, though at first she had needed persuasion before she would enter the quarters he had made his own on the aft boat-deck. Gradually a strange intimacy established itself between the beautiful woman and the eccentric reporter.

He had installed himself in the luxuriously appointed aft saloon on the boat-deck. In ampler days before the war when the ship had made the Amsterdam–Monte Carlo–Athens pleasure-run, this place had been reserved for first class passengers who wanted to give private lunch or dinner parties. Now everyone except Quigley, and herself under his tutelage, regarded it with suspicion because it had been one of the chief targets of the first Japanese air attack.

It had superb unobstructed views, even though the once grandiose ceiling was now savaged with irregular gashes left by the heavy machine-gun bullets from the Japanese Zero fighter that had found them on their first afternoon out.

Quigley had been in the saloon and survived untouched. In fact, Captain Van Steenwyjk had specifically warned the English journalist about the saloon's wooden construction and prominent position, both of which made it an inviting and vulnerable target.

Quigley, of course, took no notice at all. He was convinced that the same spot would not be hit twice, that he was destined to survive.

'If you sit here, Vi,' he had said on the first night, patting the place next to himself, 'you won't get a scratch, even if the whole Jap air force comes looking.'

In the end she joined him on the circular velvet seat where he had installed himself between two mahogany tables heavily embossed with brass and shining with age and polish. Quigley had persuaded McGough, the thin Glaswegian steward, to order a party to clean up after the raid and, as he said, the bullet scars, sinister as they were, even provided some ventilation.

Survival made Quigley manic – even he couldn't believe his luck. 'It's a mystery, but God must be saving me for some great work. I knew I was finished when they bombed Tobruk – but no, out I come without so much as a flesh wound. The same with the evacuation of Crete. The same again with bloody Singapore. The bastards will never get Quigley.'

He drank some more, considering the ways of providence. 'I pray God the old crate keeps going,' he said, finally.

They listened for a moment to the rich mechanical blend of the *Wilhelmina*'s engines. She was breaking no speed records but so far she had never stopped altogether.

'You don't believe in God, Quigley,' Violet said at last. In her bones she felt a growing confidence, but would never dare speak it aloud, except to soothe some of the most frightened children. Quigley's gloating stirred some superstitious fear in her. It invited hubris, and should be avoided. It was an invitation for things to go wrong.

'Don't you be so sure about me and God,' Quigley told her, taking a long and happy swig. 'Somebody's been looking after me – if it's not Him, then it must be Old Nick.'

She smiled, smoking her Craven A through a holder while he drank quantities of overproof rum with fresh orange juice, followed by chilled bottles of Tiger. McGough would do anything for Quigley.

As usual he had vast amounts of ready cash: presumably that was how he had managed to fight his way aboard the night they had fled the Singapore straits, the last of all the passengers, and the luckiest. From somewhere he had acquired a magnificent loose-flowing tropical suit of pale yellow silk, embossed flamboyantly with a crest and set of initials that were certainly not his own. Despite such grandeur he had failed to shave since they sailed and he looked arresting and horrible with his salt-flecked stubble of beard and sunken, malarial eyes. Like a degenerate rajah, she thought. Like a satyr.

4

An uncannily well-informed one. Somehow he had acquired a wealth of information about her life which went far beyond the casual knowledge that anyone could have picked up through knowing her over the years. He knew things she did not know herself, details, like the colour of the ribbon on her lost love-letters, which she had herself forgotten. In her uneasy state, his powers of deduction and detection seemed almost unearthly.

She had known Quigley a long time, 'for ever' as she thought, yet she had scarcely ever been alone with him before. He was a party man, someone you found at your elbow between dances, or on grand ceremonial occasions.

'Do you remember the opening of the Sydney Harbour Bridge?' he said as if telepathically. 'You were pregnant.'

'And you were drunk.'

'How else would a man survive in that country?' he responded. 'Or any other for that matter.'

He made her realise how much she had come to love her new country. She ached to be back.

She had been beautiful when pregnant, Quigley remembered, even more so probably than at seventeen when they had first met and he had written a few paragraphs about her crashing her car in Hyde Park. Soon after there had been another story about her going to a party in her night-dress, a story of such trivialising silliness that it had at once begun a fashion – for a month or two the under-twenties issued invitations to each other to attend tea-parties in pyjamas and nighties. Violet had become a 'character' via his column. He had created her – to her fury because she had been the reverse of a fame-seeker.

Violet was wonderful copy, a natural; Quigley had known this by instinct at first sight. But it went much further. There was something about her looks, some combination of innocence and challenge, that caused men to behave madly, to do anything. She set off tidal waves, all the more because she appeared unconscious of the process. It was not that she detached herself in a cold way; simply that she behaved as if all the fuss was nothing to do with her. It was other people's fuss, not her own. There was something untouched about her, which drove her forward.

Because the sensuality in her face had so intimidated him, he had made himself a kind of mock enemy from the start. He was years older, a sophisticate, not the kind to fall in love with one of the new season's offerings from the country's boarding-schools. Yet she had held him in thrall, he recognised. Instead of touching her he had made fun of her in print.

If she had that effect on him, what of others? He remembered with amusement how suspicious the other debs' mothers had been of her, and rightly. It was nothing to do with her behaviour, which had been restrained, despite his own efforts to portray her as the wildest of the wild. But the mothers were instinctively right. They knew that no husband, however jaded, and no son, however docile, was safe from folly when she came into a room. Her looks were subversive, they threatened to overthrow the established order.

'You were a radical force, Vi,' he said, 'a dangerous revolutionary without knowing it. The belle of the ball who tolled for all of us.'

She made a swatting gesture, as if he were a bothersome fly.

'I remember that joke in print. You never left me alone, did you? I was "The Girl with a Hundred Hats" or "The Girl Who Saw One Thousand Talkies a Year".'

Even dressed in a crumpled seersucker skirt and blouse she had found to wear, and looking like a kindergarten teacher, she had a powerful effect on him. Her face, with its vitality and sensuality, was as troubling as it had always been. But, whatever he said, he could no longer pin labels on her and write her up as an amusing bit of copy. She had outgrown that, even if he himself probably never would.

'We've known each other a long time, Vi,' he said.

'Too long,' she said.

She shook her head as if to make him disappear. He had always popped up at key moments in her life – like the night of the Duke of Westminster's ball on the Thames when she had first fallen in love.

Years later Quigley hoved into view again, grimacing like a medieval grotesque on the day they opened the new Harbour Bridge in Sydney, provoking her husband, as he had always done, and fixing at once on the young Gareth Mayhew. The politician's future eminence was well camouflaged by his awful, countrified clothes – a suit too small for him, and a bright tie whose misguided inspiration was the Hollywood movie magazines. There was little sign of the future statesman, but the journalist picked him out at once.

'That Ozzie politician's got his eye on you,' Quigley's voice rasped over the years. 'And I don't think he wants you for a campaign contribution, my dear. It's your body he's after, and your eyes.'

'What are *you* after, Quigley?' she asked. 'What is it you want from me?'

'I told you, I'm Boswell to your Johnson.'

'Is it sex, really? I know you keep saying so but I don't believe you. It's the funniest seduction I've ever encountered.'

'It could work yet.'

'It couldn't,' she said, and went off into the night to check the dormitories.

The moment she had gone he felt diminished, as if the energy source had been removed. Quigley was not an introspective man but now he found himself answering her question for his own benefit. He had pursued her all these years because she made him feel alive and he was fascinated to see what impact her gift of vitality would have on the world. What was now left of it. She thrilled him in the same way that he was thrilled, though he would never reveal it, by his participation in great events. She was like a story unfolding, even now.

He could never write it, of course. It would be the same even when the main actors were dead. Once upon a time he could have used her as copy but no longer. She had become too real for that. He would keep her secrets to himself. This was as close to her as he could get.

Gradually a peace had grown up between them, an intimacy Violet had enjoyed. She felt as if she had undressed in front of him long ago, and since that was in the past, further concealments were unnecessary. And in any case, they might easily be going to die. It had seemed no time for lies or pretence.

'You're a monster, Quigley,' she remembered saying one night, sipping her drink and mentally calculating how long before dark. 'You're totally without scruple. But all the same you know so much that you might as well know the truth.'

1

On the hillside the crowd wore black. The best there was, naturally.

'Forasmuch as it hath pleased Almighty God of his great mercy to take unto himself the soul of our dear brother here departed, we therefore commit his body to the ground; earth to earth, ashes to ashes, dust to dust.'

It was a grand occasion; in Highgate Cemetery the mourners numbered hundreds as a cold wind gusted among fastidious tailoring and fine perfumes. Everyone was shuffling and hunched, all muffled up against the weather like a flock of rich crows. Beyond the high walls of the burial ground a line of waiting limousines stretched nearly a mile down the hill. At the foot of the hill, submerged in an inland sea of foul vapours, London and its multitudes could be sensed rather than seen.

Violet shivered, and stamped on the frozen ground. She wished she had worn something warmer than her new knee-length black coat. Her felt cloche, the dullest in her extensive collection and the only one suitable for a funeral, barely covered her ears. She was too young to have much experience of ceremonies like this and had forgotten how much standing about was involved.

At the graveside of Hugh Franklin, newspaper magnate, the priest continued to recite, and Violet suppressed a yawn. Last night she'd danced till four with the man her father wanted her to marry. She and Peter had gone to the Embassy Club in Bond Street, where it was said that any girl might find herself dancing with a man who'd danced with a girl who'd danced with the Prince of Wales. Violet felt herself above such speculation, having already danced with the prince himself. As for Peter Ironside – 'the perfect match', as she had heard her mother call him – not only was he an inadequate performer on the floor, but the moment she allowed herself one foxtrot with anybody else, he sulked.

To put him in his place she had sat the club cat, Jackson, on her knees and told everyone that Jackson was by far the better dancer.

Next to Violet, head bowed, stood her father. Rupert Harcourt looked chastened this morning; almost reverent. In the good days gone by, before the Depression had made such a hole in his fortunes, he had briefly been the late Hugh Franklin's partner in a business based on a new paper-making process. Franklin's own achievements were wide- ranging and had included the establishment of one of the nation's leading daily newspapers. His social standing as a proprietor of the *Gazette* had made an especial mark on Rupert Harcourt's imagination. Not that Violet could see what was so overwhelming about newspapers. Now, if the Franklins had owned something that normal people like her could appreciate . . . Resisting the temptation to put her hands in her pockets for warmth, she let herself dwell on the one subject she really did know something about. It would have been different if they'd owned a moving picture studio.

As to the partnership with Rupert Harcourt, Franklin had sold out in 1928. Harcourt, on the other hand, had stubbornly, and disastrously, hung on. Now he was hoping that Franklin had remembered him at the last, and had left him some tangible memento of their shared past.

Violet was sceptical of such hopes. She had kept her doubts to herself, however; her father had made such a fuss about being seen at the funeral – as if his presence there could affect the provisions of the dead man's will. Eyes watering from the cold, she cursed her mother's invalidism. For the third day running, Sybil Harcourt had refused to get out of bed. Violet had had to accompany her father to the funeral.

She sighed inaudibly and tapped her feet in an effort to keep the blood running to her toes.

'Stop fidgeting,' hissed Harcourt without moving his eyes from the grave. 'Do you want to show yourself up?'

'If you didn't want us to be conspicuous, maybe we shouldn't have come,' muttered Violet, likewise frowning down at the lid of the coffin.

Harcourt knew she was referring to the will. His eyes furtively surveyed the faces of the other mourners; his mouth hardly moved. 'God Almighty, have you no understanding of serious matters?'

Death and its rites were the things least on his mind, as Violet knew. The serious matters that preoccupied him right now were the ones he loved most: money and status. They were also the subjects he was most squeamish about mentioning out loud, for the reason that his hold on both was incomplete. He hated to be reminded that his father had been a foreman in a woollen mill in West Yorkshire and that he himself was the very type of upstart he affected to despise. When he had come south, at the same time changing his name from plain Bob Harris, he had set out to slough off his past as neatly as a snake changing its skin. By a process partly concealed even from Violet, he had eventually shoved and insinuated his way into the upper middle class, learning *en route* to give orders in understated tones.

His social progress had had its minor setbacks, of course. Violet remembered how one day, when she had been seven years old, her parents had returned from a country weekend, with Harcourt in a particularly vile temper. Her mother later told her that while out pheasant shooting her father had killed a fox. It was a crime, Sybil Harcourt said, her own sensibilities genuinely affected. Clearly the crime hadn't been committed against the fox.

Harcourt loved money and power and status, and up to a point he was right in thinking he understood them. He believed that the first was meaningless without the other two. Marrying Sybil had obtained him a shaky foothold near the top of the class system. And money – in the boom time of the twenties – had gravitated towards him as a matter of course. In the City he'd been thought of as a 'good bet': a man with an instinct for the right deal and with his eye securely on the main chance. Under the influence of his energy and determination, anyone he wished would go along with his proposals for investment.

Now, shaken by the reversals of recent months, Harcourt's sense of practicality was deserting him. Why else should he attach so much expectation to an outside bet like Franklin's will?

And when that dream had failed, so Violet thought, she could guess all too well how she would be affected.

'Marriage is a serious matter, too – don't you think?'

'What are you talking about?' muttered Harcourt. He was furious with embarrassment that on this particular point his daughter should understand him so well. Violet was sure that, if he were not remembered in Hugh Franklin's will, his disappointment would only increase the pressure on her to marry the man of her parents' choice.

Still avoiding his eyes she exclaimed in a whisper, 'I won't marry just for you and Mummy!' Violet was feeling partly inhibited by the presence of so many bystanders, and partly protected by them from her father's wrath. 'And I'd marry *him* least of all – even if it meant you'd be ruined otherwise!'

Her father was visibly shaken with frustration and rage. As he sought in vain for words, Violet let her fear of his plans run away with her tongue yet further. 'Peter is so boring he turns me to stone. *You* may not believe this, but I can't even get carried away by his title. *Or* feel respect for his money.'

Harcourt's features were pinched with panic as he glanced around to see who might be listening. Seeking an inconspicuous way to silence her, he remembered the man who by his standing had impressed him as much as anybody there. Gesturing towards the coffin he exclaimed out of the corner of his mouth, 'Have you no respect?'

After the priest had pronounced the final blessing, it took for ever to get out of the cemetery. Voices began to be raised, as the mourners all straggled towards the main gate, waiting in turn for their motors to be driven up, and greetings and handshakes were exchanged. Though the Harcourts could claim acquaintance with most people there, Violet knew the Franklin family themselves only by reputation. Which of them, talking over there, was which? The older man with the deep tan must be George Franklin, the family's black sheep. He had quarrelled with Hugh, his father, back in the 1880s and emigrated to Australia. In fact he didn't look particularly like a trouble-maker. He had the general air of a man's man, someone more at home in a bar than a drawing-room. Standing next to him must be his wife, Daisy. She was small and compact and looked frozen.

Violet fidgeted at her father's side, eyeing the other mourners as the congregation loitered in little groups. Her eyes fell on two young men talking together near the group that included George Franklin.

The taller of them, the one her eyes were fixed on, turned suddenly and met her gaze. Some moments passed before Violet realised that he was not going to look away. She averted her face, embarrassed but reluctant to ignore him. He looked about thirty and was tall and powerfully built, with none of the willowy elegance common among well-born Englishmen of his age. His tan was so conspicuous that she guessed he must be another of the Australian contingent; George's son, almost certainly. What was his name? She tried to recall what her father had said as their car had laboured up Highgate Hill in the long cortège. James.

He saw that she was still watching him and he smiled, revealing teeth as white as a fox's beneath a neatly trimmed black moustache. His demeanour was reckless yet contained; his eyes were dark and bold. His smile broadened knowingly and Violet felt an unfocused sense of annoyance.

She waited until the Australian had turned back to his companion and, on the pretext of examining a gravestone, she positioned herself within earshot.

'Did you expect your father to be so upset?' asked the other man, whom Violet had identified as Andrew Franklin, Hugh's grandson. He was younger than his cousin, and had pale eyes, and fair hair that fell across his forehead. His looks were all the more English beside those of the Australian.

James nodded. 'They never made it up. Dad still talks about the day he got the *Sydney Gazette* up to a circulation of 150,000. He thought if he was a millionaire in his own right, old Hugh would've shown some sign of approval.'

'But there was nothing?'

'Not a damn thing. All the way here Dad was pacing the deck, praying for extra speed. He'd have swum if he'd thought it would have made any difference. Two bloody days too late.'

Violet had never heard a gentleman swear so much. Standing on a granite slab she edged closer and in so doing skidded on a patch of wet moss. She stumbled and grabbed Andrew's arm to prevent herself falling.

'I'm sorry.'

James scrutinised her with the cheerful malice of a tom-cat eyeing a goldfish. 'You must have found our conversation dull –'

'If you say so.' Violet's eyes, too, gleamed with excitement of a kind she'd never felt before.

'– for which I apologise. When you make the effort to eavesdrop, the least you should expect is to hear something interesting.'

They had no polish, these Australians. None the less, Violet wasn't going to retreat with a smile of coy apology. 'You'd better make up for it, by introducing yourselves.'

As James Franklin's strong hand engulfed hers, Andrew said, 'Harcourt? Weren't your father and our grandfather partners in something?'

Violet started to explain the connection between the two families, conscious of the Australian's steady appraisal. For her, almost every new experience had to be compared with the movies; and James Franklin's looks reminded her of nothing so much as Douglas Fairbanks in the role of a pirate captain.

After a few moments the Australian found he had stopped mentally undressing the girl and was looking only at her face. She had dark hair, in contrast with her complexion, which was as pale as a moonstone. What people noticed first, though, were her extraordinary eyes, which had been likened to those of a Persian princess. Though they were not dark, but blue-grey like a changeable sky, they were oval in a way that seemed oriental.

13

His close attention, so his manner suggested, was not a casual thing, to be given to just anyone. Violet felt impelled to justify their conversation by keeping it going.

'So who inherits the *Gazette*?' she asked.

'I do,' Andrew said, 'since my father was killed, in the war.'

'He never gave a damn for newspapers anyway,' James remarked. 'He didn't know the first thing about the business. He was too much the English gentleman for that.'

Violet had no idea what to make of James's remarks; she had never heard such talk between people who were supposed to be on good terms. She assumed it was merely a liberty he took with close family members.

She said, 'Should I see you as an example of something different to that?'

'I should have thought that was obvious. I've worked for Dad's paper right up from the bottom. He made a point of it.' He looked sideways at Andrew as if he'd scored a point. It was apparent, from Andrew's tight expression, that he didn't altogether approve of James's manner after all.

Violet asked, 'Do you still work there as some kind of menial?' She spoke with bantering solemnity, trying to seem less alert than she felt in the company of this self-possessed stranger.

He answered, in the same tone as hers, 'Not particularly.'

'So you're now too important to stay in England for very long?'

'That's right. My father doesn't care to have us leave the paper with anyone else in charge. He's damn right, too. If the boss isn't there to tickle them up a bit, everything gets slack. You have to drive a paper like a mule, with a bloody great stick in your hand.'

'But – while you're in London, will you be taking part in the season?'

'That depends on Andrew. And on whether anyone thinks an Australian is worth inviting.'

With lively complacency, Violet exclaimed, 'Oh, everyone gate-crashes nowadays. It's quite the thing.'

She took it for granted that he'd be impressed by her social confidence. Instead he remarked, 'It sounds like a game.'

Andrew, instinctively diplomatic, said, 'I expect we'll have time to go to the Duke of Westminster's ball, before Finals come up.' He was still at Oxford, at Christ Church, reading English.

Violet sensed a chance to retreat with her dignity more or less undamaged. With pretended uninterest she said, 'As parties go, it could be the most awful bore. But I look forward to seeing you there, all the same.'

As she walked away through the thinning crowd, James said, 'I want to meet her again.'

'Then why don't you? It should be no problem.'

'When did she say?'

'The Duke of Westminster's bash. Next week. I think it'll be on board the *Cutty Sark*.'

'You're sure she'll be there?'

'Everyone will be there.'

2

Sitting before her crowded dressing-table, Violet took a cigarette from a heavy silver box. Next to the box stood her old teddy bear and the silver-framed photographs of her maternal grandmother and of herself, aged two, proudly perched astride a fat Shetland pony. The lad holding the pony's bridle was Harry, her dead brother.

She inhaled on the cigarette and stood back from the mirror. She was not sure whether she liked the new cotton evening dresses from Paris: Even the world's great fashion capital had been hit by the effects of the Depression, and silk was no longer modish. This, her first cotton dress, had cost 21 guineas at Derry & Toms. It was a confection of spotted muslin, tight in the bodice but widening into an endless billowing skirt which rustled as she walked. The base fabric was white, the spots a delicate primrose yellow.

Violet sucked in her cheeks and drew herself up to her full height. The colour was good, she thought, patting the curls of her fashionable cut. She finished putting on her lipstick and rang for Aggie, her maid, to bring her a Martini cocktail.

Usually, she relished her appearance for its own sake. But tonight it both pleased and disturbed her to guess how her looks might be judged by somebody else.

She hoped she hadn't given herself away by asking all those casual questions about the Australian. One girl with whom she'd been at school had once been to a ball with Andrew Franklin; but about James himself Violet could find out very little.

'I do know he's fast with women,' the other girl had told her. 'There was the most tremendous scandal in Australia – he spent the whole night in his car with a girl, and then refused to marry her. You know what he said? The car had broken down and nothing happened so why should he get married to someone he didn't want to?'

Secretly, Violet respected him for this. Why should he be trapped by girls who played silly games? Peter Ironside, of course, would never behave like this. His correctness was one reason why she found him so tedious. He never did anything unexpected; all he did do was gaze at her soulfully and try desperately to please. He brought out a mean streak in her – but the worse she behaved, the more devoted he became. And tonight her parents had invited him to dinner before the ball. The thought of it made her ache with boredom down to her bones. It would never happen to Mary Pickford. The actress would be madly in love, or at least in terrible danger. She wouldn't be preparing to give up life just as it should be starting and settle into a marriage with someone who bored her.

Violet wished she knew more about sex. Her Granny Cameron had once or twice mentioned the subject, with a gleam in her old eyes. Sybil, however, had only mentioned it with embarrassment. Violet's girlfriends, who discussed it endlessly, spoke of risking it all for the man they loved. But they all knew that until they were married, they would do nothing more adventurous than kiss and fumble on dark terraces. Violet wondered how much of a prize virginity would be to an obviously experienced man like James. She had no doubt that he would demand it in the woman he finally decided to marry. He would want his bride to be perfect, so that he could possess her completely and exclusively.

As for the rituals that preceded marriage, Violet shared her grandmother's disapproval, though for different reasons. Violet was bored by the season. Granny Cameron, remembering the grand occasions of her own youth, found it shocking that people could literally buy their way into society. Nowadays there were ladies of rank willing to manoeuvre a girl from virtually any background through a London season and arrange for her to be presented at Court, regardless of anything except her parents' readiness to pay their bills. To her mind there had been a real season only as long as London was full of people able to hold balls in their own great houses. Now there were no more than a dozen such houses left. Violet had shared a party with a schoolfriend, in a mansion overlooking Holland Park. The house had belonged to the other girl's godmother, who was a lady-in-waiting to the queen. Violet knew that she was being auctioned off on the marriage market; she understood too that Rupert was only spending the money because he thought it a good investment.

The terrible thing about marriage nowadays, she thought, as she finished her cocktail, was that in some ways it made you free. Her father hated her to drink at home; if she had a home of her own, there would be no one to disapprove. But marriage to Peter was a high price for independence. She ought to be enjoying herself more, but the men she found most amusing were all pansies and drunks. She didn't know why Peter persisted in wanting to marry her. Perhaps her father had encouraged him behind her back. Her father seemed to disapprove of everything she did nowadays and his disapproval had goaded her into trying to shock him. She recalled his terrifying outbursts when her own coming-out year had ended in a series of minor disasters. She had appeared at a ball in her nightgown, driven a car through the gates of Hyde Park at dawn, and gatecrashed too many parties. Her father hated the Bright Young Things, as the papers called the rowdier débutantes and their escorts. He was so cold, so contemptuous of her – everything she did he took personally. 'He hates me,' she whispered to her reflection in the mirror. He's hated me, she thought, since the day that Harry died.

She didn't understand why; but she knew it was true. Her father resented the very fact that she was alive – the more so when she was enjoying herself. His grudge against her would last until she was tidily married off, bringing with her a fortune. It was as though this was the only way she could repay him for the burden of having to bring up a troublesome daughter instead of a cherished son.

She saw her own face in the mirror sadden at the memory of Harry. She had been only six when he was killed, yet her memory of him was vivid. Harry was always laughing, ready to tease his little sister. She remembered how cheerful he'd been on the morning he had crept in to say goodbye to her. He had found her in bed wearing a knitted wool hat and guffawed at her out loud. Stubbornly she had crept back under the covers, her hat still in place. 'At least it's warm,' she had muttered from beneath the eiderdown. When he had stopped laughing she had poked her head back up again. Harry was resplendent in his army uniform, eighteen years old and ready to fight and die for his country. That was the last time she had seen him. She'd never stopped loving him. He had taught her to ride and swim, years before her father thought it suitable for a young girl to sit on a horse or jump into a lake.

Violet went to the closet to pick out a pair of yellow satin dancing pumps and ran her eyes along the rows and rows of hats. She had been collecting them ever since the day he left.

The boat was lit up like a circus. Fairy lights were suspended between the masts and lanterns swung from the rigging. In the ante-room of the *Cutty Sark* the Duke of Westminster and his new young duchess were shaking hands with their guests as they arrived. The ship was crowded and noisy; at any moment the dancing was due to begin. Groups of guests loitered, peeking about them and exclaiming their hallos. They resembled a gathering of fashion mannequins – though the effect was not always pleasing to the eye. Westminster's bride – his third – was twenty years younger than himself, and the age range of the party extended from late adolescence through to octogenarianism. One or two extravagant costumes, sported by people of advancing years, were decidedly a mistake.

The Harcourts, late arrivals, accepted champagne from a waiter bearing a silver tray and continued with the conversation that Peter Ironside and Violet's father had started over dinner. Peter, himself an MP, was full of the brilliant Oswald Mosley, who, back at the start of his career, had been elected to Parliament for Harrow at the age of twenty.

'The sooner that man has power, the better,' he was announcing, alight with the rightness of his own judgement. Since Peter's opinions were never original, a lot of people in his circle shared his conviction that Mosley would – and should – one day become prime minister.

Rupert Harcourt listened, leaning slightly forward in his eagerness to hear every word and agree with it. Sybil, intent on pleasing both men, wore a similar expression. She was short and bird-like with fluffy yellow hair, and resembled a porcelain doll, cruelly aged.

Violet glanced around, finding it hard to look attentive. Politics interested her far less than individual politicians – some of them, at least. Of the ones she'd met, those whose self-confidence had attracted her had also made her more aware of Peter's shortcomings. All he was fit for was saying the right thing.

He was doing so now, ingratiating himself with her mother by criticising the new minister of labour, Margaret Bondfield, who was also the first woman to hold a cabinet post.

'Of course, she won't be able to do the job properly.' He drained his glass and looked around for a refill. 'No woman could.'

Sybil gave a sharp little laugh of agreement and glanced at Violet to make sure that she too appreciated what Peter had to say. Violet could only stare at the bubbles in her drink and pretend that the conversation was above her. She did so hope that at the end of the evening Peter wouldn't try to kiss her. He had already made one attempt, in the hall at home, when her mother and father were getting their coats. His kiss consisted of clamping his lips to hers, like wet suckers. She had managed to rebuff him, and he had sulked all the way to the ball. Surely, she thought, he must understand that I don't love him? And

Daddy – surely he must realise, too? As soon as she felt safely ignored, she slipped away.

She wandered on to the deck. Everywhere, since it was that sort of gathering, gossip abounded. Has Mrs Armstrong-Jones given birth yet? Was the Prince of Wales still enamoured of Thelma Furness? Would Thelma's sister Gloria agree to marry the American, Reggie Vanderbilt? What of Lord Westbury, who had thrown himself off his balcony in St James's Court and crashed through a glass verandah? And what of the curse of Tutankhamun, since it had been said only three months before to have claimed the life of Westbury's son?

Two haggard men in their twenties, arms linked, walked by. They seemed as intent on their conversation as a pair of bishops. Veterans of a thousand such parties, both had an uninviting pallor and could have passed for fifty, disfigured as they were by festivity – and by Fleet Street.

The younger of them exchanged greetings with Violet. She had a soft spot for Tony Quigley, despite his exaggerated account last summer of her car crash in Hyde Park. He wrote what Lord Beaverbrook had approvingly described as one of the most malicious gossip columns in the English language, Hollywood not excepted. A notoriously unsuc-cessful gambler, he had at twenty-one inherited a title and a fortune, only to lose the latter within two years. Now he wrote the Dragoman column on the *Daily Mail*, in competition with his companion, Lord Sedbergh, who worked for Lord Beaverbrook on the *Daily Express*. Each had loathed the other since Eton, when, one afternoon a dozen years ago, Sedbergh had poked Quigley in the ribs with the ferrule of an umbrella and an exclamation of 'Filthy tug!'

They had grown up the most bitter of rivals, each permanently threatened by the same possibility. Had the other obtained a scoop big enough to stop the presses at midnight and leave his competitor humili-ated – and probably out of a job? At school young Quigley had been virtually tortured by his future rival. It was ironic that their current way of life condemned them to being as inseparable as an old married couple.

Everyone tried to watch out for the two gossip writers; and everyone acted as though both men were invisible. People longed to appear in their columns; it was a sign that one had arrived. Yet everybody was terrified of what might be reported about them, or simply invented.

Violet watched them pass out of sight, each pretending more interest in the other than in their surroundings.

'I hoped I would see you here.' James Franklin's voice, immediately recognisable, made her spin round.

'Hallo.' Violet strove not to look pleased.

He leaned back on the deck rail beside her. As if it were part of the same movement, Violet felt her pulse quicken. She blurted, 'Isn't the river beautiful? Could you get to Australia if you just sailed off from here?'

'If you went to Southampton you could. Have you ever been on a sea-voyage?'

'Only across the Channel. To see the pictures and churches.'

'And that doesn't appeal to you?'

Violet shook her head. 'Not with my mama there. She's the last Victorian.'

'What about your father?'

'He's worse.' Hastily she described her father's views on daughters and marriage.

'And what do you think about a grand wedding as the conclusion to finishing school?' he asked.

'I'm not sure. I'm unofficially engaged, you know.'

'That's not much of an answer.' He stood up. She could see his breath condensing in the night air.

'*I* think you want to have fun.'

'Doesn't everyone?'

'Come and dance.'

He held her close on the dance floor, his eyes never leaving hers. Violet was conscious of his hand on her shoulder. She could no more have moved apart from him than she could imagine levitating.

'I wish we were alone,' he said. 'I want so very badly to kiss you.'

He had a gift for making her uncomfortable, as though he could see through her. The other night when Peter had suggested that they spend the weekend alone together she had turned him down almost absent-mindedly, so little desire did she have for him. But it crossed her mind that if she said 'no' to this sardonic giant he would just laugh, so well did he know his own effect upon her.

Involuntarily she returned his knowing smile. No one had ever tried to seduce her in such a direct way before.

'I'm getting married; I told you.'

'To that fool? I met him. You can't be serious. Let's go and throw him overboard.'

Violet imagined Peter, with his red face and incipient belly, falling backwards, tails billowing, into the Thames.

James went on talking, all the time holding her tightly. 'You can't marry him. He'll never make you happy.'

Hearing her own deepest feelings voiced aloud made her confused. 'I think I'd like a drink, if you don't mind.'

Releasing herself from his clasp, she looked round the room for a familiar face. Instantly there was Peter, with a glass in his hand and a look of grievance.

Stumbling slightly, he responded to her greeting and made his way across the room.

'Aren't you going to introduce me to your new friend?'

Violet mumbled the introductions. Peter slid his arm round her waist in a proprietorial manner. She wanted to laugh, thinking of what James had said.

Peter was drunk. 'I hope we're not too grand for you,' he said to James. 'This can't be quite what you're used to down under.'

Violet looked at him with distaste. She was suffocating in the crush. Was this how she would spend the rest of her life? It was too terrible to contemplate.

'I think I'll be able to cope.' James looked down at him without moving.

Peter had reached the stage of only partly understanding what was being said. He was beginning to look ill. To no one in particular he remarked, 'I've got to get a breath of fresh air.' Turning to Violet he asked, 'Do you want to take a turn about the deck?'

She shook her head. 'Oh no, it's so cold out there.'

Peter ignored her. Flushing angrily he grabbed her by the hand.

'You heard her.' James, confident and tense, planted his body between them.

Peter put his hand against James's chest. He was shorter than the Australian and with his cropped military-style hair he looked by comparison like a fat schoolboy.

'Get out of my way,' he said. Finding the other man unyielding as a tree, he pushed. Instead of backing off, James seized Peter by the wrist. His grip made Peter flinch as he struggled to free himself.

'Let go, James,' Violet quietly exclaimed. 'He's had too much champagne.'

James responded by pushing Peter hard in the chest. Peter staggered and fell against a waiter walking past with a tray of champagne. The sound of breaking glass seemed to engulf the whole party.

James stood back reluctantly.

Looking with distaste at his opponent he took Violet by the elbow. 'For God's sake let's go.' She let him guide her to the far side of the dance floor. Peter started abusing the waiter; and among the onlookers Violet noticed the pale profile of Tony Quigley. 'Hang it,' Peter was blustering, 'the fellow's a peasant.'

It was a relief to see Andrew Franklin come up and try to pacify him. 'Ironside, isn't it? I caught your last speech in the House . . .'

James was quietly exultant. 'Did you see? He's got champagne all over his bloody waistcoat. How could a man like that ever have been elected to Parliament?'

He laughed. So did Violet. Whatever happened she would never marry Peter. She would rather die.

But all about them, people were staring. 'I ought to be going,' she said, not sure if she meant it.

'Oh no, you're not. Not yet.' James took her arm, to lead her back to the dance.

'Let me go,' Violet hissed. 'You can't push me around like this.' She was worried that her parents would have seen the scuffle. Conscious of the other guests' looks, she muttered, 'Do you always behave this way with women?'

'Yes. It's infallible.'

'I'm not like the girls you're used to.'

'Too right, you're not. You're the most beautiful girl I've ever seen.' He turned her expertly on the floor, their feet in perfect time to the music. She was surprised he could dance so well.

'What are you thinking?' His voice, strong as ever, was suddenly softer.

'I was just wondering . . .' She smiled, remembering her first impression of him – that he was built more like a manual labourer than a gentleman. But his feet were as light as if he were small and lithe.

He grinned, cat-like; Violet's hands involuntarily convulsed.

'You're surprised that I can dance?'

She nodded, then laughed.

'I'm sorry, I didn't mean to be rude.'

'Not rude, just English. You see the world in a mirror. You're blind to the rest of the globe, and you think they're as impressed by the British as you are yourselves. As for Australia . . . you assume we're inevitably deficient of life's finer points. That we can't dance, or tell one wine from another, or do anything with style. You'd be amazed, if you ever came to Sydney.'

'Is that a challenge?' Violet said. She hoped she spoke lightly, so that he couldn't see how his presence drowned out everything around her.

'Call it a bet.'

'What would you bet?'

'What would you want? My cuff links? My car?'

'Is it the car you spent the night in, with that girl?'

23

James raised his eyebrows and looked at her.

'How do you know about that?'

'A friend.' Sensing dangerous ground, she wondered in vain how to redirect the conversation. Instead she said, 'I think I really ought to be going.'

'Can I drive you home? Will you risk coming in a car with me?'

She nodded. Foremost in her mind was that she had no idea how she would respond to being kissed by him. But she knew she wanted him to try.

Outside on the Embankment, James settled Violet into the leather seat of his yellow Hispano-Suiza. He reached into the back seat for a travelling rug and tucked it round her. His shoulder brushed her breasts as he leaned across her, and she caught her breath. Even through the thickness of the fox fur coat, her skin started to tingle.

'You'll have to direct me,' he said as the car roared along the Embankment. It was two o'clock in the morning as they turned into Parliament Square and circled beneath the towers of Westminster Abbey. They might have been the only people alive.

In Belgravia, at the Harcourts' large corner house in Chester Street, a single light gleamed behind the fanlight. Otherwise the street was dark. Snow had started to fall. James stretched his arm along the back of the seat, resting his fingers in the thick fox fur of Violet's coat.

She turned to look at him, and he moved towards her. She felt his moustache brush across her cheek. She wound her arms around his neck, anxious in case he went on, but dreading lest he stop. A fire seemed to course through her, melting her senses, making her weak. James pulled back and gazed into her eyes.

'You needed kissing. Badly, I would say.'

She blushed. Was it that obvious?

'I can't believe that Peter ever kissed you properly. Did he?'

'No. Oh, how dare you ask? I don't know.'

Looking at her, James almost groaned out loud. He longed to possess her, to take her there and then, in the car, with the snow settling on the windows, cocooning them against the night.

'I must go,' she said. Her body was burning too. She knew she had to get out of the car.

'Can I see you again? Tomorrow.'

'I can meet you for tea. Four o'clock? In the Ritz?' Violet turned to let herself out, but he stopped her.

'I meant it about our bet.'

'That I should go to Australia?' Violet's heart was racing. Never had she tried so hard to sound unconcerned. 'Don't be ridiculous!'

'I mean it.'

'Of course you don't.'

'Oh yes I do.'

'Then stop bluffing and tell me what the stake would be.'

'My other car.'

Violet made a point of looking unimpressed. 'Your other car must be in Australia, so that's no good.'

'Yes it is. It means you'd have to take the bet to get it. It's a maroon Delage, with silver wheels.'

'It sounds very showy.'

'You know you'd still take it, if the chance offered.'

'Of course I would. But that's not the point. Now, good-night.'

3

'Why don't you just run off with him?' Emerald Harcourt asked her sister-in-law. She had a black Russian cigarette in a long holder in one hand and a White Lady cocktail in the other. It was a fortnight since the Duke of Westminster's ball, and she and Violet were having tea at the Chelsea Arts Club.

'He hasn't asked me. And I wouldn't want to look too willing. This isn't wartime.' Violet's brother had married Emerald, a rich and independent art student, six weeks before he had been killed in France, in August, 1918. He and Emerald had met on a Thursday and married within the week.

There had been countless similar wartime romances, but not many bereaved brides had been as fortunate as Emerald. Her own comfortable income was augmented at once when she inherited Harry's considerable trust fund. This fancied injustice had always gnawed at Violet's father. When it became clear that his daughter-in-law, who hadn't even managed to produce an heir for his son, was far richer than he was himself, he refused to see her again. But Violet loved her, even though at home Emerald's name was taboo.

'But you're very attracted to him, aren't you?'

'I just don't know. I've never met anyone like him. He's dangerous, like a force of nature under stress.'

'He sounds like heaven, Violet darling. Far better than that MP, the one like a waxwork.'

Emerald's eyes brimmed with pleasure. She wore her hair twisted into two knots above her ears, in a severe style that accentuated her long face. She wasn't pretty, but she had a vivacity that was impossible to ignore. Her fingernails were long and painted a brilliant scarlet. Today she wore a patterned floral turban, baggy silk trousers and a tunic shirt. She lived in a studio with an unsurpassed view of the Thames. Her passion was painting male nudes.

'I would have loved to see poor old Peter's face when your friend who likes fisticuffs started the fight.'

'Don't exaggerate, Emerald. I never said it was a fight. James would have liked nothing better, but it was stopped in time.'

'That's not what I've heard. How too divine! To be fought for!'

Violet looked thoughtful. 'I don't know whether to be pleased or not. Even now, I don't know him that well.'

'The happiest days of my life were the six weeks I was married to your brother.' Emerald's smile was brittle. 'Don't let him go. Not if you love him.'

'But how do I know if I'm in love?'

'You'll know, darling. It's not something anyone can explain, but believe me, you'll know.' Emerald waved at the waiter and ordered another White Lady.

'Besides, if you don't make up your mind to do what you really want, won't your family force your hand? I suppose that will's been read – the one your father set such store by?'

'Heavens, yes. That's another reason I'm glad to get out and escape the atmosphere at home.'

'Even without the lure of sneaking off to see your wonderful Australian?'

'Absolutely. Ever since Hugh Franklin's will was read, Daddy's been behaving every bit as badly as I knew he would.'

'Meaning –?'

Violet set down her coffee cup and frowned. 'I heard about the will from James. We were having tea at the Ritz, the day after the ball. It was obvious what had come of Daddy's expectations, from the moment James asked what Daddy thought of the Franklins.'

'Does he blame them for his own financial trouble?' Emerald asked. 'I mean, as well as blaming me for my inheritance?'

'James asked much the same thing. He'd guessed right, of course. Daddy was amazingly overawed by Hugh, his old partner. But he also hates them all – even the late Hugh – for what's happened to him since the Depression. Quite wrongly, I expect.'

Emerald looked thoughtful. 'Mm. I suppose I can hardly say this, having come into so much Harcourt money myself; but, even now, your father's hardly broke. He had enough money for fifty men before the slump; now he only has enough for twenty.' She glanced at Violet, who said nothing. Violet's parents believed that money was an unsuitable topic for female conversation; consequently she hardly noticed the size of her own allowance, let alone the state of the family

27

fortune. 'I take it, then,' Emerald ventured, 'that there was nothing in the will for your father?'

'Not a thing. I can't understand why he thought there would be.'

'So now he's pinning his hopes on you. And the Honourable Peter.'

'Exactly. You know what he's like; failure only makes him more obstinate. And there's some business proposition involved, if I go ahead and marry Peter.' She sighed. 'Oh dear. I wish I knew what to do. I'm sure everyone's just waiting till after the family visit to Scotland.'

'Look at it this way, darling. So long as you go on seeing the lovely Mr Franklin, I'd say you were doing exactly the right thing. Presumably the tea at the Ritz wasn't the last time you saw him?'

'Oh no!' Violet responded with such cheerfulness that there was an answering glow from Emerald. 'We've been everywhere! Long walks in Kew Gardens and round Green Park. Riding in Hyde Park – James is a surprisingly bad horseman, actually: all control and no spontaneity – odd, that. Oh – and I danced every dance with him the other night at the Embassy Club; it's just as well that that sort of thing doesn't make people talk any more.'

'It sounds the most heavenly fun. But – that isn't everywhere you've been, is it?'

'Good Lord, no; I was just going to say, we've been to the pictures more times than you'd believe possible.'

'As often as that? I can't believe James is as crazy about the movies as you are – whatever his other virtues.'

Violet grinned. 'No. But to watch him, you'd never know. When he's with me, I mean.'

'Ah, now I can believe *that*!' Emerald shone with pleasure. 'That's another reason why I'm sure he must be right for you.'

Emerald was a good, generous woman, who wanted everyone about her to enjoy what she had savoured, then so quickly lost, in her own marriage to Harry. Violet herself was moved to gratitude by everything she said – Emerald understood her so much better than any of her nearer relatives.

Most important, she had said everything that Violet had wanted to hear.

Violet did not lack a mind of her own, any more than she lacked a heart. What she did need, so early in her life, was something to fill them both. Violet, on the day she first met James Franklin, was barely nineteen.

The big white house on the Black Isle, where they were going, had a view clear across the Moray Firth towards Inverness. Beyond the estuary would be bold calm mountains on which you could see changes in the weather from miles away.

Violet usually looked forward to the springtime ritual of a visit to her Granny Cameron. But this time she was craving to be homeward bound even as they set out. Boarding the early express at King's Cross, she watched Rupert and Sybil fidget through the ritual of finding their compartment, taking off their coats and hats and getting out a stack of reading matter for the twelve-hour journey north. Half her thoughts were taken up with wondering how many streets away James would be at this moment, and what he would be doing. Another part of her mind was disagreeably occupied with guessing just how closely her father would scan the pile of newspapers and magazines beside him on the seat. In recent weeks she had hardly dared peer into any of the gossip columns, for fear of what Tony Quigley and his kind might have written about her.

As the train steamed out of London she loitered in the corridor, pretending an interest in the suburban building sites overrunning the fields of Middlesex. Should she have encouraged James more fearlessly, before vanishing from town for three whole weeks? Between now and tonight, would her father's reading actually go beyond the financial columns?

Violet was divided between boredom and apprehension as they sat through a lengthy breakfast, Rupert still reading that morning's *Daily Telegraph*. The heavy cutlery jingled in time to the clicking of the wheels, and a trail of steam from the engine, endlessly forming and reforming, blotted out the view from their side of the restaurant car.

Mid-morning saw them into Lincolnshire. Violet was standing in the corridor, watching the tall spire of Grantham church advance, then recede, when her mother came up to her.

'I don't think you'd better go back to our compartment just yet, dear. I'm afraid your father's seen something that's made him just a little bit upset.'

Violet turned pink from resentment and dread. 'I didn't know Daddy ever got "just a little bit" upset. If he's only "a little bit" cross, it can't be very important, can it?'

'Oh, darling, please don't make things worse!' Sybil looked as if she might start leaking tears. 'He only wants to be proud of you. And he was so pleased, just now, when he opened the paper and saw Peter's photograph.'

'You mean, he only wants to be proud of Peter.' Violet stared obstinately out at the passing fields, her hair blowing in the draught from a lowered window. Curiosity vied in her with anger and dismay. However dramatic the offending newspaper item about her, she was blowed if she would ask about it. Let them tell her, instead.

But Sybil only retreated, looking frail and desperate. Violet stayed where she was, feeling her feet begin to hurt. She wondered if she could sit down in third class; then realised she might have to explain herself to her maid Aggie and the other two servants from their household who were travelling there. In the hope of avoiding her father a little longer, she put off lunch until the last sitting.

When she went into the restaurant car, however, her parents were there too, looking at the menu. Pride made her sit down with them regardless; and they each gave their order in an atmosphere heavy with Rupert's unspoken rage.

Just as the waiter was about to serve Violet's lemon sole, her father, still without speaking, threw down a copy of a well-known journal on to her place setting. Briefly meeting his eyes, she picked it up.

PATRIOTISM ran a heading under one of Tony Quigley's bylines.

As an example to the girlhood of Britain, Miss Margaret Wigham has decided, in the interests of economy, to have her hair re-set only once a fortnight in future, and to stop wearing stockings in the evening.

On the other hand, to stimulate trade, she had just bought four new evening dresses.

What had this typically British piece of hypocrisy to do with her? Only when Violet read on did she find the item that was threatening to make her father raise his voice in a public place.

At the Scott-Wetherby ball last night, dashing young Australian James Franklin was conspicuous by his good behaviour. Mr Franklin is best known for his involvement in a well-reported incident at a recent ball given by the duke of Westminster, at which the brawling antipodean engaged in fisticuffs at the expense of our own Honourable Peter Ironside, MP.

Violet looked up, preferring to meet her father's gaze rather than see what Quigley might have written about her. Before anyone else could comment, she exclaimed, 'Well, I can see that the gossip columnists must need James. He is a new face around town, after all.'

Her mother stared into the congealing food on her plate, pretending to be invisible. Harcourt glared at Violet. Unnerved, Violet said, 'They'll make up anything, just to fill the space. Tony Quigley is simply terrified that someone else will invent something in the small hours that he'll never be able to follow. And then he'll just have to go back to writing bad cheques.'

'Try not to argue with us, dear,' Sybil murmured, with a hasty glance at her husband. 'It is down there in black and white. And as your father points out, it has been written by a peer of the realm.'

Violet said nothing. Grimly she read on.

The lady in the case was none other than the sprightly Miss Violet Harcourt, whose name has recently been linked with that of the Hon. Peter. Does Mr Franklin protest too much, our correspondent asks, when he repeatedly denies that the insulted MP has challenged him to a duel? Says Mr Franklin, a former amateur heavyweight champion of New South Wales, 'It wouldn't be fair to fight him anyway.'

Violet looked up, ready to defend herself. Before she could speak, her father thrust another journal at her, folded back to show a photograph of James amid a group of people in evening dress. The story here was much the same. There was little the columnist could report for certain; but since James was one of London's newest and most photogenic faces, much was made of his alleged reputation as 'a wild man in a white bow tie'.

It was the same in the *Tatler*, *The Times*, the *Daily Mail*, of course, and the *Daily Express*.

Finally Harcourt, still with an accusing stare, put before Violet an article that included a photograph of her, looking flushed and cheerful at a party she couldn't identify. An up express from Edinburgh screeched past, making everything else inaudible. She read

... principal among the wild colonial newspaperman's partners on the London social scene – a Jane to his Tarzan, dare we say? – is the lovely Miss Violet Harcourt. Miss Harcourt, one of last season's débutantes, was the central figure in the Westminster incident aboard the *Cutty Sark*. She recently created the short-lived Nightie Fashion after appearing at the Londonderry ball in a white shift. 'Last year,' she was quoted as saying, 'I was only eighteen, and followed fashion to the letter. This year, I intend to lead it by the forelock.'

Miss Harcourt was also in the public eye some months ago when she was fined two pounds for dangerous driving.

In view of the colourful reputation presently being acquired by Mr Franklin, might not his friendship with the lively Miss Harcourt be seen as a meeting of like minds?

After the express had gone by, nobody said anything for some moments.

'Darling, it's not just you we worry about,' murmured Sybil. 'It's Peter, too.'

'Have you any idea,' Harcourt muttered, in an undertone that had people looking up from their entrées at tables all down the carriage, 'what this sort of thing could do to Peter's career?'

Violet knew that what really concerned them was her own career, as Peter's prospective wife. She also understood that now was not the time to say so.

'I want you to apologise to Peter,' he went on, in the quiet voice that his family and servants most feared. 'You will do so as soon as we reach your grandmother's house. I want you to write to him and promise that nothing will ever happen to provoke these sort of stories again. I also want it made clear to him that on your return you will come to some definite understanding with him.'

Violet wished in vain to point out that everything she'd just read was old news warmed over. Avoiding her father's eye, she said, 'May I telephone him, instead? I'm sure Granny won't mind me making a trunk call. For something like this.' It had occurred to her that a letter to Peter was something her father might ask to see. He might even demand to dictate it himself.

'It would save delay, Rupert,' Sybil urged, in a low voice.

Harcourt made a dismissive gesture of agreement. Violet's lack of resistance had left him disarmed. 'I suppose,' he grumbled, 'you haven't stopped to consider how your mother must be embarrassed by all this nonsense?' At his side, Sybil said nothing and looked duly mortified.

It was too much to bear with patience. Violet cast her table napkin aside and made an excuse to leave for a few minutes. In the privacy of the lavatory she fumed, then grew worried. She had been right when she told Emerald that her parents would force a decision on her just as soon as they were back in town.

Within a few hours of their return events would threaten to move fast. Violet would be due to leave again after only a few days, on another family visit. If she wanted to thwart her parents she would have to take an initiative of her own. There was no other way.

Sybil passed James a cup of weak china tea. He drank it in one go. She refilled his cup and passed him a plate of thinly cut sandwiches which were even smaller than the smoked salmon and egg mayonnaise triangles they served at the Ritz. In his well-cut tweed suit, with a fob watch-chain across his chest, he might have passed for an athletic stockbroker. Violet could imagine his clothes hanging in a cupboard, with her own nearby, and blushed at the thought.

'How do you find England, Mr Franklin?'

'I find it rather old-fashioned,' he said, sitting back on the low velvet chair and hitching one foot on to his knee. He seemed to fill the room with his presence.

Sybil bristled and Violet inwardly groaned. It was all her fault that James was here. Her first act on returning from Scotland had been to send Aggie round to the Franklin house in Little Venice with a note inviting him to tea. Now here he was, looking like a caged animal – the more so for being on his best behaviour. She had been silly to hope that if her mother would only meet him they might get on. And in only a few days' time Violet might have to leave town again, on a duty visit to an aunt in Oxfordshire.

'Have you been to the opera, the theatre, or to Aintree for the National?' You should be grateful, Sybil's tone implied, that English culture has so much more to offer than the outback.

'I caught Noël Coward's *Cavalcade*. I'm not a great theatre-goer. Oh, and I also sat next to Evelyn Waugh in the Ritz.'

'They say his books are shocking,' Sybil replied. 'And also that he's converting to Rome.'

'He didn't mention that,' James said blandly, and winked at Violet. He gave Sybil herself his winning smile.

She seemed to be immune, however. With a cough of unease she stiffly left the room to order more tea. Violet knew why her mother hadn't asked the maid to perform this menial task. Sybil, whose breath already smelled of gin, was in the habit of leaving at such moments for a secret drink.

James leant forward.

'If we left now, we could be on the boat by dinner time. You don't need anything. It's so easy. It has to be better than this . . .' He gestured at their surroundings. The drawing-room had been elegantly furnished with original Chippendale pieces. The whole effect, though nowadays shabby, was light and pleasing. Now, however, Violet saw it through new eyes: an inbred, stifling place.

James reached for her hand. 'I want you.'

Violet didn't know how to answer him. She wanted him too; but she couldn't say so; not out loud, and certainly not in her parents' drawing-room. His hand, stroking her palm, made her tingle. She felt overwhelmed and confused.

Before she could reply, Sybil reappeared with a full teapot, and the familiar tang of spirits on her breath.

It was lucky that at least Violet had had excuses to be out so often. Even though she had officially 'come out' the year before, the fact that

33

she was single meant that she was still invited to take part in the social whirl. The season was gearing up for the summer fling, when every weekend would be spent at some sporting function: Ascot, Henley, Goodwood. Even now, in early April, there were luncheons to attend, tea parties, at least two cocktail parties every evening and almost always some kind of dance or dinner party. Fittings for clothes and hats, and visits to the hairdresser, supposedly accounted for the rest of Violet's time.

Of course, following Tony Quigley's various revelations in the national press, there would be little further point in being clandestine. As James was taking his — rather early — leave, he said, 'I've asked Violet to go riding with me tomorrow morning.' He hadn't, but he knew she would accept.

'Oh, that will be nice,' said Sybil. She was evidently flustered, though, at the uncertainty of what her husband would say if he found out. As if her fears had conjured him up, as James was about to open the door Harcourt entered the room.

Harcourt was big and fleshy, as tall as James; but where James was hard, Rupert was soft and flabby.

He sized up the Australian, briefly shaking his hand.

'So you're the young man that caused the fracas at the Westminsters'.' There was no humour in his voice. Without waiting for a reply he made his way to the drinks cabinet.

'Speaking as a newspaper man myself, I can tell you, Mr Harcourt, that gossip columns are notoriously inaccurate.'

'I told you none of it was true,' said Violet, standing next to James, her head level with his shoulder.

Rupert showed no sign of having heard either of them. 'I see you're leaving,' he remarked over his shoulder to James. 'Don't let us keep you.'

James left the room without a word.

Violet was surprised at both of them. Her father had been embarrassing, certainly; but she had expected James, in particular, to lose his temper.

Downstairs in the hall, while James was putting on his hat and scarf, she said, 'I'm sorry my father was so ill-mannered, and I'm sorry too that you've had trouble with the gossip columns.' She hesitated, weighing an unknown risk, before adding, 'You shouldn't be seen with so many pretty girls.' While she'd been out of town, she'd been troubled once or twice to read descriptions of him keeping company with other women.

Again, he gave no sign of being offended. 'You know you're the prettiest girl in London as far as I'm concerned.'

He put his hands on her waist, pulling her closer. His lips brushed her forehead. She was struck by what a paradox he seemed: both more gentle and more violent than other men she knew. She shivered in apprehension and leant her head against his shoulder, feeling the softness of cashmere against her cheek.

James caressed her back, his thoughts running on what, suddenly, he had decided to tell her tomorrow. Throughout the weeks she'd spent in Scotland he'd been asking himself, was he going to have to marry her in order to sleep with her? He had never thought much about getting married before now, but what other way would there be? Violet wasn't likely to let him make love to her in the back seat of a car, or in a rented hotel room in the middle of the afternoon.

Now, too, the unwelcoming behaviour of her parents served only to concentrate his sense of purpose.

After he had gone she loitered, wondering how to interpret his behaviour, and reluctant to face her parents. The hall was lofty and elegant, with a black-and-white tiled floor. A Regency sideboard stood beneath a large mirror. On the table was a bowl of out-of-season roses, and a silver tray for visitors' calling cards. Once the tray had been piled high. Nowadays it was usually empty, and its polished surface winked in the lamplight. Faded William Morris paper covered the walls, an exotic design of flowers and birds in reds and greens. Violet sighed. Rupert should have sold the house long ago. But he had hung on, as though this outward symbol of wealth would convince others he was doing fine. It didn't and he wasn't. Everywhere there were signs of age. Curtains fraying at the hem, chair covers worn and shiny on the arms, wallpaper peeling at the edges.

But damn it, thought Violet, as she ran upstairs, anxious to get to her room before being trapped by her mother, it's my life. And life doesn't start till you find the right man. It has been destiny, she thought, as she started preparing for that evening's party and undressed for her bath. Destiny that I went to the funeral. Destiny that he came to England in the first place. I can't ignore it. If I do, the door to the world will be closed to me.

It was eight in the morning on Rotten Row.

Mounting up at the livery stables behind St George's Hospital, James and Violet had walked their horses across the busy traffic at Hyde Park Corner, through the Wellington Arch and into the park. James's size and weight bore down on his bay gelding. He had no trouble controlling the animal but he had little natural ability as a rider. The horse seemed frightened of him, cowed by his bulk. In contrast, Violet was a skilled horsewoman. Her black mare pranced under her, making a pretence of shying at the first daffodils poking up through the grass. Once they were inside the park, the noise of the traffic faded. Mist lay in belts beneath the trees.

In silence they walked their mounts side by side down the broad avenue. Violet wore a small frown, noticing nothing but her own thoughts. Her family seemed less likely than ever to find James acceptable. Also she was uncertain whether she mightn't have to leave town again for a few days, on a visit to Oxfordshire, to her horsy aunt Henrietta. And within the next few hours James was due to join a yachting party off Cowes, as one of the guests of a paper manufacturer with whom Andrew did a lot of business. Surely time was running out for her?

James too seemed preoccupied. After a minute or so, during which he several times looked carefully at Violet, he spoke.

'I'm going to have to return to Australia. Dad and Mum are leaving in three days. I can't wait much longer.'

Violet involuntarily gripped the reins through her yellow string riding-gloves. Her mare, startled, danced sideways.

James pulled up his horse roughly, the bit jarring in its mouth. His eyes flashed, and beads of sweat had formed above his moustache.

'Will you come with me?'

Violet avoided his eyes. Yes, of course she would go with him. But was this a proposal; did he love her? She turned her mare in his direction and looked up. In the chill morning the steam from the horses' nostrils was like dragons' breath.

James leant forward in his saddle, reaching for her hand. 'Answer me.' His voice was urgent. 'God damn it, Violet, look at me. I love you. I'm asking you to marry me.'

'I love you too,' she said. Her voice was barely a whisper, and tears shone in her eyes. James leapt from his horse, leaving the animal to wander.

As Violet kicked her feet from the stirrups and leaned to jump down facing him, he lifted her to the ground and embraced her. She was so light, he thought: hardly bigger than a child.

'Let's go to your father. Now. I want to get married as soon as we can.'

He squeezed her to him, and she gasped as she felt the breath forced out of her. Taking her face in his hands, he greedily kissed her mouth, her eyes, her neck, her hair. The horses stood obediently beside them, blowing clouds of hot breath.

'Stop it! The cavalry is going past.'

He kissed her again.

'Of course you wouldn't care about that,' she said.

'And neither should you.'

'I must tell Father myself,' she said, minutes later, as she took hold of the horses by their trailing reins. 'It will be better coming from me.'

James took his reins from her and swung himself back into the saddle. 'Are you sure?'

Violet laughed. 'You just want to see the look on my father's face.'

'It's not that. I just don't want to lose you.'

Violet looked at her parents' house from across the street. She felt in love with the world. Nothing could stand in her way. Time was her friend now that she had found a purpose.

She sang to herself as she dodged through the cars, ignoring the hooting of a taxi. Inside the hall, she pulled off her gloves and coat and went up the stairs two at a time, past the dour portraits of two centuries of Camerons, portraits of her mother's family. She hated them, all the more as her father liked to pretend they were part of a venerable ancestry of his own. 'I'm free of you,' she said to the line of reproving faces.

Her mother was seated beside the fire in the first-floor drawing-room. Once in her presence, Violet felt her confidence evaporate. She wanted to step back on to the street, to recapture her feeling of buoyancy. In this room, in front of her mother, she felt like a child.

'Where have you been?' Sybil showed no welcome, only anxiety. Today she looked smaller and more doll-like than ever.

'In the park, of course,' said Violet, glancing down at her jodhpurs. 'You were here, Mummy, when James and I arranged it.'

'With that Australian? I hope the two of you didn't go riding on your own?'

'He's asked me to marry him.' Violet wished it weren't still early, so that she could have a drink.

'Goodness.' Sybil sat up. The magazine on her lap slid to the floor. 'But he's so . . . so . . .' She gestured vaguely. 'How embarrassing for you.'

'I said yes.'

'You can't marry him! He's . . .'

37

'Not our type. A foreigner. Not like precious Peter. I know all that and it doesn't change anything.'

Sybil walked to the cocktail cabinet and poured herself a gin and tonic. Her hands were shaking.

'I think I'll have one too,' Violet said.

When Sybil had gulped down most of her drink she turned to Violet with a look of pleading. 'Darling, please think sensibly. Marriage lasts for ever; this is just a fling. You won't be happy with someone from such a different background.'

'Not so different. His father was born here. No one can say that the Franklins aren't perfectly respectable.'

'They're a new family. You know your father will never allow it.'

'The Franklins aren't exactly descended from the Normans, I grant you. But what were the Harcourts three generations ago? They were down a coal-mine, weren't they?'

'Don't ever let your father hear you say that.'

'He's not marrying James. I am. I love him. Doesn't that count?'

'It won't in ten years' time.' Sybil topped up her drink. She wished that Rupert would come down from his dressing-room.

'Mummy, how can you understand? *You*'ve never felt like this.'

Sybil sat down on the window seat. She hesitated before speaking.

'I have, you know. I was in love too when I was your age. He was a lieutenant in the 1st Leicesters. We met at a ball. We fell in love at first sight, or very nearly. He died of diphtheria in a camp in Natal before they even saw a Boer.'

'Oh, Mummy! I'm so sorry!'

'Don't be. We would never really have suited one another. I was caught up in the romance and the glamour of that time: the war; the uniforms; all that patriotic feeling.'

'So then Daddy came along and married you for your money?'

'That's a beastly thing to say. You know it isn't true.'

'I'm sorry,' Violet said again. But it *was* true. Even she knew Rupert had run a number of mistresses on his wife's money. And now he had lost most of it. What a mess. She shuddered to think of her own life turning out like her mother's.

'I know our marriage isn't perfect,' Sybil said as if reading her thoughts. 'But you'll be surprised how quickly you learn to make the best of things.'

'I never will,' Violet exclaimed. 'And I won't be sold to the highest bidder either. Don't pretend that Daddy loves Peter for himself. No one could.'

Tears of helplessness started in Sybil's eyes. She had never been able to deal with her daughter. How she wished she could summon up the conviction to make Violet wait; that Australian was so full of himself. But Sybil had lost her daughter's trust long ago. And time, which at present was Violet's friend, was Sybil's enemy. It had made her afraid. She had never really loved Rupert, it was true. And over the years she had come to hate him – but never so much that she found the courage to cross him.

'Darling, you must do what you can to forget this young man. I don't want to sound unsympathetic, but there's no point in mentioning it any further.'

'I won't. I can't. Help me persuade Daddy. Please.'

Violet's eyes were beseeching. Sybil hadn't seen that look for years – not since Violet was thirteen and had begged not to be sent back to boarding-school. Naturally they had taken no notice, and in the end she had simply run away. Sybil averted her eyes. She couldn't meet that accusing look from the past.

'Has somebody died?' Rupert Harcourt took in the tense atmosphere in the drawing-room. He sat down by the fire, slyly kicking Sybil's spaniel which was snoozing at the foot of his chair. 'And why, pray, are you having a cocktail party at this time of day?' He turned to Sybil. 'And shouldn't the girl be packing to go to her aunt's?' This was how he often referred to Violet, even in her own presence.

'Daddy, I want to get married.' The alcohol had hit her empty stomach like a bullet and she felt giddy and reckless. Nothing must stop her.

'In that case I think I'll join you. I'm glad you and Peter have made up your minds.'

'It's not Peter I want to marry. It's James Franklin.'

'That Australian? The one who punched Peter? The know-all from Botany Bay?'

'But I love him. And he didn't punch Peter; I already told you. And you've always said you liked the Franklins.'

'Doing business with a family doesn't mean you want to marry into it. And that's not the point.'

'So what is the point?'

'You're unofficially engaged to Peter Ironside. And I won't have my daughter marrying an oaf.'

'Are you saying that you won't give your permission?'

'I am.' Harcourt's face was flushed and his breathing was erratic.

'Don't you care about how I feel? Don't you care that I love him?'

39

'No.' There was no limit to his contempt. Watching him, Violet wondered if he looked like someone about to have a heart attack. She half wished he would.

'I will marry him, with or without your permission! Oh, Daddy! Oh God, won't you even look at me?' Violet was in despair. 'You've never liked me, have you? You've always resented the fact that it was Harry who was killed and not me.'

With a surprisingly swift motion for such a heavy man, Harcourt darted towards her and slapped her across the face: a stinging blow that made her eyes water. 'How dare you talk to me like that! Now get out of here, and see that your packing is done. You can go to your aunt Henrietta's tomorrow morning.'

Violet ran sobbing from the room.

Rupert sat down on a small ornate chair which creaked under his weight. He looked steadily at Sybil, still out of breath. 'How could you have encouraged her, by inviting that lout into my house?'

'Oh, but Rupert, I didn't do anything of the sort.' Sybil's eyes were rheumy with unshed tears. 'How can you say that? You're cruel to her and to me too.'

'Don't you start too. You can't want such a marriage any more than I do. I'll have a word with Peter. If he and I handle this right, then she'll have to toe the line. She won't humiliate herself by breaking things off in public.'

'Don't be too hard on her, Rupert. She's our only child.'

'She'll thank us in the end. Now, I don't want to hear any more about this.' He looked at his watch, an important man in a hurry, then stumbled against the spaniel, who was dozing unnoticed.

'Why does this dog always follow me around! It smells. We should have shot it years ago.'

Sybil looked at the clock on the mantelpiece. Still only ten-thirty. If only Rupert would leave the house, she could help herself to another drink.

4

Violet was laying out her clothes on the satin counterpane: summer wear, mostly. Helping her was Aggie, her maid.

'Will you be warm enough, Miss Vi, with just those things?' Aggie wanted to know, viewing the selection of beach clothes and frilly muslins on Violet's big bed. Aunt Henrietta's big stone house in Oxfordshire was notoriously underheated, in addition to lacking every other twentieth-century convenience. It didn't even have a telephone.

'Perhaps.' Violet's tone was despondent.

Aggie looked again at her. The two girls, mistress and maid, were the same age. But Aggie's inborn shrewdness, and the wider social experience she'd gained from earning her own living, made her seem the older by far.

'Shall I pack some other things as well? I mean, choose them for you – since you don't look too cheerful, if I may say so?' As Violet's servant, Aggie felt able to speak more freely than was often the case with people in her kind of job.

'Yes – yes, please do.' Violet glanced at Aggie's broad, almost-pretty face. Should she tell her what half-formed notions were in her mind? Or would they sound ludicrous, at this stage? 'And there are several other things I want to take. As well as clothes, I mean.'

Aggie was too tactful to probe much further. But her curiosity grew no less at the sight of the extra luggage Violet wanted to include: some inherited pieces of jewellery, mainly of sentimental value, that she would never wear in the country; her old teddy bear; and the photographs of her grandmother and of herself on her Shetland pony with her brother Harry.

Their preparations were nearly complete. Meanwhile it was impossible to ignore Violet's manner. She was both energetic and absent-minded, to the point where Aggie felt some remark was called for.

'Are we going for longer than usual, Miss Vi?'

Violet hesitated, craning to see if her stockings were on straight.

'Aggie, don't mention this to my parents, will you? Or anyone. But . . . what if I told you I was going away altogether?'

Aggie looked solemn. 'If you might be going somewhere else for good, would you take me? I wouldn't mind if it was overseas, even.' Though Violet had concealed from her parents how much time she'd spent with James, it had been less easy to hide such details from Aggie. Already it had occurred to Aggie that the good-looking man who'd come to tea might be behind a lot of small changes in Violet's behaviour.

Violet sat down on the bed. Aggie's question gave her pause. Several desperate plans had shaped themselves in her imagination; but she still had little idea how to put any of them into action. Practical details jostled, in Violet's head, with thoughts of how her predicament reflected the latest Fairbanks' movie.

But there was one thing she should have remembered: Aggie's future. With Violet gone, on whatever terms with her parents, Aggie would be out of work. Without references, among three million others now unemployed, she would never find another position. And if Violet left home without her father's blessing, he would refuse Aggie a reference, from no other motive than spite, simply because she'd been Violet's maid.

He himself was never slow to remind his house staff that they were lucky to have a job, during a depression. He paid Aggie a miserly ten shillings a week, and allowed her two days off each month and a holiday every other Christmas Day. Luckily he'd never discovered that Violet made a point of doubling Aggie's wages, out of her dress allowance. Low wages, so Harcourt always said, were the basis of the economy, keeping inflation in check and guaranteeing what he called 'the social order'. It made no sense to Violet. Her own allowance, which seemed magically to expand to cover any frivolity she wanted, made the extra ten shillings look irrelevant.

Violet knew, however, that it made a lot of difference to Aggie. It grieved her now to think that she'd originally given Aggie the money out of nothing better than disobedience to her father.

She asked, 'Are you sure you want to come? I'm not just leaving the country: one way or another I mean to go all the way to Australia.'

'Of course I do. You're my only friend in this house.'

Violet felt a further twinge of guilt. She should have remembered that Aggie's life was all the more insecure for her having no family. She looked at Aggie's strong face, in which there was more friendliness than fear. Something also prompted the thought that if she were going so far from home, even to marry the man of her choice, it would be better to go with an ally like Aggie at her side.

'Aggie, I need your help. Oh, I'm in such a mess!'

Aggie was squatting on the floor, putting wooden shoe-trees into a pair of walking shoes. She looked up at Violet. 'Of course I'll help. What can I do?'

'Can you ask Max to deliver a letter for me? It could be terribly urgent.' Max was Aggie's current boyfriend.

'Who to, Miss Vi?' Aggie, smoothly and automatically, went on with what she was doing.

'It's the man I intend to marry. And I don't mean Peter.'

Aggie shot a glance up at her, and Violet grinned. She knew Aggie didn't like Peter.

'Who's that, Miss Vi?'

'He's an Australian. His name is James Franklin.'

'When you marry him, is that when you'd be thinking of going to Australia?'

'Somehow I must get there, yes.'

The letter was written, and Aggie had hurried out and given it to her boyfriend, at the nearby mews garage where he worked.

Meanwhile the car was shortly due to arrive, to take them to the country.

'Are you ready, Violet?' Her mother sidled into the room, looking jumpy. Normally Harcourt expected his household to carry out his wishes by guesswork. Today, though, he'd told Sybil in great detail what he wanted her to say to Violet. 'See that she leaves in the right frame of mind, will you . . .'

It never occurred to Sybil to object. All she hoped, for everyone's sake but above all her own, was that she didn't have betrayal written all over her.

'You look much better,' she said. Bracing herself, she added. 'Don't be too angry with your father. He only wants what's best for you.'

Violet remembered that line. Sybil had produced it in support of her father after Violet had run away from school. He didn't understand me then, and he still doesn't, she thought, striving to keep up her confidence. She tried to think instead of James. If only he hadn't had to go to Cowes. It might be two whole days before she could talk to him on the telephone.

'Peter will forgive you,' her mother went on, sitting on the stool in front of Violet's dressing-table and fingering a silver-backed hairbrush and comb.

43

Violet glanced at her. What did she mean? 'A few days in the country and you'll feel quite your old self again. And besides,' lowering her voice, though there was no one to hear them, 'things may not be as – well, as inflexible – as they seem, shall we say?' Fear of her husband had dictated Sybil's words. But sympathy for her daughter made her say them with feeling. She really did want everyone to be happy. Especially if it meant they'd leave her in peace.

Violet was radiant. 'Oh, Mummy! Do you mean that? Seriously? No – no, really – do you?' She knelt at her mother's side and embraced her. 'And is that what Daddy says, too? Really?'

Sybil avoided her daughter's intent, rapturous gaze. 'Darling, not so fast, please! I only said things *might* be changed.'

'So he won't object to James after all? And he'll give up bullying me about poor old Peter?' Already the thought of escape was making Violet feel less unkindly towards her unwanted suitor.

Sybil reddened, uneasy. 'Let's just say that if you do what he wants for now, and go to Aunt Henrietta's, where you're not, well, in his sight all day – well, then, as I say, I'll see what little ways I can find to influence him.'

Violet put an arm round her mother's shoulders and kissed her.

'Oh, Mummy! I knew you were on my side really. Of course I'll do what you want, now I know everything will be all right.'

Sybil forced a smile, looking at her daughter's reflection in the mirror. She was so lovely, she thought; so young and unknowing. Rupert was right: any course of action was worthwhile, to save her from herself.

But after Violet and Aggie had left, she went to her room and wept until she was nearly blind.

Several merciful hours were to pass before the next stage of Sybil's ordeal. It was late that afternoon before the phone signalled the call she had been expecting.

As she snatched up the receiver her face was foolish with anxiety. '. . . no, Mr Franklin, I'm afraid Violet is not here.'

'What time do you expect her back?'

Sybil coughed nervously and wished she hadn't left her drink upstairs in the drawing-room.

'She's gone away, Mr Franklin.'

'Gone away? What the hell do you mean?'

'Please don't use that sort of language with me. Violet is in the country. There's obviously been a terrible mistake. She cannot marry you, of course; that's out of the question.'

'Mistake?' His voice was so loud that she had to hold the receiver away from her ear. 'She has agreed to marry me. Now, tell me where I can find her, or I'll come straight round and wait there till she comes back.'

'It won't do you any good,' Sybil said, surprised at how calm she sounded. 'Violet doesn't want to marry you.'

'I won't accept that unless I hear it from her.'

'I assure you, she'd say exactly the same thing. Good day, Mr Franklin.' Sybil replaced the receiver with trembling hands. She looked at it for a moment, then took it off the hook. She couldn't deal with another call like that.

Rupert returned home late. He was pleased with the day's progress. Peter had just rung him back to confirm that there was, as he had hoped, a seat for him on the board of a brewery in the Midlands. Meanwhile he had seen to the newspaper announcements personally, only one issue later than he'd hoped. It had been a damned ticklish thing, arranging everything in time. Peter had been in his constituency, of all places, and it had been hell's own delight getting in touch to tell him in advance of Violet's 'acceptance'. Harcourt got out of the cab and turned to pay the driver.

He was stepping back on to the pavement when his arm was grasped from behind. Swinging round, he found himself face to face with James Franklin. The Australian, deliberately or through clumsiness, was standing on his foot. He let out a cry of pain.

'How dare you!' he said, struggling in vain. Rupert found that he was effectively trapped, on the pavement outside his own house.

'I have been ringing your bell for the past three hours. No one in your godforsaken household has the decency even to come and tell me where Violet has gone. I've given up expecting to be invited in. But I've got you now, and I'm not letting go until you tell me where she is.'

'I suggest that you stop manhandling me, if you expect an answer.'

James removed his foot, but he kept his hold on Rupert's arm.

'My daughter did tell me she'd foolishly agreed to marry you.' Rupert dusted his lapels, frantically trying to think of a way out. This lunatic might kill him. 'She considers she's made a mistake, and she has asked her mother and me to sort it out for her. She's too embarrassed to talk to you herself.'

The Australian stared at him, a hint of uncertainty in his face. 'Try to consider it this way,' wheedled Rupert. 'Mrs Harcourt and I don't want you to think disrespectfully of our own daughter. But your

45

experience,' attempting a smirk of man-to-man complicity, 'must tell you how unreliable most young girls of her age can be.'

'Is she here? At least tell me that.'

'No. I give you my word on it. She left this morning.'

James looked closely at him for a moment longer. Then he let go of Harcourt and walked away down the street.

Andrew Franklin was careful not to talk too much as he sat opposite his cousin at breakfast next day. Presumably James's ferocious silence had something to do with the Harcourt girl. But it was clear that it would be futile to ask.

'Are you coming to the *Gazette* for a last visit?' he asked. 'I have to be back in Oxford tonight.' James, in a mood that had reduced everyone about him to silence, had announced his intention of sailing next day for Australia with George and Daisy.

James nodded, and Andrew tactfully averted his eyes. What could have happened? He had been up in Oxford for the last three weeks but he'd seen an item in Tony Quigley's column describing Violet and 'her dashing young Australian' dining by candlelight tête-à-tête at the Café Madrid.

His mother had also encountered the two alone at the new play, *The Apple Cart*. She had even observed that they had left at the interval – London society was no place to conduct a secret affair. In this case it had not lasted very long, Andrew thought. She was worth watching, that girl. If she could dispose of his handsome cousin in three weeks flat, then that idiot Ironside, if he was still in the picture, could look forward to a bumpy ride. Andrew had been taken with Violet himself, and was secretly amused at James's discomfiture – he had been too damn cocky from the start.

The car eased its way through the traffic in Piccadilly Circus, stopping for the crowds hurrying out of the new underground station. James stared listlessly out of the window. After leaving Harcourt outside the Chester Street house, he had weaved his way from pub to pub, drinking neat whisky, washed down with tepid local bitter. He had a dim recollection of getting into a fight with someone; an equally painful memory of later paying a girl he had met in Leicester Square and going with her to a room above a tobacconist's shop. Her hair had been red; likewise, her heavily rouged cheeks and lips. He had picked her because she was everything that Violet wasn't. He'd shouted at her after making love to her violently, and he recollected that the prostitute had been crying when he left. It was only the third time in his life that he had had to pay for sex. The first time had been in Sydney, the second in Singapore when he had got drunk and decided to investigate the myth that oriental women had no pubic hair.

His head was still throbbing, and every sight about him felt like a personal assault. Cabs and motor cars jostled with open-topped omnibuses. Advertising slogans hung from the buildings like ceremonial flags, cluttering the once stately façade of Regent Street. Taxis stood bumper to bumper, sandwiched between the buses. HEINZ IDEAL PICKLE glared at him off the side of a bus. James felt suffocated by the noise and the crush. He needed a drink.

If it was all her father's doing, then why hadn't she written by now, or telephoned?

When he had come to this morning, seeing the world through his fog-bound hangover, his first thought had been to ask the maid if there had been any calls, any letters.

'No, sir,' she had replied. Seeing her scrutinise him, he wondered, did he look that bad?

The *Gazette* building towered over the end of Farringdon Street between Ludgate Circus and the Thames. It was ten storeys high, a world within itself, a machine made of metal and human flesh, which communicated news from round the world to its 450,000 readers every day.

From the basement car-park an elevator took James and Andrew up to a lobby lined with blue marble. The effect of such a room was austere, but it was alleviated by a vast map of Victoria's empire as it was in 1892, the year when Andrew's grandfather, Hugh Franklin, had built Empire House. The map was twenty feet wide by twelve feet high and made of semiprecious stones. The seas were brilliant lapis lazuli. England was set in dark-green jade, India in quartz, Canada in pale-blue soapstone. The map had taken two years to construct and until it was completed, Hugh had refused to consider the building officially open. So for six fraught months in 1891 the newspaper had been printed on the newly assembled print plant in Empire House, but written and compiled in the old *Gazette* building in Gray's Inn Road.

The doorman touched his cap to Andrew in a formal gesture. Then his face split into a grin and he held out his hand to the young man, whom he had known since Andrew was two years old, arriving at the *Gazette* perched on his grandfather's shoulders.

Andrew returned the older man's handshake, noting with pleasure that his uniform – a dark-green twill, edged with thin gold braid – was impeccable and that across his chest gleamed the medals he had earned

47

in the Great War. Bill had lost his left arm at Aix-la-Chapelle and, as he was never slow to tell anyone, almost lost his life too; yet his disability hardly hindered him.

The lobby was bustling with people: reporters dashing through the front door with stories, messengers bringing photographs.

On the sixth floor the editor, Harry Nelson, rose from his desk as James and Andrew came in. James had got to know him well over the past weeks. He liked the slow-speaking Englishman, who had a quick brain.

'I've only come to say goodbye,' he told him. 'I'm off tomorrow.'

'Are you sailing via Suez?'

'I suppose so,' James replied, staring down through the window at the leaden waters of the Thames.

'Except maybe I won't,' he decided suddenly. Before leaving Little Venice that morning he had found that the *Orontes*, on which his parents were sailing, had no spare berth. 'I know that route too well. I'll ask your secretary if she can get me a berth via Panama. I've yet to see the Americas.'

'Go right ahead,' Nelson said. 'I'd commission a piece on your travels, but we're concentrating on domestic news now everything's so tight.'

'Thank God. I loathe writing,' James said. 'How tight is it? It seems to me that you've come through the Depression pretty well so far.'

'We have. It didn't look good when we had to close during the General Strike – that was nearly a fortnight. But we haven't lost a day's publication since.'

The print shop was dusty, heavy with the peculiar smell of wet ink and paper. Huge linotype machines squatted round the room. The pots of molten metal were so hot that the printers could warm up their sausage rolls before lunch just by placing them against the metal containers. The keyboard operators worked furiously, producing words they had no time to read and digest. The skeletons of the pages for tomorrow's edition were beginning to take shape: outlines for the positions of pictures, the size of headlines. The arts pages would be the first to be finished, then the features and the social pages. The front page and the two main news pages wouldn't be completed until late into the night, allowing the maximum time for collecting news.

They watched a features page being assembled, slugs of type being arranged on the stone. The forme, as it was known, then went to the foundry, where the dirt and grime left from the ink was thick on every surface. There it was cast into a curved metal plate. From this, the page would actually be printed later in the day.

From the composing room, James and Andrew made their way th ough to the room housing the presses. This was a world that had barely changed since printing in Fleet Street started in 1499. The head of the print union, John Newman, greeted them warmly, and hustled them into the heart of the print shop, where a test run was just starting. Newman looked at his watch. He always kept it running five minutes fast, which helped his nerves when he thought he was going to be late for a deadline. While he spoke the machines started turning slowly. These initial copies would not be sold to the public; they were to test the ink strength, a job which Newman always supervised personally. 'It's crucial to ensure that all pages have the same ink flow,' he said, holding aloft the page, looking at it and through it, not bothering with the words. Andrew and James knew the process, but they also appreciated that John enjoyed displaying his rule of the print room. 'See, there's a shadow here. That means the ink is flowing too heavily on the other side.'

'Give me that!' Before Newman could respond, James had snatched the page and was scanning it with a look of incredulity. It took Andrew a moment to realise that James was examining not the standard of printing but part of the text itself.

Looking over his cousin's shoulder he saw that James was staring, aghast, at an entry under FORTHCOMING MARRIAGES. A dozen couples were listed; at the head of them, as befitted the heir to a baronetcy, came 'the Hon. Peter Ironside'. Next to his name were the words that had first caught James's eye.

'Miss Violet Louise Harcourt.'

Andrew took the page from James who stood, stupefied by his own growing rage. Leading Newman aside with as few words of explanation as he could manage, he saw to it that the document was taken away for re-inking with as little comment as possible.

Tentatively he went up to his cousin, having hurriedly completed James's farewells on his behalf, just before the presses were due to start up and drown out every other sound in the room. 'You look as if you need a drink.'

In response, James turned and led the way at the moment that the machines hit full speed. For once, assaulted by the noise, Andrew involuntarily stepped back. The power of the machines could be felt throbbing through the floor.

He followed James up Fleet Street, which was crowded at this hour with newspaper vans. They turned into El Vino's. It was packed with journalists and the air was thick with smoke. James ordered a bottle of hock and quickly drank two glasses. He was just pouring a third when the pallid Tony Quigley appeared at their table. Without waiting for an invitation Quigley pulled up a chair.

'Drowning your sorrows?' he said, putting down his own glass of champagne and lighting a cigarette.

'What the hell are you talking about?' James turned his bloodshot eyes on the journalist. Quigley had a thin scar running from one nostril down to his jawline. His eyes were hooded. Even if he tried not to, he would always look debauched.

The gossip writer spread his hands. 'Violet Harcourt's engagement, of course. Is it true that it's being announced tomorrow? I'll be writing it up when it is, and I wondered if you had anything to add.'

Several other onlookers in the crowded bar were watching James. His features were immobile despite his anger and humiliation. Andrew knew how he must feel – like a man kicked in the stomach by a horse. He also knew what his cousin must be thinking: little bitch.

Quigley's eyes never left James's face. He leant over to fill the Australian's glass.

'Just a fling then, was it?' he prompted.

'That's right. Nothing serious. Anyway, I'm leaving for home tomorrow night. I wish them both luck.' James met several curious stares nearby with a blank look. He wanted nothing more than to punch the odious Englishman on his slack jaw.

Quigley had taken out a notebook.

'So, you're returning to the Australian *Gazette* tomorrow. What have your impressions of England been, Mr Franklin?'

'I think we've been through this before. All I'd like to add is that I'm glad to be going.'

Aggie's boyfriend, Max, whose only two loves in the world were his motor bike and Aggie, picked himself up off the ground and tried to stand. He couldn't.

His right leg gave way beneath him and his heavy frame crashed back on to the tarmacked road.

A few yards away his pride and joy, a BMA 350-cc motor bike, lay on its side, its front wheel spinning deliriously in the air, its back one hopelessly buckled. A long skid mark stretched behind him up Lavender Hill. He had lost control of the bike when he swerved to avoid a stray dog, which suddenly nipped out into the road in front of a milk van.

Desperately he had put his left foot to the ground, trying to prevent the bike from charging across the road into the opposite pavement. But he was moving at over thirty-five miles an hour and the weight of the bike, coupled with the force driving him forward, had tipped the bike over on to its right side. After that he wasn't really sure what happened, except that he seemed to go on skidding down the centre of the road heading straight for a car coming up the hill towards him. With a supreme effort of strength, he freed his legs from the machine and rolled sideways towards the relative safety of the pavement on the left-hand side of the road. The car screeched to a halt, missing the bike by inches.

The driver, a loud young man, was leaning out of the window, yelling at him. He tried to answer, then remembered nothing more, apart from excruciating pain in his leg.

The next thing he registered was the face of a nurse bending over him. He was in hospital and his leg was suspended from the ceiling by a series of complex wires and pulleys. He ached from head to toe. 'What time is it?' he mumbled, through a stiff, bruised jaw.

'Ten o'clock in the morning. You've been asleep for twenty-four hours.'

'Twenty-four hours?'

The nurse smiled. 'You were only semi-conscious when we brought you in here. Then we set your leg – a bad break, that one – and we had to knock you out. You've been sleeping since then.'

'My God, the letter.' Max struggled to sit up, but the nurse pushed him firmly back on to the pillow.

'No moving for you for a long while.'

Hanging over the back of the chair by the iron bedstead was Max's coat. In its pocket, by now badly crumpled, was the envelope bearing James Franklin's name.

Aggie'll never forgive me, he thought as he drifted back into a drugged sleep.

Violet was on her way down to join Henrietta for a cocktail before dinner. This was her second night in the country and already she was bored by her aunt's conversation.

Henrietta was a big-boned woman with small eyes and big hands and feet. Her only interest was horses; and mounted, in a black hunting coat, long black skirt and bowler with black veil, she made an imposing figure. She was a brave rider, though hard on the horse's mouth and rather too free with spurs and whip.

Unfortunately there was no other subject worth talking about to

Henrietta. Years of knowing her aunt had taught Violet how to deal with her and they had evolved a relationship in which Violet asked the questions – How high did you say the fence was? Is he going better in a Pelham bit? – and Henrietta answered with enthusiasm.

Violet looked at the drawing-room with a degree of perception she would not have had a few months earlier. It – and her aunt – looked so English, and not in a way that Violet altogether liked. The sofas sagged, rather like Aunt Henrietta's bosom, which was usually wrapped in a shapeless fawn twinset spattered with dog hairs; her stockings were habitually wrinkled round her ankles, too, and her sensible brown shoes were always muddy. On a table between the windows silver-framed pictures of the family fought unsuccessfully for space with larger photographs of horses. The old turkey carpet was dowdy and slightly shabby; a case of what the English – when covering up for lack of funds – liked to call impeccable taste.

Why hadn't James sent a telegram? Violet was too proud to try to telephone him. After all, he would by now have had her letter and if he didn't bother to contact her, then surely it must mean that all his overtures of love were as insubstantial as the freezing wind which whipped round Henrietta's bleak house. She'd written in such a rush that now she could hardly remember what she had said. All she knew was that it had been full of phrases like 'I can't live without you'. She wondered whether she had managed to put him off by this outright declaration of love.

At least Aggie had made an excuse to run down to the local garage and try to telephone Max – though he wasn't on the telephone at home either. He lived with his parents in a tiny terraced house in a street on the south side of Clapham Common. There wasn't even an indoor toilet, let alone a telephone. Aggie would have to leave a message at the local pub, if she was to find out whether the letter had been delivered.

Henrietta was in the drawing-room already. 'You're a sly one!' she exclaimed. 'Why didn't you tell me about it last night? Or were you waiting so that the announcement would be a surprise?'

Violet failed to guess what her aunt was talking about.

'Oh, my dear! There's no need to be shy about it! Why didn't you say it was in today's *Times*? I've only just noticed it! Now tell me: have you decided yet on a date?'

Violet stared at her aunt in terror. 'Have you got a copy?'

'But of course! It's right here.' Henrietta scurried over to a side-table. 'I hope you've given instructions to reserve some copies as souvenirs.'

Violet studied the entry under the heading COURT CIRCULAR. She looked with horror at her own name, feeling her aunt's eyes on her.

'I'm not sure when the wedding will be,' she said, grabbing at the first words that came into her head. She felt so angry she thought her head would burst. How could Sybil have let her father do this? Had James seen it? Did he believe it? The thoughts chased each other in circles, finding no answers.

'Miss Vi!' At the door Aggie was signalling urgently. Never could Violet have been more thankful to be interrupted.

In the chintz-furnished guest bedroom, Aggie was looking anxious. It was cold enough for her breath to be visible.

'Oh, Miss Vi, Max has had an accident!'

Having phoned the number she'd been given for the hospital, she was able to tell Violet exactly what had happened.

'. . . Yes, he's going to be all right. But your letter –'

To Aggie's surprise, Violet clapped her hands together and smiled for the first time since they had left London. 'Oh, Aggie, thank heavens! Don't misunderstand me: I'm sorry Max has had an accident; but that explains it. No wonder James hasn't sent a telegram – he will have seen the announcement. Don't you see? Now I can telephone him.'

In the nearby village the garage was just shutting shop when Violet panted in and asked to use the phone.

A few moments later, in the grimy corner where the telephone stood, she replaced the receiver with trembling hands. He had gone. That very afternoon. At this moment he would be aboard the liner in Southampton. For an instant Violet thought she was going to faint, in a sprawl on the oily floor.

Picking up the receiver again, she asked the operator to try to find the number of the *Orontes*. There was an agonising delay before she could even get through to Southampton. After a series of clicks and different voices somebody finally asked, 'You want to speak to someone on board?'

'Yes,' she shouted down the crackly line.

'I'm afraid that's impossible. The gangway has already been raised.'

She walked back to Henrietta's house with tears running down her face. Just hold on, she told herself, having sneaked unobserved into her bedroom. From now on, everything will simply be a question of self-control. Violet was clear in her mind about what to do next, even though her spirit was aching. She confided to Aggie such plans as she had so far made.

That night, as soon as she was the only person still up, Aggie made her way to Henrietta's library.

In among the books on gardening and the finer points of the horse, *Debrett's Peerage* and old copies of *Country Life*, she found an atlas. Australia was the furthest place in the world that you could go to. Aggie's only travelling so far comprised trips to Brighton with Max, strapped into the side-car and loving and loathing every scary mile of the run. The thought of going 10,000 miles was hard to accept.

But she was part of this mad escape plan, wedded to going with Vi as truly as she had once thought she was pledged to follow Max.

Next morning started early: Violet had been unable to sleep, and Henrietta was going out with the Heythrop, whose meet was five miles away. 'Borrow a horse if you like,' said Henrietta. 'Perfect spring day.' Violet watched her tucking into eggs and bacon, to be followed by quantities of toast and marmalade. The only item Henrietta skimped on before a day's hunting was coffee. 'It's so hard to get off the horse and go behind a bush when you need to.'

'Yes; thank you, Henrietta, I might go out for a ride.' Violet tried to sound unexcited. Outside the sun was shining weakly. In Australia, it would be hot. She wondered how she would adapt to spending Christmas in sun and August in rain.

'Have you packed your own things, Aggie?'

Violet looked doubtfully at the clothes hanging in the guest-room wardrobe. All her Parisian outfits, including the short-skirted one by Chanel that she was wearing, would be far too conspicuous.

Standing in the doorway, Aggie was awaiting instructions. 'Yes, Miss Vi.'

'You've got to stop calling me Miss Vi. From now on we're just two girls going to Australia.'

'How are we going to get there?' Aggie was trying not to look nervous.

'We'll go on a ship. First, though, I suppose we might need to get some money.'

Like many daughters of the well-to-do, Violet herself never seemed to have much cash. Her dining and dancing had normally been paid for by some young man; her transport was provided by her father. Otherwise she had a weekly allowance, like a child's pocket money. It would never have occurred to her to acquire any savings. For the first time she realised that Aggie probably had more real money than she did.

Aggie had been thinking the same thing. 'I've got some put by. You know, for a rainy day. Thanks to you, I've saved up almost £30.'

'Thank you for the thought; but you'd better keep it. When we get to London, we'll go to a pawn shop and sell my jewellery. Don't look so shocked, Aggie.' She grinned. 'Call it Father's unwilling dowry.'

Violet looked at the contents of her little jewel case. A necklace of cornelians. A bracelet set with opals. A diamond pendant and a pair of diamond stud earrings. She had no idea which item was the most valuable. But they were all she had with her, and there was no going back to the house in Chester Street to get anything else. She cursed her sheltered upbringing, which had led her simply to accept the fact that she had diamonds and gold.

'Now, Aggie, I want you to go and tell Cook that your mother is ill, that you have to return to London and that I have given you permission to go.'

'But I haven't got a mother.'

'Cook's not going to know that, is she?'

Violet rode out of the stable yard. Broomstick was her favourite horse, a bay thoroughbred gelding who had once won at Badminton. He was twelve years old now, and his fiery nature had been tempered by age, which had also turned the black whiskers round his muzzle silvery white. But he was still full of courage, would take a fence as well as any four-year-old, and wasn't against the occasional skittish shy when something fluttered in the hedgerow, or a car roared by at speed.

Below Henrietta's square Georgian house with its unruly garden a long expanse of grass ran down to a stream. The watery sun had started to warm the frozen earth, and the ground was perfect: just the right amount of give to be kind to the horse's legs, but not enough to make the going laborious. Violet urged Broomstick into a canter.

'Running away, running away.' The words were in time with Broomstick's strides. She wouldn't let herself think of what would happen if James rejected her when she arrived in Australia. She concentrated on reminding herself that whatever awaited her it would be better than life in London without him.

At the stream she slowed to a walk and turned down the valley, making for the main road south to Oxford. Just before the road there was a difficult jump, where a small hedge concealed a drop. Many a horseman had tumbled there, seduced by the prospect of taking the hedge at speed, only to find the ground unexpectedly opening up on the far side. Violet had jumped it often, forewarned of its trick. All one had to do was slow the horse right down immediately before, so that the animal had time to see over the jump to the drop and adjust his strides accordingly.

Broomstick neighed in anticipation as the hedge drew close. Violet debated whether to have one last jump, but decided against it. Broomstick chafed at the bit, shaking his head in eagerness, as she reined him in.

'Whoa, boy.' She smoothed his neck and slithered to the ground. From her pocket she took a pair of nail scissors.

The girth was made of webbing rather than leather and the scissors cut easily through its fabric. Violet frayed the severed edges. It wouldn't fool anyone for long; but it would do the trick for a few hours.

Pulling the heavy saddle from Broomstick's back, she threw it into the long grass by the hedge. She led the horse to the fence and turned him round several times, so that he trampled the grass, leaving heavy hoofprints.

Then she slapped him on the rump, shooing him away as she did so. He looked at her with puzzlement, and for a moment stood his ground. Then, obligingly, he flicked his tail, bucked and turned back into the field at a gallop.

Violet watched him go. She pulled off her bowler hat and shook out her hair. Then she threw the hat into the hedge alongside the saddle. She wriggled out of her long black riding skirt: underneath she wore a red wool skirt which, though expensive, was plain enough to be inconspicuous. From her jacket pocket she took a red scarf and knotted it round her neck. The scarf and skirt did not match; she was confident she could now pass as a country girl on her way to town for the day.

Aggie was waiting up on the main road. She carried a battered leather suitcase, which had once belonged to Violet's mother and which Aggie had rescued from the rubbish tip. Inside it were their combined possessions.

'Oh, Miss Vi, thank heaven you've come. I seem to have been waiting ages.'

They started down the road to Woodstock. Their plan was to get a charabanc to Oxford and from there a train to London. In cash, Violet had a pound, borrowed from Aggie against the moment when she could sell her jewellery.

As the charabanc was pulling away from the Bear at Woodstock, Aggie commented, 'You ought to wear a hat, Miss Vi.'

'Aggie, don't call me miss. Someone might hear. Why should I wear a hat?'

'Well, all girls of our station wear hats when they go out.'

Violet looked around the bus. Aggie was right; she was the only girl without a hat. Her lustrous black hair shone like a beacon. Hurrying from the bus station in Oxford to catch the London train, she bought a hat at random. It was hideous, but so much the better.

In London, she needed Aggie's advice again.

'This was the shop my mother went to.' They had stopped in front of the window of a pawnbroker's shop in Pimlico. It was crammed with items: watches and jewellery, china and glass, a box full of wedding rings, two men's suits on tailor's dummies, and a lady's fur coat draped inelegantly across a chair. Two complete sets of silver cutlery were pressed up against the glass. Violet studied the display with fascination. She wondered how many ruined fortunes the shop represented and how many desperate people had made their way into its dark interior, willing to sell their family's heritage for hard cash. While Aggie, from tact, lingered outside, Violet pushed open the door and went in.

The pawnbroker listened to what she had to say, glanced at the opals, then examined the diamonds through an eyeglass. Though he made a point of looking indifferent, he realised at once that a dealer he knew in Hatton Garden would pay a high price for the earrings and pendant.

First, though, he needed to gauge how desperate the girl was. Despite her ludicrous hat she was clearly from a good family. She didn't look like a thief in any case; but the odd question in that direction might still frighten her into accepting a low price.

'Well, young lady; these are quite good stones.'

He removed the glass from his eye and fixed Violet with a stare.

'How did you come by them?'

'They're mine; who else's?'

'That's what they all say. I'll just look in the book.'

He extracted a large black volume from under the counter and ran his eye down several pages. He knew the diamonds weren't on the black list of stolen goods, but the book always unnerved customers regardless. Violet twisted the signet ring on her little finger. Her palms were moist.

'Seems you're in the clear. A hundred quid for these,' indicating the diamonds. 'And I'll make you a present of a tenner for the bracelet.'

Violet drew in a sharp breath. Whatever the jewels were worth, she had enough sense to realise that the man was probably offering her less.

'But they're worth far more than that. I'll tell you what I'll do,' she bluffed. 'I'll take the same for the opals and cornelians together as you've offered for the diamonds.'

The pawnbroker wondered if she was in the family way. It was a definite possibility.

'A hundred and ten, and that's my last offer.' He held out his hand for the jewels.

'No. That's robbery. I'll not sell for anything less than £250.'

The broker put away his eyeglass with a look of uninterest. 'I'm sorry: it's my final offer,' he repeated, turning away from the counter. This was the moment when most people changed their minds. Just last week he'd bought a silver dinner service for only £25.00. It had been worth well over £100.

Violet blinked back tears of humiliation. 'Just as you wish,' she said proudly, striding out of the shop. 'I'll go elsewhere.'

The broker watched her go. She'd come back. They always did.

There was only one farewell Violet wanted to make.

'How lovely to see you, darling,' Emerald exclaimed as she ushered them into the riverside studio in Chelsea where she lived.

'I've just discovered this wonderful new cocktail – a Bosom Caress-er. It's as sublime as the name.' Without waiting to be asked, she poured them each a generous glass. Aggie tried not to look amazed at her skintight dress, draped in several yards of pale mauve feather boa.

Emerald's apartment, too, was a surprise to anyone unfamiliar with such places. On the mantelpiece were rows of invitations. They were unlike the usual stiff white AT HOMES, occasionally brightened with an embossed coat of arms, which had been part of Violet's own life since she turned seventeen. 'Winnie and Fifi are making a little Whoopee on Saturday Night. Do come and Bring a Bottle!' Violet wondered whether Winnie was short for Winston or Winifred but didn't like to ask. Next to their invitation was an elaborate card made up of a jumble of words cut out of newspapers and gaudily painted in scarlet, yellow and black. 'It's adapted from Marinetti's "Futurist Manifesto",' Emerald said, following Violet's gaze. 'Divine, don't you think?'

Violet nodded. She had never heard of the 'Futurist Manifesto'. Emerald was always catching her out like this and unwittingly making her feel ignorant.

Prominent amid the room's organised chaos was a half-finished oil painting of a naked man reclining on crimson cushions. Seeing it, Aggie blushed. 'I think it's time women painted nudes, don't you?' Emerald said, trying to put her at her ease. Cigarette and drink in hand, she took an appraising look at a detail of the brushwork.

Emerald was a collector, as well as a painter in her own right. On the crowded walls of the studio hung a series of voluptuous female nudes painted by D. H. Lawrence. She had bought them up a few years before, after the police had raided an exhibition of his work. There were simple line drawings by the French painter Jean Cocteau, two Picassos painted in the early 1920s when the artist was all but unknown, a grotesque portrait by Augustus John, two Nina Hamnet drawings, and a small painting by Henri Matisse for which Emerald had paid less than fifty pounds. It was largely because of Emerald's activities as a collector that Rupert Harcourt was forever accusing her of squandering the money she had inherited from Violet's brother Harry.

'So what brings you here, on this unspeakably cold night?' It was obvious that she hadn't seen the marriage announcement. Sitting down on the sofa beside Violet, she smoothed out the wrinkles in the elaborate shawl which covered the chintz upholstery.

'It's James.' Violet brightened at the certainty of Emerald's sympathetic understanding. 'There's been the most terrible disaster, but everything's going to be all right.' The words spilled out in a rush, as she explained what had happened since the moment in Hyde Park three days ago when he had asked her to marry him.

'So, you see, I simply must go to him. I have to go to Australia.'

'Of course you have,' Emerald replied easily, as though she were talking about a trip to Cornwall. 'But, Violet darling, you'll need some money, won't you? I can get you a thousand to be going on with, first thing in the morning from the bank if you like. Tonight, you can stay here. It isn't the Ritz,' turning apologetically to Aggie, 'but at least it's warm.'

Aggie stared, feverishly calculating in her head. At her present rate of pay, to earn £1,000 would take her forty years.

'Oh, Emerald, that is kind of you!' Violet sipped her cocktail, feeling relaxed for the first time in days. She had half believed her plan would sound ridiculous; but Emerald could make anything seem possible. 'We'd love to stay the night – wouldn't we, Aggie? – but I really don't need any money. I've got lots. I've just made a rather good sale of some of my jewellery. The buyer' – even in Emerald's hearing, Violet was too

59

self-conscious to say 'pawnbroker' – 'was a bit sticky about meeting my price. But he got far more cooperative once I'd made a show of walking out on him.'

'Well, that's wonderful. It sounds as though you've taken care of everything. Oh, Violet, I do want you to be happy. I think this James Franklin sounds splendid. I can tell you love him.'

Emerald, like Aggie and Violet herself, took it for granted that Violet had a basic understanding of money and its value.

They fell to talking of the future over more cocktails, wreathed in the smoke from Emerald's endless Turkish cigarettes. Glass in hand, in a comfortable armchair, it was more than Aggie could do to stay awake. In her sleep she dreamed of rocking waves and windswept sails and a new world on the horizon.

5

Fifty yards beyond the stacks of canvas wardrobe trunks awaiting porterage from the platform of Southampton railway station the SS *Carthage* lay at anchor, her high prow visible above the shipping offices and warehouses.

At the ticket office Violet and Aggie learned that there was no boat to Australia for another three weeks, so Violet bought two second-class tickets on the starboard side of the first boat going east. The *Carthage* was due to sail for Singapore that night, and from there, the clerk assured them, plenty of boats would be going to Australia. It was clear that he had mentally marked them down as members of the 'fishing fleet', the nickname given to eligible daughters from impoverished families, on their way east in search of husbands.

From the deck they watched a tearful woman on the dockside bidding farewell to her children, a boy and a girl. Agitated by their mother's distress, they too were starting to cry.

'It won't be for long, darlings.'

The little boy, who couldn't be more than eight, stood his ground bravely. 'Yes, Mummy. And I'll take care of Alice.'

He put his arm round his little sister's shoulders and Violet felt a lump come into her throat.

She wondered if a search party had found Broomstick and how long it would take them to become suspicious about the girth. It seemed as though much more than twenty-four hours had passed since she had been severing Broomstick's webbing with a pair of nail scissors.

'Will you write to your parents?' Aggie asked, leaning on the deck rail beside her. Down on the dockside crowds of people were waving hats and newspapers held like flags, to friends or loved ones who were sailing. Everyone on board except them had someone to see them off. For a moment Violet felt desolate. To avoid communicating her sudden sense of foreboding she smiled as she replied.

'I'll write to Mummy. You'll have to post it before we sail.'

Her father, she was sure, would try to blame her mother – would blame anyone rather than himself. Poor Mummy. If only she had some of Emerald's toughness. Just thinking about her mother made her want to cry. Though she was not entirely sure whom she was crying for, her mother or herself. She turned to look at Aggie. The other girl's thick brown hair was blowing back from her forehead and her cheeks were ruddy.

'You had better write to Max, too.'

Aggie nodded. 'I'll miss him. But Max won't have any problem finding another girl.' There was a pause and then she said, 'We've come this far, we can't get cold feet now.'

'You're excited?'

'Yes; yes I am.' Aggie knew she must put on a brave face; if she didn't, they might change their minds in the few hours before the *Carthage* sailed. She took a deep breath, sniffing the salty air mixed with the portside smells of tar and rope, oil and smoke.

Violet looked at her in surprise. She had expected it to be Aggie, not herself, who found she had doubts at the last moment.

'Dear Mummy,' Violet began. She paused and chewed her pen. They were in their tiny cabin below deck and Violet was perched uncomfortably on the edge of the lower bunk. 'Please don't be angry with me. I had to go to James. I love him and I can't live without him and neither you nor Daddy would understand. I don't know when I will be back.'

She looked at her watch. In five minutes the steward was coming round to pick up last-minute shore mail. She read through what she had written, deciding that it was probably the most inadequate letter of her life. But how could she explain to someone like her mother, who had never, as far as she knew, taken a risk or a gamble from the moment she was born?

'Thank you for everything you have done for me,' she wrote, then thought about crossing it out. It sounded pathetic. 'I love you very much, so please try to understand. Do not worry about me, I will be perfectly all right. Agnes has come with me. I will write when I reach Sydney.'

There was a knock on the door and the bright face of the second-class steward looked into the cabin.

'All ready, girls?'

She handed him the hastily sealed envelope bearing her mother's name and address.

Before the *Carthage* had even entered the Bay of Biscay the storms began. Aggie and Violet lay on their bunks, alternating between the top and the bottom depending on which of them felt more ill. For the first three days of the voyage neither of them was well enough to eat anything.

Lisbon, their first port of call, brought a few hours' relief; and Violet even felt sufficiently recovered to leave the cabin, to instruct the wireless engineer to send a cable ahead to the *Orontes*, now nearing Port Said.

Once back at sea, however, their discomfort was almost as bad as ever.

Their cabin was on the lowest deck, below the water line. Aggie seemed indifferent to the absence of natural light, but Violet felt panic rising every time she thought of the mass of water swirling and roaring a foot or so away from her head. On the second day, rough seas notwithstanding, she could bear her incarceration no longer. She put on the black coat she had brought from Aunt Henrietta's and told Aggie she was going on deck.

'I can't come with you, Vi.' Aggie, on the lower bunk, was gaunt and pale from hours of retching into a bucket.

'It would do you good to get some air.'

The boat lurched steeply. 'I'm going to be sick again!' Aggie gasped. Violet looked away, nauseated even more by the smell than by the movement of the boat.

The deck was deserted as she pushed open the heavy sea-tight door and stepped outside. A strong wind was blowing down from the north, whipping the sea into endless white horses. She pulled the coat round her shoulders and breathed deeply. The cold air caught in her throat, but revived her. Holding on to the deck rail with her gloved hands, she watched the water stream powerfully past.

Five young soldiers walked by, side-stepping the piles of empty folded deck chairs which the wind had blown over. One of them doffed his cap at Violet.

She smiled back; shipboard life evidently suspended all need for formality. She wandered along the deck, alternately walking freely, then rushing to grab the handrail when the boat dived into a trough.

Second-class passengers were allowed to walk only round the stern of the boat. Halfway up the long deck, a heavy gate barred the way into first class. Violet looked through it, then turned to retrace her steps. After a few weeks she was going to be deathly bored with this walk.

'Curse it.' An exclamation from behind made her turn round too quickly so that her feet skidded on the wet deck. She collided with a well-dressed man who was holding on to the edge of a lifeboat, trying to regain his balance.

'I'm sorry,' she said.

'My fault entirely.' The stranger adjusted his hat with his free hand. 'Ben Schiff at your service. Recently of New York City, bound for the Orient.'

He seemed to expect a reply.

'Violet Harcourt. Recently of London, bound for Australia.'

Ben shook her hand. Though he was burly, his bulk was not due to fat. His dark eyes were arresting.

'I wonder if we can get back again,' he said conversationally, pointing to the gate. Evidently he assumed she too was travelling first class. Violet had noticed that he looked well dressed, in a light-brown coat of thick cashmere.

Because of the pitch and roll of the boat he courteously gave her his arm. They walked towards the stern of the boat, Ben keeping his other hand on the deck rail.

'What takes you to Australia?' he asked. 'Family?'

'In a way,' Violet replied quickly. 'And you? Do you have business in the Orient?'

'I plan to. I'm in oil. In Texas. And there are some mighty big fields under the South China Seas which haven't yet been seized by Royal Dutch. For the moment, you could say I'm wild-catting.'

'What does that mean?'

'Oh, just an expression to describe prospecting for oil. Would you like to join me for a drink?' They had walked round the stern and were standing at the gate on the other side of the boat.

Violet blushed. 'Actually, I'm travelling second class.'

Ben raised his eyebrows and looked at her. 'We'll soon take care of that.' He pushed open the gate and ushered her through.

Inside the first-class saloon, uniformed Chinese waiters padded silently on the lush red carpet. The furnishings were brocade, heavy and fussy, but the chairs were deep and comfortable. Violet sat down gratefully while Ben motioned to a steward.

'A bottle of the usual, Tran. And this young lady is my guest. Make sure she always has what she wants.'

Violet watched, curious. No money had changed hands; yet she was sure Ben had already selected and paid Tran to take care of him on the trip. There was a sophistication about Ben quite unlike the foppish worldliness shown by Peter in knowing his way round the Bond Street night-clubs. Ben Schiff seemed a man who could take on the world with masterly grace. Yet, at the most, he couldn't be more than thirty.

The Krug champagne was icy cold. Ben raised his glass in a toast, and settled back in his chair. Violet looked at him.

'How did you get into the oil business?'

'My father used to make deals – taking ten per cent of the sale price – between countries with oil to sell and giant corporations who wanted to buy it. I decided to go it alone. I'm no middle man.'

'So the Depression didn't hurt you?'

'Oil is a commodity – it endures. That's not saying we weren't hurt. Even Rockefeller suffered, after he bought equity stock last October. Your family were involved in the crash?' Violet was aware of the shrewdness in his dark eyes.

'Yes.' Violet explained how her father had invested in paper-making shortly before the whole venture collapsed. She hurried to add, 'Oh, but he wasn't wiped out.'

'Aside from all those it destroyed, a few people found going broke was good for them. I think it concentrated their minds.'

Violet was unsure how to answer him. 'I don't think it was good for my father. He couldn't adapt. And he couldn't face people so easily.'

As she was preparing to return he asked, 'Will you join me for dinner?'

'I'm not sure if I ought to . . .'

'Because we only just met? Because we haven't been formally introduced? Don't be so English.'

Violet's hesitation was brief. She was reassured because he'd promptly described himself as a married man. She was also tempted at the thought of an excellent meal.

'Thank you. I'd love to.'

The cabin still smelt stuffy when Violet returned, but she was pleased to see that Aggie was looking better. She sat down on the edge of the lower bunk, listening to the beat of the engines and the regular creak of the metal plates and woodwork.

'Aggie, we've got a problem.'

'Another one?'

'Oh, it's not really serious. I need some clothes.' She explained about Ben's invitation to dinner.

Aggie swung herself off the bunk and dragged out the suitcase.

'Three silk shirts; your red skirt; a yellow silk skirt; two cotton dresses; and a jacket.'

Violet looked gloomy. 'So I've nothing for the evening.'

Aggie leaned over and pressed the buzzer to summon Arthur, the steward.

'Hmm,' he said when he arrived. 'Clothes, is it? Well, if you promise to keep it quiet, I'll give you the key to the theatrical locker.'

Violet was all delight. 'Oh, Arthur, could you?'

The theatrical locker was a converted cabin down in the hold. It was thick with heat from the nearby engine room. The noise was deafening. 'Cor, how do they work down here?' Aggie exclaimed.

Arthur unlocked the door and switched on the light.

'It's a treasure trove!' Violet's eyes widened. The room was bursting with crinolines and charleston dresses, swords and sabres, military uniforms, and a multitude of hats.

'I expect you'll want a needle and cotton,' Arthur said, opening a cupboard in the wall. 'I'll leave you to it. But don't forget to lock up! It's more than my job's worth if anyone finds you've been here.'

The girls started sorting through the costumes.

'Look at this, Aggie.' Violet held up a long, close-cut dress in silk. The fabric had been cut on the cross, so that it swirled softly out at the hem. Violet slipped out of her skirt and jacket and, clad only in her camisole, pulled on the dress.

'It could have been made for you. I wonder what something so nice is doing here?'

'Mm,' said Violet, pleased. 'And how about this?' She held up a length of dark-green crêpe de Chine labelled 'Maid Marian:scene 3'. 'I bet this could be made into a simply marvellous skirt.' In fact, Violet herself hadn't the least skill as a needlewoman.

'I could turn that into something really pretty,' agreed Aggie. 'I'm a good seamstress, though I say it myself.' She was looking through a pile of assorted helmets and boots. From underneath she suddenly pulled out yards of cerise tulle. 'Look at this! Now, if we drape this round your left shoulder, leaving the right one bare, then gather it in a bow on the right side, pull it in at the waist . . . wait, here are some pins.' Violet stood still, while Aggie pinned up the folds of material. 'Now where did I see those flowers?' Aggie muttered, searching through a box full of elaborate costume jewellery. 'Here we are!' She pinned a silk camelia to the left shoulder and stood back. 'It looks a treat. What a pity there isn't a mirror down here.'

'Aggie, you're a genius! With all these things, and you to help me, I could have enough clothes to last a whole voyage in first class.'

At a quarter to eight Tran came to collect Violet, knocking softly on the cabin door and presenting her with a single fresh rose. She pinned the white flower to her dress, before being escorted along the bare corridors of second class, through a heavy doorway and into the world of first class.

Ben was waiting at the top of a flight of red-carpeted stairs. He wore a short white dinner jacket over straight black trousers. A red silk hankerchief flowed from his breast pocket. He looked both powerful and distinguished as he and Violet walked through the crowded staterooms towards a reserved corner table.

'We'll be sitting with the captain tonight at dinner,' he said. 'I hope you won't be bored. It's hardly the Embassy Club.'

'You know the Embassy?' Violet was delighted.

'Sure; I know it well. Luigi Naintre is a fine restaurateur, though not above a bit of sharp dealing. When he owned Ciros in Orange Street, and served champagne after hours, he charged prices you wouldn't believe. Twenty-five shillings for one bottle!'

'You hate to be overcharged?'

'I'm a money-maker – I'm rich, but I want to be richer.'

The captain's table was set on a raised dais at the far end of the dining-room. Violet found herself seated next to a high-ranking military officer of florid appearance, and opposite a drunk tea-planter from Malaya. In contrast to much of the conversation, the food was excellent and Violet ate ravenously. A rich fish soup, made from prawns, mussels, clams and crayfish tails, was followed by *fillet de boeuf carbonnade* served with tender honeyed carrots, glazed peas and a potato soufflé. Next came grilled turbot, and for dessert there was a choice of *crêpes suzettes* or fresh fruit. With the *crêpes*, Ben, who was evidently knowledgeable about wines, suggested she try a glass of chilled Château d'Yquem. The sweet, aromatic wine and its fruity but sharper aftertaste delighted her.

'Do you think this compares with dinner at the Ritz?' Ben asked, signalling to the waiter to refill her glass.

With a look of seriousness that he found delightful, Violet considered. 'The room's not so pretty. And of course there isn't anyone I know here, except you.'

Ben roared with laughter.

'I don't see what's funny,' she said, all surprise.

'I meant the food, not the diners, you goose. I suppose if someone told you about the Independent Labour Party you'd want to know why you hadn't been invited.'

Violet flushed. 'I am grown up, you know.'

'You're certainly on the way,' Ben replied, waving over a waiter to bring cigars. 'It's a helluva shame the English still feel they have to bring their daughters up as if they had cotton wool between the ears. Do you know that poem Alan Herbert published in *Punch*?' He quoted:

> 'I like them fluffy, I freely confess,
> With fluffy blue eyes, and a fluffy blue dress,
> And fluffy fair hair, and no brains at all. . .

That's what a British gentlemen expects from the woman of his dreams. Fluff.'

'Actually, I do think you're awfully rude.'

'You have to remember I haven't enjoyed the benefits of Eton.'

'That's obvious,' she said, bright with pleasure at the company of this strange man. 'Where did you go to school, since you're clearly better educated than I am?'

'I didn't go anywhere,' Ben said. 'My father insisted on private tutors. He didn't trust schools. I had American teachers, French, Spanish, German – everything except British. He said the British were going to lose their empire, and he didn't want me to learn any bad habits from losers. He was a very competitive fella', my dad. He liked to finish first.'

After dinner they listened to the ship's band running through its repertoire: Cole Porter, Irving Berlin and the old Vincent Youmans hit, 'Tea For Two'. The *Carthage* slid through the calm night as Ben led Violet expertly round the floor to 'What Is This Thing Called Love?' Were they doing this on the *Orontes*, she wondered.

By the time the evening was drawing to a close, it was clear that Ben knew everyone on the first-class passenger list. More, he knew every officer, the gym instructor, the masseur, the chef, the chief steward, the three-man committee who presided over both the weekly and the accumulative sweepstake in which passengers wagered how many nautical miles the *Carthage* would cover, and even Arthur, their own cabin steward down in second class. His occasional disparagement of their fellow passengers made Violet both uneasy and intrigued. True, as a collection they might well be far from inspiring. 'Many of them know each other out East,' Ben said. 'Or they've met before on the boat. That tea-planter guy, who was at dinner – he's trying to have an affair with the tall Frenchwoman wearing a flower in her hair. She's the wife of an official in Saigon. She'll be in his bed all right, before too long.'

Violet exclaimed, and he looked at her. 'It helps pass the time.'

She wondered unhappily if James was 'passing the time' with someone's wife.

As Ben was lighting his last cigar of the evening he seemed about to say something, then hesitated.

'So how are you enjoying being a runaway?' he asked eventually.

Violet blushed. 'How did you know?'

Ben shrugged massively. 'From the papers. At Lisbon I had several brought on board. I hate being out of touch.'

'What papers?' Violet clutched his arm. 'Please show me.'

'Now?'

She nodded. Rising, Ben led her out on to the first-class promenade and along the deck. His stateroom was on the expensive port side, which was more sheltered from the sun while they were eastward bound. It had none of the claustrophobia she and Aggie endured down on deck three of the big ship. His spacious cabin was at least four times larger than theirs and resembled a luxury hotel suite. In their underground cell there was only harsh electric illumination; here, net curtains fluttered in front of the sliding doors that gave on to a private verandah with a sun umbrella and, beyond, ocean merging with sky.

Here was luxury and coolness; but also a sense of organised work underway. A large desk, transferred from the purser's department and covered with charts and other documents, took up the centre of the cabin. Large-scale maps had been fastened to the walls.

Beside the desk were two stacks of newspapers. Ben began riffling through them, discarding copies of the *New York Times*, the *Wall Street Journal*, the *Los Angeles Times*, the *Financial Times*, the London *Times*, the *Daily Telegraph*, the *Gazette*, *Le Monde* and the *New York Herald Tribune*. Violet stared in amazement.

'Do you read them all?'

'Yes,' he said, over his shoulder, 'and I guess you'll end up doing the same.'

'What on earth do you mean?'

'Okay, I'll tell you.' He turned round, raising one eyebrow. 'If I've got the story right, you're running away to Australia to join the heir to a newspaper magnate. Am I right?'

Violet was lost for words.

'You don't have to look so goddam scared,' he said, amused. 'I'm no clairvoyant — but one of my articles of faith is finding out what's going on in the world. Your story's here, in the *Daily Mail* of three days ago, and also in the *Express*. I must say, you've gotten yourself great headlines.' He held up a copy of the *Mail*. '*Débutante – Runaway Mystery*,' he started to intone.

Violet seized the paper from him. A photograph, taken some time during her coming-out year and used in one of Quigley's articles, showed her leaving a ball. She was on the arm of a young man whose name she had now forgotten. At least it wasn't Peter.

'Of course we're absolutely aghast,' her mother was quoted as saying. 'Her engagement to Peter Ironside had only just been made public, when she simply vanished. But we wouldn't dream of assuming that she eloped with her Australian friend, having read his statement that their friendship was at an end.'

Violet felt a coldness spreading out from her stomach.

'Have you got the previous day's *Mail*?' she managed to ask. Ben passed it to her, and she turned to Quigley's column, where a picture of James seemed to bound up off the page.

'When told about Miss Harcourt's engagement Mr Franklin expressed surprise. Asked about his own relations with the young lady, he replied, "It wasn't an affair, just a fling."'

Violet sat down on a sofa. She could feel her legs shaking.

'What's the matter?' Seeing her face, Ben poured a glass of brandy. She took it and gulped it down.

'It's nothing,' she lied as he picked the paper off the floor and started to read the story. She watched him, not knowing what else to say.

He finished reading and looked at her, guessing her thoughts. 'Cheer up. You shouldn't believe everything you read in the papers.'

'I know,' she said miserably, sitting down again on the sofa.

What could James have meant? Was she following him for nothing?

'Your parents tried to stop you marrying this Australian guy?'

'Tried? It sounds as if they succeeded,' she said bitterly. 'He just packed up and left the country.'

'After seeing your engagement all over the papers? It does sound as if Quigley rubbed his nose in it.'

'You know him?'

'A nodding acquaintance, which is to say closer than I care for. You should never talk to gossip writers, not even to say you're not talking.'

As Ben put his stack of papers back in order, he glanced several times at Violet's face. Her troubled eyes were huge.

'We could send a radiogram at the next port of call,' he said.

6

At Port Said, where a number of passengers disembarked, Ben had booked a cabin for Violet in first class.

She had protested. 'I can't afford it.'

He made as if to contradict her. 'But I can. And it's cheaper than paying the stewards every time you cross over no man's land!'

'I don't know how you get away with it, Vi.' Aggie, looking serious, was sitting next to Violet on the lower bunk. 'You never even seem to worry.'

'That's not true. I do worry about what's going to happen. And about accepting his hospitality.'

Aggie sighed. The excitement of the voyage was wearing off. In the lower deck other passengers' servants, together with the poor emigrants and regular soldiers, spent their days boozing and playing deck games. Tugs-of-war with officers from first class took place almost daily; so too did lotteries on how far the ship had sailed in the previous twenty-four hours.

Meanwhile she was worried about Violet.

Aggie was less sophisticated, but in many ways far smarter, than Violet, whose upbringing had cushioned her from the world. Violet expected people to wish her well as a matter of course. How could Aggie explain that this wasn't the case – that the world was full of people who would cut off Violet's little finger merely to steal a gold signet ring? Aggie feared for her, loving her like the family she did not have. She worried, too, at the thought that it was upon Violet that her own future depended.

Violet tossed aside her copy of the *Carthage Times* for the week of 25 July. She and Ben were sitting out on deck in canvas chairs. Both wore solar topees against the vertical sunlight. The tropical sun had brought out copper gleams in her dark hair and a few freckles had appeared across the bridge of her nose. She was wearing baggy shorts that stopped just above her knees, and a sleeveless cotton shirt. Her slender arms had tanned a deep brown. Her eyes were bluer than ever.

She looked at Ben.

'Why do you choose to travel by sea when you could go by aeroplane? It surprises me that you're prepared to waste the time.' The monotony of life at sea was beginning to affect almost everyone about them.

'It's a good opportunity to work. Out here,' waving his hand towards the ocean, 'is the only place nobody can call you up.'

'Doesn't your wife ever come with you?'

'Very rarely. Litzie hates leaving Paris.'

Ben had briefly mentioned that his wife spent a lot of time in the French capital, where she was involved in some kind of political activity.

'Because of her interest in politics?'

Ben grimaced. 'You could say that. Two years ago she went to Palestine and became a Zionist. I wish sometimes she'd gone somewhere else.'

'What's that?' Violet thought Ben's wife sounded terrifying.

'Someone who believes in a national home for the Jews. The British agreed to the idea in 1917, or that's what she says. I think they've got her fooled. Sure, they support the idea – but only if it doesn't prejudice the rights of anyone else who's been settled there all those centuries since we Jews got the hell out.'

'You sound as if you disagree with your wife.'

'Do I look like I need a national home? My ancestors escaped from the ghetto. We've been three generations in America, and done very nicely. That's my national home. Litzie, though, and Dad, they used to fight like wildcats on the subject. She thought he was a bad Jew. I guess I'm more on his side. He thought she was just dumb, not to see all the trouble she was storing up for the next generation.'

'Don't you love her?' Ben frowned, ignoring the brashness of Violet's question.

'Yes but I don't have to love her politics. She's also a Red.'

'My God!' Violet had never encountered a communist. She had heard plenty of talk, though, about the danger they posed to decent society everywhere. 'Where did you meet her?'

'In Paris, when she was studying at the Sorbonne. She was raised in Vienna. Her father has a bank there. As a matter of fact he has quite a few banks.'

'Does she like America?'

'She thinks we're reactionary barbarians. Not that that matters. Even though it's my home, neither of us is there very much.'

How could such a marriage work? Ben saw the puzzled look on Violet's face and laughed.

'You could call it a modern marriage. We like to lead our own lives.'

'What about children?'

'She doesn't want them. There's never a week when Mom doesn't make some pointed remark.'

'Don't you mind?'

'Yes. But it could still happen some day.'

As the miles of ocean slipped by, Violet's thoughts alternated between her mental image of James and the photographs she had seen in Ben's stateroom of his beautiful blonde wife, who was doubtless intimidating. For the first time in her life, Violet found herself thinking, I must seem very boring in comparison.

Meanwhile money, always in Aggie's thoughts, was beginning to worry Violet too. Not much arithmetic was needed to see why they should feel anxious. They had thousands of miles yet to go; but their original £200 had already dwindled to a total of £82 5s. 6d.

Ben, misled by Violet's ignorance about money, had no idea she might be financially at risk. It was purely from sporting instinct that he had persuaded her to bet a whole pound on the ship's lottery and guess the ultimate length of their voyage.

'I've been doing some calculations,' he said one evening after dinner when they were sitting up on deck, watching the stars at mid-heaven above them.

'I'd never have guessed,' Violet said. Ben's calculations had become something of a joke, but none disputed their accuracy. He had even been barred from entering the daily and weekly sweepstakes on how far the *Carthage* sailed, after he'd won three days running.

'You can kid me as much as you like. But I'll tell you one thing. We're going to dock late, maybe half a day, maybe more. Once I'm back on land I can't afford to hang around. I reckon I'll have to climb on board the seaplane for Surabaya the moment we dock or I'll miss my drilling team.'

She turned to look at him.

'I planned to make sure personally that you and Aggie were fixed up OK before I left.'

'We'll be all right.'

'You don't know the Orient, and you don't know how you'll travel on to Australia. You call that all right?'

Violet didn't answer. She stared helplessly before her, bewildered at the warning in his voice.

Above, the broad span of the Milky Way shimmered and danced. The moon hung low on the horizon, so close it seemed the *Carthage* would steam straight into it. What did he mean?

Ben reached out and squeezed her hand. His touch broke her fragile self-control.

'I'm frightened.' She spoke in a whisper.

'Shhh,' he soothed. 'If it doesn't work out, I'll come and find you. That's a promise.' She had no idea how he would find her, or how he would keep such a promise, but she was comforted none the less.

'Don't let them change you, Violet,' he said softly. 'You're worth more than this whole ship put together.'

She fell asleep beside him, while the ship steamed onwards into the waxy moon.

Asia has skies like no others in the world: vast, luminous blues reflecting equally brilliant seas. After England, even the clouds seemed wilder, higher and more grandiose.

In the distance, a smudge of land: the passengers clustered on the starboard side, watching as the black shape materialised into the tiny island of Pulau Wey, at the tip of Sumatra. First a line of surf became visible, breaking on a yellow strand; then the green of palm trees, glittering in the sun. The atmosphere was giddy with good cheer. Relief at seeing land was coupled already with nostalgia for the life on board.

People exchanged addresses, promising to meet again back home or for drinks in the Palm Court at Raffles Hotel in Singapore.

It was like the end of term at school, Violet thought, when you willingly forgave your enemies in the sheer joy of the impending vacation.

Ben put his arm round her shoulders. Immediately after disembarkation in Singapore, he was leaving by seaplane for Surabaya. Violet knew she would miss him. They were waiting on deck for the results of the voyage's final lottery, she with feelings more uncomfortable than mere curiosity.

Every noon since departure, Violet had staked her sixpence on the daily lottery without success. She had also invested the more significant sum of five shillings on the bigger weekly draws – and again lost every time. The last draw of the journey was to be made shortly before the *Carthage* steamed into the harbour at Singapore.

Violet staked a full pound on this final lottery. To guess how many miles the *Carthage* had sailed since leaving England, she had followed Ben's advice and worked out an average of the miles sailed every day, bearing in mind that according to his calculations the *Carthage* would arrive in Singapore just over half a day late. She sealed the envelope containing her estimate and dropped it into the bin.

Others were also waiting anxiously for the results. Several young men who had spent too freely at the bar were warily eyeing the bridge, waiting for Captain Stainforth to appear.

Ben was to make the draw. He stepped forward to read out the final distance.

'Voyage of . . . 8,860 miles.'

They were now in sight of Singapore. Violet caught her breath. Her estimate had been for only nine miles less.

Methodically Ben opened the envelopes in the bin, discarding all those that were outside 250 miles of the final distance, and putting to one side those that came within the range. Within a few minutes he had a small stack. He went through them again.

At length he held up just one. 'The winner is the young lady who guessed 8,851 miles,' he said. 'Miss Violet Harcourt.'

Violet stepped forward amid applause to collect her prize, aware that several pairs of suspicious eyes were trained on her. Her friendship with the American oil man was well known. Ben handed her the envelope containing £60 – equivalent to a £1 bet from each first-class passenger.

She thanked him, averting her eyes. To him it was a game, but for her it was a serious matter. She suspected that the same was true for a number of passengers, because as she resumed her seat she was surprised to meet looks of downright hostility as well as envy. The sweepstake had become a focus during the long, empty days. Winning the last one, The Grand Draw, was something that many had imagined themselves doing.

The docks at Singapore were vast and filled with animation and urgency, despite the damp heat that made one welcome any breath of wind. Produce vied with machinery for loading space, and there were great piles of fruit, much of it unfamiliar, stacked under netting along the wharfs.

Below the prow of the great liner Ben's luggage stood in rows upon the quay. He too was sweating, as the porter put Aggie's meagre suitcase on the ground beside his extensive luggage.

Ben's predicted docking time for the *Carthage* had been exact: as he had feared, in order to rendezvous with his drilling crew he had to leave for Surabaya immediately. He was none the less reluctant to leave her.

'I insist that you go,' she said, trying to laugh. A pile of bananas swung through the air, moving precariously towards a nearby ship.

'Make sure you go to Raffles, won't you?' he said. 'The head porter is called Rajid Singh. Mention my name and he'll see you come to no harm.' All around them was the chaos of the Orient: Chinese, Malays and Tamils, and the British, with their mandatory solar topees.

She returned Ben's strong grip. 'We'll be all right! This place is full of sahibs and memsahibs all eager to help English girls in distress.'

'If you say so.'

Violet wanted to laugh at the concern in his face. 'Go, Ben, or you'll miss your seaplane and you'll blame me forever.' She tried to sound cross.

'OK. Look after each other,' he said – to Aggie rather than both of them – and climbed slowly into his rickshaw. Violet waved suddenly, sad to see him depart. Raising his hat in salute, he disappeared into the crowd.

The shipping clerk was English. He was tediously precise and took his time, looking up details in well-thumbed timetables and consulting his watch and calendar. They had two choices: either to wait a week and catch a liner which was even then *en route* from Hong Kong to Sydney, or travel in two days' time on a tramp steamer which accepted ten passengers along with its cargo of rubber. The latter option was half the price. Violet didn't hesitate.

'You won't find the company much to your liking, young lady,' the clerk said.

'It's only for nine days. We'll manage.'

The rickshaw man set off for their hotel at a tremendous pace. Violet sat back in the bumpy seat and took in her surroundings. She liked what she saw; Singapore lacked the menace of the tight little streets she'd seen when she went ashore with Ben at Port Said, and the open faces of the Chinese contrasted with the covert hostility of many of the Arabs they had encountered. The noise and the bustle, too, were inviting rather than intimidating. She was longing to get out, to walk off her sea-legs and the sense of claustrophobia that had built up on the boat.

At Raffles they booked a double room. A uniformed servant led them up the vast staircase to the first floor. Their room opened off a long narrow corridor. Inside, one door led to the bathroom and another to the sleeping area, which had two narrow single beds positioned under the window. Glass doors led out on to a tiny balcony, which overlooked a garden. Purple and orange bougainvillaea flowered in profusion, and yellow canna lilies grew in clumps. They ought to clash, Violet thought, but they don't. Like the native women here, who wear such exotic materials, their colours blend perfectly.

'Come and see this,' Aggie called from the bathroom. The plumbing was primitive. On one side of the white tiled room stood the jambon, or lavatory.

'Europeans call them thunderboxes,' Vi said, who'd learnt the expression from Ben. 'I expect we'll get used to it.'

On the other side of the room was a huge ceramic receptacle full of icy cold water.

'You ladle this over yourself instead of sitting in a bath. It's wonderfully cold. They call it the Shanghai Jar.'

The gloss and glamour of Raffles was apparently reserved for the public areas downstairs. The paintwork in their room was peeling, and judging by the stain on the wall a water pipe had recently burst. But below their balcony was the wrought-iron roof of the Palm Court. A clientele of Europeans, fashionably dressed, could be seen seated at small white tables, listening to the tinkling of a piano. The hotel was a world apart, untouched by the seething city outside its walls.

'I'm going out for a walk,' said Violet, changing her shoes. She noticed Aggie's look of alarm. 'I'll leave the money with you,' she added, 'and just take a few dollars. But I've got to have some exercise. I know we all walked miles round the deck each day, but it isn't the same as actually going somewhere.'

The doorman, clad in a starched white uniform, with a red turban and an impressive red silk cumberbund, saluted as Violet sauntered down the oval steps on to the forecourt. The driveway encircled a lawn with dissected flower beds whose plants bloomed in flamboyant profusion. Tall palm trees swayed in the light breeze.

Outside the hotel she turned off the wide main road and almost immediately found herself in the narrow streets of the native Chinese community. The little shops sold an abundance of beautiful things: bowls painted with dragons and mythological scenes, teapots with circular cane-wrapped handles, vases painted in the Chinese style, fans and parasols in bright hues, and wonderful rolls of silk. Violet was absorbed. She strolled slowly along, stopping to admire the merchandise, seduced by the easy manner of the tradesmen, who didn't hustle her or insist that she buy, as the Arabs in Port Said had done.

She stopped in a small café and drank a glass of freshly squeezed limes, enjoying the sharpness of the taste. She hardly noticed the time passing and it was only when her feet started to protest that she considered turning round and heading back to the hotel. She stood at the junction of four small roads wondering which way to go. The scene was the same whichever way she looked. She quickened her pace, aware that with the dwindling of the light the area had grown menacing. Chinese faces which she had smiled at in the afternoon now seemed frightening and strange. The roadway turned sharply downhill.

At the bottom of the hill she found herself on the banks of the Singapore River. Junks and sampans nestled and nudged each other. There was a sickly smell of rotting fish. The tropical night, which has no dusk, descended: it was by now almost completely dark. There were no other Europeans in sight and Violet felt a mounting sense of panic. She cursed her stupidity for coming out alone. Small shapes swarmed in the shadows. A rat ran across her left foot. She screamed out loud and jumped backwards, tripping on a pile of greasy ropes curled beside the water's edge.

'You lost, little memsahib?' The heavily accented voice was close to her ear. She clutched the thin material of her cotton dress closely round her, wrapping her arms round her breasts, shivering in spite of the sultry heat which the night had scarcely diminished.

'What way to Raffles Hotel?' Unconsciously she adopted a stilted pidgin English, pronouncing her words carefully.

The man laughed and moved round in front of her where the light from one of the neighbouring boats fell on his face. He was a thickset Chinese, with narrow eyes and a fleshy mouth. When he laughed she could see a row of gold teeth, hungry and menacing.

'Long way to Raffles. I show you.' He held out a hand, black with grease and dirt. He wore a pair of baggy brown pants and a grubby white singlet, which exposed powerfully muscled arms.

'No, I find the way. Alone.'

He laughed again and as he did so, four more men appeared out of the shadows. She felt naked under their gaze, almost paralysed with fear. She turned to walk away, catching her foot on the rope again and stumbling forwards. One of the men grabbed her arm, gripping her, his fingers biting into the flesh above her elbow.

'You come with us.'

Violet started to shout, but the sound was cut short by a rough hand over her mouth.

He pulled her away from the river, down a narrow passage and through a doorway. Inside the room a light flickered and gasped. The walls were smeared with oily fingermarks, on the floor was an old rattan rug and in the corner lay a mattress covered by a stained sheet.

Roughly the man pushed her backwards on to the mattress. She curled herself into a ball, pulling her dress down over her knees. With

78

her other hand she stuffed her small leather handbag into the space between the wall and the mattress.

The sailor who had originally approached her stepped forward. He pulled at her arm, tugging her upwards till she was standing.

From his pocket he extracted a long, curved knife. He ran his finger along the blade, watching with satisfaction as a thin line of blood spurted from the pad of his thumb. Violet recoiled from the sight, imagining the knife cutting deep into her throat. He pressed the blade against her left breast. She stayed absolutely still, terrified that movement would cause the sharp point to slip.

The knife eased under the cotton fabric, its steel edge cold on her naked breast. He cut through the material and slid the knife downwards, splitting the dress in two like paper. Then he cut across the shoulders. She stood there in her camisole, the lacy edges of her knickers reaching to mid-thigh. He eased the knife slowly and deliberately between the fabric and the middle of her breasts, then cut downwards. The garment fell apart. Carefully he tweaked away the thin straps that held up the camisole over her shoulders. She was scarcely breathing by now, horrified by the slowness of his movements, by the methodical way in which he had mutilated her clothes.

She was now completely naked and she drew one arm across her breasts, and placed the other hand across her dark pubic hair. The men stood back, at ease and prepared to take their time. They walked round her, studying every inch of her body, commenting in their own language on what they saw. The sun had left sharp tan marks on her arms and legs. The older man ran the knife delicately round the lines, then roughly pulled her hand away from her crotch.

Without exchanging a word, two other men seized each arm, forcing her backwards on to the mattress. The rough cotton grated against her skin. Her eyes were wide with terror. She was convinced she would die; somehow the thought seemed to help, seemed to take her away from the horror of the scene in which she was involved, as though she were watching it from a point on the ceiling.

The knife blade eased between her legs. She parted them involuntarily. The Chinese sailor moved the sharp point across her vulva, opening the soft pink skin. Time stood still. She had no idea how long they stood there, just looking at the most intimate part of her body, while the fat Chinese gently moved the blade to and fro.

If I move I'll die, she thought, willing herself into total immobility. He stood up and roughly pulled down his trousers. His thick penis was marbled with blue veins. She bit back her gasp. Bile rose in her throat;

she could hardly breathe. Blackness descended but then the room wheeled back into focus and the momentary respite of semi-consciousness faded. She screamed out loud, throwing herself sideways against her captors' hands. Their laughter was full and deep. They pressed her against the mattress, one to each arm, one to each leg. The two men holding her legs stood up, pulling Violet's body upwards with them. She was spreadeagled and powerless to move.

The man peered at her vagina, pushing into it with his fleshy finger. He smiled as he met resistance. He pushed his finger upwards, turning it round. She squirmed with pain, tears springing to her eyes, blood to her mouth as she bit her lips in anguish.

He placed his swollen organ at the mouth of her vulva and pushed forward roughly. The pain was unbearable. It seemed to be splitting her in two. He ground inwards, till the hairy muscles of his legs were wedged between her thighs, his coarse skin rubbing against her soft white flesh. Then he moved backwards, and forwards, slow thrusts which gathered momentum. She felt a curious sensation as his semen discharged deep inside her, its wetness mingling with her own blood, which dripped steadily on to the dusty floor. He pulled back, smiling in satisfaction.

The other men took their turns, pinching and pummelling her flesh in their excitement. Vomit rose in her throat and she gagged, unable to keep it down. The pain was unbelievable. She screwed her eyes shut, conscious of the foul taste in her throat, and the thrusting between her legs, threatening to tear her in two. She was no longer aware of how many hands were holding her, pushing her legs apart, ramming into her. All she could hear was the throaty laughs and guttural exchanges, the panting in her face - it was like being devoured by wild animals. A hand pulled at the nipple of her left breast, twisting it like a screw. She tried to turn aside, to turn away from the menace, but stronger hands held her still, her legs were forced yet wider apart, till her knees were almost touching her shoulders. Then a new pain, something penetrating her from behind. She screamed as a cramp of agony coursed through her. Yet another of them was bearing down, forcing himself through the tight muscles of her body.

The other men were laughing. She felt her skin start to tear and for a moment she blacked out, falling limply on to the dirty sheet. He drove home, grunting and gasping with his own exertion. She was impaled, she thought, returning to consciousness. The pain was so intense that she dared not move as he pushed backwards and forwards, ripping delicate skin. Then a final shudder and he fell forwards on to her, his beery breath against her cheek. She turned her face to one side and bit back another scream as he pulled himself out of her.

He made some comment to the others as he stood up, accepting a bottle, and taking a long swallow which made the muscles jump in his emaciated throat. She was repelled beyond words. It had been like coupling with a creature that had no human quality. She felt herself convulsed again by sobs and by spasms of pain and shock. Perhaps I'm going to die, she thought; perhaps they've killed me.

They sat down in the far corner, passing the bottle between them, oblivious of her now; she could have been a dirty sack in the corner. She pulled the grey sheet round her knees, seeking to cover up her nakedness; trying to disappear altogether.

Covertly she watched them, conscious of a new terror. They could hardly let her go, could they? Now they had used her, would they just keep her there, lying on the filthy mattress, till they wanted her again? Or would they just cut her throat and dump her body into the river, along with the rotting carcasses of fish and rabid dogs that floated amid the junks and sampans? In the end, they would have to.

The thought gave her energy. She had to get away. Somehow she must convince them that she was not going to try to escape, lull them into ignoring her for a moment. She closed her eyes and willed her muscles to relax. Little by little she slowed her breathing, till it was easy and deep. She relaxed her hands, allowing them to open.

From the corner she could hear them talking. Someone threw a bottle into the corner. Still she stayed quiet. One of the men walked across the room, his heavy footprints creaking on the wooden floor. He touched her leg with his toes. She bit back the scream and the shudder, languidly shifting her leg an inch or two, as though moving into a more comfortable position.

He turned back to his mates and said something. An argument ensued. Probably they were trying to decide how deeply asleep she was. She had no idea what time it was; the whole night might have passed. Aggie would be in a wretched state. Would she have called the police?

She heard them standing up and moving around. The door opened and a draught of cool air filled the room. She was conscious of shafts of light; it must be dawn. Maybe they had to go to work. She waited till the noise had died away and the door had closed again; then she risked opening her eyes.

Only one man remained. He was crouched in the corner, squatting on his haunches, picking his fingernails with the edge of the knife blade. His head was bowed, and he was not looking at her. He yawned, a loud exaggerated noise, then stood up. She peered at him through her eyelashes. He left the room by a door at the back and returned a moment later with a blanket. In the far corner, by the door to the alleyway, he lay down and rolled himself in it, wedging his body up against the door, forming an effective human lock.

Violet watched him for some minutes, feeling a terrible tiredness creep over her, as she listened to his steady breathing. She wanted to sleep, to pass out of the reality of the room and all that had happened there. She dug her nails into the palm of her hand till it hurt.

She coughed lightly. The man did not move. She coughed again, more loudly. Still no movement. Carefully, she raised herself on to her elbow and studied the room. Light was now pouring in through a high window overlooking the alley. If I can get away now, she thought, at least there will be people on the streets, some chance of escape in the crowd.

By the side of the bed was a cheaply made cupboard, its door hanging loosely on one hinge. Her shredded dress was unwearable. She opened the cupboard door, wincing each time the wood creaked. Still the man slept on. Now for the first time, she could hear noises from outside, shouts and bangs of daily activity from the port. The smell of hot soups brewing wafted through the window. She peered into the cupboard. A jumble of colourful materials lay on the bottom. She extracted a long rectangle of patterned fabric – a sarong, she realised; the garment that Chinese men often wore wrapped round their waists. She stood up and tied it round her; at least she was covered. She picked up her bag from behind the mattress. She wondered why they hadn't bothered to look for it and realised with horror that they were probably waiting till later. In spite of the humid warmth in the room she was chilled to the marrow. She looked round for her shoes and slipped them on hurriedly.

Her legs ached and the insides of her thighs felt as though they had been pounded by hammers. Her head was giddy and she found herself shaking uncontrollably.

I must pull myself together, it's my life, my life, she told herself.

There was no way out through the front door; the sleeping Chinese made that impossible. She opened the door at the back of the room, finding herself in a dank corridor which smelt strongly of urine and a sickly sweet odour which she couldn't identify.

At the end of the corridor were two doors. She turned the handle of one of them. It was locked. The other opened into a tiny room, bare except for four wooden stools and a straw tray bearing two thin pipes.

The smell was almost overpowering. A small window was set in the wall. She stood on one of the stools and reached up. The window opened easily in its worn and rotted frame. Outside she could see the pale-blue morning sky. She balanced two stools on top of each other and heaved herself upwards.

A rainwater barrel was standing just outside the window. Violet pulled herself upwards, swinging one leg through the window and down on to the edge of the barrel. Seconds later she was on the ground, straightening her sarong. She was standing in a tiny alleyway, so narrow that if she held out her arms she could touch the walls of the houses on both sides. It was filthy with litter and rubbish and stank of human excrement. Violet felt her stomach turn. She retched, vomiting into the gutter until her stomach hurt and bile ran from her mouth. Leaning against the wall to stop herself shaking she looked up and down the alley. At the bottom, the river slid by, gentle in the pastel morning light, reflecting the palest of pinks. She turned up the hill, breaking into a run, picking her way through the mounds of festering refuse which seemed to be everywhere. Round two corners and she was in a wider alleyway, where traders were opening their shops, putting chairs outside, hanging up silks and cottons, arranging spices in long trays. Their stares filled her with pain and shame.

Two Chinese women walked past, carrying cooked crispy ducks by their feet, denuded carcasses like embryos. One of them smiled at her and she felt an unreal sense of calm come over her. She was free. She had survived. Violet walked on uphill, moving as in a trance, barely aware of her surroundings.

Clothes, she thought, I mustn't look conspicuous when I get back to the hotel. She held on to this practical thought, conscious that if she let go now, she would run and start to scream. It was as though she had woken shuddering from a dream, or was looking on from outside herself; as though someone else was guiding her footsteps and setting her face in a denial of the terror within.

From a small shop, she bought a cheap shirt of cream Laotian silk, and a crimson skirt with a tie belt. In the back of the store, she put them on, the Chinese woman in charge of the shop helpfully folding the fabric of the skirt into two neat folds and pulling the ties behind her back. Thus equipped Violet turned uphill again, and within ten minutes found herself back on the broad highway outside Raffles Hotel. The doorman hardly blinked as she slipped past him into the lobby, and upstairs to her room.

Aggie opened the door at the first knock and flung herself into Violet's arms.

'Where have you been? I've been so worried. I thought you must be dead!'

'I'm perfectly all right, Aggie. I ran into some people from *Carthage* – that nice teacher who liked walking. We explored and explored and then by the time we'd had dinner it was too late to get home on my own through the streets, so I stayed in their hotel.'

The lies came out effortlessly. Violet was conscious again of feeling like two people.

'But it's only seven-fifteen in the morning.' Aggie looked at her, perplexed. There were shadows under Violet's eyes, and her cheeks were hollow, as though she hadn't eaten for a week. 'And the police have been looking for you. The hotel manager was ever so worried. I even tried to contact Ben.'

'He'll be in Surabaya by now,' Violet said quickly. 'Anyway, as you can see, I'm fine. I'll just get changed and then I'll see the manager.'

'Perhaps you could just see him now . . . he was so upset. He thought you'd been murdered.' Aggie was still not reassured. Violet wasn't herself at all; more like a puppet. Aggie wondered if she had been drugged – you heard of things like that in these places.

The manager of Raffles was English. He listened patiently to Violet's story of how she'd come to spend the night in another hotel, to avoid the streets after dark.

'Why didn't you get a rickshaw to bring you here? Your maid was beside herself with worry. And we've had half the Singapore police force combing the area for you.'

Violet smiled, but the gesture felt like a grimace. She struggled to imagine how she would behave if her story was true. 'I met up with some friends from the boat. They invited me to play bridge and somehow or another the evening passed very quickly.'

He gave her a cold, queer look, full of disapproval. He probably thinks that I spent the night with a man, she thought. Little does he know how near and how far from the truth his suspicions are. She wanted to laugh hysterically.

'I do apologise for all the trouble I've caused.' She made a point of meeting his eyes. If I can just hold on another minute, she said to herself, fighting the desire to laugh and cry and pound the wall with her fists, I'll be all right.

His features softened. 'I'm very glad you're safe,' he said. 'Just don't underestimate the east. We're the invaders here and many people don't like us. Take my advice and don't go in the bazaar again on your own.'

Violet stood on the white tiled floor of the bathroom, ladling water out of the Shanghai Jar over her head and shoulders. There were bruises and ugly red welts all over her body. Her self-control was finally ebbing and she retched, her stomach cramped with pain and revulsion. Hastily she threw more water over herself, kneeling on the floor and rubbing the rough carbolic soap between her legs and over her breasts, trying to work up a lather in the cold water. I'll never be clean again, she thought, in rising panic. Every muscle ached and the tendons in her inner thighs felt as though they had been stretched and twisted into knots.

It was all my fault. My fault that I was silly enough to be out alone, my fault that I didn't listen to Ben. She could hear her mother's voice from the night before her first proper dance, embarrassed and embarrassing, so that Violet had pretended not to listen. 'Men can't control themselves once a woman's gone too far. That's why they're so different from us.' Sybil's little-girl voice had been prim, and yet excited by what she was saying. 'So a girl must never go too far, never, never, never . . .'

And that is what I've done, Violet told herself, shaking now with cold from the water, but still scooping it up, pouring it over her hair, sponging it between her legs. I just stood there, didn't I? I could have run, at the moment when the man with the knife asked if I was lost. I could have run. I asked for it. It was all my fault. I stood there, on my own, at the docks, in the night, and I asked for it. I'm as guilty as they are. I could have screamed. If only, if only . . .

The wild, shaming thoughts ran round her head until she was near to howling out loud. She was no longer a virgin. She could never offer that to James. Everything she had dreamed of was ruined. He'll never want me, she thought. Even if I lie, he'll know. Men always do. It was another thing that Sybil had emphasised, in that same voice Violet had hated, girlish and knowing at the same time.

I'll never tell anyone. Anyone. But it won't help.

She laid her head against the hard cold wall, feeling water drip off her hair, down her back, running in little rivulets between her breasts. She watched the drops as if they were swollen tears on her cold skin, but she knew that it was too late to weep now. Tears would have been a consolation perhaps, but her wretchedness was too acute. Violet looked at the floor and thought that she would never weep again.

85

7

The *Mary Rose* rounded the headland. Their voyage from Singapore had been stormy; at times the winds had been so high that great seas had flooded over the vessel. Aggie had been terrified.

Violet, however, had accepted it all with resigned calm. Day after day she had sat huddled in the corner of her bunk, oblivious to their discomfort, her eyes fixed on the heavy swell of the sea as it crashed against the boat and turned the porthole opaque. All Aggie's cautious attempts to talk to her had failed. For most of the journey Violet had stayed in the cabin. She ate almost nothing.

How could she go to James now? Could she lie? Even if she tried, she was sure she could never behave as if nothing had happened. Whatever she said, there would come a moment when he found out that she was no longer a virgin. She could not even think of herself as the same person. Lying on her bunk, she felt waves of loneliness wash through her. If only James had been there to offer consolation. But even if he were there, it was something she would have had to face alone. The only way to deal with it was to pretend it hadn't happened.

Their first sight of Sydney was of the lighthouse at the mouth of the great harbour. The ship slipped between two headlands and into the calmer waters of the bay. From the water they could see small inlets and hills, with rows of roof-tops stretching down towards the breathtakingly blue sea. Within the headlands, deep watery fingers reached inland between 200 miles of richly wooded banks. Ferries zigzagged to and fro. It was early spring here; yet it felt as warm as a summer's day back in England.

'Oh, my word, it's good to be home,' said one of their fellow passengers as they stood on the deck. The other people making the voyage on the *Mary Rose* were all Australian. Five businessmen, two of them travelling with their wives, and a priest, who had spent much of the time at sea telling his rosary beads and murmuring Hail Marys while the ship ploughed and heaved. The ship steamed towards the naked girders of the almost completed Harbour Bridge.

'It was a running joke in the town that the two ends would never meet,' one of the women told the girls. Violet gazed upwards at the giant steel structure, two great claw-like arms just touching each other 500 feet above the water.

In the cabin Aggie tidied her clothes, straightened her hat and dabbed a little spot of rouge on each cheek. The weeks at sea had done her good, turning her sallow complexion into a tan. She had persuaded Violet to help cut her hair the night before, in rows of neatly bobbed curls; and she in turn had trimmed Violet's hair.

Violet, however, had been listless and indifferent to Aggie's attentions.

'Don't you want to look your best? For when you see him?'

It was the nearest Aggie had dared come to asking a direct question about James. 'I suppose so,' Violet had replied, hardly bothering to look in the mirror.

Now, as they looked down at Circular Quay, Aggie was worried. In a few minutes they would be disembarking; and she still had no idea of Violet's immediate plans.

'In the old days,' said their friendly companion, 'there would have been rows of men, ringers and so on, waiting at the docks to see what women were getting off. They were so hungry for women, they'd marry them before they'd even left the port.'

'Did the marriages work?'

'You'd be surprised. There's many a legend says they were the best ones going. It was a hard life, though, in the outback.'

Violet clutched her suitcase and stepped on to the busy wharf. In a way their surroundings were a disappointment. They could have been in Antwerp or Tilbury, so much did the dockside resemble any modern city in Europe. But there was comfort, too, in the familiarity of the scene. She looked at Aggie, noting the worried crease between her brown eyes, and the hint of panic in her smile. Violet knew she had to pull herself together and stop behaving like an automaton. What had happened had happened. She couldn't put the clock back – though, oh God, she had striven to, lying awake in her bunk on the *Mary Rose*, imagining that she had run at the crucial moment, or screamed more loudly.

She tried to smile and to put some determination into her voice.

'We'll go to a hotel for a few days. We need to recover from the voyage before we get in touch with James.'

87

There was a row of taxis: big cream-coloured Fords, and sedate hansoms.

'Excuse me,' Violet said to one of the drivers.

'What d'yer want?'

'To go somewhere, of course,' Violet retorted.

'I can see that. But where do ya want to go?' Suddenly he grinned. 'You're pommies, aren't you? Don't get many of them coming in on the *Mary Rose*.' He leant across and opened the front door. 'Get in then.'

Violet climbed into the front and Aggie into the back. It was more like going for a ride with a friend than hiring a driver.

They left the docks and turned into a wide thoroughfare like a smaller version of Oxford Street, lined with shops.

'So you want to find suitable lodgings for young ladies,' said the cabbie.

Violet nodded and explained their immediate needs. They drove on through a suburban area of single-storeyed houses with red roofs of corrugated iron. Each home had its own garden, surrounded by wooden picket fencing or a parched hedge. Brown, healthy-looking children played on the wide grassy roadside. It was September, and familiar spring flowers like daffodils were in bloom next to more exotic plants: canna lilies and strangely shaped trees with red tufty flowers. The cabbie said they were corals. From a distance their naked branches looked as though they were hung with Christmas tree ornaments.

Violet nervously adjusted the angle of her blue felt hat. Until Singapore, she had been longing for her first sight of the new country where she had planned to make her home with James. Now she was shivering with apprehension. James had wanted her, she was sure, because she was what her mother would have called pure. She kept remembering something he had said one evening in the Embassy Club. A group of girls had walked past. Their dresses were slinky, cut on the cross, and shimmered in the pink light. All of them were tipsy – no, beyond that. One, unsteady on her wedge heels, had bumped into their table and almost fallen. The girl's lipstick had been purple, but so thick it was nearly black. Her dress was short enough to look like a chemise.

Violet had followed James's sardonic stare. 'You've got some choice types here,' he said. 'Where do they dig them up?'

But she knew all the same that he had been aroused. She could well imagine him with a girl like that. But only for one night – he would probably kick her out next morning.

In Violet herself he had seen something different. And now he would have been wrong . . .

Violet looked over her shoulder, hoping to catch a last glimpse of the sea, but it was out of sight. Their surroundings had changed again. It seemed to Violet that Sydney wasn't a single town so much as a series of villages, some on the seaboard, others continuing inland.

Eventually they stopped in a suburb of small houses and gardens. It all appeared recently built, and the road looked as though it turned into a track not much further on. The driver had taken them to a guest house in an area known as Strathfield. It was run by 'an aunt' of his, and was apparently a good place for ladies on their own.

'She'll treat you well. You'd get a crook deal in the town,' he said as he drew up outside.

The guest house was called Belle View. There was a garden of worn grass, with yellow flowers blooming in a scrubby hedge.

A sturdy woman in an apron opened the door. Violet had been thinking of inspecting the accommodation; but the landlady's straight, not unfriendly gaze told her that she herself needed to pass some form of inspection.

The moment they stepped into the narrow, spotlessly clean hall Violet was sure they had found what they needed. They could have their meals, breakfast and tea, and two rooms for £1 a week each. When she offered to pay in advance, uncertain whether it was the right thing to do, the landlady, who introduced herself as Nona Vickery, a widow, said: 'Friday night's rent night here. You can wait till then.'

As soon as the girls had unpacked, Nona was knocking on the door to tell them tea was ready. In the front room, next to doors opening out on to the makeshift porch, where the household sometimes slept in the hot weather, a table was laid for five. Nona was serving up a thick mutton stew, with boiled potatoes, cabbage and carrots. She too sat down in front of a large plate of food, after pouring out cups of strong Indian tea.

'The other places – they're for my brother Jack and his mate, Bill,' she said, eating heartily. It transpired that both men also lived there, and worked in the moving-picture business. Nona herself was a war widow, whose husband had taken several years to die from being gassed.

At the mention of the movies, Violet looked up.

'Do they have a theatre?'

'A picture-show is what they've got. They haven't the capital for any fancy frills. But there's money to be made in the pictures, especially now they're talkies.' The words sounded as if she was quoting someone else. 'Jack says, now there's more people out of work every day, they'd all want to go to the pictures – if the prices went low.' Noticing how Violet had grown attentive, she asked, 'You keen on the pictures too?'

Violet was telling her, when a door banged and they heard loud male voices.

Jack Maguire was not much bigger than his sister, but as soon as he entered the room he filled it. He wore a bright check jacket going shiny at the elbows, and a new bow tie covered in yellow spots. He looked younger than his sister, but his curly hair was starting to thin.

His companion was a quieter individual altogether, with a thin frame failing to fill a black suit that had known better days.

'Good evening, ladies.' Jack doffed his straw hat with a courtly flourish. He marched to the verandah, boots ringing, and came back with two big bottles of beer.

At table the men – Jack with a froth moustache on his upper lip – were themselves soon talking about the movies. Jack asked Violet what films had been on in London when she and Aggie left. She remembered a particular afternoon in Berkeley Square with James, and mentioned *The Love Parade*.

Jack's eyes shone. 'Jeanette MacDonald and Maurice Chevalier. It's one of the new musicals by Ernst Lubitsch. It's not been here yet – but you can buy the music.'

'What are the most popular films in Sydney now?'

'Oh, I'd say *The Singing Fool*. When Al Jolson sings "I'm Sitting On Top Of The World", you feel wonderful. When he weeps over his dying son, the audience wants to weep too. Tear-jerkers are good films for times like these – they take people out of themselves. That's the kind of film I want to show. Everything from Hollywood. You wouldn't believe that town – just ten years ago it was a village, now they've got actors like Douglas Fairbanks making £3,000 a week.'

'Have you been there?' Aggie asked, her eyes wide with amazement at the thought.

'Jack just thinks he's been there. He lives in his own Hollywood,' Nona said, laughing.

Their shared obsession revealed, the conversation ran on for hours. Jack knew the stars, producer, director, composer and scriptwriter of every talkie ever produced. It was not just a hobby, nor even just his trade, but a passion. As far as Violet could make out, he had spent his whole life working in what he called 'the picture business'. Bill, who never spoke more than two words, was his partner; and to hear Jack talk you would think they had voyaged through every township in Australia to carry the gospel according to Hollywood.

What exactly they did in this line of business became clearer when Bill sat down at the upright piano. He could play for as long as Jack talked – he was no star, but he carried hundreds of melodies in his head, as well as special sound effects like thunder or galloping hooves. Aggie was entranced. It was not long before Jack started to sing (he was no virtuoso either, but an enthusiastic bar-room tenor), and Aggie shyly joined in. Once started, she looked ready to go on all night.

Eventually Violet pleaded exhaustion and retired to her room. She lay listening to the music through the thin wall. The people in this house seemed ready enough to accept her, but would they be as friendly if they knew the truth?

And what was she going to say to James?

8

Violet woke late next morning, to the smell of frying and the sound of Aggie laughing out of doors.

In the yard, Jack, Bill the pianist and Aggie were eyeing a ramshackle truck. At first it reminded Violet of a motorised horse-box. Looking closely, she saw that one side was decorated with a garish hand-painted pattern of silver stars. The legend MAGUIRE & SOUTH – THE LIMELIGHTERS was evidently an amateur job too, because the last three letters, instead of being pillar-box red, had only been given a black outline.

'We ran out of paint.'

It was the longest sentence she had heard Bill speak. 'Jack said we needed to change the name – we used to be called "The Silver Screen".'

'What's "the limelight"?'

Jack laughed, astonished that anyone could be so ignorant. 'Oh, my word, you ought to know that. It's the light you get when you mix the ether with the oxygen.' Seeing Aggie, too, look puzzled, he added, 'The limelight is what you see the pictures by. You know – the special light? It's soft and dandy, not like electricity. When you go electric you get a hard light, harsh you could say. Of course the change-over was bound to come. Which means bit by bit the electric boys are running us off the road.'

'C'mon, Jack' – Bill seemed more talkative in the mornings – 'not "running". "Have run." '

As she sat down to breakfast, Violet decided it would have to be today that she went to see James. The romantic reunion she had spent so many hours imagining would be an ordeal. But it was one that had to be confronted. There could be no alternative – or none she could discover. After all she had come thousands of miles to see him. She could not avoid doing so simply because the encounter now terrified her.

'What are you young ladies doing today?' He and Bill were off to Hardcastle Street, to bargain with a bankrupt theatre owner in the hope of bringing down the price of his premises. 'I'll show you the Roxy if you like. She's beaut; you ought to see her.'

Before Violet could say no she saw Aggie's eyes on her.

'You go, Aggie – if you want.'

'Oh, I do,' Aggie said. 'I'd love to see it.'

Violet made her own excuses, and saw them off with relief before dressing herself with extra care. She put on a pale-lilac dress, one of Aggie's most successful on-board creations. The colour set off her grey-blue eyes, making them luminous. Aggie had even managed to concoct a matching hat which sat prettily on her shiny black hair.

She felt she was dressing not only for James, but for everyone about him. Once, she had relished meeting him in intimate surroundings, but now she was reassured to think that at least she would be presenting herself to him in a more or less public place.

The *Gazette* building was extraordinary in its splendour. In the spacious entrance hall, polychromatic marble friezes led the eye up towards a pillared gallery. Violet could see that the architect had been thinking in terms of a cathedral – and after all, hadn't James told her that the *Gazette* was the most important newspaper in Australia; the only one with the power to make or break a prime minister?

He had spoken of the *Gazette* with the same preoccupation as Jack, back at the Belle View, when on the subject of Hollywood. 'You must realise it's *The Times* of Australia. One of the great newspapers of the world.'

'Pardon me, if it's not too much trouble.'

As she hesitated in the crowded lobby, Violet was pushed to one side by a young woman. The girl wore an expensive perfume, applied with abandon. She walked quickly, evidently no stranger to the place. Her clothes were striking: she must have been by far the best-dressed person in the building. She wore a striped knee-length cotton dress secured by a wide white belt and carried a matching leather pochette bag. Her fashionable shoes were black, with wedge heels, and buckled straps across the arch of the foot.

At the bottom of the staircase to the gallery, the girl stopped to ask the uniformed commissionaire a question.

'I'll tell Mr Franklin you're here, miss.'

The girl turned round, loitering, head and shoulders above the crowd, on the second step. From a distance she was lovely. Close to, however, there was something not very nice about her face. Her lipstick was very dark, almost black.

Violet's hands went dry suddenly and she felt her throat tighten. It wasn't the same person; but in dim lighting this could have been the double of the girl in the Embassy Club, the one who had drunkenly fallen, almost ending up on James's lap. She stood, staring up at the girl, whose face wore an expression of eagerness. Then suddenly she sought to hide.

James had come through the door. He entered hurriedly, with a look of pleasure; for a moment it seemed as if he were about to take his visitor in an embrace. He was more deeply tanned than he had been in London, and even more handsome. His immaculate business suit could only partly disguise his athlete's build.

Violet had forgotten the extraordinary physical sense of his presence. She flushed with mingled excitement and trepidation. Fearing that he might turn and see her there, unbecoming and red-faced, she shrank further out of sight behind a pillar.

The two were talking and laughing, their heads close together. It soon became evident to Violet that there was no likeliood of her being noticed by James.

She turned and forced herself through the crowd. Outside the ponderous swing doors the light in the street hurt her eyes. She leant against the wall of the building, trying to catch her breath. Beside her was a plaque, set into the brickwork. 'The *Sydney Gazette*. Proprietors: George Franklin and Son.'

A beggar standing by the doorway held out his hand. 'I haven't had a square meal since last week.' His clothes hung off him and there was a thick stubble on his chin. Violet dug into her bag and gave him sixpence. He stared in amazement. Within seconds a horde of other beggars had clustered around her, and she had to fight her way past them, breaking into a run. She came to the bottom of the hill, and the great panorama of the waterfront. Sinking down on a bench, she felt her legs trembling, and prickly sweat leaving patches under the arms of her dress.

James hadn't waited for her; he hadn't believed that she would come. He had replaced her with another woman, an awful woman of a type he must secretly find exciting. And now I'm in no position to be superior about her, she thought miserably. No matter what that girl's life had been, she could have experienced nothing as degrading as Violet's own humiliation during that night in Singapore.

She was brimming with rage: towards her parents for their lack of understanding, and towards Ben for being absent when she needed him in Singapore – even though part of her knew none of them was really to blame. Her anger with James was even stronger, a sense of outrage that frightened her. But even that was nothing compared to the anger she felt towards herself. She had been a fool. She deserved what she had got.

Violet made her way home as slowly as possible. Only when in her room did she give way and weep. After a time she fell asleep. When she awoke there was a new resolve in her. James had to be forgotten – she could never think of seeing him again. It was impossible, too, to think of returning home. She would have to make a new life for herself and Aggie where they were; she would have to find a job. But how? None of the women she had known had ever worked, unless you counted her mother's charitable committees, or Emerald's mysterious relationship with the world of art galleries and auctions.

None the less she was surprised to feel the faintest optimism inside herself. She would show the world that she was not a complete fool.

Violet washed her face and went into the hall. The sun had almost set, but it was still very hot. Nona was laying the table for tea, tutting under her breath that Jack was late again. But then the door swung open and the three of them walked – almost danced – into the room.

Jack put his arms about Nona's waist and swung her round.

'We've sold it. The farmer from Richmond has agreed to buy the wagon.'

'For how much?' his sister asked, drily.

'Forty-five pounds!' He sat down to his tea, grinning with pleasure.

Aggie, too, was looking cheerful. 'The Roxy's wonderful, Violet,' she said. 'Big and beautiful, just like Jack said.' Both girls had quickly found themselves on Christian-name terms with their hosts.

He flashed her a quick smile of appreciation.

'So do you think you will buy the cinema?' Violet asked.

'Another hundred pounds and we'd be away.' He paused, seeing Nona's reproving glance. 'Let's just say we're on to some luck, what with the wagon selling so well and all.'

'If you bought the cinema, how would you manage it? Can it be turned into a success, even during the Depression?'

'Yeah, of course it can! If it's managed right. Chris charged too much – that was his first mistake.' Noticing that Violet, too, was looking at him with interest, he turned to her and explained. 'Old "Chris" Christiansen, he used to be in circuses and prize fights and all sorts; his

95

name was everywhere. He bought the old Roxy Theatre a couple of years back, to use for talkies. It was a bargain too, and a bigger bargain now.'

'A bigger white elephant, you mean!' Nona said.

'Not the way I'm going to run it. Chris doesn't understand pictures. To be truthful, he's still a circus man at heart. Monkeys is what he likes, and koalas.'

'He's seven months behind with the mortgage payments,' Bill added.

'That's why it's so cheap,' Jack said triumphantly. 'There'll never be another chance to get a theatre, a real picture palace, for £200 down and £30 a month. It's a steal.'

'Except that you haven't got £200,' Nona said.

'Is it really so cheap?' Violet found herself saying. An idea was taking hold of her. She added, partly for her own benefit, 'Since the Depression, property prices have collapsed in London. My father says it's the perfect time to buy – as long as you've got the capital.'

'Sure it is. I know a lot of people don't have money now; but all the more reason why they want to go somewhere to get their minds off their troubles. They'd come all right, but they've got to be able to afford it and they've got to feel it's a good place. Chris had let it run down. Paint peeling everywhere.'

'And the seat covers were in rags,' Aggie joined in. 'And there's no curtain across the screen; and the carpet's something shocking.' She spoke so earnestly that Violet found herself smiling.

Violet put down her knife and fork. 'Aggie, can I have a word with you?'

In her bedroom they both sat down on the bed. It was the moment Violet had been dreading since she fled from the offices of the *Gazette*. She was responsible not just for herself, but for both of them. How would Aggie take the news that they were going to be doing . . . what, exactly?

'Aggie, I'm not sure how to tell you this. I don't want you to be worried.'

'Yes, miss?'

Aggie had stopped calling Violet 'miss' in front of the others; in their new setting it seemed more natural. Alone with her, though, she reverted to the old form. It made Violet feel worse, because even more responsible.

'I've decided that I don't want to get married just yet. We're going to have to stay here and find work.'

'Stay here, miss? In Belle View?'

96

'For the time being.'

'Oh, thank goodness. You made me think we'd have to leave.'

Violet was hugely relieved. She was also surprised. It was out of character for Aggie – unlike herself – to be unperturbed by their lack of security.

'I've been thinking about what to do. We've over a hundred pounds. We could try and invest in a business. What would you think?'

'I only know about working for a wage. Investing – that's man's talk.'

'But what about staying here?'

Aggie said quickly, 'I like it here.'

Violet took a deep breath. 'Aggie, I'm thinking of offering to go into business with Jack and Bill. Would you work in the cinema if I did?'

'Oh yes,' Aggie said, sitting up straight. 'Have you told them?'

'No. I don't even know what they'd say. They hardly know us.' Violet's smooth brow knotted with concern. 'They may not want us.'

'Your money is as good as anyone's,' Aggie said staunchly.

From the lounge they could hear the tinkle of the piano and the sound of laughter. Aggie avoided Violet's eyes. She herself wasn't frightened in the least by the thought of working, and the prospect of staying delighted her. But Violet had never worked in her life. What did she imagine she could do for a living? And why this change of heart? Had she seen Mr Franklin today? Had he been nasty to her – he was a very attractive-looking gentleman, but there was something cruel about him. It was to do with Singapore, Aggie was sure of that. Something had happened. Perhaps she had had an affair with Ben, perhaps he had secretly stayed behind and met her and now she was pining for love of him? He was a married man, after all.

Violet got hastily to her feet. 'Shall we go and ask them about our investment?'

'Oh yes!' Aggie was all delight.

Violet smiled in response as bravely as she could. She had lost all sense of whether the scheme was madness or not. Indeed she seemed to have lost touch with everything. All she could think of was that pushy girl, with her reek of scent. Just get through the days, she kept on thinking, and maybe I'll grow to love him less. Maybe in time I'll even forget him.

9

'Tomorrow, we can start painting.' Jack jiggled the keys to the Roxy in the palm of his hand.

From his seat in the corner of the front porch, Bill smiled. It was he who was in charge of the accounts, and his methodical mind had ensured that every penny was accounted for.

'I'm glad you've got Bill on board this ship,' Nona said. 'He'll keep an eye on you.'

Negotiations for the purchase had gone through quickly. Christiansen was relieved to be rid of the cavernous building on Hardcastle Street, considering it to be nothing but a financial millstone.

'Here's to future luck and prosperity. To all of us.' Jack raised his bottle of beer and drank deeply.

Six weeks from Violet's arrival at Belle View, she, Jack and Bill had become partners in the Roxy Cinema. Together with Aggie and Nona, they were celebrating.

Violet cleared her throat.

'Now that I'm a partner – officially, that is – I have a couple of suggestions to make.'

Jack looked up. His reserve about going into business with this pommie girl had gradually evaporated. Her suggestions were always worth hearing: thrifty and original.

'If the Roxy is going to be the best cinema in town, we have to look smart. And that means more than just a coat of paint. I've been looking around in the last few weeks. I've been to the Parade, the Empire, the Odeon. Their staff don't wear uniforms; you can hardly tell the difference between the girls who sell the tickets and those coming to see the show. So, if we're going to be better, that means uniforms for the staff. For us, I should say,' grinning at Aggie.

'And the next thing is publicity. A week before we open with a new title, we must have a free showing for the reporters from the Sydney newspapers. Show the film in the morning and then give them drinks and lunch. All newspaper men like to feel they're privileged.' She thought of Tony Quigley. He was always boasting that he had never paid to see a film or a play from the day he started work in Fleet Street. 'There's no benefit giving them complimentary tickets once the film is open to the public – it's no longer news.'

'But, Violet,' Jack objected, 'we'll be paying rent for a film for a whole week without earning any money from it.'

'Yes. But all that week the critics will write about it. It's a form of free advertising.'

'Doesn't sound free to me,' Jack said, taking off his hat and furtively flicking a comb through his hair. It was getting thinner every day.

'Please let's try.' Violet turned to look at him. 'It's sure to work.'

'I don't much like it, but I'll go along with it. Just for a while. Uniforms are a good idea, though.'

'How much will they cost?' Bill asked.

'Very little. Nona, Aggie and I have decided we can make them up here. If we use a smart pattern out of a fashion magazine, we can use a fairly cheap material and get away with it. They won't cost more than fifteen shillings each, and we only need three.'

Bill looked thoughtful. 'It's a good idea. I don't know about these lunches, though.'

'They'll cost much less than buying an advertisement in the paper,' Violet answered quickly. 'And again, we can cook the meals here, and take them down to the cinema.'

She and Jack meanwhile debated for hours on which film they were going to show at the opening of the Roxy. They didn't argue about where the film should come from; there was, they both concluded, only one place. Never mind that the film industries of Germany and France were producing masterpieces; they were determined to stick to Hollywood. Their choice, finally, was Greta Garbo in *Anna Christie*. The film hadn't been shown in Australia and it was Garbo's first role in a talkie. Already she had made ten silent films – all great successes.

Five days before opening night they held a lunch for journalists from the *Gazette*, the *Sydney Morning Herald*, the *Telegraph* and the *Star*. Each journalist had been sent a printed invitation, requesting that he bring a guest. Violet resisted Jack's enthusiastic attempt to introduce gimmicks like '*Hollywood comes to Sydney*', printed across the top of the invitations. Instead, she settled for simple wording and presentation.

Violet was to run the cash desk, Aggie would sell ice creams, and Mavis, a local girl, would be showing people to their seats. All were dressed in their new uniforms – chic day dresses of pale-green silk, whose colour looked cool in the hot weather. The dresses had low waists, full box-pleated skirts, and matching scarves which tucked over one shoulder. They were sleeveless, but could be worn with a shawl. The Roxy itself, clean and fresh in its new coat of paint, was also in shades of green, so that the effect was like stepping into a vat of cool water. Meanwhile Nona and Aggie had sewn till their fingers blistered, making new curtains for the screen. Violet had designed them in an ambitious rainbow pattern, using seven different fabrics and exceeding Bill's budget. But when they were finished and hung, in a blaze of colour, everyone agreed that the expense had been justified.

The moment came for the lights to be dimmed. Bill started to step up the organ, his feet pumping furiously. As the strains of 'John Brown's Body' died away, the curtains parted, in response to a mechanical lever operated off-stage by Jack. He then had to race round the back of the theatre into the control room. The credits for *Anna Christie* appeared on the screen within thirty-five seconds of the curtains opening. Jack had sworn that the effort would eventually kill him and was resolved that their next improvement should take the form either of a new stage-hand or a new projectionist.

The film was received as enthusiastically as they could have wished, and its closing credits appeared on the screen to loud applause. Afterwards Violet and Aggie ushered their audience into a side room for lunch. There was a duck pâté, made out of half a fowl that Jack had poached from an inland lake up north, egg mayonnaise, a side of cold roast lamb, clams from the bay, and a whole large mountain trout in aspic with cherries popping out of its mouth. The newly baked bread was fresh and crusty, and served with butter curled into neat rounds. Violet was delighted that Aggie had turned out to be such a resourceful cook.

Moving amongst the guests with the practised charm that came to her so readily on social occasions, Violet answered most of their questions with the spontaneity of personal interest. 'Yes, Miss Garbo was born in 1905 in Stockholm.' 'Yes, her parents were very poor; she was working in a barber's shop when she was only fourteen.' Watching the reporters take notes, it occurred to Violet that it would be a good idea to prepare information about the stars of their films. It could only lead to more inches in the papers.

Over the next few days, all the papers carried an item about the new Roxy. Words like 'elegance', 'charming surroundings' and 'excellent ambience' peppered the articles. They also gave details of Garbo's life and the full plot of the film. Violet was delighted, but Jack was wary.

'They tell you the whole story,' he complained. 'People won't want to come now.'

Violet smiled and crossed her fingers.

Five days later, she was turning people away. By ten minutes to six all 250 seats were occupied. She was gratified to see that everyone had turned out in their best, however frayed. Already the Roxy had acquired a certain class, setting it apart from the other cinemas in town. Locking the cash register she sneaked into the back of the auditorium. An expectant hush prevailed. Bill took his seat, fidgeting with his new bow tie – white with green polka dots, in accordance with Violet's colour scheme. He placed his fingers on the keys. The strains of 'John Brown's Body' began to fill the theatre, and Violet could almost feel the ripple of pleasure that spread through the crowd.

They were agreed that already the Roxy had met with a success that deserved celebration. That evening Nona cooked a special supper. Afterwards, on the verandah, Jack opened the bottles of Resch's beer with greater abandon than usual. He was more jubilant than any of them. Nona watched him, a cautious smile on her lips. In the past, her brother's enthusiasms had led them nowhere. She had always known that he was like their father: a great one for plunging in.

Aggie, by contrast, had not cast doubt on a word he said. Observing them, Violet felt herself grow lonely; and she excused herself early from the sing-song without which no festive occasion at Belle View was complete.

The Roxy, she thought as she undressed, was going to be a success, though there was a lot still to do. Meanwhile her head was full of ideas – certainly fuller than Jack's. The difference was that she kept them to herself until the right time came.

But why, at this moment of all, had it come upon her so painfully that she still longed to see James? She missed him desperately – she could have killed herself, to stop feeling like this one moment longer.

Lying in bed she re-read two recent letters from home, if that was still the right word for England. Emerald's was the more amusing, as well as the more sympathetic. From Violet's earliest childhood, Emerald had shown a talent for understanding her young relative. 'I wish Emerald had been my mother,' Violet found herself saying. Emerald had written:

It's your life and I daresay it's best if you live it as you want. But Vi, darling, are you as happy as you say? I wouldn't have liked to take on a new world like that at your age, but then at your age I was already married and a widow, and to be honest it took me a few years to get over Harry, if I ever did. I suppose I'm still a widow, and always will be.

On the subject of Violet's parents, Emerald's response to Violet's questioning was surprisingly cheerful.

Your father takes it like everything else – as a personal affront. As you know, I don't like speaking to the man (there's no point pretending otherwise); and when I broke my rule not to do so he was just as wretched as you'd expect. He said that you weren't his daughter, and never had been, that kind of nonsense. I asked him if he'd ever heard of King Lear, and so there was a row, just as I knew there would be. I enjoyed that – it was as lively as a night at the Chelsea Arts Club, only without the conversation being so good. He said the only people I liked were gipsies, which was pretty rich. Your mother, of course, just sat there and agreed with every word he said. She gave up being anything but 'Her Master's Voice' long ago. Harry and I would never have been like that – or do you think all marriages end up the same way? Anyway, the evening ended unsurprisingly, with your father sulking, your mother a bit tiddly, and old Emerald in disgrace for interfering.

The last paragraph had been in capital letters:

ARE YOU REALLY HAPPY? REALLY AND TRULY? HAVE SENT £200 IN YOUR NAME TO BANK OF NEW SOUTH WALES, PITT STREET, JUST IN CASE. GIVE IT TO SOMEONE DESERVING IF YOU DON'T NEED IT.

Her ending made Violet cry.

With my love, always and forever, Auntie Em.

The other letter, from Sybil, was mostly about how badly 'your poor father's' feelings had been hurt, after he had done so much for Violet. In response to all Violet's plans for the Roxy, she had merely asked, 'What could you know about business?'
But the real sting came at the end of her letter.

I was not at all surprised to learn that your 'marriage' had been abandoned; because when your father wrote to Mr Franklin, not once but three times, Mr Franklin didn't even have the common courtesy to reply. You said Mr Franklin came from a good family in his own country. But your father and I suspected all along that he was the kind of person who was only interested in taking advantage of your inexperience, to pass the time while he was on holiday. We both knew that in Australia it would be a different story. Only someone immature would have been taken in by such a type. Now you've learnt that for yourself, by far the best thing would be to come home . . .

There had been more. But now, at the end of what should have been a day of triumph, one hateful phrase kept running through her head.
'In Australia it would be a different story.'

Now that the cinema was operating there was less work to do than in the two months of preparations. There was a showing three times a day: once at 4.00, again at 6.00 and a final evening showing at 8.00 p.m. Each one attracted a different crowd. The afternoon performance was filled by women and unemployed men, and occasionally a smart-looking gentleman with a younger woman: some member of the business class taking out his mistress, no doubt. The six o'clock show brought in children, who would rush home from school, gobble their tea and then make it to the talkie before bedtime. Mostly the children were eager and excited; a trip to the cinema in these hard times was a rarity, and more than once Bill had obliged some parent by playing 'Happy Birthday' on the organ before the curtain parted. In the evening, couples would line the seats, holding hands in the dark, grateful to be able to go out somewhere that wasn't going to break their budget.

Almost six months after the cinema opened, the Depression showed no signs of lifting. Violet suggested that they introduce a lunchtime screening, with special rates for the unemployed. Bill was against it.

'It will give the cinema a bad name,' he protested. 'And anyway, we're doing good business as it is.'

Violet was adamant in her decision, and finally she talked Jack and Bll round to her point of view. In early March of 1931 the Roxy started special shows at 1.00, charging an entrance fee of only a few pennies, and every day the theatre was full to capacity.

'It won't be popular,' Bill warned.

'But it's already popular,' Violet protested.

'That's not what I mean.'

The takings each day were now sizeable. There was plenty of money to repay the mortgage and to pay a good salary to Aggie, Nona and Mavis. Every day they turned away young girls who asked for jobs. They hired a new organist, an Irishman called Kelly Keefe, who sang and played with some skill, so that the ten-minute prelude now became a twenty-minute performance. Two reporters wrote of Kelly's musical ability, and he soon became a major attraction in his own right.

Having money in her pocket again delighted Aggie, particularly since she was earning far more than in London. She spent extravagantly on new clothes and hats. Such items were hard to find during the Depression, but Aggie had a knack of ferreting out a bargain. Violet, on the other hand, hoarded her money. This was the first time she had ever earned her own living. Every penny seemed worth far more than a pound given to her by her father – not that he had ever given her much cash. Young ladies often didn't carry money when they went out; men were supposed to pay for everything.

Meanwhile nothing would have induced her to spend the wages she paid herself on clothes, and it was odd to find herself admiring a new dress that Aggie had bought. In the past, it had always been the other way round. Aggie was a new person: an equal.

The days passed quickly; Violet was so busy that she spent little time thinking about anything except work. There was always something that needed to be done – instantly. The men, particularly Jack, liked to tell strangers they encountered at lunchtime nearby in 'the hotel' that they really ran everything. But when it came to the three of them working together they made no attempt to deny their dependence on Violet, even less the fact that it was she who was truly their jack-of-all-trades.

'Violet can do anything. You've got to hand it to her,' Bill said expansively one night after their ritual evening beers on the verandah. Success, Violet noticed, had mellowed him, just as it had unexpectedly steadied Jack. Now that he had a little money Jack was more cautious than she imagined him in the nomadic days when the men had nothing to lose but their unconventional mode of transport.

'Too right.' Jack gave her a smile. 'She's handier than you with that Paragon. Next thing she'll be in Hollywood making the pictures herself.'

They were paying tribute to one of her minor triumphs. Their new cash register, a Lamson Paragon, had jammed, causing Bill to spend most of the morning trying to find the salesman who had talked him into falling in love with this latest piece of English-made equipment. Jack had teased him, having favoured a rival American machine which was slightly cheaper and far more fashionable. He was a lover of everything American, and there had been a fierce argument before Bill's choice had prevailed; Bill was the person who most used the cash register, after all.

And today Violet, wielding a screwdriver, had been the one who had fixed it. Not only had it been working for the matinée, but Bill's face had been saved. Sometimes it struck her that she was more grown up than either of her male partners. They were far more likely to fall in love with toys or gadgets; also their feelings were more easily hurt. By general agreement it was she who was the directing force in the business, as well as the diplomat who helped everyone get along better. It seemed a lifetime away from her débutante existence in Belgravia.

One evening after closing up the theatre, the four of them were silent as they walked back to Belle View; Bill and Violet in front, Aggie and Jack bringing up the rear.

In recent months Aggie had blossomed, her normally optimistic self now a fact, rather than a brave front she put on in hard times. She and Jack had grown close; though Violet, taken up with each day's frantic activity, had scarcely noticed.

'We'll have to keep it quiet for longer.' The whisper from Jack was louder than he thought.

Violet, overhearing, determined to ask Aggie what was up, before they retired to bed.

Aggie got undressed that night in a hurry. As she slipped into her long cotton night-gown, she seemed unusually thoughtful.

'What have you and Jack got to keep quiet about?' Violet finally asked.

'Oh, nothing, Vi,' Aggie answered quickly.

'But, Aggie, we've never kept secrets from each other.'

Aggie looked at her without answering. Singapore lurched into Violet's mind, and she shuddered. 'It's something to do with Jack, isn't it?' she persisted.

Aggie nodded. 'We've been courting. Secretly. He's asked me to marry him.'

Violet sat down quickly on the edge of the bed. Aggie and Jack. Her only two friends, except for Nona, who worked fourteen hours a day and usually went to bed when she was finished, and Bill, who could go two days without a word. It was unbearable. She would feel so lonely.

Aggie sat down beside her and put an arm round her shoulder. 'Nothing will change. Except that you and I won't be sharing this wardrobe any more!'

Violet looked up and smiled.

'I *am* pleased for you; it's just that it's a shock.'

Nothing could be the same again. Aggie would have all the happiness. It must have been going on for months – almost from when they first arrived. She had never noticed, despite the number of times that Aggie and Jack had made excuses to stay on late at the Roxy, to work on the book-keeping or clearing up. She herself had been too tired by then to do more than trudge home through the streets of Strathfield, to find Nona already in bed.

She squeezed Aggie's hand. 'Jack's a good man. You both deserve a very happy life.'

Aggie smiled. 'Yes. I've been lucky . . .' She let the words hang in the air. For a moment she wondered if Violet was about to offer a confidence of her own. Aggie knew she was still preoccupied with thoughts of James; but did she love him? She even knew that Violet kept a collection of press clippings about him, mostly society pictures that made the most of his brooding good looks.

But Violet said nothing.

10

Violet was at the till a few days later.

'Two tickets for the four o'clock show.' The confident voice, a bit louder than was strictly necessary, was one Violet could never have forgotten. Trembling, she glanced up from Bill's Paragon, straight into James Franklin's astonished eyes.

Even at such a moment they retained the penetrating, almost ferocious look she had been trying to recall ever since she had last seen him.

And now he was there; she could have touched his hand through the grille. Her eyes clouded with emotion; speechless, she felt a surge of happiness such as she had not done since they had been together in Hyde Park so long ago.

James stared at her, unbelieving, as if she had risen from the dead. She hoped she was smiling. It was going to be all right, she thought; now, everything was going to be fine.

Then to her horror she realised James was not alone. Someone behind him, a woman, was saying: 'That girl's very slow. Is she ill or something?'

His companion was a girl tanned so brown that she could have been an Indian or a Maori. Her eyes were turquoise. She was looking at Violet with the contempt due to an inferior failing to carry out a simple task. As if James were her creature, she put her narrow, dark hand on his arm, flaunting their closeness. Violet, overcome with jealousy and humiliation, felt herself blushing a deep, hot colour that she knew must make her look like a schoolgirl.

James looked like a boxer trying to shrug off a heavy blow. 'I had no idea you were here. They told me . . .'

'We haven't got all day.' The people standing in line behind him and the girl were restive. 'What is this? A picture house or a debating society?'

'Oh, c'mon, James.' The girl tried to tug him away. 'C'mon, you're keeping everyone waiting. I'm waiting too.'

She spoke with an exaggerated inflexion Violet had heard the cleaners use, a soft low-class Sydney accent delivered on a rising inflexion so that each sentence sounded like a question. The moment her lips moved, much of the sharp symmetry of the face was lost: she seemed voluptuous, yet ordinary. Violet knew in a flash why James had brought her here – he was ashamed of her. He'd thought there would be no one he knew attending a matinée at this obscure theatre.

'Has Bill's famous Paragon jammed again?' Aggie had come to see why the flow of ticket-holders had been interrupted.

'Take over for me,' Violet said. She turned and ran, straight out of the doors on to Hardcastle Street.

Aggie stared for a moment in the direction of the street, then hastened to deal with the queue. She hoped there was not about to be a disturbance. On the far side of the lobby a tall man and a dark girl were quarrelling so fiercely that Aggie wondered if he was going to hit her. There was the kind of violence between them you sometimes saw on the streets when closing time was called in the local hotels. Yet they did not seem at all drunk, and they were both well dressed, especially the man.

'What do you mean, you don't want to see the film? You invited me. You've paid for the tickets. And *I* want to see it.'

James tore the tickets in two and threw them into a nearby ashtray. 'I've changed my mind. I'm going to put you in a taxi.'

The girl looked at the ruined tickets with fury.

Aggie closed up the till and walked over. At first she couldn't place the tall good-looking man; then she recognised him and it all made sense. It did nothing to lessen his anger that the girl was beginning to whine at him, close to tears. Aggie heard him mention a taxi again and stepped between them.

'I'll get one for you if you like.'

James looked at her blankly. They had passed each other once on the stairs at Violet's London home, but clearly he didn't recall her face. In any case she now looked different, full of the confidence that Australia, and Jack, had released in her.

'Thank you.' He flashed her a polite smile, revealing perfectly white teeth beneath his trimmed moustache. It changed his face entirely, she realised, as she walked to the door. She hailed the driver of a yellow Packard, who slowly turned his vehicle around.

'Where to?'

'It's not for me. Can you wait a minute?'

Inside, the girl was crying and James's face had taken on a bruised dangerous look. He took out his wallet and peeled off a handful of pound notes which he thrust towards her. There were an awful lot of them, Aggie thought. The girl crammed them into her bag and said very loudly, 'You bloody bastard.'

'I've got a taxi waiting,' Aggie said. She was determined not to let James slip away.

'You bastard,' the girl said again, and walked out with dignity.

James smiled at Aggie as if nothing had happened.

'Thank you. Now tell me where I can find Violet Harcourt.'

Aggie was about to reply when Jack put his hand on her arm.

'Who wants her?' he said to James. 'Are you a friend of Violet's?'

'Miss Harcourt and I are old friends. I want her address.'

Jack took off his hat and swung it round on his index finger. It was a gesture designed to irritate; he had taken an immediate dislike to this loud, condescending stranger. Maybe Violet wouldn't want to see him? Enough men fell for her, God knows. Although on the majority she had an unusual effect, as if her beauty was too much for them. A lot of them never approached her at all, but simply hung around. This cove, though, had plenty of confidence.

'It's all right, Jacko,' said Aggie. 'Mr Franklin knows Violet from London. I'm Aggie, Mr Franklin. I'm Miss Harcourt's maid, or I used to be.'

'Not any more you aren't,' Jack said unnecessarily.

'How is she?' James asked. 'What was she doing here?'

'She's a partner,' said Jack. 'If it's any of your business.'

James ignored him.

'Oh, Miss Violet is fine, Mr Franklin,' Aggie hastened to say. 'I know she'll be very pleased to see you. I'll write down the address.' She turned towards the ticket counter to find a pen and paper, leaving James and Jack glaring at each other. Inside the cinema, Kelly's organ solo was rising in crescendo.

She handed him a slip of paper and watched his elegant figure as he strode into the street and jumped into a maroon Delage.

Jack looked on, his hard expression unchanging as James drove away. 'A real gentleman. Talks like a bloody pom, down his nose. I hope Violet will thank you for that.'

'She will,' Aggie said.

'She scooted off like a rabbit. Can't see that was exactly a big welcome.'

'That's because she was surprised,' Aggie said, crossing her fingers behind her back. Violet looked as if she'd received a blow. 'She'd have been furious if I'd done anything different. You didn't like him, did you?'

'Do you like him?'

'He's a gentleman,' Aggie said cautiously. 'And very handsome.'

Jack made a noise of disgust.

Violet ran a bath and stripped off her clothes. The cool water calmed her, and at length she felt her heartbeat slow down.

She regretted the impulse that had made her flee back to Belle View. 'I'll never see him again,' she told herself. The thought filled her with panic. Her courage had failed and she had made a fool of herself. Running as if she had something to hide. Unfortunately, she knew only too well that she had.

She stayed in the bath till the water was cold. Then she got out slowly, delaying getting dressed and stretching out the time to avoid thinking: what if he doesn't come?

In the kitchen Nona could be heard preparing tea; Jack and Aggie generally came home during the six o'clock performance, leaving Bill and Kelly in charge. Violet had told her she was feeling faint. She wondered what to say now – and what to wear; if he didn't come, she didn't want to be left all evening looking like a wallflower. But if he did . . . She couldn't complete the thought.

The loud knock on the door made her jump, even though she had been expecting it. She put her ear to the bedroom door and listened to Nona walking across the linoleum in the hallway towards the front door.

'Miss Violet Harcourt, please.' The voice was deep and strong, but Violet detected nervousness. She leant against the door-frame to steady herself. Nona knocked on her door.

'There's a gentleman to see you, Vi.' She sounded puzzled.

Violet went over to where her clothes and Aggie's hung side by side in the cupboard. She took her blue and white spotted dress off its hanger and slipped it on, fastening the buckle of the broad navy belt. Thank heavens she had this good dress, she thought, as she checked her make-up in the mirror and dabbed scent behind her ears. She felt quite calm as she finished her toilette. She had waited for this moment for months and a few more minutes did not matter.

She stepped out into the hall. James was standing framed in the front porch. She walked towards him, conscious with every step that she was irreversibly changing her life.

He reached out and touched her cheek with his hand. His gesture was curiously hesitant, as though he were trying to convince himself by touch that she really existed. She moved closer, forgetting Nona's presence in the hallway. He pulled her to him in a quick, strong embrace, and murmured in her hair, 'Let's go, out of here, somewhere. On our own.'

It was a second chance for her. She could have found an excuse and called on Nona to lend her support. She could have said, 'Wait, we can meet tomorrow.' But Violet did not have the strength for denial or delay.

Without bothering to collect a coat or hat, she went with him down the steps from the porch and across the minuscule front lawn. The maroon Delage he had spoken about laughingly after the duke of Westminster's party on the Thames was parked on the rough road, its shiny wheels with silver rims wedged into the ruts left by the old pantechnicon. He opened the door for her and she settled herself on the soft leather of the front seat. Violet watched him jump into the driver's seat with an athletic grace uncommon in such a large man.

'This is impossible to believe, like something I've dreamt,' he said. He wore a wild grin of triumph.

'I know.'

'I've dreamt of kissing you,' he said. And then she was in his arms again, and they were sharing a long kiss which left her giddy and almost bruised.

She felt her spirits lift as she leant back into the luxury of the leather seat and James drove them away down the street. The wind blew through her hair. He said nothing, but it was better that way. The experience of being together could be savoured more easily without nervous exchanges.

There was safety, too, in just driving, without talking. She had no idea where they were going and she didn't want to ask. She just wanted him to remain silent, to stay within the spell cast by the early evening and the steady noise of the car and the beauty of the long waterside vistas beneath them. This was what she had dreamed about.

'We're going to the boat,' he said at length. 'It's moored in Middle Harbour. The office use it for parties and I go there sometimes. The boat's lovely.' He turned towards Violet, including her in this statement. The boat was at anchor against a small jetty. She was a 60-foot white cruiser, decked out with lights. James introduced Violet to his skipper, Les Sheedy, and showed her into the saloon. He poured champagne and then touched her glass with his own. 'To us.'

They kissed. 'You're more beautiful than I remember,' he said, as they drew apart. 'And I've tried to remember you every night.'

'I've tried to remember, too.'

She was looking into his eyes for something she could not find. Then he kissed her again and for the moment she forgot all her fears.

'We must talk,' he said. 'Tell me from the beginning what happened.'

'The beginning?' She moved away and sat down on a small sofa, looking out of the porthole at the sunset streaking the Pacific as the boat cast her moorings and made for the open sea.

'I need to get a picture in my head. At first I thought you were going to marry Peter Ironside. Then I find you in the Roxy picture theatre. I can't get over you being in Sydney at all. I imagined you in the south of France or Italy or Greece. But Sydney . . . in the Roxy. That's too much to take in.'

'But not England –'

'Not since I heard from your father.' From his wallet he took a piece of paper. 'Read for yourself.'

There was a single sheet, with her address on the top. How funny to see it there. It was creased; clearly James had read it several times. Her father's unmistakable handwriting, tiny and spider-like, covered one side only.

Dear Mr Franklin,
  In reply to your last communication, I'm taking the time to inform you that Violet is now back in Europe having realised that she made a mistake concerning her association with you. I am sure that after a period abroad with her sister-in-law she will have recovered her health and sense. She will be travelling indefinitely and has asked that you should not try and communicate with her – she has suffered enough as a result of your ill-considered intrusion into her life.

Violet put it down. 'Did you believe this?'

She was overcome with astonishment and fury. Even after her father's deception over the 'engagement' to Peter Ironside, it was hard to believe.She found herself trembling with rage.

'At first, yes. It reached me just as I was leaving to catch the train for Southampton.'

He looked her in the eye as he spoke. Yet Violet knew that somehow or other he could have made greater efforts to discover the truth. He had tried, certainly; but not that hard.

'When I reached home, of course, I got your letters – I came via Panama because I couldn't face weeks on the boat with Mum and Dad. So I've been expecting you – every day.'

He said this accusingly. Violet thought, no, that's not true; you weren't expecting me the day I went to the *Gazette*. Sensing that the conversation was getting dangerous, she reached for his hand.

'Does it matter now? I'm here and you're here.'

'Of course it matters. What happened to you? Is there someone else? Did you meet someone on the boat?'

'No, there isn't. There never has been. Oh, James, I had such an awful time.' She moved closer to him and he put his arms around her. Violet started to cry with relief. She was going to be able to tell him about the nightmare of the rape, and he would see that it was not her fault. He did still love her. Thinking this she suddenly felt an extraordinary lightness.

'It's all right,' he said consolingly. 'Don't be afraid.' With one hand he smoothed her hair and with the other he gently rubbed her back. 'But you must see the only thing I could believe was that you didn't love me any more. That you'd found someone else. Someone on the boat, perhaps . . . Thank God there's been no other man. That's the one thing I couldn't stand.'

She stiffened in his arms, terrified of what she had so nearly done. She had been on the point of telling him the truth, and losing him forever.

'Tell me what did happen,' he said. 'Did you miss the boat, or what?'

She accepted the proffered lie eagerly. 'We were robbed in Singapore. I suppose a lot of people are.'

'I see . . . So – no Peter and no one else? You're still mine?'

She laughed, anxious to shift the topic.

'I wouldn't marry Peter in a million years. Not if I had a thousand lives.' They both responded as though her exaggeration were amusing. Violet could see that James too did not really care to explore the whole truth. He did not want to spoil a happy ending by learning too much about what had gone before. Like her, he wanted to preserve his passion – and his illusions.

He poured her more wine. 'So that disposes of Peter – in spite of what I read in the papers?'

She almost quoted words of Ben's that came into her mind. 'The papers get everything right. Except anything you happen to know about very well yourself. Then they get everything wrong.' Instead she shrugged. She didn't want to risk introducing a hint of Ben when she was with James. 'The papers! You should know about *them*.'

He laughed. 'I'll tell you one thing. If I ever see your father again I'll kill him with my bare hands.'

She saw a shadow pass over his handsome face, despite his bantering tone.

'Can't we go up on deck?' she asked hurriedly. James tucked his arm round her waist and they went out into the night air. The stars were thick above them, a million gleaming points in a never-ending blackness. They were moving silently through the still night water, scattering phosphorescence behind them like confetti. A big ship, like a moving island of colour, was travelling across their path, heading for Sydney harbour.

'It's the *Mauretania*,' James said. 'It used to be the flagship of the French line.'

'She,' Violet corrected him, looking at the searchlights playing along the liner's deck. Now they could hear music too, an echo of an orchestra coming to them in fragments across the water. 'Boats are always women.'

It was Ben again. Violet couldn't get rid of him. She turned to James with her face lifted, to exorcise the wrong image.

'She's not as beautiful as you are,' he said.

When they stopped kissing, the *Mauretania* was so close that they could make out movement along the deck under the multicoloured lights.

'So there wasn't anyone else?' James said, holding her.

'There wasn't anything in the past,' she said nervously. 'It doesn't exist. There's only now.'

It was very nearly true; almost completely true now, with the music clearer every second across the water. Yet even with his arms around her and his lips on hers and then his voice asking her to marry him there remained those terrible things she could never forget and never talk about. She knew then that they both had secrets from each other which would always remain untold.

She tried to make her fears go away. 'Yes, I love you,' she said, and almost meant it with all her heart.

11

Belle View, the little house in Strathfield, and Bellevue Hill, one of Sydney's most exclusive areas to the south-east of the harbour, were forty minutes apart and, so Violet thought, separated by a few thousand miles. At the end of three weeks she had made the transition from one to the other so completely that it was hard to imagine she had ever inhabited that other Australia.

James had been anxious for an early marriage – so much so that if they had followed his first impulse they would have eloped to Queensland and gone through a ceremony over the first weekend, abetted by a magistrate in Brisbane James knew from his schooldays. A few moments' thought, however, had changed his mind. They would do things 'the right way, have a big party, enjoy ourselves'. It was decided that Violet should spend the intervening weeks living with his younger sister, Bunty McGrath, and her husband, Dick.

Dick was waiting for his father to let him take over the family hardware business. He and Bunty had no children, despite many efforts, including, as Bunty soon confided, the power of prayer.

Bunty filled her empty days playing golf at a fine club in Rose Bay, and going to charity lunches, organised and attended almost entirely by women, where the guests kept their gloves on till it was time to eat.

Violet had forgotten what it was like to fill in time like this. To Bunty, though, it was positively taxing to undertake a round of golf, a visit to a hat shop and a fitting at the dressmaker's for Violet's wedding dress.

'I'm exhausted,' she said after one such expedition. 'What a morning. So busy.' Bunty threw herself into an overstuffed chintz armchair, and rang a small bell for the maid. She was a tall woman of great elegance.

Violet could not help but think of life at Belle View, rising before six and carrying on, some days, for another fourteen or fifteen hours.

'If the unemployed were ready to work half as hard as I do,' Bunty was saying, 'the country would soon be on its feet again.'

Violet could not forbear to answer.

'I don't agree, Bunty. When I worked at the cinema I turned away literally hundreds of girls who wanted jobs. They would have worked if they could.' Sometimes she thought that her six months working at the Roxy had taught her more about Australia than Bunty would ever know.

Bunty raised her well-shaped eyebrows.

'Nonsense. I know they don't really want to, because that's what Dick says.'

Violet sighed and gratefully took the dry Martini that the maid brought in. Since the move to Bunty's she had started to look forward to drinks before lunch. She found herself wondering how things were going at the picture theatre. Violet had already learned during her time at Bellevue Hill that, as a topic, her life as a working woman was never a success. She sipped her first cocktail of the day with relief. No wonder her mother drank. It was a way of making the time pass.

'Violet, are you listening?' Bunty had a notebook on her knee and was writing down another of her endless lists with a small gold pen. She was ferociously organised to deal with the tiny details of her life. Though only twenty-five, she sometimes reminded Violet of a type of English county lady in her sixties. 'You must have some visiting cards printed. And we must assemble your going-away trousseau. I don't suppose you've been told where James is taking you for your honeymoon? It would be helpful to know if it is to somewhere hot or cold.' Bunty put down her pen and smiled to herself. 'Just think of it. When you're getting married here in Australia, everyone in England will be putting on their hats for Ascot.' She said the word 'hats' with relish, as if they were something to eat with cream.

Violet found it easier to get on with James's parents, George and Daisy, and her first visit to them had been a success.

James had called from the office to say that he would be late. So she had driven to their house with Bunty.

'I'm so glad that Dick's not in newspapers,' Bunty said, as their car rounded a broad sweep in the drive. 'We never knew, when we were first growing up, what time Dad would be back.'

'Did your mother mind?'

'She must have done, mustn't she? I would,' Bunty replied. 'We're here. Don't be frightened of them. Dad has always had a soft spot for pretty women.' The car laboured up a steep incline, crunching over the gravel, and came to a stop outside a columned porch.

Killymoon had been built in 1900 to celebrate both the new century and the first year that the *Gazette* had showed profits. It was a square two-storey building, with a dark slate roof and with tall chimneys at each corner. On the ground floor a covered verandah surrounded the house on three sides; you could dance straight out on to it from the ballroom. There was also a first-floor verandah, on to which the bedrooms opened. Violet saw that here was a house where people always wanted to sit outside.

The garden was even more pleasing than Killymoon itself. It was laid out in the English style, with herbaceous borders and immaculate lawns which had been mown so that light reflected off the grass in broad alternating swathes. But even at the end of the growing season it didn't feel like an English garden. The flowers were too rich and almost indecently large. The yew hedge which circled the garden was overrun by lantana, whose pink and white flowers looked like tiny daisies. There were so many, they almost obscured the dark waxy foliage of the yews. Everything seemed to flourish out of all control: great banks of nasturtiums, hydrangeas like coral reefs, and roses as big as cabbages.

Violet's obvious pleasure prompted George to say, 'Why don't I give you the full tour?'

She nodded with delight and set off arm in arm with her future father-in-law.

They walked past a fountain in the form of a cherub, water gushing from his mouth. Up in the coral trees parakeets twittered. George said, 'The view down to the harbour was splendid when we first came here. On Saturdays, when the children were young, we used to go for picnics on the beach. What meals we used to have!' He patted his stomach and smiled ruefully. 'I'm under doctor's orders not to eat so much. Ales and wines, German sausages, fowls and hams and tongues. Tarts and cakes and fruits.' His eyes were like James's, deep-set and brown. He still had a full head of hair, though it was liberally shot with grey. 'Let me show you the tennis court. James is a wicked player, but I suppose you know that.'

With Daisy, too, Violet got on well from the start. Daisy had pale-blue eyes and her grey hair was tied back in a knot. Deep lines ran from her jaw to her high cheekbones; she looked older than her sixty years. She was calm and self-contained, capable of bursting into peals of laughter or of instantly giving her full attention to whoever was speaking. Violet sensed that her marriage with George had been a great success. James's parents were a cheerful, outdoors couple, who showed a tolerant approach to their children. It was clear that they liked Violet and they swiftly made her feel comfortable. At first she had felt uncertain of their response, particularly when she had to say that her parents would not be coming; but they took it all in their stride. It was with reluctance that she got up at the end of the evening to leave.

May turned into June and the weather grew colder, with blustery winds scattering the last rose petals in the garden at Killymoon. Then, before Violet knew, it was the eve of her wedding. At Bunty's house, alone with her hostess, she was trying to calm herself, as she sorted and packed her clothes. Laying everything on the bed for the maid to put in her suitcase, she felt sad that her mother wasn't there to help her.

When she had first read her mother's letter saying that neither Sybil nor Rupert would attend the wedding, Violet had been angry. Now, she was unhappy and not a little scared. Would James know that she wasn't a virgin? Even though she knew intellectually that the rape had not been her fault, she carried the sense of blame around with her like a mighty weight. All her girlfriends had always believed that men could tell, without fail. Whether they were right, Violet simply did not know. She couldn't ask Bunty; indeed, she couldn't ask anyone. At times the need to confide in someone was so great that she wished she had told Aggie what had happened straight away. It was too late now.

12

The wedding was as James wished, a lavish, even ostentatious affair. It was not simply a rich man's occasion, marked by niceties like the champagne, whose vintage predated the Great War (his father's idea) or the naval band (a contribution of Bunty's). The celebrations had a sheer profusion and an opulence that might have been taken as *nouveau riche*, in another family.

Newspaper proprietors of the Franklins' standing had their own special style, a bravura quality that often stemmed from a patriarchal megalomaniac figure heading the board. George Franklin, especially in retirement, was not like this. For all his unassuming manner, however, he was a connoisseur of power, politics and the world of business. He was also a man with a lot of friends; and on this occasion, spurred by Daisy, his wife, he had mobilised them freely to do honour to his son and his son's bride.

He had taken a great fancy to Violet from the start, a feeling he was pleased to find reciprocated by her. Some weeks passed before he was able to identify the affinity between them, and then it had taken Daisy to point it out – on the day George received an ungracious letter from Rupert Harcourt declining to participate in his daughter's wedding.

'I can't understand any father treating a child like that,' he said.

'You mean *you* wouldn't treat a child like that, because your father did as much to you. I don't recall your family attending *our* wedding?'

George had come to Australia virtually an outcast. He had been very young, and unable to avoid stupid quarrels with his father. He too had arrived penniless in a strange country and he too had married impetuously for love. When he and Daisy had started married life they had bought their first furniture second-hand. It was a pleasure to George that his son's situation, forty years later, was so superior.

The reception at Killymoon, George's mansion on Bellevue Hill, was to be attended by 400 guests, from the governor-general downwards. The toast to 'The Bride and Groom' was to be proposed by a former state premier, a skeletal but still imposing figure in his seventies, who owed his long-forgotten election to George Franklin and the *Gazette*.

Only a small number of those invited had met the bride before the ceremony, and almost none knew anything about her absent family. Yet neither the bride's apparent lack of kin nor, by implication, an absence of money, raised any aspersions. Instead even the most sceptical onlookers were moved by Violet's looks that day. She shone with a piercing yet serene beauty which many of those present remembered for the rest of their lives, and which immediately resolved any unspoken questions about the marriage. This was self-evidently a love match, a union based on the natural attraction between two unusually fine examples of human beauty and health.

They were, as guests repeated to each other, 'a wonderful-looking couple', 'a striking pair'. No wonder the bridegroom's parents were so obviously delighted. 'They'll have beautiful children.' There was also frequent comment on Violet's poise and style. 'She'll make a good hostess' was another remark that went the rounds. 'She knows how to talk to people.'

Violet kept thinking, this is supposed to be the happiest day of my life. But I'm frightened. Frightened of being alone with James.

And despite the admiration all about her, she was secretly ill at ease. She felt embarrassed that her parents had declined to come and that she was contributing no money towards the occasion; she was also discomforted to find herself, at her own wedding, virtually friendless. Only Emerald had received the news with pleasure; but her reply was another thing that had worried Violet. She was, she said, too ill to undertake the long journey; maybe she would come for a visit the following year. She sent Violet an emerald necklace which Harry had given her at their own wedding, with a note saying, 'He would have wanted you to have it.' It sounded like a message of doom.

Aggie, on catching sight of Violet in her wedding dress, had gasped. She wondered what on earth it must have cost. It was made of eggshell-white silk from Thailand, heavy and luxurious. The full skirt billowed out into a long train which rustled as Violet walked. Her waist looked tiny. Tight sleeves which ended in vee-shaped points over her hands made her arms look as slender as a child's. Seed pearls decorated the neckline and the hem and were scattered across the gauze veil like dewdrops.

On someone plainer the dress would have been a disaster; it would have swallowed her up in its own beauty. But Violet wore it like a princess. As the organ music stopped, heralding her arrival at the church, heads turned and stayed turned. Every eye was fixed on her as she walked slowly up the aisle to stand beside James. She seemed completely in control, as though she had rehearsed the scene many times.

James smiled at her, and Violet managed to smile back. There was something inevitable about this moment, and had been since they first met. Though not technically lovers – something James had been trying to remedy almost daily throughout their engagement – she felt that there was already a biological connection between them. There was no doubt of his passion for her and if that was the same thing as love, then she too was in its spell.

Yet looking at him now she thought how little she knew him and how great was her dependence on this man and his family. She knew that 400 pairs of eyes were on her, that it was too late to run; but in a way it had been too late from the start, from the moment they had caught each other's eye in the cemetery on Highgate Hill.

They stepped forward towards the vicar. Violet felt as if she had dived off a very high board into a swimming pool. She looked at James; but instead of catching her eye he was exchanging a whisper with his friend Billy Sorrell. It must have been to do with the ring, because James took something from Billy and slipped it in his waistcoat pocket. There was a complicity between them, a kind of subdued prankishness, from which Violet was excluded, related perhaps to the fact they had been at school together. Then James turned and squeezed her hand and a current of desire ran through her.

He was so handsome in his tail coat, he might have been modelling it. He looked perfect, she thought. A perfect stranger.

The church was absolutely silent as the vicar began: 'Dearly beloved, we are gathered together . . .'

Bunty sighed, and wished that her own husband looked more distinguished. The broadness of Dick's chest and the length of his arms were a combination to daunt the most expensive tailor; and his carroty hair militated even against formality, let alone elegance. It was three generations since the McGraths had been near a plough, and her father George had reminded her once that the McGrath industrial empire, founded on a chain of hardware stores in New South Wales, could buy and sell the *Gazette* several times over. Yet it was her cross to be married to someone who always looked, in James's sardonic words, 'as if he's just come in from milking the cows'.

She looked around her. The preparations that had preoccupied her for weeks were coming to a triumphant fruition. Everything was as James wanted. The flowers were perfect, the music was just right and the bride looked beautiful. The dress was a stunning success – and so it should be, Bunty thought, recalling the number of visits to the dressmaker for fittings. She had been so nervous at her own wedding that she could hardly remember much about it. It had been enjoyable playing a major role in her brother's without having to be the star. The only thing out of keeping was the presence of Violet's strange friends from the picture house. She looked across the aisle to where they were sitting, up near the front of the bride's side of the church. It had been a mistake to invite them. But Violet had insisted – even though, as Bunty knew, James had been against the idea.

They were an odd pair. The girl, who must once have been Violet's maid, was dabbing her eyes with a white lace handkerchief and holding on to a vulgar-looking man. He must be the one called Jack. What on earth could Violet have been doing for so long with these nondescript people? At least the girl was wearing a pretty dress, with a smart white straw hat decorated with long silk ribbons. She must have learned her good taste from Violet. Bunty looked enviously at the size of Violet's waist. From behind, the dress showed off her figure to perfection.

She was pleased that her priest would be at Killymoon for the reception. Kieran O'Fallen had not only married Bunty and Dick; he had given Bunty instruction in the faith during the three years of their engagement. Dick's family were strict and influential Catholics, and although she had taken his religion there were still McGraths who treated her like an interloper. Bunty felt their reserve all the more strongly because so far she and Dick were childless. The hurt of this had made her go to great trouble to make Violet feel at home; and though Bunty found her a strange girl, not at all what she had expected, she was prepared to be happy, because James was.

She had always adored James. As a child his name for her had been 'Slave' and indeed as far as she could she had fulfilled his every wish. It was not just a question of love, but the only way to get any peace. If James was balked, then life was a torment for everyone. When he got what he wanted – when it was a day like today – he was the most enchanting person in the world.

The organist pounded out the opening bars of 'The Wedding March'. Bunty blinked back tears as James and Violet stood for a moment on the altar steps. They stepped into the aisle to start their triumphant walk out of the church. Violet's veil was thrown back off her face and her eyes were unnaturally bright. Their hands were tightly clasped. Bunty could see the thick band of gold on Violet's fourth finger.

James looked at Violet as if she were a prize he had won. Watching them on the church steps a few moments later as they lined up for photographs, Bunty could not help a moment of trepidation on behalf of the bride.

Her husband's thoughts were echoing her own.

'It's a long way home to Mummy,' Dick said in her ear. His eyes too were on Violet.

She elbowed her consort in the ribs to show her disapproval, and Dick let out a yelp. 'Cut it out, Bunty,' he said, pretending to be aggrieved. 'Can you imagine what it would be like – being married to your brother?'

It took almost two hours for Violet, with James at her side, to receive all the guests in the reception line at Killymoon.

'Now you've met everyone in New South Wales,' he said, brushing his forehead with a silk handkerchief. 'I notice the governor-general knows your family.'

'He said he used to hunt with the Heythrop, so he would have known Aunt Henrietta. I wish one of them had come, James – I'm sorry.' Now that the effort of meeting the guests was over, she felt isolated.

'Cheer up, you're better without them,' James said. He put his arm around her shoulders in a reassuring squeeze. One of the military-looking waiters in white ducks was passing, and James took a glass and raised it. 'Here's to you. You're a Franklin now. You belong to us.'

'You've done all right, Vi,' Jack said, looking up at the cut-glass chandelier that hung from the ceiling of the ballroom. 'You wouldn't know there was a depression, would you? Not here, anyway.' His eyes widened briefly. 'Is that the governor? Sir Philip Game?'

Violet nodded and shuffled her cream satin shoes on the parquet flooring. She took a smoked salmon canapé from a waiter and held out her glass for more champagne.

'You'll never need to be a business lady again,' Jack said.

'I might. Although James isn't very keen on women working.'

'And when has that stopped you?' Aggie was flushed with wine and excitement. Her cheeks looked hot.

'Aggie, leave the girl alone. It's her wedding day. All the same, Vi, there'll never be anyone who's a patch on you when it comes to the pictures. There's a great businesswoman lost today.'

'How does it feel, then? To be the new Mrs Franklin?' Father O'Fallen's face was close to hers. He had piercing blue eyes and aquiline features.

'Wonderful,' Violet replied. 'I've never seen you in your uniform before. If that's the right word.'

O'Fallen made a low bow, the wide black skirt of his soutane touching the hem of her wedding dress. His face was momentarily obscured by the brim of his black biretta. The priest had not been at the church, only at the party.

'*Alii situs, alia licita,*' he said.

Violet looked puzzled.

'It means, my dear Violet, there's a time and a place for everything. I have to make the point today because I'm like Daniel in the den, or a rose among the thorns.'

Violet looked questioningly and O'Fallen did a comic, martyred expression.

'A solitary Jesuit among the Protestant establishment of the state. With a few exceptions, I'm pleased to add.'

'You don't try and convert people, do you?' Violet asked.

'I have no such mission,' O'Fallen said. 'I certainly don't think your husband would like to be converted. Or not at this stage of his life.'

'He wouldn't, I'm sure,' Violet said, smiling. 'Do you feel lonely in the—' she glanced at the guests in their extravagant fashions '— the den?'

'I forget I'm lonely, because of all the people,' O'Fallen said. 'I expect we're alike in that. You have been very lonely, I think?'

'Not any more,' Violet said, looking round for James. She suspected that the priest understood her all too well, but she certainly did not wish to exchange confidences with him. He knew far too much already. She was convinced that by some priestly alchemy O'Fallen also divined that the bride was wearing a white dress to which she had no right.

'It's time we were off. Time for us to change.' James bowed his head lightly to O'Fallen, answered the priest's smile with one bordering on lasciviousness. Violet blushed.

Aggie was standing at the bottom of the stairs.

'Do you want me to help you change?'

Violet nodded, and took her arm.

'How nice, Violet; your old maid.' Bunty, who'd been loitering, had stepped into the hall. 'I was going to volunteer myself, but I'm sure you'd rather have . . .'

Violet realised that Bunty had wished to be asked. She was always disappointing Bunty in some way. Now, too, her sister-in-law's snobbery, or perhaps mere conventional sense of rank, was affronted by the relationship between Aggie and herself. There was nothing to be done about it, Violet thought, running up the stairs as if they were an escape route. She needed to relax, before the next stage of the celebrations, with someone she knew well; and Aggie was the only one.

'Shall I run you a bath? I think you have time,' Aggie said.

'Yes, but I want a drink first. There in the corner. Why don't you give me a Martini and have one yourself while I get these tight shoes off.'

She laughed at Aggie's expression. 'I asked for a tray of drinks there,' she explained. 'I knew I'd need something after those guests. I couldn't believe there'd be so many . . .'

'Lovely people,' Aggie said. 'Very grand, except for Jack and me. Nona and Bill were right not to come; they wouldn't have felt comfortable. I saw Mrs McGrath, your sister-in-law, giving me a funny look in church.'

'I hope you didn't take any notice. Bunty's got a good heart.'

Aggie grimaced. 'No, I didn't,' she said, busying herself with the last suitcase. 'But I'll tell you one thing, Vi. There'll be times over the years when you miss old Belle View. No matter how happy you are as Mrs Franklin.'

In the bath Violet lay back and remembered her departure from Belle View, seven weeks before. She had woken up one morning in her tiny room to the sound of Nona's voice raised in astonishment.

'You wouldn't read it in a book.' It was an expression Nona reserved for the near miraculous. 'Come and look, Jack; and someone wake Vi.'

It was an act typical of James – impulsive, dramatic, a bit exaggerated. Some time after returning her to Belle View, he must have remembered their conversation in London at the Westminsters' dance, and woken the chauffeur. Thus, at seven-fifteen that morning, Nona had found the Delage outside the bungalow, open and overflowing with flowers. The colours were magnificent, like a coral reef trapped in a box.

Violet walked down the path. She smelt roses and lavender, orchids and camellias.

Nona's face was filled with suspicion, as if the strange object might explode in their faces. 'The man – a chauffeur – said it was for you.' She sounded uncertain. 'He said there's a letter.'

There was an envelope propped on the polished mahogany steering-wheel.

Darling Violet,
   You've won our bet, and I always pay up when I lose.
   Love, James.

'What are you going to do?' Nona asked.

Violet giggled, all happiness. 'Put the flowers in water. Give me a hand.'

'Aren't you going to say what this is about?' Jack asked, after Nona and Aggie and Violet had filled all the vases in Belle View, and even the sink. 'Who are they from?'

'Oh, Jack,' she said, smiling irrepressibly. 'I've won a bet, that's all.' Seeing him look aggrieved, she took his arm.

'James Franklin has asked me to marry him. I've said yes.'

Aggie hugged her, her eyes wide with delight.

'How wonderful, Vi. When is it to be? I'm so happy for you. We'll both be brides together.'

'I'm not sure when. We only decided last night.'

The girls kissed each other, laughing. 'What a relief,' Aggie said. 'I did so hope this would happen. But I'll tell you one thing – I'd given up hope.'

'My God, Vi,' Jack said. 'Are you sure you know what you're letting yourself in for?' Even though Aggie had explained that Violet and James had achieved a long-awaited reunion, his face was full of concern.

'I've never been so happy.' As she said it, she thought, it's almost true.

'We'd better celebrate,' Bill said.

They drank Violet's health in beer; Bill played 'Here Comes The Bride'; and for a few minutes it was one of Belle View's most boisterous celebrations. Then the atmosphere unexpectedly changed, and even Jack became quieter. It was as if they had all realised at the same moment that they were also celebrating a farewell.

'I don't suppose you'll be staying here much longer?' Jack said, wiping a line of froth off his upper lip. 'Now that you're engaged to marry someone like that.'

'I hadn't managed to think that far,' Violet replied.

'I'm sure your Mr Franklin has,' Nona said, with a shade of disapproval. 'He won't want his bride living down here with people like us. He'll want you somewhere more . . .' She hesitated. 'More fitting.'

Violet didn't know how to answer. She hadn't thought until now that by marrying James she might lose the friendships she'd made at

Belle View. It was a place where she had felt safe. The thought came to her unbidden that perhaps she would never be so happy again. She rejected it impatiently. From now on there would be James.

Jack, sensing her distress, came over and put his arm round her shoulder. 'Don't worry about us, Vi. We'll just have to get by without you. It's a good business now, nobody's going to starve. And remember one thing – you'll always be able to come back here.'

'That's right, Violet. Always.' Aggie kissed her again. Both girls were crying. It was sad beyond words that her life with Jack and Aggie, Nona and Bill, had ended, all in the span of less than a day. Belle View had become part of her past. Walking round the scrubby garden for the last time, Violet tried to imprint it on her memory. She didn't want to forget a place where she had found happiness and love.

There was a knock on the door. Daisy's voice said, 'Can I come in?'

'I'm ready,' Violet called, dabbing on some perfume. She hastened to let Daisy in.

'Thank you for a lovely day – it's all been due to you.'

Daisy kissed her warmly. 'It's been our pleasure – Bunty's too. She's delighted to have a sister. Now – James is waiting downstairs. It won't do to keep him waiting, especially on his wedding day.'

Violet kissed Aggie goodbye, clinging briefly to her. Downstairs a crowd had assembled on the steps of the house. George squeezed her arm. 'You make me wish I was younger,' he said, grinning mischievously.

'Have a wonderful time, Violet.' Bunty kissed her and whispered, 'Don't forget – it's never worth arguing with James.'

Then her husband was beside her and hustling her down the steps and into the back of a green Daimler. There were no JUST MARRIED placards or tin cans attached to the bumper – James's friends knew him too well to play practical jokes. All the same it was a mellow and in some cases boozy party who cheered them away down the drive.

At the aerodrome they boarded the aircraft with which James, despite sceptical protest from George, had recently equipped the *Gazette*. It was piloted by Les Sheedy, the same handsome, polite man who with white cap on his head instead of flying helmet and goggles had acted as skipper of the *Gazette*'s motor-cruiser.

'I hope you enjoy this, Mrs Franklin,' he told her. 'It's likely to be a bit rough over Bass Strait.'

'Good thing Billy got too drunk to come with us,' James said. He was in high good humour. 'He's terrified of flying, you know.'

It was Violet's first flight, and she herself was excited. Inside the aircraft, James had installed comfortable seats and carpets; even so, the fuselage was draughty and the noise deafening. They soon tired of shouting at each other above the roar of the engines. James opened a bottle of champagne and filled Violet's glass. He wrapped a blanket round her and, exhausted after the wedding, she fell into a restless sleep, hardly waking for the refuelling stops at Albury and Melbourne.

When she did wake up they were flying over Bass Strait. The plane was bouncing up and down in a storm, creaking and protesting. Lightning flickered past the windows. She reached for James's hand and he gave her a reassuring squeeze.

'Don't worry,' he shouted, 'it won't last.'

The plane dipped downwards, breaking beneath the clouds. Below, she could see the grey sea flecked with white horses and furrowed with troughs. They flew on towards Tasmania.

They were to spend their honeymoon in a mountain lodge belonging to James's best man, Billy Sorrell. Billy owned the biggest wood pulp company on the island, and it was he who supplied the *Gazette* group. The house was magnificently sited, with a mountain range behind it, and a view of a lake. The waters of the lake had a blue-green clarity that reminded Violet of glacier-fed pools she had seen in the Alps.

A meal was waiting for them, and in their bedroom there was more champagne. A log fire blazed in the grate. While James disappeared to the bathroom Violet sat watching the shadows from the firelight. It reminded her of home. She hadn't sat in front of a wood fire since leaving England, and the lush, green scenery of Tasmania made her think of Europe too. From the bathroom she could hear water splashing into the tub. The moment was approaching when she could no longer shelter behind her supposed innocence.

James came out of the bathroom, wearing a silk dressing-gown loosely tied round the waist. His hair was wet and slicked back from his forehead. As she got to her feet, he took her in an embrace. He started to undo the buttons at the back of her dress, easing his hands in under the silk, and running his fingers down her spine, feeling every bone and contour.

She pushed him away and looked up at him.

'No – wait. I must get changed.' He let her go reluctantly. When she came back into the bedroom she was wearing a white satin dressing-gown over a matching night-gown. James was looking out of the window, down into the valley. He held out his hands and she came towards him uncertainly.

Her lips parted beneath his, as she stood pressed against him. Quickly he undid the ribbons holding her négligé in place and pulled the thin straps down over her shoulders. Then he uncovered her completely, circling her nipples with his tongue. They hardened and she felt heat between her legs and groaned. He knelt and moved his mouth downwards, covering her with kisses, nibbling her flesh, grazing her with his moustache. His hand parted her legs and she backed away from him towards the bed.

James stood up and threw off his dressing-gown. Gently he laid her on the bed.

'You're beautiful,' he said, gazing down at her. He saw the fear in her face, and he leant forward.

'Don't be afraid. I love you.'

He bent her backwards, lifting up her ankles, playing his tongue along the soles of her feet, then down her legs. He moved on top of her, covering her body with his. She looked up at his face, only inches above hers. Suddenly she was back in that filthy room in Singapore. She was gripped by terror. He would never understand. His body was heavy on hers and she tried to move away but he was too strong. Despite her fear she was starting to respond; but he was hurting her, with a strong grip which held her immobilised. He parted her legs abruptly, and forced his fingers into her. He had risen to his knees and seemed to tower over her like an animal. Her first response, a hunger on the surface of her skin like an irritation, retreated to a deeper part of herself.

Involuntarily, she strained towards him, trying to hold herself open, but his face blurred again, and the expression in his eyes, the panting breath, reminded her overwhelmingly of the other time, the terrible one on the docks that she had tried so hard to forget. For a moment she could hear the Chinese voices again and their guttural cries and there was the same paralysing fear.

'Relax. I won't hurt you. My darling,' he said. But she hardly heard him.

She felt James steady himself, as though he were expecting resistance. Then he was pushing into her. First pushing with ever-increasing pressure, and then thrusting harder and harder, on and on like a machine that would never stop. His breath was gasping and harsh close to her face but she felt as if he had gone away from her. The hunger in her body left her too, evaporating under this relentless physical onslaught. Her whole body hurt, pummelled and squeezed and wrenched.

After a long time he cried out and she was detached enough to think that Chinese and Australian men produced the same raucous unearthly noise at the moment of climax. Then he collapsed across her. She tried to push him away but he was a dead weight, crushing her breasts and shoulders.

'I can't breathe,' she said.

He lifted himself up on one elbow and looked down at her with narrowed eyes. For a long time he didn't say anything at all.

'That wasn't the first time, was it?' he hissed. 'Who was it? Peter?'

She didn't reply. It was as bad as she had feared; worse.

'Was it some man on the boat? How many, Violet?'

She turned her head sideways on the counterpane, trying to avoid the pain and disgust in his eyes.

'Why don't you tell me the truth? I have the right . . . What were you playing at in that theatre? Was there someone there? One of those larrikins with big boots?'

'No, no. Why are you asking these crazy questions?'

As she turned to face him she could feel him stiffen again and he started moving in her. Immediately, it hurt.

'Let me go.'

His hands held her still, while his hips continued to move. 'Tell me the truth.'

'Stop it,' she said. 'You're hurting me. Please.'

Her eyes were afraid, her body taut. James watched her face as, with short, quick thrusts, he hammered into her, as though he were trying to drive right through her into the bed. She stopped fighting him and lay there, tears smarting in her eyes. What could she say? Would it be better to invent a lover than to tell the truth? He bit at her nipples, and she put up her hands to cover them. Roughly, he pushed them away.

'Answer me, Violet. You're my wife, damn it; I have a right to know.'

'I can't tell you anything, James. Please don't ask me. I love you. Isn't that what matters?' she said.

He lifted up her hips, working himself deep inside her, forcing her thighs apart till she thought she would break in two. 'I thought you were different,' he panted, 'but all this time you've just been pretending to be a coy little virgin.'

She started to moan in pain.

'Does that feel good?' he said bitterly, working his fingers between her buttocks and forcing them upwards.

She recoiled as she felt his thumb try to break into her. 'Please stop,' she pleaded; but he went on jerking into her.

Violet was obsessed with a longing to tell him. But something held her back. She could not speak. She was heartbroken.

'Keep your secrets!' he hissed into her face. 'Maybe it's best if you do.' His voice was hurt as well as angry. He pulled himself out of her as if suddenly eager to sever all contact. She winced with pain.

James started to dress.

'Where are you going?' Violet pulled the counterpane around herself, still shuddering with distress.

'Somewhere I'm going to be better appreciated. Right now, that's almost anywhere.'

She could see the pain in his eyes, and she put out her hand to touch him. He brushed her away.

'It's a bit late for that,' he said, reaching for his coat. As he left, he told her, 'Don't wait up.'

There was a finality about his words. She had been right to be afraid – that night in Singapore had ruined her life. Nothing could ever be right again. Her bruised body hurt, and at last Violet began to weep. He was too arrogant, she too proud; she could never tell him the truth.

James appeared for breakfast next morning with a sardonic, composed air. Superficially he behaved as if nothing untoward had happened. Violet noticed, however, that his eyes had dark shadows beneath them – he looked as if he had come from a night's debauchery, though where he had found it in this deserted place Violet could not imagine. She longed to reach out to him, but she was too scared to make the first move.

James had arranged for Billy, who had come down from Devonport that morning, to show them the sights, as if the prospect of being alone with her all the time was unwelcome. Violet, too, was relieved to see Billy's amiable big man's face. He drove them, in a Bentley especially designed for rough country, to a lodge looking down on a landscape of tall Huon pines. Billy's logging camps had left their mark in patchwork tracts of bare scrub, denuded of everything but stumps like gravestones. It saddened Violet that trees a thousand years old were reduced to wood pulp, to print papers like the *Gazette*, whose life-span was twenty-four hours.

They had a picnic near a waterfall and when a gang of loggers passed Violet was subjected to a barrage of raucous whistles. To her surprise James put his arm round her, the first sign of affection he had shown all day. He liked it when other men admired her; and yet he was jealous, of her supposed past most of all.

Although he made a ritual of resistance, Billy gave in to their joint demands that he should join them for a long and elaborate dinner. Violet drank enough champagne to enjoy his stories of the old convict settlement on Van Diemen's Land — but after he had driven off recklessly down the dirt road into the valley there was nothing between herself and James but an oppressive silence.

Her second night as James's wife was as violent and painful as the first. He seemed determined to treat her as the whore he thought she was. Later she would be unable to remember at which point during the honeymoon he initiated a habit that was to persist. He would get undressed in his dressing-room, make love to her until she was exhausted and he was satisfied, and then go off to sleep in another room, or sometimes disappear for the rest of the night. The sound of his car driving off in the small hours was to become part of their life's pattern.

What she was to remember was their visit to a prison in a village called Richmond. There were all manner of relics from convict days, including a stone bridge of great beauty, built at speed to service the local mines, whose construction had cost scores of lives. There was a triangle, where convicts had received many thousand lashes, and a gibbet, where summary justice had been administered. Worst of all, there was a burrow-like cell block reserved for women prisoners.

It included a black hutch of stone, with a door two feet thick, where 'incorrigible' women had been kept in solitary confinement. When Violet stepped nervously inside, James closed the great door as a joke. Standing in the cold darkness she had experienced claustrophobic terror so acute that she had nearly fainted. Outside she heard the men laughing, and when the door was finally opened she flung herself at James and tried to scratch his face.

Billy was shocked, and profuse with apologies. James looked at her complacently; she could see though that he was excited. Later he made love to her violently in the car, having got rid of his friend on some pretext. She realised that her fear was an aphrodisiac to the husband she had only just started to understand.

In later years she often dreamed of the destroyed trees, and also of the women who had been incarcerated at Richmond, transported thousands of miles in chains for some trivial or desperate offence, and used by men as pack animals or whores. The stricken faces she imagined haunted her. And sometimes Violet dreamt that she herself was the convict, forbidden light and warmth in that dungeon of stone, while outside the gaolers laughed and drank their beer.

At last their time alone together was at an end. James made no effort to conceal his impatience to return to Sydney. The moment they were back at Killymoon he was out of the car, leaving Violet to deal with their luggage, and deep in conversation with his father about a *Gazette* leader that had appeared in his absence. She noticed that they were talking, as he had talked with Billy in Tasmania – endlessly, it had seemed – about a new faction that had appeared on the political scene.

'I assume you wrote the leader?' James was saying. 'I was delighted to see it – it's time we shifted that bastard Lang. He'll turn this place into Russia in three years.'

George laughed and greeted Violet with a kiss. 'Your husband is a great man for exaggeration.'

'Is he?' Violet said, turning to greet Daisy. Yet again she found herself thinking that her husband was someone unknown to her – and the more she found out, the more unsure of him she became. Disillusion seemed to have killed his love and she had no idea how to restore it.

At tea with Daisy she tried to confide a little of what was in her mind. 'I wish I wasn't so ignorant. When James is alone with me I think he misses people to talk to about politics and so on.'

Daisy observed the drawn look on Violet's face. At first she had put it down to lack of sleep. She began to wonder how unhappy her new daughter-in-law might be.

'I don't expect he wants to talk to you about politics, my dear. Political women are not popular here. More than that, they're hated; feared a bit, too, I wouldn't be surprised.'

'Why?' Violet asked.

'Probably because they make men feel threatened. Men do like to feel they're in charge of all the important things in the world.'

'But isn't it true?' Violet said. 'After all, they do run all the government, the newspapers and the businesses.'

'I suppose so.' Daisy poured more tea. 'But when you were doing your lovely theatre – do you know I went there last week? – you didn't find it very hard, did you?'

'Oh, I enjoyed it.'

'I've often secretly believed that women could do it all as well, or better. You've no idea what women here learned in the war.' She glanced up with a smile. 'But please never speak a word of this to Bunty – she'd think I'd turned into a suffragette.'

'So you don't think James would be more interested in my company if I learned about politics or business?'

'Oh no, he'd hate it,' Daisy said with a kind of pride. 'He's very masculine and he likes to argue – he always has. You are just the kind of girl he's always needed. Someone beautiful and graceful, someone with style.'

'So my business is to be pretty and keep quiet?'

'I think you can do what you like within reason,' Daisy said. 'After all, those things men believe are life and death are usually nothing like so important as they think. I often think business is a game they play, like cricket. We are the people who make their lives – I've done everything for George; I even put out his towel and shorts every night so he can go swimming at dawn. If I hadn't done that for forty years he'd never have been able to find them himself. He can run a paper but when it comes to living, he's about seven years old. And so, I'm afraid, is James. I can see you're beginning to find that out.'

They went up to dress arm in arm. Violet thought that Daisy might understand much more about their honeymoon than she let on. It was a comfort to have found a friend.

Three weeks later, Violet drove over to Belle View to deliver Jack and Aggie's wedding present. For her own wedding, Aggie had given her a hand-embroidered bed jacket, a comparatively humble object among the opulent – and sometimes hideous – gifts from total strangers. These presents were not a token of friendship, since most of the donors had never met her. Violet had felt as though she had been wrongfully chosen as the recipient for hundreds of prizes she didn't deserve, awards for her supposed cleverness in marrying a man notoriously swift on his feet when other women, not to mention their mothers, had tried to tie him down. Violet had seen respect in the eyes of some female guests, as if she had beaten them in a race by the use of superior, probably English, cunning. It made her feel cheap, all the more as she was burdened by a fear that she had been far from clever at all.

Her ambivalent feeling about her own presents had made her uncertain what to give Aggie and Jack. Then, to her delight, it occurred to her to buy them a new car. They needed one: Jack had recently put a down payment on another theatre in a suburb some miles away and, though there was a train service, the schedules were erratic. It would be a real improvement in their life, something they could use and enjoy constantly.

George's chauffeur, Sean, had picked out a second-hand blue Packard, which had cost fifty pounds and looked almost new. Violet had decided against a new car, for fear that it might seem ostentatious.

The Packard, following behind her to Belle View with Sean at the wheel, looked very stylish and American. Jack would be delighted, she thought.

The Delage was too big to manoeuvre easily along the familiar, still uncompleted streets, past houses with names like Angel's Rest, Sunny Spot, and the somewhat sombre Journey's End. Drawing up outside Belle View she had a moment's regret at having brought the ostentatious Delage – perhaps it would have been better to have driven the Packard herself and then got a taxi home.

But it was too late now. She was ringing the bell, and Sean, dressed in a dark uniform and wearing a peaked cap, was standing by the door of the Packard. It was cold, and she shivered as she stood waiting for someone to answer.

Nona smiled when she saw Violet, but she didn't embrace her. She stood to one side to let her in and Violet saw that the whole house had been re-decorated. Gay curtains hung at the windows, there was a new grandfather clock in the hallway, and on the walls were smartly framed photographs of the family. Violet ran her eyes quickly down the line of faces, and was disappointed not to see herself included there. The pictures were a sign of progression. The first showed Jack and Bill beside their wagon. Then came a shot of them outside the Roxy in Hardcastle Street. Another picture showed Aggie standing in front of the curtains of the Roxy stage, her face animated and exuberant.

Nona excused herself, saying she would put the kettle on, and Violet timidly approached the living-room door. She could hear the sound of the piano and people singing from within.

Kelly was playing, and Jack and Aggie, arm in arm, were singing.

They didn't hear her enter and she stood in the doorway for a few moments, listening to the words of the song.

I've heard men say so often, they could love their wives alone,
But I think that such foolish men must have hearts made of stone,
Now my heart is made of softer stuff, it melts at just one glance,
A pretty girl can't look my way, without a new romance.
Oh, I could love a million girls, with every girl a twin . . .

She stepped forward into the room and instantly Kelly stopped playing.

'Violet!' Aggie cried.

'Don't stop for me,' she said. 'Do go on – that's a terrific tune.'

'Just something we're rehearsing for tonight's show,' Kelly said, closing the lid of the piano.

'Where's Bill?' Violet asked.

'Doing the accounts,' Aggie said. 'He's down at the Roxy. But don't let's talk about that — how are you? You look wonderful.'

Violet blushed. She was wearing a crisp black skirt with a white shirt, etched by black cuffs and finished off with a black bow at the neck.

'I'm fine,' she said. 'But I'm not sure that I'm cut out to be a lady of leisure . . . I was thinking of coming back to work. Maybe doing those write-ups you were so keen on, Jack?' They all looked at her blankly.

'Is something the matter?' she said quickly.

'It's a bit of a surprise, that's all,' Jack said. 'We understood that you were tickled pink not to have to worry about our small-time ventures any more.'

'What makes you say that?'

'When you decided to sell your shares . . .' Jack began.

'What?'

He coughed and looked embarrassed. 'You mean Mr Franklin didn't tell you about his letter?'

Violet looked confused.

'He wrote to us last week, saying that you'd be selling your shares.'

There was a silence. Jack looked worried.

'You're not angry about it, Vi? It makes sense, doesn't it? You spend more on a hat than . . . you know what I mean. It's a different world now.'

Nona came in with the tea-tray. To conceal her chagrin Violet said, 'Can't we have tea in a minute? I've got something for you.'

They went out on to the porch and there was the new car. It reminded her of the morning that James had sent the Delage.

'Is that for us?' Aggie cried. 'Oh, Violet, isn't it smart! And it's perfect for Jack getting over to the new theatre.'

'Hold on,' Jack said. 'Hold on a minute.' He was frowning. 'I can't accept something like this, you know that. How can I?'

'But it's exactly what you need. And it's not just for you, it's our wedding present,' Aggie said, taking him by the arm.

Awkwardly, Violet put the keys into Jack's hand. He recoiled as if she had offered a tip he was too proud to accept.

He opened the door and climbed in all the same, peering at the dashboard. Aggie got into the passenger seat, making a mock curtsey to Sean, who was holding the door.

'Isn't the leather wonderful, Jack? I love the smell.'

'Reckon so,' Jack conceded. But he made no attempt to start the car, and got out with the keys still in his hand. He's going to give them back to me, Violet thought. Oh God, I've done the wrong thing again.

'C'mon, Jack. You can't hurt Violet's feelings.'

'I won't take it back,' Violet said. 'Sean's got all the documents and they're in your name. It's yours already. I don't need it – there's plenty of cars at Killymoon.'

'That a fact?' Jack said flatly. 'Reckon you won't miss it, then.'

There was a silence and through the window they could hear Kelly monotonously playing 'Chopsticks'.

'Thank you, Violet,' Aggie said, kissing her. Jack was walking back to the house, having put the keys in Aggie's hand.

'You know how it is,' she said. 'Jack's very proud. But I've got to stand by him now. He's all right, really.'

'I know,' Violet said. 'I'm sorry I can't stay for tea.'

Driving back, her heart was already hardening against her husband. How dare he interfere so! By the time the Delage turned into Hardcastle Street past the Roxy, she had brushed away her tears and repaired her make-up. She had hoped to find herself visiting home. Instead she had discovered that her blighted marriage threatened the only friendships she'd made in her own right. She had not even taken her coat off. The only thing that had stayed with her was Kelly's silly, tinkling song, 'I Could Love A Million Girls', and now she could not get it out of her head.

13

'The baby will get quite tipsy if you go on like that.' Daisy put down her petit-point tapestry and looked carefully at her daughter-in-law. 'I know this will sound interfering – but you are drinking a lot. It isn't good for you.'

'I don't drink much.' Violet quickly turned her eyes away from Daisy and looked at the tennis court. James was poised to serve the first ball of the second set. He had taken the first set with difficulty from Keiran O'Fallen.

She hated anyone noticing how much she drank. Please let the baby be a girl, she prayed for the umpteenth time. She couldn't bear the thought of producing a child who would grow up to be like James.

They had been married for nine months and the estrangement that had started on their honeymoon had never healed. Sometimes she still saw him looking at her with a gentle, unguarded expression; but it was too late. His bitter violence had destroyed something in her, replacing her natural optimism with a wary cynicism. She felt isolated and frustrated at Killymoon, especially now, with a great lumbering belly. Bunty tried to be friends, but her idea of a good time was shopping for clothes, which was useless for Violet in her present condition. She hardly saw Aggie, and sometimes she didn't leave the house for days on end. Even her work of writing press releases for the Roxy had ceased for the present, notwithstanding her determination to continue as an active partner in the business.

James's attempted interference, and the fearful scene that had followed, had served only to strengthen her purpose. The baby was due in two weeks' time. Violet was simultaneously longing for her pregnancy to be over, and intimidated by the prospect of birth and motherhood. Once a mother, she could no longer call herself young.

The doctor had said that she shouldn't drink. Not that it had occurred to him that a decent woman would drink, except champagne at a wedding or a glass of wine with dinner. Of course, there were unfortunate women who drank, just as there were women who had got divorced or went insane. Violet couldn't bring herself to take his advice seriously. She could always disguise the smell by gargling with cologne. Men were allowed to drink, after all; no one complained when they had a few too many — and anyway, drinking made her feel less melancholy about the state of her marriage.

Nowadays James was courteous even in private. But Violet never lost the feeling that he was covertly watching her. She knew if she met his eyes she would see that speculative, waiting look — a terrible patience that she did not understand, largely because patience was not a trait James seemed to exhibit in any other area of her life. She wondered again if it was all her fault, if she had somehow trapped him by evading the subject of the rape in Singapore.

He hadn't married her for money, or for a title, or for her position. In Sydney, on the terms of his own class, she had been one of the least eligible women around. He had married her solely because he had wanted her, and he couldn't have her any other way.

She knew he was anxious about the baby — and more enthusiastic about it than she was. When the doctor had told her she was pregnant, her initial reaction had been disbelief. Surely babies didn't result from the nights of semi-rape she had known with James. Briefly, she had shared his delight. But even his occasional gestures of reconciliation now seemed fated not to succeed.

The previous night he had come home early from the office with a gift for her. She had been in the bedroom, resting, when he arrived and knocked on the door.

He sat down beside her on the edge of the bed.

'You must be suffering in this heat.'

'I feel like an elephant. I wish the baby would hurry up and be born.'

She said it accusingly, as though it was his fault alone that she was pregnant. He took a slender box out of his pocket and put it in her hands. Inside was an elegant pearl clip. It would look perfect on the new season's fashionable black dresses, Violet thought — except that she was so fat.

'For the mother of my child,' James said, leaning down to kiss her. Sometimes nowadays he was very sentimental.

'I'm not a mother yet,' she said. She knew it was not a gracious reply; but the previous night James had failed to come home at all.

She fingered the jewelled clip. He often bought her lavish presents — but usually as peace offerings, to make up for coming home so late that he'd found her asleep.

'Thank you for this. It's lovely. But I'd rather see you occasionally. I do wish you'd come home earlier – I get so lonely.' Even before she spoke, she was aware of putting another barrier between them.

James stood up, the cold, closed look back in his eyes. 'By God, you can be ungrateful.'

He slammed the door behind him. Violet lay back on her pillows. Pain throbbed in her back. She held the clip in her hand until it became sweaty to the touch.

Today, 19 March 1932, a big event was due in the city's history; and at Killymoon the first of several visitors was joining the household in its own share of the celebrations. Andrew Franklin and James had discussed a sponsored flight from London to Sydney as long ago as James's visit to England, two years before. Now it had become a reality. Andrew was also here to join the grand occasion of the opening of Sydney Harbour Bridge. The flight had been timed to arrive in Sydney on the day the bridge was formally declared completed.

At breakfast in the dining-room at Killymoon, Andrew could talk of little but the flight – and of its pilot. Petra Maybeck, flying her converted De Havilland solo, had become an overnight sensation. Her syndicated articles had described each stage of her journey with a self-absorbed verve that was irresistible, and her pert face, becomingly framed in a helmet, was as familiar as the prime minister's.

Violet was ambivalent about meeting her. I must seem so boring in comparison, she thought. She was conscious of lumbering around like a penguin, now that it was her ninth month of pregnancy; easily tired, more easily tetchy.

'What do you think she'll be like?' Daisy asked Violet out of Andrew's hearing.

'Tough and leathery, I expect. She has a fierce look, like a man.'

Daisy looked at her thoughtfully. Violet's edginess was due to more than just her pregnancy. She knew James now slept in his dressing-room; but plenty of men did that when their wives were heavily pregnant. They ought to have been happy, she thought. In so many ways they were well matched: attractive and intelligent, popular in Sydney. Yet Daisy knew Violet was often wretched, and while she never heard the couple argue, she sensed a reserve between them that certainly hadn't been there before they were married.

On a side-table in the dining-room was that day's edition of the *Gazette*. A picture of Petra Maybeck stared up from it. God, how Violet envied this free stranger. Petra had come within a few hours of breaking the record for a solo flight from London to Australia, set up by Amy Johnson in 1930; and over the last few days Violet had watched Andrew willing her to succeed. Unfortunately mechanical failure, in Thailand, at the border town of Pedang Bezar, had held her up, and she had taken an extra two days to reach Sydney. She had arrived secretly the night before, landing on an airstrip to the north of the city. As far as the crowds were concerned, her first sight of the country was to be today, when she would swoop between the Heads at the mouth of the harbour, and fly up under the bridge.

It was clear that Andrew was besotted by Petra, and Violet, influenced by the hollowness of her own marriage, was surprised to find that she felt jealous. Andrew's arrival had in any case raised her spirits. Despite his preoccupation with Petra, he still found time to show more interest in Violet, as a woman and a person, than any other man in her life nowadays.

He had changed since she had last seen him, though in a way that she admired. 'If we'd met on the street,' she confided to Daisy, 'I don't think I'd have known him.'

'Running your own business has a way of making you grow up. George says there's nothing like it for sharpening the mind. He's terribly impressed by Andrew too.'

For today's historic occasion, it was partly on Andrew's account that she felt encouraged to make an effort even at this late stage of pregnancy. She wore a dress of heavy linen which hung in full soft folds across her stomach. It was pale French blue with a lace collar and cuffs. Her felt hat was in a matching shade of blue, trimmed with flowers on one side. She stood up in front of the mirror: given the circumstances, she looked her best. The baby kicked and stirred inside her. Two days earlier she had felt it drop downwards in her womb, settling into position in her lower pelvis, ready for birth. The midwife, Mrs Flannery, a bird-like woman who looked barely capable of lifting a suitcase, but who was in fact wiry and strong, had examined her quickly and said that they could expect the new arrival any day. Violet liked Mrs Flannery, who had delivered more babies than she could remember and who exuded a no-nonsense approach to the business of childbirth. She had told Violet quite bluntly to expect it to hurt. 'There's no point in being unprepared. If you're ready for the pain, then you'll find it far easier to cope with.'

Violet paused to pluck a single hair out of her eyebrows and studied her face critically in the mirror. The only thing to be said for pregnancy was that it made one's skin glow, even without make-up. She had other reasons for wanting to look her best today. Not only would all of Sydney be there to see the bridge declared open: several hundred guests from overseas would be present – including Ben.

I'm nosy as hell to find out how you and married life go together so I'm coming to see for myself. No, to level with you, I've been striking oil in Indonesia. And Litzie's agreed to quit politics for six months and join me on a run through Singapore and Sydney. So we get to see the opening of that famous Bridge . . .

Violet had folded Ben's letter neatly and hidden it beneath one of the purple velvet trays in her jewel box. She had never told James about her friendship with Ben; the moment when it would have been possible, before they were married, had come and gone. Now, she was sure that if she did mention him, he would assume they had been lovers. Sometimes she wished they had been . . .

The Killymoon party made ready early to leave for the bridge. George helped Violet into the front seat of his Daimler, and drove them all slowly down the hill, taking exaggerated care on the bends. They passed along the shore, from where they could see the magnificent lines of the great steel bridge. The water was calm and sparkling blue.

In the area set aside for dignitaries, their seats had been reserved in the front row. Violet scanned the crowd for Ben, disappointed to see no sign of him.

A broad red ribbon was stretched across the roadway up to the bridge. Red bunting hung from the support beams of their awning, and flags flew. Violet twisted round in her seat, nodding politely to a host of well-known faces. It was as though the whole country had turned out for the occasion. At her side Andrew was scribbling observations in his notebook with a gold-tipped pen.

'Keep quiet,' George was saying, 'they're about to cut the ribbon.'

Jack Lang stepped forward to cut the ribbon. In his hand he held a pair of exaggeratedly large scissors. With a flourish he prepared for the ceremonial gesture. At that moment the crowd shifted, and Violet saw Ben seated three rows behind, next to the American ambassador. She raised her hand in greeting, flushing with pleasure as she saw his face split into a grin.

A cry from behind the watching crowd shattered the silence, together with the sound of hooves clattering on the tarmac.

'Long live Australia! Freedom for all!' A horseman was galloping up the roadway, brandishing a sword. From astride an 18-hand black steed he sliced the ribbon with a single blow, and vanished amid a general buzz of astonishment.

The crowd were still exchanging startled remarks when there was a new drama. Its first intimation came as a sharp throbbing noise in the eastern sky. The sound grew in intensity, until it concentrated around the opalescent white form of Petra Maybeck's De Havilland. She was apparently flying directly at the bridge and everyone on it.

Only at the last moment did it become clear that Petra's plane, a tiny object against the bridge and its setting, was going to fly just beneath the newly connected girders. Only fifty yards away, the wings dipped sharply, first left, then right. There was a brief hubbub in the crowd, who at first thought something was wrong. Then they realised it was a salute, even as she was passing beneath their feet and under the bridge, to start a soaring climb out across the harbour. Turning in a broad arc, Petra repeated the performance from west to east, while the bridge and both shorelines rang with cheering.

Violet turned to Andrew. His face was a study in relief, and he was laughing with joy. Now that the inauguration party was under way, the guests were milling about, talking and being served with champagne. The waiters were bringing tray after tray of glasses, and almost everyone was a little drunk.

Violet emptied her glass thirstily, as she exchanged greetings and chatted with a succession of the Franklins' Sydney acquaintances. She was feeling queasy and the weight of the baby resting in her pelvis made it wearisome to move from the same spot.

'Hullo, Violet. I thought we'd run into each other down under.'

The drawl was as familiar as the unhealthy, nightbird's face. It was Tony Quigley, the last person she'd expected to see. Champagne glass in hand, he was swaying on his feet.

'My God,' she said. 'You're all we need.'

'It's a good occasion, isn't it? I enjoyed the Johnny on the black nag. When it comes to inaugurating a bloody great girder the Aussies are unbeatable.'

'What on earth are you doing here?'

'It's a stunt. The RAF are flying me round the world – I'm supposed to be writing about the "Seven Wonders of the Empire", this thing being one of them. Actually such matters bore me to death. I've reached the conclusion I'm a serious person, a philosopher. I like to stay close to things that matter, and I don't think bridges and dams and transcontinental railways matter a damn.'

'What does?'

'The things I usually write about. What most people try to pretend is trivia. Who knows whom, who's after whom, who's been where.

143

Births, marriages, deaths. Falling in love, falling out again.' He gave her a wink and nodded towards James, who was talking to the governor of New South Wales and his wife. 'If you immerse yourself in those things, day in, day out, you can tell when a marriage is going wrong by the way a husband looks at his wife across a room – or across a bridge if you prefer. Sometimes I know what's going to happen to them before they do – it's frightening. Many's the morning I've sat at my desk trying to imagine the next society marriage crumbling on the ski-slopes in St Moritz, a name or a face has come into my head and, by God, you'd be surprised how often the people I think of are in the courts before the year's out.'

'How could you possibly know such a thing? You're unbelievably arrogant.'

Quigley gave her his knowing leer. 'But I observe you don't get on with your awful brute of a husband. You'd have done better with that feeble Tory MP who was following you like a dog. Didn't take long for the Great Romance to go wrong, did it?'

'Shut up, Quigley. You're drunk and awful. Isn't there anywhere in the world I'm safe from you?'

'Probably not. Remember, I was the first person to immortalise you in print. The night you crashed in Hyde Park. It's like a baptism. I'll probably be around to report your will, and attend your funeral. The last rites of the press.' He gave his barking laugh.

'You're inhuman beyond belief,' Violet said. 'Do you put it on, or are you really like that?'

Quigley was unabashed. 'Ironic, when you think of it. You marry that bully boy, and endure hell on earth as the price if I'm not mistaken and –' he paused to arrest a passing waiter '– and all for nothing. You could have waited a couple of years and done what you liked. Gone for that yokel in the yellow tie who can't take his eyes off you, for instance. You used to like politicians, didn't you?'

Violet, feeling none too sober herself, could not resist following the direction of Quigley's eyes.

Gareth Mayhew. She knew him, but only by sight.

'Someone just told me he's going to be prime minister after next. Not that it matters a bugger – I mean, an *Australian* prime minister's not exactly the president of the USA, is he? – Ah, that's the man I'm after. Young Andrew Franklin, your gifted cousin. The one who's having it away with that very naughty lady aviator. Or didn't you know?'

'Is this country as crazy as it looks? I mean, that goddam pantomime with the horse. Tell me what's going on, will you?'

Ben had worked his way through the crowd, and was kissing her cheek. His face was full of pleasure. The first impression was exactly as she remembered: an overwhelming vitality.

'You look beautiful – far more beautiful.' He examined her face keenly, as if to verify his words. 'It's a joy to see you.'

'Welcome to Australia. It's lovely to see you too.'

'C'mon. Let me in on the secret. Who was he? One of your talkie extras, or what?'

'No. Probably a political stunt. But I'm not allowed to say more, being a half-witted female lacking the intellect to understand these mighty matters . . . It's kind of you to pay me compliments, but the truth is I'm as fat as a house. I'd introduce you to my husband, but I see he's too busy. Talking more politics, I expect.'

She had imagined confiding her unhappiness to Ben. But now he was there, as neat and self-contained as ever, she was reluctant to reveal what she had known since the wedding night, and maybe even before. She was prattling with nervousness – if only she could say something true and simple: 'I've made an awful mistake.'

'I'll introduce my wife then. She enjoys politics too. Can't get enough of it as a matter of fact.'

Violet recognised the face that had shone from the state-room photographs, only an older, tauter version, a woman who looked as unhappy as she must look herself.

'This is Litzie.' Violet was surprised to see herself assessed and rejected in one glance by this beautiful and somehow desperate stranger.

'Ben has told me all about you,' Litzie said. The way she said 'all' implied that it didn't amount to much. 'I expect you would like a nice talk about babies, but I'm the wrong person for that, unfortunately. I have none, and I don't intend to change.'

She glanced at Ben as she spoke, as if to punish him. Poor Ben. Here was a new aspect of his life, one that obviously didn't run like clockwork.

'Litzie's views are a bit too progressive for Australia,' Ben said. 'I'm afraid she's just explained to your premier that he's not a socialist at all, as he fondly imagined, but a tool of the capitalist cabal.'

'James calls Lang a Bolshevik,' Violet said. 'That's why Lang's going to have to resign soon.'

'*Bolshevik*,' Litzie exclaimed, almost spitting with derision. 'He wouldn't know what the word means, and I don't suppose you do either.'

Ben said, 'I had one helluva job persuading Litzie to make this trip. And all it's done is confirm what she knew before she left Paris.'

'Aren't you going to introduce me to your friends from overseas?' It was James. For once Violet was pleased to see him. He was a very handsome man, she had to admit that. She performed the introductions and the two men looked each other over as if they were about to negotiate a contract.

James made no attempt to conceal his hostility. Violet wondered whether it was because Ben was so spectacularly well dressed.

'I hear your newspaper sponsored that stunt.' Ben waved a manicured hand to indicate Petra's flight. 'It's a smart idea. You'll sell a lot of extra copies.'

James gave a shrug – he was not about to discuss how his paper was promoted with a know-all American he had only just met.

'What brings you here, Mr Schiff?'

Ben explained his part in the oil business, and Litzie said, 'He's a capitalist. He doesn't know the species is about to become extinct. Tell me, please,' she said to James, 'this New Guard that people are talking about. Are they your local fascists?'

'That's not the right word,' James said. 'The New Guard are nationalists, patriots, members of the "Returned Servicemen's League", many of them – what your husband's country calls "Veterans".'

'They sound familiar to me,' Litzie said. 'Frustrated unemployed riff-raff. Members of the petite-bourgeoisie with a weakness for playing soldiers. Tell me what your New Guard think about Jews. That's always a sure sign.'

James looked as though he would have liked to hit her. Violet reached for another drink, wishing they served something stronger than champagne. It was a totally incompatible group. Thank God they weren't at her dinner table.

'You should discuss matters like that with a politician,' James said, stepping back to include a stranger in the circle. 'Here's the very man. Gareth, meet my wife, and these visitors from foreign parts. This is Gareth Mayhew, one of our up and coming men. My wife, Violet, and Mr and Mrs Schiff—'

As James went through the ritual of introduction, Violet looked at Gareth Mayhew. He was beginning to be spoken of as 'the coming man'. Violet, at one remove, had come to know a lot about this awkward yet powerful man whom everyone treated with such respect. His origins might be obscure but his future, as nowadays George and

James often remarked, was clearly going to be distinguished. It always amused Violet that the two male Franklins were so possessive about Mayhew. He was like an ungainly foal they had purchased because of secret knowledge about its blood line – every subsequent success had been a tribute to their own acumen.

The Mayhews came from a long line of Methodists, none of whom seemed to have enjoyed any worldly success. Gareth's father had turned his hand to a series of business ventures and systematically failed to make any of them pay. Lily, Gareth's determined mother, had watched her husband fail time and again – at garages, furniture stores, a smallholding – and sworn that her eldest son would break the family mould.

She had taught him to read before he was four and to play every sport that didn't involve a large expenditure of money, and she had coached him academically. She was rewarded when he won an open award to the Fort Street High, considered the finest state school in New South Wales.

The school was located some distance out of the city, at Taverner's Hill on the Parramatta Road. When Gareth started there, Lily moved the household out to Taverner's Hill, where Gareth's father set up in business yet again, with a novelty shop.

From Fort Street Gareth had gone to Sydney University, where he took a first in law; and from there to Phillip Street, where he did his articles. Phillip Street, the legal centre of Sydney, was the scene of a formidable social pecking order. Wentworth Court, where he started out, seemed to him unbelievable, like something in Dickens. He found that he had to rent a couple of store-rooms and paint them himself. His fellow lawyers evidently liked that sort of thing: it made them feel part of what Mayhew had been heard to describe as 'your fine old pommy tradition'.

Litzie, pitching straight in, asked him about Australian political parties. He looked at her, Violet noticed, with a warm, almost sexual attention.

'So, you say the United Australia Party here is the same as Conservative in England, or Republican in America? And you are to the right of that pathetic little man' – she meant Lang – 'who presumes to call himself a socialist? That means you are a reactionary! Yet with your silk shirt and loud tie you are yourself the epitome of a provincial arriviste.'

Mayhew grinned broadly. The fact that he refused to take her seriously made Litzie even angrier.

Violet, in the dutiful role of social wife, intervened to ask why he had gone into politics.

'It's logical for a lawyer, don't you think? The law is all to do with getting things to work, finding ways to enable some goal or other to come about. Politics is the same kind of thing. If you want to do something there's no better way. Except, maybe,' giving her an ambiguous smile, 'to be born rich, like your husband.'

Violet was uncertain whether he was motivated by self-interest or by altruism. Nevertheless she was flattered by the look of directness with which he answered her.

The most striking thing about Mayhew was his eyes, which were a deep oceanic blue. Men as good-looking as this were often so laconic they scarcely spoke at all. Mayhew, on the other hand, was almost too eager to impose himself, too active, too eloquent. Now he took her hand and said something conventional. It was strange because amid the social hubbub around them they looked at each other and exchanged a message. It was as if they had said to each other, 'We will be friends one day, but there is too much going on now.' A time will come, Violet thought, with an unexpected shiver of excitement.

She felt a twinge of selfish pleasure when Litzie, turning her attention towards James, left them to talk uninterrupted. Queasiness and fatigue were making her feel unequal in any case to being diplomatic. Gareth Mayhew's magnetic eyes expressed concern.

'Are you all right? Do you want to sit down?'

'I do; but I'll keep going to the end.'

'Don't let that German woman worry you. I'm not sure she's the full quid.'

Violet's first impression had been right: he seemed genuinely attracted to her, even in her present condition.

'Nice to speak to a real lady,' he said. 'Not someone who's up to her ears in a lot of Marxist flim-flam she doesn't understand. Her husband's too big for his boots too. Typical Yank.'

Violet wanted to defend Ben, but she hadn't the strength.

'Do you know he had the nerve to tell me that Australia would be economically dependent on America in twenty years? And that I'd better remember his name because one day I'd need his help?'

'Ben can be a bit overpowering,' Violet said.

'The Americans have no breeding. They're like us, a raw, new country; but at least we haven't been settled by the scum of Europe. No wonder they've got so many gangsters.' He started to tell her about his own ancestry – he evidently wanted to emphasise that his ancestors hadn't been convicts. They had arrived in Adelaide in the 1830s, as part of a group who were determined to set up a utopian society where everyone was equal. There was something a bit pompous about him; yet it did nothing to make him less attractive. James, joining them, also listened with unusual attention – even with deference.

Meanwhile the party was breaking up. At the first opportunity Violet moved across to where Ben was saying goodbye to the American ambassador. To her regret she heard him saying that next day he and Litzie were taking the train north.

'We're going to take a look at some prospecting companies I've an interest in,' he confirmed as soon as Violet was alone with him. 'Litzie will hate it, I expect. She hates everything about this place.'

'So I saw,' Violet said. 'It's not so bad.'

'Nowhere's bad if you're happy. Are you?'

'I don't know. What a question.'

There was a silence. Ben said, 'Litzie's grown away from me. I left her alone too long when I was trying to make my pile, and now . . .'

'She's very beautiful,' Violet said.

'She believes in a better world and I admire that. Only . . .' He paused.

'Only what?'

'I guess she's fed up with me. She's in love with someone else. A communist, obviously. When we were in our twenties in Paris it was different. But then we lost a child. I don't know why I'm babbling like this. I must have drunk too much.'

'It's the champagne and sun. Everyone's drunk. I think I want to get a lot drunker. Do you wish you hadn't married?'

'I guess not. Too late to whine about it now.'

On the way home to Killymoon the pains started.

Violet twisted on the rubber sheet, praying for some way to stop the waves of agony. Mrs Flannery's warnings about the pain of childbirth had been no preparation for the reality. Violet's eyes fixed on the ornamental carriage clock on the mantelpiece. Four minutes to six in the morning. The contractions were coming every three minutes. She clamped her teeth round a piece of towelling and readied herself for the next one. By the side of the bed stood a gas cylinder and a black mask, which she had refused. The mask was more frightening than the pain – like being in a black cell.

Mrs Flannery wiped the sweat off Violet's forehead with a cloth wrapped round lumps of ice.

'It won't be long. You're almost ready to start pushing.'

One minute. Two minutes. The hands of the clock moved on as the pain started again.

'Bear down with the next pain; you're doing wonderfully.'

Her crooning voice was comforting. Violet's legs opened and she pushed till she felt the blood vessels in her neck stand out and threaten to burst. It was six-thirty.

'I can see the head. Just one more.'

Then a slithering feeling and a miraculous end to the pain. In her arms, Mrs Flannery held a pink mewling baby, the long bluish umbilical cord still attached to its belly.

'It's a boy!' The midwife cut the cord and tied the ends. She wrapped the baby in a towel and passed him to Violet, who looked down nervously at his puckered face. A son!

'Help him. He wants milk.'

Violet rubbed the tip of a fat nipple against his mouth and in seconds he was sucking, gently at first, then with growing strength. He was so tiny, barely a foot long, and in her arms he weighed almost nothing. The effort soon proved too much and the baby shut his cloudy blue eyes and drifted off into sleep on her breast.

'I'll wash him,' said Mrs Flannery.

'No. No, leave him here for a few more minutes.'

'Shall I fetch his father?'

'In a minute.' Violet stroked the soft downy hair on his head. She felt wholly at peace. This was her child – she felt as though James had had nothing to do with his creation. How could she have thought that she wouldn't love a boy – she had never felt love like this for anything. Opening his wrinkled hand, she smiled with delight when his fingers closed around one of hers. She looked at the clock. Ten minutes to seven. She hadn't even noticed that it was daylight.

Even in the Franklin household a private telephone call was an event, when it came from the other side of the world.

It was for Violet, resting in bed two days after the birth. Lifting the receiver on her own extension, she was amazed to hear her mother's voice, just as the baby's nursemaid had said it would be. Sybil must have taken the very first opportunity to call, after receiving the telegram.

Her mother sounded potentially tearful, much as Violet would have expected. She also sounded happy, indeed grateful, that she now had a grandchild. But there was an evident shadow behind her pleasure.

After they had exchanged news concerning each other's health and that of the baby, there came a significant-seeming pause.

Sybil said, 'As I say, I'm very well. But . . . oh, poor Emerald. I went to her funeral the other day, you know. Your father said he wouldn't have it, but I thought, well, one of the family ought to be there.'

'Her funeral?' Violet was overwhelmed. Not even Sybil's depressing manner had prepared her for anything like this.

'I wondered if you already knew, dear.'

'Emerald is dead?'

'I expect you'll be hearing from the lawyers, you know. The fact is, she left everything to you. And in spite of all the money she used to spend on pictures I don't think she can have been, well, particularly hard up, shall we say. I wouldn't ever say this to your father, but I always quite liked her as a matter of fact. I know I only met her a few times, but she always made me laugh.'

In a tone of apology, as if partly responsible, Sybil went on to give the details of Emerald's protracted final illness. Violet wept soundlessly into the receiver. She was stricken at least as much for herself as for Emerald. All through her pregnancy, which had seemed at times to be going on for years rather than for months, one of her greatest joys had been that, now, Emerald would surely want to visit Australia, to see the baby. At last, Violet had thought, I really will have something of my own to show her. She had pictured Emerald's expressions of delight so clearly, it was as if their reunion had actually taken place.

When Sybil had rung off, having sounded less affected or inconsequential than she'd done for years, Violet lay back on her pillows and sobbed. In the next room the baby started to cry.

Joy and sorrow: who would have thought that one could feel so much of both?

14

After Samuel George Franklin's arrival in the world, the months seemed to pass by almost unnoticed. It was a time of nappies and bottles, nicknames and bedtime stories, and Violet found herself completely absorbed by the world of the nursery. Adult life was kept at a distance; and for the time being she was happy with an arrangement that some part of her knew would be temporary.

Daisy was a constant figure; a mother-in-law who never, or almost never, made Violet feel that she was being criticised. Daisy delighted in her grandson, and she and Violet kept a close check on what they called 'the baby boom' among their family and friends.

Aggie was the next – her daughter, Joy, was born in 1933; and eight months later she was expecting another baby. Like Violet, Aggie had devoted herself to motherhood, with an enraptured and mellowed Nona fulfilling the role that Daisy occupied in Violet's family. Andrew and Petra, who had married a year after the historic flight, wrote to say that they too were expecting a child; and Daisy at once added this old country addition to her knitting list.

Fifteen months after Samuel's birth, Violet herself had another child: a daughter, Elizabeth Emerald. Violet soon gave up her attempts to refer to them by their proper names, and they were henceforth Sam and Lizzie.

The summer of 1934 came in fast and brought long hot days. The children were restless in the heat and Lizzie cried pitifully every time she was put into nappies. Sam was walking by the time he was a year old, and fearlessly ran across the lawns of Killymoon, uncaring of his frequent falls and tumbles.

George took particular delight in his grandchildren. He spent hours playing in the garden with Sam, throwing balls for him, rolling him over on the grass, even constructing a sand-pit. Sam in turn adored his grandfather. The closeness between the two of them delighted Violet all the more because James's own relationship with the children was perfunctory. He was too busy, he saw them too seldom, and they were still too young to capture his interest. For much of the time, he used the house only as a hotel, basing his working life round an apartment he had bought in Macquarie Street, within a few minutes of the office.

Violet knew that he worked long hours. 'It's only what his father used to do,' Daisy tried to explain. 'They never saw their father when they were small, or only on high days and holidays. It's the price of employing a lot of people, George says.'

But it was more than that. James had not slept with his wife since soon after Lizzie was conceived. Violet had no illusions about James's sexual drive and was certain that he must have another woman, maybe several. Since they lived in almost separate worlds she tried to dismiss the matter from her mind. Her sadness at the wreck of their marriage had largely disappeared, leaving in its place only emptiness.

Keiran O'Fallen confirmed her suspicions.

The priest had 'just dropped in' one evening in November at the cocktail hour, and Violet found herself alone with him. He began by talking politics.

J. T. Lang had gone, to the relief and delight of everyone at Killymoon, but the Australian economy was no closer to coming out of the Depression. 'I don't know what this is going to do to a generation of Australians,' O'Fallen said. 'Even the birth rate is falling.'

'Except here,' Violet laughed. 'In fact, Franklins all over the globe are busy producing babies.'

'I hope you're going to have some more?'

'That's a very personal question. You're not my confessor, as far as I know. And not James's either . . .'

'No, thank God,' O'Fallen said.

'What do you mean by that?'

'I mean that as a priest and a friend I have your family's interests at heart. There's a lot to be lost here,' he replied, looking away from her into the garden. 'I thought you were such a sensible person.'

'I don't understand you.' She stared, challenging him to respond.

'You ought to love your husband, Violet. Because if you don't . . .'

'You mean my husband has mistresses, don't you? I know that. He always has, and he always will. I can't influence James; after all, I'm his property. I'd like to change the subject, if you don't mind.'

Later on that night, Violet heard James let himself into his dressing-room. She got out of bed and opened the connecting door. She caught him, literally, with his pants down, and almost laughed at the spectacle of her husband trapped in a tangle of trousers and braces.

153

He looked up and said sharply, 'Is anything wrong? Are the children all right?'

'Oh, they're all right, not that you'd care.'

'You've been drinking again.'

'No, I haven't,' she replied, though she felt none the less that her attack was weakened. 'Father O'Fallen was here tonight. I daresay you didn't expect him to tell me that you have a mistress.'

'He's lying.'

'How dare you say the priest is lying! *You* are lying! I know it's true – it's the reason you never come near me.'

'The reason I never come near you, my dear little wife, is that you're frigid. I sometimes think I must have been bewitched, to think you were different. I'd never known any English girls, before you. Silly, isn't it?'

'You hadn't the faintest idea of what I was like, and you didn't try to find out.'

'Leave me alone. You're drunk and I want to go to sleep.'

He pushed her back into her room. Violet heard the key turn in the lock and ran to her bed, throwing herself down on the pillows. 'I hate him, I hate him,' she sobbed through clenched teeth. She pummelled the pillow, wishing that every blow was smashing into James's face.

On a morning just before Christmas 1937 Violet ran down the stairs at Killymoon, whistling softly under her breath. She found Daisy alone in the dining-room. Her mother-in-law looked frail these days. Last winter she had had a bad attack of bronchitis, which had left her, even in hot weather, with a hacking cough.

'Where's George?' Violet asked, helping herself to coffee from the silver pot on the sideboard.

'Still swimming,' Daisy answered. 'He's taking a long time this morning.'

Violet caught the hint of worry in Daisy's voice and drained her coffee in two gulps.

'I'll go down and join him. I could do with the walk. I love the beach in the early morning.' She kissed the top of Daisy's head. 'Look after the terrible duo for me, won't you?'

George was a man of meticulous habits. In recent years he had grown more punctual, more regular about every little thing he did. He moaned if breakfast was even five minutes late ... Violet's thoughts were moving ahead of her, and she broke into a jog trot down the path that led from the end of the garden. By the time she reached the road beside the golf course down to Rose Bay she was running as hard as she could.

The beach was deserted, except for an old man walking along the edge of the water, beachcombing. The waves were breaking quietly in the still morning air.

She stared wildly up and down, then kicked off her shoes, and ran up to the old man. 'Have you seen anyone swimming?'

He scratched his head. 'Can't say that I have.' He bent his head to his task.

'This is serious. Someone came swimming down here early this morning and hasn't returned.'

The old man looked out at the sea and slowly shook his head. Violet cursed her luck. Trust the only person there to be a half-wit, who wouldn't have noticed a battle cruiser till it was on the beach beside him. She turned and ran the other way, her feet slip-slapping in the water.

Her eye was caught by a bundle lying a few feet from the sea. She increased her pace. George's blue towelling beach robe. Daisy had bought it for him after the doctor had recommended he take up regular swimming for his health.

'Oh God!' Violet squatted down on the sand, fingering the material. She couldn't bear anything to happen to George. He and Daisy had been far more like a mother and father to her than her own parents had been. He must be alive. He must be hiding somewhere.

But there was no movement on the flat expanse of sand. Clutching the robe she ran on down the beach towards Point Piper. Nothing. She was trembling with exhaustion, but her feet still seemed able to run, and she took the steps back up to the road two at a time. She must raise the alarm. But how could she break the news to Daisy?

Up at the house, Daisy was standing on the verandah staring down the path to the beach. Her eyes lighted on George's robe, and Violet saw her body sag as though hit by a bullet.

'We must get a search party. Don't worry, we'll find him.' Violet ran on into the house to the telephone. The coast-guard answered immediately. She went back on to the verandah and held Daisy in her arms, feeling the thin body limp against hers, the strength drained away. Daisy still hadn't spoken, hadn't cried. It was as though she knew there was no hope.

The news spread. Soon the beach was full of people who had voluntarily joined in the search. They covered miles of coast, looking for clues. But as night fell, the chief of the rescue operations took James and Violet aside to tell them it was useless to go on.

'He could have been taken by a shark. No one saw it happen. There's little chance of finding any traces.'

Violet started to sob. James's face was drawn.

'There's no possibility that he has just gone off?' The rescue chief was apologetic. 'I'm sorry, but I have to ask.'

James shook his head. 'No, no chance of that. Don't even mention such a possibility to my mother.' He kicked at the sand and turned, taking Violet's arm. For a moment their own differences were forgotten. 'We'd better get back to the house.'

Daisy was perched on a rattan chair on the verandah, looking out towards the sea.

'She's been sitting there all day,' Violet said, as they came up the path.

'I don't know what she'll do without him.' James quickened his step up the incline, skirting past the fountains, the neatly turned borders of flowers. Everywhere there was evidence of George: his work, his passions, his hobbies.

'Mother.' James knelt by the old lady, who seemed crumbled and diminished. 'They've called off the search. We'll start again in the morning.'

'No,' Daisy said. 'I know he has gone. I want you to stop looking.'

'Come inside, then. Have you eaten?'

Daisy shook her head, but stood up when James took her arm. Standing alone on the verandah, Violet clutched the railing and wept. Not so much for the dead, as those left behind.

The shock waves caused by George's sudden death were slow to settle. Everyone was caught off guard. Violet watched as Daisy shrank behind the protection of an invisible wall which she had thrown around herself. She answered questions by rote, replied politely to queries about her health, laughed at little Sammie's jokes. Yet she was acting as though by remote control, and there was an aching sadness about her which filled the house.

James soon found the atmosphere intolerable. Using the excuse of an increased work load now that he was in charge of the *Gazette*, he absented himself more and more from Killymoon, returning late at night, leaving early in the morning. For a time, he and Violet even ceased giving dinners, something that he had formerly enjoyed.

The house was left to the women and children – and to O'Fallen. The priest played with the children, chatted to an unresponsive Daisy, shared a drink with Violet. Bunty's dependence on him increased, as she tried to deal with her own sadness at her father's death. O'Fallen never again raised the subject of Violet's marriage or James's extramarital life. She had to admit she was grateful for his company, and there existed between them an uneasy truce.

'How is your mother-in-law?' he asked one day at the end of January. They were playing ball with Sammie on the tennis-court, which had been one of his grandfather's favourite spots throughout hours of patient games with him.

'No better. She really has lost the will to live. I'm beginning to believe in broken hearts.'

O'Fallen smiled thinly. 'It might be a help to take her away for a bit. Is your house at Palm Beach finished yet?'

Partly in response to the dissatisfactions of her married life at Killymoon, Violet had been supervising the building of a second home – all her own, as she thought of it – in the form of a beach house, twenty-five miles out of the city.

'Almost. We could sleep there now, if we didn't mind camping out.'

'Why don't you take her there? Killymoon lives and breathes George. I think that while she stays here, she's expecting him to walk in at any time.'

'I'll try.'

Violet accepted O'Fallen's suggestion without much confidence. To her surprise, Daisy readily agreed, and the following morning they packed the car with food, blankets, sheets, swimming costumes and toys for the children.

Before they left Daisy asked Violet to come in to George's study, a room that had been deserted since the day of his disappearance. It still smelled faintly of his cigars. On the wall was an ornate oil painting. It showed a little boy wearing a suit. His hair was neatly parted in the middle, in the style of the Victorians, and he had a cravat round his neck. He was standing in the middle of a glade, a tiny figure at the foot of tall trunks. His face was round with terror, and his mouth was parted as though emitting a silent scream of fear.

He was lost, somewhere in a deep tangle of undergrowth and trees.

'I want you to take that as a present and put it in your house,' Daisy said. 'It's out of place here now. George always loved that picture, even though it's not worth anything. It's a copy of a famous McCubbin picture in Melbourne.'

Violet had never cared for the picture. But she was touched, and kissed Daisy as she thanked her.

The children were happy and excited. The day was clear and fine, and the sun was already hot when they rolled down the drive shortly after eight-thirty.

It took them just under an hour in the Delage to arrive at Palm Beach, where the new house was now complete except for its furnishings. Gareth Mayhew was also building a house there, as it happened; but otherwise the place was almost without trace of man's presence. The last thousand yards consisted of a rutted track which tested the big car's springs, and then they were at the site.

Sammie and Lizzie rushed out of the car and scampered up to the door and into the main room. Violet and Daisy followed them, amid the children's delight as they inspected the bedrooms, peered out of the windows, and ran back on to the verandah to see the view.

The Pacific Ocean thundered in along the sandy shore, transparent like glass, and tinged with green. As each wave gathered force near the shore, the tip of its crest would arch upwards and outwards and then slowly start to fall, scattering droplets of water, then finding yet more strength, start to break and roll into a perfect hollow tube, till that burst too and the foaming mass of water battered down on to the sand, scattering spray in its wake.

Huge clouds hung on the distant horizon like magical castles in a faraway fairyland.

Violet knew she had been right to insist on this place. It would be wonderful for the children – and for her too. Better, she thought, to be alone out here with the sea and the birds, than stifled in Sydney with James.

Daisy went back to the car and carried in the painting. When they finished hanging it, on the wall in the main room, Violet took three steps backwards and looked up at the boy in the forest.

Gratitude notwithstanding, with Daisy she found it impossible –and needless – to be insincere.

'It's always made me shudder,' she said quietly.

Daisy, too, was looking up at the picture.

'When George first went off to prospect for gold, he discovered a fear of the big spaces. He figured out then that there were two types of Australians – one kind that could deal with the space, who revelled in it and challenged it; and the others, the majority, who pulled away from it and clung to the towns like limpets to a rock, who needed big cities like Sydney where they could pretend that all that vast outback just didn't exist. He bought this painting just after James was born.

'George always thought that the children would be overwhelmed by the wilderness, by the terrifying natural world of Australia. When they were young, he always kept us in the city. That's why, even though I wanted to, we never built a place like this.'

Daisy walked over to the window, and stared out at the sea.

'Now nature has come back and taken George. So all his worrying was in vain.' She gripped the window sill in both hands and bent her head, tears falling. Violet went over to her and embraced her thin shoulders, feeling her body heaving.

At length Daisy collected herself.

'It's better for the children to learn the power of the wilderness, rather than be protected from it.' She looked up at the picture. Light bounced off the canvas, and played on the terror in the small boy's face. Violet trembled. Could she protect her children, any more than George had been able to protect himself?

'George always thought that the danger lay on the inside, in the bush,' Daisy said. 'He was always so confident of the sea.'

The ocean, her grandchildren and the lost child in the picture, together had finally broken down Daisy's reserve. The contact that had eluded Daisy's own children, James and Bunty, and her friends in Sydney, was made with her daughter-in-law. Her own grief, she realised, had been a burden to others. On their return to Killymoon, that fact was brought home when she overheard the children's nanny telling Sammie to 'shut up' before he went into the house.

'Why?' he demanded in a plaintive voice.

'Because Granny doesn't want to be disturbed.'

At that, Daisy went out on to the verandah and picked up her grandson. 'No, darling; you make all the noise you want. Granny is feeling better.' She smiled gratefully at Violet across Sammie's head.

'Have you been ill, Granny?' Sammie demanded.

'Yes. I have been a little ill.'

'But you're not going to die, are you?'

'No, I'm not going to die. I'm going to live to watch you grow big and strong. Just how Grandpa would have wanted.'

15

'Violet would like it very much, if you could come to dinner here on the 21st . . .'.

James was perched on the edge of the desk, speaking into the telephone mouthpiece in his loud, confident voice – a voice too resonant for têtes-à-têtes, and ideally better suited to addressing people in groups. Violet, passing the open door of what had been George's study, winced at the sound.

'We'll be sending you a card, then. No need to reply formally.'

He rang off and she went into the room where she had sat so often with George. She missed those quiet chats with him. Now the study was nearly always empty, though Daisy made sure there were fresh flowers every day, as if she were still fighting the aroma of George's Havanas.

'Who would I like to come so very much?' she asked lightly.

'Gareth Mayhew,' James replied, without looking up from his address book. 'You've nothing against him, have you? Most women seem to like him.'

'Nothing at all; I rather like him, too.'

It was true. If all their guests were company as good as the politically ambitious Gareth, with his astute lawyer's mind, her role as the Franklin hostess would have been a joy. Gareth was now one of their fixtures and, for Violet, a major consolation for the grand dinners James was again constantly arranging at Killymoon.

Violet herself generally enjoyed entertaining – but she wished the pressure of appearances were less intense, and the guest lists less carefully weighted. James never invited someone he had just met and liked, or anyone waiting to arrive in the world. Every man or woman who came was someone. He was adept at mingling business and pleasure, at putting people under mild social obligations, and charming them for purposes which sooner or later involved a business interest. Sometimes there were three dinners a week – for senators and judges, for a railway magnate or the owner of a shipping line, for bankers and the closed-faced lawyers who advised them, and for a variety of politicians and other political people – including members of the present government, even though the *Gazette* theoretically opposed them. James also gave dinners for people whom Violet thought of as 'up from the country'. These were Australia's real aristocrats, the owners of properties on which untold quantities of livestock roamed areas so vast they were more like whole countries than any farm Violet had encountered in Europe. The graziers were a species of old Australian baron, and they brought with them the eccentricity as well as the self-reliant bluntness that came from living in such grandeur and isolation.

George had built up a network of friends and contacts over the Killymoon table with the help of his wife as hostess. But Daisy had also been something more – she had been George's ally. Although she had appeared so disarming that the most nervous of wives was soon confiding some intimacy, Daisy had been as sharp as her busy knitting needles. She had a knack for getting people talking, and George never made a business move involving someone she knew without first asking her opinion.

Now Violet was playing a similar role to Daisy's, only a far more glamorous one. It was also, as she saw, subtly diminished. She was expected to be more beautiful, more elegant, more exciting than Daisy had ever been; and there was no doubt that she was. Yet James never asked her opinion, nor sought her advice.

'My function,' she complained to Daisy, 'is entirely decorative. All he wants is for me to look beautiful and make sure we serve the best dinner in Australia.'

'No mean achievement,' Daisy replied. 'But you mustn't just tell me. He's the one you should talk to – boys never listen to their mothers. At least, James never did. He just ran out of the room while I talked to empty air.'

James was doing something similar to her, Violet thought. What he got up to once he had hurried out of the house, often soon after dawn, was as great a mystery as the empty heart of Australia. If it had not been for the parties, Violet wondered whether he would ever have come home at all.

The dinners apart, Violet was occupied entirely with her own life, at the beach, or in town, or with making plans for the children. James was as ignorant of her life beyond Killymoon as she of his; and the house itself might have had nothing to do with him. All he asked was that it functioned perfectly, as if by magic. He never so much as looked at the houschold accounts Violet kept, a task Daisy had relinquished with a mixture of reluctance and relief. James simply signed the cheques, only examining the big bills, which, to Violet's annoyance, he would always round down by a few pounds. 'We pay promptly,' he said when she commented. 'They're damn grateful to give us a discount.'

Violet organised the running of the house quite differently from Daisy; but the old lady had nothing but admiration for her daughter-in-law's various improvements and economies. According to Daisy the three big ledgers labelled 'Killymoon' which Violet verified once a week would have delighted George. 'Nothing pleased him more than well-kept accounts – you'd have made a great businesswoman, Violet.' Violet was struck by the irony that she had largely given up a business, in the form of the Roxy, for a marriage that had itself become nothing more than a business arrangement.

To escape from the emptiness and effort of her life with James, Violet was now occupied most of all with the completion of The Cottage, as the beach house was to be named. She made every excuse she could to go out there. Not least in the hope of meeting Gareth Mayhew checking the progress of his own property. He had rather grandly named it the Southern Cross, even though it was what he called bachelor quarters, with just three bedrooms. It was far smaller than The Cottage, which, so he teased her, should really have been called The Mansion. The two buildings had taken shape together, and though so far he and Violet had not met there, she always looked to see how his house was coming along.

One morning she was walking along the beach, luxuriating in the place, and in her own solitude. She was wearing tan baggy trousers and an open-necked shirt, with a silk scarf tied round her neck. She wriggled her bare brown toes in sand as fine as sugar. Every so often she saw strange jellyfish like little transparent octopuses spread out on the wet sand, their clear tentacles tinged with pale green hues. On the rocks at the end of the bay an albatross perched, its long sharp beak pointed at the waves, its eyes scanning the water. As Violet watched, the heavy bird lumbered down the rock, beating its wings, then picked up into flight, soaring up high, only to turn and plummet downwards, like an arrow. Cleaving the water with its sword-like beak, it emerged moments later with a squirming fish.

A lone voice, almost lost in the sounds of the breeze and the exhausted surf, was coming from the uncompleted shell of Southern Cross. Intrigued, Violet drew closer.

'Speaking, as I am, before so many who are pledged to judge this issue otherwise, let me, in conclusion, demand of you just this . . .'

Through a window-frame as yet unpainted and unglazed, Gareth was standing alone in a room with walls of raw plaster. In his hand was a sheaf of papers, and hanging from a nail in a beam was a mirror large enough to reflect his head and shoulders.

He spoke the last words a second time, banging his fist on an invisible table, and Violet started to clap.

'Bravo! I've discovered the secret of your success.'

Gareth was startled, but not too much to laugh at her. 'Too right,' he said, having invited her inside. 'But I suppose I could have been caught out before now. I've been doing this for weeks.'

He handed her a piece of paper, bearing a row of unemployment statistics in enormous type. 'It's easier if you haven't time to learn it by heart.'

Violet was fascinated. 'How long does it take you to learn a speech like this?'

'Not long – I've always been able to repeat anything I've read. People say I could have made a living as a memory man on the stage. The problem is inflexion and pauses – you see it says "Pause Here" once or twice.'

'I never thought you rehearsed.'

'I didn't for the bar, because there it doesn't work. What you need as an advocate is a conversational kind of voice. If you pull out the *vox humana* stop with judges in Australia, God help your client. They like pleadings which are, well, English. Gentlemanly. You can bellow a bit at a witness sometimes, if he's obviously lying, but even then I liked to be pretty calm. Soothe them down, you know; ingratiate yourself a bit so they make little concessions you can work away at later. The judges understand that. But they've got no time for advocates who perform like Nellie Melba . . . Why are you laughing?'

'From pleasure, at how unselfconsciously you enjoy talking about yourself!'

He laughed too, delightedly.

'But you're practising now,' she said.

'That's for politics. It's funny, but people like their politicians . . . well, larger than life. You need a style that's more theatrical. I've improved a lot since I've been coming down here, or so my secretary says. She calls these rehearsals my singing lessons – but at least I don't have people rushing in thinking I've gone troppo . . .'

'Except me.' Violet's smile lingered as she gazed at him.

163

'You're welcome any time.' He returned her bright, still look, his blue eyes narrowed against the fierce light outside. The sophisticated Mrs James Franklin blushed and looked down at the bare floor. To change the subject she said, 'When will you be ready?' She indicated the unfinished building in which they stood.

'When I can afford to put the men back on. Being in the government has cost me most of my income. I've had to withdraw from various things, in case there might be a conflict of interest. And the government doesn't pay its members half so well as the Bank of New South Wales reimburses counsel it keeps on retainer . . .'

He sighed and pulled the pockets of his trousers out. 'So you see,' he said, 'the poor man's broke.'

Violet left him to perfect his speech. Later she saw in the *Gazette* that it had been a success.

James meanwhile had paid no real attention to her house-building project, until the crates arrived from England containing Emerald's pictures.

It was an astonishing and even puzzling collection, and the more she unpacked the more Violet was overwhelmed by her sister-in-law's range of taste. Emerald had spent two years as an art student before war started in 1914, one in London and the other in Paris. Thanks to her own family's money, she had already been rich by comparison with most of her fellow students. As early as 1913 she had bought her first painting, to help the painter Harry McVey. McVey remained obscure, but she never disposed of his splotchy, Sickert-inspired head of a landlady.

Indeed Emerald had never disposed of anything, good, bad or unclassifiable. In the annexe to her studio a Modigliani had hung next to a Rouault and a Côte d'Azur hillscape painted by Emerald herself in homage to Cézanne. 'There's only one word for my collection, darling,' Violet could hear her benefactress saying in her gravelly voice. 'It's eclectic. "Every school and no school", Augustus John says. School of Emerald, I tell him, darling.'

Along the verandah Violet had half-a-dozen canvases propped up as if in a street exhibition, trying to decide what she would hang at The Cottage. James appeared on his way to the car and let out a bark of laughter when he saw the big Dali collage. 'Call that art?' he said. 'Sammie does better than that.' Violet decided at once that she would hang the Dali in the dining-room.

'Now that's something else,' he remarked. 'Very warm indeed; look at her . . .' It was a big Lawrence nude, one of the three that Emerald had helped smuggle from an exhibition in Mayfair closed by the police as an outrage to public decency. It showed a woman against a background of vine and olive. One arm was held up towards the sun in a gesture of pagan invocation; the other was bent back, with her hand braced against the side of her neck. It was an absurd and probably uncomfortable pose but its intention, which was to emphasise her round breasts, succeeded perfectly. The pose was at the same time abandoned and submissive; the woman's face wore an expression of ecstasy.

'That's what I call a proper dirty picture,' James said, glancing round to see if they were observed. 'I assume you have no plans to hang that anywhere in Killymoon?'

He was laughing and his face was flushed, but there was also anxiety in his voice.

'Not here – at the beach.'

James shrugged. 'I suppose if it's somewhere people won't see. The bedroom, for instance.' He laughed again, derisively, and made a quick move towards her. Violet knew that he was about to squeeze her breasts and she stepped sideways, fending him off.

For a moment his hand brushed her bare shoulder. She lingered beneath his touch, guiltily. She had been thinking of hanging some of the pictures in the bedroom; but not for James's benefit. Recently her confused thoughts about Gareth had included her bedroom at the beach. She was taken off-guard by James's reaction. It had been so long since he had expressed any sexual interest in her.

'Erotic art is lost on you. If you can call that art,' James's rough fingers massaged her shoulder blade. His voice was bitter, with an underlying tension.

She moved away from him, aware that at last she was almost unmoved by his opinions, and even by his pain. But she was not free of him yet.

'Why don't you give them to a museum?' he said in parting.

What did he know of art? she thought, hearing his car start. Again she heard an echo of Emerald's voice. 'Do whatever you want in life but don't spend it with Philistines, my dear. Like your father, they know nothing of either beauty or love.'

It was James, rather than Violet, who instigated The Cottage's house-warming. A week after Violet had finished hanging the pictures and stowing china, he announced that he planned to come out there.

'Gareth told me yesterday that his house is now at a stage where he can occupy a couple of rooms. If we have a party to open the new house, it will encourage Gareth to spend more time there.'

'Good idea, James,' said Violet evenly.

James's enthusiasm for bringing Gareth ever closer into their lives was, as Violet supposed, to do with politics. It was not simply that the *Gazette* supported Gareth's party. James shared the ardent conviction of many that Gareth Mayhew was the man to bring Australia out of the doldrums.

'I've already invited Dick and Bunty. We haven't seen them in a while.'

James looked at Violet. She had been drinking more than usual that day, because James had been at home all afternoon.

'You don't bother much with my relatives, do you? Bunty was complaining the other day that she never saw you at the golf club.'

'My God, that's priceless!' Violet put down her glass so hard that it splashed. 'Have you any idea of the kind of people who spend their lives there? Is that the height of your ambition for Mrs Franklin? You wouldn't expect your mother to be there playing bridge five hours a day.'

'She wouldn't be drinking gin all day. And be nicer to Bunty; she thinks you don't like her.'

Violet knew he was in the right. Bunty meant well; she was what Daisy would have called 'a good soul'. Yet there was a deadness about Bunty's idle world which repelled her – the more so because it mirrored the equally dismal, enforced idleness of another section of the population.

She remembered the journey they made to stay with Bunty's parents-in-law on their enormous new property in Queensland. For the children it had been an adventure because it meant occupying a private railway car of their own. But on the way up the north coast, running through sugar cane and cabbage palmetto and tropical lakes stained brown as strong tea, she had seen a squatter camp. It had been established in a shanty town by the rail track, with almost naked children playing in the white dust. On the Queensland border, not far from the railhead where they changed trains, there had been a similar desperate little community of cane-cutters, surviving in huts made of old cans and hessian sacking. 'No-hopers,' James had said, as if commenting on a characteristic of the Australian fauna.

He himself seemed like an animal of a different species – distant, indifferent to Violet's feelings or ideas. At the same time, her growing independence made him uneasy. She now spent an increasing amount of time at The Cottage – mainly, so she told herself, to forget the similarities between Bunty's life and her own. With the party there to look forward to, furnishing and decorating her new house had become a passion. It was wonderful to be able to start from the beginning and to have everything she wanted, instead of things burdened with family history. She chose snowy white bed linen and fluffy white towels, and porcelain soap containers for the bathrooms, patterned with delicate flowers. Curtains in the bedrooms matched the carpets, whose chintzy patterns were echoed in the seat coverings. Violet had wanted an overall effect that was bright and light – but that would also be intimate and protected, particularly when the winter southerlies turned Palm Beach into a wild, even frightening place. She planned to do a lot of cooking there and had also taken great care over the kitchen, which glowed with copper saucepans imported from France. She had spent a year making lists, she told Daisy on the day the first furnishings were delivered. There was almost a complete crate of silver: more, Daisy said with amusement, than they had acquired at Killymoon in nearly forty years. 'It's a beach house you're furnishing, not an English country mansion,' she said, unpacking what turned out to be a set of Royal Doulton egg coddlers nestling in a bed of straw.

Violet blushed. 'That's no reason not to be comfortable. Anyway, I'm indulging myself.'

Daisy turned her attention to a dozen small Waterford cut-glass bowls. 'These are lovely – heavens, and is this Copenhagen china?' She looked at the individually hand-painted plates, in porcelain so fine it had a blue transparency. 'You've gone to so much trouble; I wish I had your energy.' Daisy sighed with pleasure. 'All these wonderful things – they're just made for entertaining.'

'Oh, Violet, I'm just longing to see your house. Everything I've heard about it is delicious.'

The Rugby Tourer swung over the great bridge and headed north on the Pacific Highway. Bunty wore matching shirt and trousers and her hair was tied back in a checkered scarf. She looked expensively dressed, in the latest fashion for the beach; but somehow she failed to look cool and elegant. 'And Gareth Mayhew is coming. He's far more attractive since he became attorney-general.'

Violet wondered if the flowers had survived that she had planted round Gareth's beach house. She had done it without telling him, digging bright bougainvillaea and hibiscus plants into earthenware tubs along the sun deck.

Bunty prattled on. 'I saw him last week at the Black and White Ball.

You shouldn't have missed that, you know. He was dancing with Anne Summerskill – is that serious, do you think?'

Violet's hands tightened on the steering-wheel. Anne was pretty; she had the right background, too.

'I have no idea.'

'I hope he doesn't make his secretary jealous.' Bunty giggled.

'What do you mean?'

'Oh well, people always said that Miss Bosworth . . .' Bunty faltered. However, the church had offered her a kind of excuse for such talk. 'It was Father O'Fallen who mentioned it to me, as a matter of fact. He said they'd been together since Gareth first went into politics.'

'He would.'

Violet looked anxiously at her own reflection in the rear view mirror. That morning, waking up after too much to drink the night before, she had noticed the first signs of age – ghostly crows' feet around her eyes. Thankfully, they were once more invisible.

At Palm Beach Bunty disappeared into the house to 'explore', and Violet unpacked the car. She had planned the food with particular care for this, the weekend of the house-warming. Tonight they were having a salad of quails' eggs and leeks, followed by an artichoke risotto, and passion-fruit ice cream. One of the major contributions she had made to the Killymoon dinners had been the food – far simpler but more interesting, Daisy freely confessed, than the menus she herself had written.

'Violet! It's extraordinary. Not, well, not what I expected.' With mingled amazement and doubt, Bunty took in the long wooden building, constructed on stilts, and surrounded by a wide sun deck. The lines of the house were clean and sharp, the angles hard; it looked very modern. Violet had had it designed so that the bedrooms on the first floor as well as the rooms below all opened on to a verandah. Even though it was mint new, the house had nothing raw about it. Yet she saw that to Bunty's eyes it looked somehow foreign: not English, precisely, but alien in some other way.

All Bunty said, though, was, 'It's very spacious, isn't it? Not like the usual beach bungalow.'

'That's how I wanted it,' Violet said. 'After all, it's entirely my own house.'

Inside she looked round her with satisfaction. It was an incongruous building, she had to admit, on a coastline where no one, except for Gareth, had ever thought to establish anything more permanent than a hiking tent. The polished floors of Tasmanian oak were covered with

Turkey carpets; the sofas and armchairs were deeply padded, and softened by pale chintzes. Table lamps would shed soft pools of light in the evenings, and the huge fireplace and Swedish wood-burning stove, which would ensure adequate winter heat, dominated one wall. But the biggest surprise, in that lonely place, were the pictures: the Nina Hamnet drawings, the strangely contorted Dali and the swirling Modigliani of 'Red Horsemen in Flight'.

George's cherished copy of the McCubbin was now hanging on the stairs. Bunty walked over to it.

'So this is where it's got to. I wondered where it was.'

'Daisy gave it to me after he died. I didn't like it at first. Now I do. It gives everything else a sense of proportion.'

Violet paused; Bunty was clearly upset at this visible reminder of her father. She went and put her arm round Bunty's waist.

'Come on, let's have a drink. And there's time for a swim before the others get here.'

Bunty returned the hug. 'I'm glad we've had this time together.'

Violet poured two glasses. 'Here's to us.'

'Here's to The Cottage.' Bunty giggled. 'I must say it's a pretty big cottage.'

Violet almost replied that Gareth had said the same thing.

The men – James, Gareth, O'Fallen and Dick – had been to see what O'Fallen facetiously called 'the Mayhew residence'. From the verandah Violet and Bunty watched them returning along the beach. They all wore baggy trousers and sandals, and James sported an old yachting cap stained with salt. They were joking among themselves as they approached the house. Reaching the path that led up from the beach, they fell into an arrowhead formation with Gareth coming up the verandah steps as if it were his natural right.

Violet was sitting in a cane chair, her bare arms deeply tanned. She was slim, not a pound overweight. Even casually dressed she looked, Gareth thought, like a model; like an illustration from the English glossy magazines scattered on the low tables of wrought iron in the spacious main room. Back in Sydney, Violet had found the tables in a scrapyard in Paddington. Having originally been brought to Australia as ship's ballast, they provided an authentic touch of Regency England.

Violet too was authentic, Gareth mused. No wonder James appeared to have fallen for her so precipitously.

'It's like coming home,' he said as Violet came to greet them. He flopped into a deck chair beside her, accepting a chilled cut-glass goblet of Pimm's. The glasses, like their contents, had been kept in an ice-box.

The drinks were garnished with crushed herbs and slices of orange, lime and cucumber. He stretched his long legs contentedly. 'You're a perfect hostess.'

There was an unexpected stranger at dinner. Rex Pountney, a dapper, unashamedly down-to-earth figure from the western suburbs of Sydney, was Gareth's political agent. There was an emergency which needed Gareth's immediate attention. Pountney showed no embarrassment as he apologised to Violet for the intrusion, and insisted on spending an hour closeted with the attorney-general. The rest of them loitered, drinking on the verandah, and savouring a special excitement in the atmosphere. The wildness of their surroundings, with the comfort and style of the house's interior, put everyone in high humour. It was a novelty and a treat.

When Gareth and his political aide reappeared, Pountney breezily accepted Violet's invitation to stay for dinner.

'As you can see, we're not going in for black ties at my new house,' Violet said, glancing at James with the thought that he might be displeased. But James merely looked genial and announced, 'The man's come so far, the least we can do is feed him.' Normally, such a man at his table, in lurid tie and flashy suit, would have been anathema. Yet where Gareth was concerned, James was eager to do any kind of favour.

The conversation stayed with politics.

'Mr Pountney is also famous in his own right,' O'Fallen volunteered over his whisky and water. 'Since before the war he's been the man who decides who's elected in Parramatta.'

'Ancient history, Father,' Pountney said, refusing a cocktail and asking if there was any bottled Sydney Bitter Ale. 'It's the next war that bothers me.'

'You think there's going to be one?' asked Dick. He had recently joined the naval reserve at his wife's behest and was training regularly.

'Too right I do,' Pountney said, raising his beer schooner towards Violet in a gesture of appreciation. 'I'm too old to go this time, thank God. But there'll be plenty of others who will.'

'I refuse to take it seriously,' Bunty said, 'and I certainly don't like talking about it all the time.'

'I thought you were the one who got Dick to sign on.' James always relished showing up the women around him as irrational.

'That was because I don't believe it's ever going to happen,' Bunty answered, playing the card James wanted.

'I hope you're right, ma'am,' said Pountney, 'because if Herr Hitler and Mr Chamberlain can't agree, I know one thing. It's going to cause a lot of trouble in Parramatta.'

The dinner was a scene of good cheer, but the topic would not leave them alone. Over the quails' eggs James asked Gareth for his own, informed view. Violet observed how everyone broke up their private conversations to listen.

'The British are playing for time, that's clear. They hope Hitler will give them the leeway to rearm properly before he embarks on war. They also hope the vicious little demagogue will back off once they've built up fighter planes capable of resisting the air force he's been trying out in Spain.'

'But if there's war, will Australia follow the empire?' asked O'Fallen.

'Australia's constitutionally part of the empire. Of course we'd follow.'

'Supposing people thought the war in Europe was nothing to do with Australia, or that it would destroy us for twenty years like the last one?' the priest persisted.

'That's what people in Parramatta say, especially the Irish,' contributed Rex Pountney, who was getting rather drunk on white Bordeaux. 'With apologies to our beautiful hostess, a lot of people aren't as patriotic about the British Empire as they used to be.'

'They will be – once the shooting starts,' said Gareth.

Violet looked at the table through half-closed eyes. She was seated at one end, with Gareth on her right. James sat at the other end. Through the flickering light of the candles he looked pleased with life. Everyone seemed at ease, despite the inherent gloom of the conversation. The mix of shirt-sleeves for the men and the formality of silver and fine food suited everyone.

'Hitler's leading the fashions, whatever you think of him,' Bunty contributed. 'Girls are wearing German costumes and the European magazines are packed with articles about Aryan good health and outdoor living.'

'The British press censor the real facts,' James said. 'Here it's publish and be damned. Australians knew a lot more about Mrs Simpson than the British, for example, until the moment of the abdication.'

'A wicked business,' said the priest. 'The press should have done their duty.'

'To make him give her up, or to encourage them?' Violet asked quickly.

'He should have done his duty too, of course. To the people and the crown. Don't you agree, Gareth?'

'All I can say is I'm glad I wasn't in his shoes at the time. I hope the poor blighters are both happy. I expect they'll find life very hollow.'

The first guests to arrive for the house-warming next day were Billy Sorrell, over from Tasmania, and his latest fiancée – his third, according to James. They were early; none the less Billy was already drunk. He staggered out of his bright yellow Mercedes coupé and dragged his escort, Marjorie, up to the sun deck by her arm.

Introducing her loudly to everyone in general, he then left her to fend for herself. She was pertly blonde, with a snub nose and porcelain complexion.

'What a darling place,' she exclaimed, accepting a drink. 'You must be Violet. I've heard so much about you. Oh – and is that Gareth Mayhew? I've been longing to meet him.' She took a hasty gulp of Pimm's and walked unsteadily over to him. Violet covertly turned to watch her, but was interrupted by the arrival of several cars full of guests who must have teamed up in a convoy on the long stretch of deserted road leading out to Palm Beach.

Gareth wound up the gramophone, and the rhythmic sound of Cole Porter's 'Let's Do It' started all the recently arrived guests dancing.

'It must be the heat,' he said to Violet. 'They seem to be getting drunk very fast.' For once, Violet herself was surprisingly sober. She had a glass of lime juice and ice and felt no inclination to get drunk.

In the corner Marjorie had started an earnest conversation.

'Men's clothes are so awful,' she was saying. 'They wear such ugly things, like uniforms. Billy says you can tell a man's politics from the clothes he wears. New Guarders and fascists all wear green pork-pie hats. Communists always go bareheaded. What do you think, Gareth?' she said, grabbing his arms as he walked past her.

'On your reckoning, I'm a Red.' Violet caught his eye and flashed him a sympathetic smile.

She went through to the kitchen to get some more ice. Overhearing his voice, she paused, stooping before the ice-chest, and lingered to listen.

'How do you entertain, then? I mean, how can you be a single man and a successful politician?' Gareth was being questioned by Mostyn Delf, an old friend from his early career as a lawyer.

'Dunno exactly; it's a mystery. Rex says you have to make an advantage of your weaknesses; and that being a widower is part of my charm. The ladies of Parramatta all think I need looking after – that's why they vote for me.' Gareth had married young; following the death of his wife after a few months' illness, he had remained a widower for many years now.

Violet heard Rex Pountney's laugh. 'If you need an escort there's always la belle Bosworth. She'd do anything for Gareth here – even marry him. But Gareth isn't the kind of fella who lets sheilas get in the way of his career. Not like that pom king of England.'

'Pom ex-king,' Gareth said, and they all laughed.

'You'd think the poor sod would have understood the rules,' Pountney said. 'Now, Gareth enjoys power and privilege far too much to piss 'em away like that. Don't you, sport?'

Gareth must have moved off at this point, because it was in an undertone that Violet heard Mostyn say, 'Useful to have such a good friend who owns a newspaper.'

'Yes – he does need Franklin for his leadership campaign. The *Gazette*'s already made him the most popular politician in Australia. And with the *Gazette* behind him Gareth can fight for the party leadership, and win in a dawdle.'

'Why does the *Gazette* support him so unconditionally?'

'Search me, sport. If Mr High and Mighty Franklin wasn't such a one for the ladies I'd think he was one of – you know.' Pountney gave a conspiratorial laugh. 'As it is, Franklin must just believe in Gareth, like the old biddies do in his constituency. Strange old world, isn't it?'

Violet didn't wait to hear any more. Was this the only reason that Gareth cultivated their friendship?

She took the ice out on to the verandah. Down beyond the beach some of the guests were swimming, while others were attempting a drunken game of volley ball on the sand. Billy was trying to kiss Marjorie in the corner while Dick looked on.

'Dick's right,' Billy said to her.

'Right about what?' Marjorie said with annoyance.

'That underneath all that finery, you've got the finest pair of knockers in New South Wales. That's why I love you.'

Violet went over to refill Marjorie's proffered glass. At the sight of her, Billy stopped manhandling Marjorie. He made sure, however, that Violet did not pass his own glass by, even though he was already reeling.

As the fierce heat of afternoon turned to an evening of blissful warmth, Violet leant over the verandah and watched the men in the water. James, as strong a swimmer as his father had been, was further out than the others. Dick, with his red hair, was easy to track, diving into the big breakers thirty yards from the shore and coming out on the other side shaking his head and blowing. O'Fallen had equipped himself with a surfboard, a short one like a child's, and was skilfully riding the occasional wave, not in the usual standing position, but lying along the board as if it were a toboggan.

Gareth was the first to come out, and stood in the shallow water looking at the ocean as if it belonged to him. He had none of James's obvious physical strength. But Violet could not take her eyes off him. What was it about him that she could not resist? Was it, as Bunty had suggested, the attraction of power? Whatever it was, Violet could sense its force at fifty yards as though the two of them were close enough to feel each other's breath.

It was almost dawn before the last of the guests departed. Billy, incapable of driving, was snoring on a sofa while Marjorie went upstairs to one of the children's beds. Bunty and Dick had retired some time earlier. Eventually even James took himself up to bed.

Violet and Gareth were finally sitting alone on the verandah. Above them the Southern Cross spread out, faintly now, across a huge sky with a tinge of light. It was like watching the sky dying, Violet thought, rather than the birth of morning. There was something ominous about this moment that was neither night or day.

Gareth reached out and took her hand. 'I'm in love with you,' he said, quietly.

'I'm a married woman,' she answered. But her tone was an invitation. She got swiftly to her feet and stood holding the verandah rail.

'You feel it, too, don't you?'

She laughed nervously, pushing her hair back from her forehead. 'Yes. But I'm afraid. It could go so wrong for you, for everyone.'

Gareth went up to her and put his hands on her shoulders. She leant back, resting her head against him.

'Don't be. You only live once. We've got the beach. Why do you think I built my house?'

'I never let myself think that far.'

'But you wondered, didn't you?' His voice was like a touch, and she could feel his breath on her neck.

'Is it so obvious?'

'It is to me. God, I hope you did. I've loved you for so long. Since I met you, the day they opened the Harbour Bridge.'

She turned to face him and he took her slender body in his arms. He buried his face in her hair; then she felt her mouth parting under his.

Violet pulled away and took his face in her hands.

'You have your answer. I love you too.'

He leant forward to kiss her again. Gently she resisted.

'Stay here with me,' he said, his strong voice kept low with an effort.

'Not now. Not this weekend. I want it to be perfect for us.'

He held her close again.

Above, someone – her husband, or the priest – could be heard stirring in his sleep. She wanted to laugh out loud, from fear and joy and a tumult of other feelings; but above all from the sheer happiness of knowing he loved her.

From somewhere among the eucalyptus behind the house came the repetitive, liquid call of a nightjar. The Pacific waves rolled and crumbled along the thinning darkness of the unquiet shore. He placed his hand on her breast and she laid her own upon it, in a gesture of intimacy she had not known before.

He had said what her heart longed to hear. But there was another part of her that was sunk fathoms deep in dread. She wanted not to care: about James, or society, or Gareth's own momentous career. She desired him more than she had wanted anything; for him, she was ready to defy the world.

'WAR!' screamed the headlines in the *Gazette* and every other newspaper.

Two weeks later, on 12 March Germany had invaded Austria. The day after, Hitler announced that Austria, the land of his birth, was now a part of the German Empire. His next move seemed likely to be a take-over of the Sudetenland. The French were talking of a military response if the German army crossed the Czech border, but Chamberlain refused to commit himself to supporting them.

Suddenly Gareth was spending all his time in Canberra, the raw new capital he loathed. Violet was in a turmoil of anxiety. How would they ever manage to be alone together? She fretted through the days, carrying on her life with the children, and playing her part in a series of Killymoon dinners where even the women talked only of rearmament and what 'the Russian Bear' was going to do. She felt as if her hostess smile had been painted on her face, and that one night she would get blind drunk and scream out precisely what was in her mind.

So restless was she that one afternoon when Bunty suggested a round of golf she was waiting in the clubhouse thirty minutes later.

'Why your sudden interest?' Bunty asked as they were teeing up at the first green.

'I used to enjoy a game when I was younger – in England,' Violet said, preparing her own shot. She sliced it nevertheless and the ball shot off into the rough. Violet bit back her exclamation of annoyance and set off to retrieve it. As she walked across the fairway, she saw Bunty's perfect ball soar into the air to land 60 yards from the green. Her sister-in-law came to help her find her ball.

'I did enjoy your house-warming,' Bunty said, as Violet prepared to hit herself out of the rough. 'If you weren't a happily married woman, I'd think that Gareth was attracted to you.'

'Nonsense,' Violet said, regretting her impulse to join Bunty. 'Gareth is a family friend. Well, really a friend of James.'

'True – James has done a lot for Gareth, and so did George.' They were talking on the grass of the fairway, parched and brown after months of summer sun. Violet's ball was still far short of Bunty's, so again she went first. She tried a number seven iron from her golf bag and positioned herself carefully. The ball clipped into the air and landed on the green, rolling to a stop only 12 feet from the hole.

'What a shot,' Bunty said. 'You ought to play more often – you could be the ladies' captain if you kept at it. Does Gareth play – we could get him to make up a four? Dick has never had any interest in golf. He can't think of anything but his boats.'

Violet seized on the new line of conversation eagerly. 'You didn't have a chance to see the inland lagoon behind the beach. We're going to build a jetty – it's a splendid natural harbour.'

'Will James bring the big boat there?' Bunty asked, taking out her putter and leaving herself with a four-footer which she tapped in professionally.

'Oh no; it's far too shallow. James much prefers to stay at Middle Harbour. That's what he calls proper sailing.' Violet was really thinking about Gareth. She prayed that Bunty couldn't see the flush on her cheeks, as she missed a putt that would have gone down effortlessly when she was eighteen.

'You need to practise,' Bunty said again. 'You can't waste your whole life at Killymoon, you know.'

It was a week before Gareth was seen at Killymoon – to James's pleasure he invited himself for a drink. He appeared looking travel-worn in a crumpled suit and tie that did not match.

'I've come straight from the plane,' he said, with a glance at Violet she was sure her husband must have noticed.

However, the only thing on James's mind was a letter he wanted the politician to see. It came from Andrew and contained all kinds of alrming information Churchill had passed to him.

'He couldn't print any of this in the London *Gazette*,' he said, handing the letter to Gareth. 'The rise of panic would have been too great. You'll see it adds up to an indictment of the whole rearmament programme. Too little, and too late, Churchill says. He thinks America's the only hope – them, or a war between the Reich and Russia.'

The two men were absorbed – if it hadn't been for the look in Gareth's eyes, when she met him in the hall, Violet would have wondered if she had dreamt the night at the beach.

'What about the Japanese?' James wanted to know. 'Do you honestly think the British will give priority in the East?'

'Not on the day after they're invaded by a few panzer divisions.'

'Shouldn't we be rearming, as Churchill says?'

'I can't talk about that now.' Gareth slipped a confidential smile at Violet as she refilled his glass. It made her uncomfortable to be in the presence of both men. She was amazed at how easily Gareth was able to carry on as though nothing had happened. It was part of his politician's skill never to seem in the wrong.

James briefly had to leave the room to take a telephone call. Gareth leant towards her, touching her knee with his hand. 'Sunday night?'

'I'll try.'

'Do more than try. Succeed.' He looked into her eyes, whose colour always seemed to be changing. Violet reached down to take his hand, then moved back guiltily as she heard the door opening.

Conversation turned to the forthcoming general election.

'I'm glad you're so confident,' James said.

'Oh, we'll win – unless there's a last-minute scandal, or old Rex Pountney's got his sums wrong.'

'And we'll back you to the hilt,' James replied, 'as we always have done. If you try a shot for the leadership . . .' He raised his glass in Gareth's direction.

'No comment. All that's far too premature, and I don't want anyone flying kites. If there's any suspicion that I'm rocking the boat on the eve of a national election I'll be the former attorney-general before you can say a schooner of bitter.'

They both laughed, and Violet saw them exchange a look of complicity. She felt a wave of hoplessness. Sometimes she thought that Gareth needed James more than he needed her.

On Sunday afternoon Sammie and Lizzie both wanted to come to the beach.

'You have school in the morning,' she said to Sammie, who was holding on to her knees.

'But I don't,' wailed Lizzie. 'And summer is nearly gone, and soon we won't be able to go at all.'

'I want you to look after Granny,' she said, extricating herself and shutting the car door. She smiled brightly at them through the window, churning with guilt and excitement, and drove off fast before she could change her mind.

As she turned the Rugby Tourer on to the track down to the beach house, he was waiting on the shore.

'I thought you'd never come,' he said, helping her out.

They went towards the house, her head cradled on his shoulder, his heady masculine smell making her feel faint.

'Are you sure?' he said. 'Do you love me?'

'Yes, more than anything. More than my life,' she answered, knowing that it was indeed her life she was playing with and his too. Indoors he picked her up in his arms and carried her upstairs.

The Lawrence nudes stared down at them as he laid her on the bed. He undressed her slowly, his eyes full of wonder. It was worse than any hunger or thirst, this yearning of flesh, and Violet strained towards him, meeting his kiss which burned her mouth.

He broke away, to kiss her neck and then to hold her at arm's length for a moment, gazing at her body as if he was trying to imprint every part of her on his memory. 'So that's what you look like,' he said. 'If you knew how I've imagined your body. It's as though I knew it all, every inch of it under your clothes.' His hands stroked her forearms, feeling the fine downy hair, gold from the sun. Then his mouth moved downwards until it covered her nipple. She felt his lips, then his tongue, caressing, tickling, biting. Violet felt herself teetering on the edge of an unknown feeling, filling her breasts, her stomach, her throat, a longing that invaded her whole body, a need, so intense that she would die if it wasn't fulfilled.

'Are you afraid?' he said, meeting her liquid eyes which seemed blue-grey in these short moments of twilight.

'A little,' she said. 'But don't stop.'

He traced his tongue across the flatness of her stomach, kissing and nibbling. Her legs parted as his mouth moved inside her thighs. Violet's body was so sensitive now that she experienced every flickering touch on the delicate skin inside her legs like a tiny stab. His fingers stroked her gently, parting the lips of her sex.

Violet tensed herself, wondering if it was possible to feel more than this, and knowing that there was more to come. She caught her breath as his finger eased into her, gently at first, then with a small thrust, and then another. She could not help exclaiming as he began to move his hand faster and harder, with a deliberate insistent rhythm that became more like a sound than a feeling, a sound merging with the thunder of the surf. He was using his tongue now as well as his fingers, and then she felt his lips against her own hidden skin, and then his mouth licking and teasing and finally engulfing her.

'Go on,' she exclaimed. 'Whatever you do, don't stop!'

The waves of pleasure rolled inside her, centring deep down somewhere, like a volcano, gathering itself, ready to erupt. She shut her eyes, seeing sparks behind the lids. He mustn't stop, he mustn't stop. Her fingers wound into his hair. Then the peak of ecstasy, coming like great rolls of pain and pleasure, jerking her body and mind in bliss.

She opened her eyes, and met the wanton, fulfilled expression on the face of the big Lawrence nude looking down at her. Now she knew how the model had felt. She was so filled with relief and delight, that she began to laugh. Finally, she understood all the lovers of the world.

'Why are you laughing?' he said.

'Because I'm free – you make me so happy,' she answered, reaching up to kiss him.

'Now?' he said. She felt every muscle start to tremble as he lowered his body on to her.

Her thighs gripped his waist as he entered her, but still he was gentle – she could not believe that anyone could be so patient, easing only a fraction of himself into her at a time. The emptiness inside her, like an opening anemone, was aching to be filled. He watched her face, looking down at her. She tried to raise her body to his, but still he wouldn't bury himself in her. Then, when she thought she could bear it no longer, he thrust himself deeply in her, his arms cradling her head, his mouth covering hers, his tongue searching. They were moving in easy unison, inseparable in their mounting passion. Violet felt it building and soaring again inside her, the same need, only shared this time, and it was as if she were being lifted out of the room, and even out of the world altogether. She heard herself cry out as she passed the peak and she felt Gareth's whole body stiffen and strain on hers. Then he too was riding the wave which neither could halt, moving frantically now, as if they were on fire. At his climax, she heard him call her name and she buried her face in the warmth of his neck, holding on to him for fear she would die.

They slept, and woke in the early evening. Gareth stretched himself beneath the sheet which covered them and lazily pulled Violet to him, a gesture so familiar and relaxed that they could have been sleeping together nightly for years. They might be married, she thought, properly married, not the travesty she had experienced. They might be together always on a wash of domestic sensuality, familiar, dependable passion and fulfilment. This is enough, she thought, waking with my lover, my beloved lover, why should I ask for anything more? 'I love you,' she said, and it was like a sigh. She curled against his hard body, relishing the feeling of his skin.

'I'm hungry,' he said, leaning on one elbow and looking down at her.

It was too abrupt for her – she would have preferred a slower awakening; she would have liked him to kiss her. She responded nevertheless.

'Let's swim first,' she said, sitting up and swinging out of bed, easy and proud of her body for the first time. She had never walked around naked in front of a man before and now, as they swam through the waves in the early evening light, the water rippling off their naked bodies, she marvelled at the feeling. Now she could look at his body and now she could have it, again and again.

The moon rose on the horizon, waxy yellow, and so low that its sharp edges mingled with its reflection on the ocean. The successive breakers were so heavy they might have travelled halfway round the world to disintegrate furiously on this beach. The land noises of cicadas, a rasp that could fray the nerves, and the rustle of the trees behind The Cottage, stirred by end-of-summer winds, blurred into the sea-sounds. Violet realised that she could smell the salt surf tang with the scent of eucalyptus simultaneously. Never in her life had she felt so languorous and yet so alert. After their swim, she cooked omelettes and made a salad, and took a bottle of chilled white wine out of the ice-chest. They ate and drank on the verandah, sitting close together.

She would die of loving him, she thought, looking at Gareth in the moonlight, his thick hair slicked down by the water. As if reading her thoughts he reached out and pulled her to him. 'You're cold. Come back to bed, darling.'

He left at dawn. Violet woke to the busy rustle of papers. Through half-closed eyes she watched him already dressed, rearranging the contents of his briefcase.

'Do you have to go?'

'Yes – the plane for Canberra leaves Sydney at 8.30.'

He kissed her, longingly, as she reached up to try to hold him.

'I love you,' she said.

'I love you too. I won't say goodbye and I can't say when I'll see you again.' He paused, reluctant to break away from her.

Violet felt desolate at the prospect of his departure. She tightened her embrace.

'Let me go,' he said, laughing.

He kissed her quickly and then was gone. Seconds later she heard his car start up and the crunch of the wheels along the driveway.

She was no longer sleepy. The morning light was strong and she looked round the room with new eyes. The nudes stared peacefully down. They made her smile in self-recognition now. She dressed quickly, in cotton trousers and shirt, and busied herself tidying up the remains of dinner, polishing glasses, fixing things up. When she could find nothing else to do, she made a strong cup of black coffee and sat out on the deck. Would he always leave like this, she wondered? Would he always be able to cut off so abruptly? I don't care, she thought. Any moment with him is worth the risk and the possible pain. It has to be. It's the biggest thing in my life.

She drove back to Sydney slowly, dragging out the time before she had to confront Killymoon again. On an impulse she pulled off the road and drove into a small park. She got out of the tourer and sat down on a bench. A Jewish family were having a picnic at a rustic table near a wishing-well and a set of concrete toilets.

The father wore Hassidic clothes which must have been hot and uncomfortable; his children seemed unhappy and his wife looked harassed. Violet felt a wave of sympathy for the family, refugees no doubt, jettisoned from some strange ghetto in Europe into this alien country. Like me, she told herself, remembering the day she had first arrived in Australia, scared and bruised from the rape, uncertain of James, of everything.

But I'm cured of that now, she thought. Suddenly she had realised that her fears about sex, about whether she could ever enjoy it, had vanished. She felt a wave of love for Gareth, so strong that she wanted to weep. Getting back into the car she turned on the ignition. As the engine idled, she sat for a moment longer, looking at two Australian children laughing at the Jewish boys' little black hats. One of the Jewish children started to cry, and she found herself thinking of Sammie and Lizzie. Quickly, she put the car in gear and backed out of the parking space. Whatever happens, I mustn't hurt the children.

That afternoon, trying to take up the routines of life at Killymoon as if nothing had happened, Violet received a letter from Ben.

Litzie has gone to Vienna to try and get her parents out of Austria. I'll probably have to bribe half the Third Reich to get her back. I've heard one Jewish joke which made me laugh – among the hundreds now being told in Europe.
  'Who is the most desirable woman in the Third Reich?'
  'An Aryan grandmother.'
  I gather your friend Quigley got into trouble trying to interview your abdicated monarch in exile. He maintained that Edward had been in Berlin trying to chat up the Fuhrer.

Violet folded the letter and put it away. Thoughts of the troubled world at large jostled with an awareness of her personal feelings. However happy Gareth might make her, the narrow life they shared would always be fraught with insecurity. How she wished Ben were here to talk to.

16

Violet let herself into the fusty little house in Parramatta. Dunroamin wasn't all that different from Belle View, except that Rex Pountney was a bachelor who had gone on living in his mother's house after the old lady died, and he was by no means a fastidious housekeeper. Nona would never have put up with rows of ale bottles in her back garden. Also the streets here were narrower, and the gardens smaller than Belle View's patch of reclaimed scrub. Through half a dozen sets of net curtains, Violet was conscious of prying eyes.

Gareth arrived twenty minutes later. Instead of his usual Homburg he was wearing a check cap pulled low over his eyes. At the sight of him she was helpless with laughter.

'You look like a burglar!'

'Just as long as I don't look like the next leader of the National Party.'

As a curtain raiser to the general election, three months away, Gareth's party was to select a new leader. The present head of the party, old Willy Lyons, had become increasingly ineffective in opposition. Meanwhile he had exercised the old man's prerogative in making up his mind slowly and then changing it, as he veered between securing the succession to Gareth, and nominating Gareth's rival, Lynch Meldrum. A combination of lampooning by the *Gazette* and bargaining by Gareth had now made Meldrum stand down, in return for a promise of the defence portfolio and the deputy leadership. So now it was Gareth against the established party leader. The old man had held on, as one observer put it, 'because he can't think what else to do'.

Violet said, 'If they saw the next leader like this, wouldn't there be a scandal!' Gareth was already tearing off his shirt and tie.

It was impossible for them not to speak of scandal. In the struggle for the party leadership, Gareth's personal advantage was small; and he was desperate that no last-minute upset should undo it. Now more than ever he was walking on eggshells. It seemed to Violet that nothing could have been more difficult than arranging to meet him.

Afterwards, he said, 'I think I'm going to win.' He was resting on one elbow, looking down at her. 'It's hard to believe. A kid like me. Dreams – everyone has dreams, every poor kid. And now . . . in a week I'll be the leader of the opposition, unless there's an earthquake. And then . . . it makes you dizzy.'

He smiled at her. 'Almost as dizzy as you do,' he said, taking her in his arms again.

They left separately with elaborate precautions she half enjoyed. The encounter made her feel cheap, like a girl in the office smuggled away with the boss for an afternoon. But the risk was exciting, and the sense of crossing a borderline into delinquency made her see how tired she was of the hostess and good wife act James demanded from her. If only it weren't for the leadership crisis, during which Violet had felt that Gareth might just as well be on the moon. There were times when, secretly, she wished he'd stayed a lawyer.

It was the evening of the final result in the leadership election. Before she went to say goodnight to the children, Violet went down into George's old study and tuned the wireless to Canberra. An announcer was saying that Gareth was the favourite for the impending vote and trying to persuade Lynch Meldrum to tell the public which candidate he supported. As she went upstairs Violet heard the shadow finance minister saying something about confidentiality. On the landing she paused, and found she was trembling. Supposing Gareth lost; would he turn to her for comfort, or might he even blame the Franklins?

But if he won? She made a vow that whatever the outcome she and the man she loved were not going to be separated much longer.

'Is Daddy home?' Sammie asked, when she went into his room.

'Yes, darling.'

'Will he come and say goodnight tonight? I missed him last night.'

'He's been very busy.'

'You're always saying that. I wanted to show him my new train.' Sammie wound his arms round her neck and burrowed his head in the hollow of her shoulder. 'You smell nice.'

'So do you,' Violet said, hugging him back and stroking his sandy-coloured hair.

'You do love us, don't you, Mummy?'

'A million times, darling.' She kissed him on the cheek and laid his head on the pillow. 'Sleep now. School tomorrow, and it's swimming.'

'Do I have to go – if it's still raining?'

'We'll see.' Violet switched off the main light, hesitating over the night-light which glowed in the corner. James didn't approve of Sammie having it on through the night.

'Can you leave it on?'

'Yes,' she said.

'Night night, sleep tight . . .'

'Don't let the beetles bite,' Violet answered, falling into their nightly routine.

'If they do, don't bawl . . .'

'Take a spoon and gobble them all.'

She closed the door so that James would not spot the glow and went back down the corridor to her room to change. Along the wall hung portraits of stern Victorian gentlemen whom George had liked to claim as his English ancestors. Daisy had told Violet that he had actually bought them in a lot from an auction. George could get away with jokes like that. She knew James hated them and, were it not for Daisy, would have consigned them all to the bonfire long ago.

In the study, James and Daisy were listening to the big wireless. Violet feared that Daisy would be reminded of George gathering them all together on Christmas Day to hear the king's speech from London.

'It sounds as if he's got it,' James was saying. He sat hunched towards the machine as if he was going to nudge it with his shoulder. No matter how well-cut his clothes, no tailor could disguise his heftiness. The commentator's voice was raucous with excitement; he made the proceedings sound like a horse race.

The static was so heavy that Violet could scarcely make out a word. James, who had been fiddling endlessly to try to get better reception, squatted down on the carpet, his ear against the loudspeaker in the set. His face wore an expression of excitement and anxiety. 'C'mon, Gareth. You can beat that old wind-bag with one hand tied.'

Violet tried not to meet his eye. How much easier it would be, if her husband did not appear genuinely to support her lover.

I don't care, she thought. She went to the cabinet to pour herself a drink, and turned back to the wireless as they began to announce the votes.

'William Albert Lyons 151, Gareth Mayhew 181. I declare Gareth Mayhew . . .'

The rest of the sentence was obliterated by applause and static in equal combination.

'He's done it!' James shouted.

A bottle of champagne was sent for. Bright with triumph, James filled their glasses and proposed a toast.

'To Gareth.'

'To Gareth,' Violet repeated, and drained her glass.

17

The streets of Hobart climbed steeply from the banks of the Derwent River's broad estuary. It was a setting whose theatricality immediately struck Violet as a good film location. With Dick and Bunty she had flown to Tasmania to join James for part of Gareth's campaign in the general election.

Billy Sorrell's pilot, Mintie, banked low so that his passengers could admire the neat shingle roofs, and the sunlight reflecting off the water. Hobart was a considerable town, yet it looked dimity and dwarfed against the natural splendour of Mount Wellington, as if the Tasmanians had only gained a toehold. Mintie descended until they were only a hundred feet above the estuary. Violet could see the piles of bamboo fishing traps, like giant lobster pots, and dozens of small boats.

From the air, the gold and green of the Tasmanian pastureland was unlike anything she had seen in mainland Australia. It was so reminiscent of what Daisy called 'the old country' that Violet thought, I must go back one day, just to see.

Bunty, who saw England as a shrine of social observance, believed that Violet must live in a state of permanent regret at being cut off from Ascot and Wimbledon. The truth was so different. It had been astonishingly easy to turn her back on the place, far easier than she had expected. But Bunty was right in so far as she now missed the frivolities of her old life there – its variety, and the sense of the unexpected, which probably had had most to do with being eighteen. That her parents were far off was usually a cause for a heartfelt 'Thank God' – particularly when, once or twice, she had allowed herself momentarily to imagine her father's reaction to her relationship with Gareth.

No, the sudden nostalgia was not for her family; rather there was a stirring in her for the old *place*, for the look of the countryside, its modest scale, its sense of antiquity and solidity.

Mintie circled the Fox Moth once more over the town and landed in a cloud of dust on a grass strip beyond Battery Point. There was an old but highly polished Bentley waiting to take them into the city.

At the hotel the first person they saw was Cissy Greeley walking through the lobby with a notebook in her hand. Cissy was a reporter who worked for the *Gazette*. She had been sent to interview Violet after her wedding and later, after James had insisted on deleting all the references to Violet's work at the Roxy, Cissy had telephoned to apologise. She had sounded so genuinely distressed that Violet had impulsively invited her to lunch.

Cissy was down to earth and in many ways she reminded Violet of Aggie. She was buxom without being overtly sexy, a country girl who had come into the city. But, as Violet had got to know Cissy, her original perceptions had changed. Cissy was very ambitious. She supported a widowed mother who lived alone in the Blue Mountains and she herself had been abandoned by an Italian husband whom, she confided to Violet, she had married in a 'fit of passion which had swept her off her feet'.

That sentiment, at least, Violet wholly understood, and they struck up a friendship which Violet never mentioned to James. Cissy was brighter and funnier than Bunty and her circle of friends at the Rose Bay Golf Club. Violet would dutifully attend Bunty's functions, but often she made excuses and went to a film matinée with Cissy instead. Cissy wrote the film reviews for the *Gazette* and Violet, as an extension of the publicity work she still did for the Roxy, contributed to Cissy's articles anonymously.

Cissy was looking slimmer and far better dressed than the last time Violet had seen her. It turned out that she had been travelling with the Mayhew campaign.

'I'm doing politics now.' She was as exuberant as a schoolgirl; Bunty instinctively withdrew from her familiarity.

Violet wanted to know about the campaign.

Cissy looked offended. 'Didn't you read my stuff from Melbourne and Adelaide?'

'You made it sound as if they were throwing roses under his feet,' Violet said placatingly.

'It's the war issue that's set the campaign alight,' Cissy explained. 'He's taking a big chance. The voters don't like being warned they're for the high jump and that all they can do is tighten their belts, get ready to join the army, make sacrifices – all these nasty, uncomfortable prospects.'

'I think he's right about the war,' said Dick. 'Everyone in London's talking like that – everyone who knows anything. I reckon he's just telling 'em the truth.'

'Even if it is the truth I'm not going to think about it,' Bunty remarked with a force that made them laugh. 'I'm off shopping and then it's lunch at the Yacht Club. Anyway, Dick's too old to fight.'

She waited though, curious despite herself, as Cissy described how Gareth had dominated a stormy evening at Adelaide University, turning the heckling to his own advantage.

'His timing is beaut,' Cissy said. 'It's as if those guys were his own stooges they'd planted in the crowd. It's as good as a stage show.'

Violet realised with a sense of jealousy that Cissy too had fallen under his spell. Now that Gareth was a public man she would have to share him with a great constituency of people who would never come as close to him as Cissy had done, people who had only heard him speak on the wireless or had seen him on the newsreels at the picture theatres.

'You wait till you hear Gareth speak,' Cissy was telling Dick. 'He's changed – I'd never have believed it was the same man.'

Even Bunty was curious to take in scraps of gossip about Gareth and his campaign – notwithstanding that she felt it was bad luck to mention the chance of war, as if talking would make it happen. In recent months Gareth had managed to capture everyone's imagination, not for his policies, but for himself. There was something vital and modern about him, a piquancy of intelligence and a physical presence, that made the government seem mediocre, conservative, old.

'I think he'll win,' Bunty said. 'All our friends say James backed the wrong horse, but I think he's had a lot of foresight.' She was, as ever, the adoring younger sister.

Violet had no doubt that in judging the country James was far ahead of many of his fellows. She wondered why he had supported Gareth so wholeheartedly from the start. Personal affection? Shared convictions? A sense of affinity? My God, if only he knew. The one consolation she could draw from Gareth's extreme caution was that her husband would never find out. It was impossible in any case to imagine how James would react because she continued to find him a mystery.

He was obsessed with his work, and increasingly ambitious; yet what was the point of his success? It did not make him happy, or certainly not in the home. He loved his children, but he still played no more than a symbolic and awe-inspiring role in their lives. Sometimes he would not see them, except when they were asleep, for days on end. He was a stranger to them, involved with the pursuit of – what, exactly? Surely not money, nor power – he often said he would have hated politics as a career. He had strong opinions about most things, and yet Violet could not see him as dedicated to converting people to a point of view, as Gareth certainly was. There was something child-like in his approach to work, as if he were going through a schoolboy craze. She had understood the patronising note in Gareth's voice when he had spoken once of James 'pursuing his plan to own more newspapers than Hearst'. Gareth had made James and his business plans sound like Sam and his cigarette cards of Australian cricketers: Bradman, Macartney, Fleetwood-Smith. Sam would play with them deep into the night if allowed, just as James, working round the clock, was always the last to bed and the first to rise. Even on vacation he could never pass over the chance of a deal, a meeting, a conference. He was absent from their group now, having talks in a private room upstairs with the proprietor of the *Hobart Times* before the rally began.

Cissy was right. Gareth looked different. He came on to the platform to rousing cheers – and to something behind them: a new sound, rising up from the base of the platform and echoing round the hall like a mighty line of surf. 'Gar, Gar, Gar,' they chanted.

'My God,' whispered James when the noise had subsided. 'It's like a war-cry.'

Violet could find no reply – she was overcome by the atmosphere and by Gareth's effortless domination of the assembly. They greeted him like a film-star, and listened with profound, almost brooding attention.

Even his voice was hard to recognise. Sometimes it was soft and almost wheedling; mostly it sounded rusty and rough, as if his vocal chords were under strain. His delivery had also changed. In some school-hall along the campaign trail he had deserted his dry and argumentative lawyer's style. Instead, his delivery was reminiscent of Lloyd George, 'the Welsh wizard'. There was something Celtic and lyrical about Gareth's voice now. He varied his tone like a singer, sometimes almost shouting, sometimes speaking so softly it was scarcely more than a whisper. Violet listened, awe-struck.

When it was over she was cheering madly with the rest. As the Franklins' party worked their way towards the exit, she listened to the crowd's reactions.

'Give me a straight-out answer. Why can't we let the pommies fight their own battles? Hitler's not got a claim in to Tazzy, has he?'

'Is this bloke all for conscription then?'

'Too right he is. We'll get a free pair of boots any road.'

'He's right about not kiddin' ourselves about the future, all the same. He tells it straight.'

Violet realised she had failed to follow Gareth's argument. Had he said 'conscription' outright? Certainly it was there by implication; moreover he had somehow made the idea attractive. He had managed to present the threat of war as uplifting, a hard but invigorating tonic, just what the nation really needed. It had been closer to a sermon than a political speech.

She saw for the first time what a skilled actor he was. His style was well judged; yet he had retained a country awkwardness which had moved these unforthcoming people who, normally taciturn themselves, were not easily impressed by the gift of the gab. What they had witnessed was a consummate performance, a piece of theatre. How much of him was real – even the side he showed to her?

Careful arrangements had had to be made about their party's late supper. 'Gareth doesn't want anyone to take pictures of him with a glass in his hand,' Cissy explained. 'He can't afford to annoy anyone now for the wrong reason.'

At every turn Violet found herself confronted with a new reality of political life. They spent three and a half hours just waiting and eating and getting in and out of cars, during which she and Gareth were alone for no more than a couple of minutes, in an ante-room to the hotel's private salon.

'You look so beautiful,' he said. 'Not being able to kiss you is driving me mad.'

Some perverse instinct made her say, 'At least you recognise my face. Is it always going to be like this?'

Violet and Gareth drove back next afternoon to Billy Sorrell's house at Glendevon. They were accompanied by Dick and Bunty, who then took the old Bentley on into Devonport to register their entry in the round Tasmania yachting race. James was staying on in Hobart to sign documents that the lawyers had been notarising overnight. Violet learned, from a conversation between Dick McGrath and Mintie, the pilot, that James now owned the three leading papers on the island.

'He's going to be the biggest newspaper man in Australia if he keeps ridin' 'er like this,' Mintie said. 'Mr Sorrell reckons it's a bad moment to take so much on.'

'I know,' Dick answered. 'But it makes sense. He says everything's going dirt cheap now. They'll all go lower yet if the worst happens.'

The butler answered the door, and told them Billy was out riding till six o'clock.

'A whole afternoon,' Violet murmured. 'Our luck must have changed.'

'I know mine has,' Gareth said.

Later, amid the tousled sheets on his bed, she rolled over and looked down at him.

'What were you going to tell me?' she asked, her face still bland with contentment. 'I want to know what's going to happen to us when you're elected. You were going to say something last night.'

'It's still not "when", it's "if". All the experts insist I'm mad as a cut snake to say a war is even possible. "Tell 'em what they want to hear, mate, the first rule of politics." The knives will be out for me, if it goes wrong.'

'But they wouldn't cheer and yell like that if you'd really forgotten the first rule of politics, or whatever those horrible old men Pountney drinks with go on about?'

'Too right.' Gareth gave her a wicked grin. 'You know more than any of them. *You* can see a winner when it comes out of the paddock.'

His voice was still hoarse and loud from incessant use. It was hard for him to scale himself down to being in one place with one person.

'But what about us?'

'When I win there'll be London. I'll have to go quite soon after the election. When I return, you could come and work for the government.'

'Doing what?'

'Chairing committees, figurehead stuff. At least you'd see me.'

'What kind of committees?'

'Mobilisation of women during the war, rationing, information. Does it matter?'

'Well, yes, it does. I'll have to think about it.'

'That's thanks for you,' he said. He rolled her over till he was on top of her, flattening her breasts. She could feel the hardness between her thighs and tried to push him backwards.

'I want to talk to you.'

'And I want to make love to you.'

Later they too went riding through the Glendevon fields. All Violet could think about as they walked back up to the house in the evening shadows was that, whether Gareth won or lost, she was in trouble. If he won, he'd never have time for her, and if he lost, he'd be a changed man. It was like the foolishness of people saying 'Did you marry James for money?' How could anyone answer that? People were what they were. And without their money, or their success, or whatever else distinguished them, then they would have been different.

18

Returning home, Violet camped out for a few days with the children at Palm Beach, falling into a daily rhythm of sun and surf and beach picnics taken in the shade of the scrubby palms.

News of Gareth's campaign came from afar, and she heard reports on the wireless at dusk as if from a foreign country. Violet never forgot this time. Sam and Liz were delighted to be back at the beach, and pleased to have an uninterrupted spell with Violet. Liz was showing the first signs of real beauty, with straw-coloured hair, and huge eyes in a small face. She was naturally neat and tidy and fussed about her clothes and her room, forever arranging and rearranging her books. But she was subject to swings of mood and had a nervous habit of flicking her hair out of her eyes whenever she was upset. Usually any unhappiness had to do with some real or imaginary harm to one of the animals in her life – she was passionately attached to anything smaller than herself, even spiders.

Sam was quite different; it seemed a miracle that they got on so well. He habitually bit his nails to the quick, and always had a button missing from his shirt, or a rip in his trousers. He was swift to enthuse, and equally quick to lose each passion, except when it came to collecting something – anything, from cigarette cards to pine-cones. His last school report had almost reduced Violet to tears – James had been furious. Sam refused to concentrate, his teachers said, and he was forgetful and untidy.

Yet he was also endearing, even if not so immediately attractive as Liz. There was something joyous about his enthusiasms, his initial ability to pull other children into his imaginative schemes. He loved to start telling stories which Liz was supposed to finish. Sam's tales were often horrifying, peopled with weird creatures. Liz would attempt to carry on the tale, but Sam found her versions too tame for him.

But they never tired of each other's company. Violet could have watched them playing on the shore for ever, without needing anything else.

Meanwhile Gareth's campaign entered its last days. She told Cissy, briefly staying with her at the beach, about Gareth's offer of a job.

Cissy had laughed.

'He's not slow to find space at the public trough for his friends, is he?'

'Don't exaggerate. He didn't say anything about a salary.'

'If you're not paid, then it's not a real job. What are you going to do, anyway?'

'It sounds very formal – sitting on committees, or organising women's mobilisation groups.'

'You should grab it. Women always have opportunities to do things in wartime.'

It was the night of the election results, at the Constitutional Club in Parramatta. Violet arrived before James, expensively dressed as he said the occasion befitted. She caused a minor stir as she arrived in the Bentley and made her entrance along a white-tiled corridor smelling of stale beer, old dust and carbolic.

The club, a mid-Victorian mansion in some need of renovation, was grandiose, with elaborate balustrades, and stained glass windows bearing heraldic escutcheons of dubious authenticity. For many years now it had served as the National Party's Sydney headquarters.

The main room was filling up with people, their shoes echoing on scruffy parquet flooring with marks from chairs dented into its surface. There was a big, unsteady-looking stage, on which the platform was already busy. Bunting in the ANC yellow and blue hung round the galleries. The press were sitting near the stage, shrouded in cigarette smoke.

Violet found herself in the midst of several hundred Mayhew supporters, most of them local workers and sympathisers, who were drinking beer or tea according to sex and consuming sandwiches piled on trestle-tables and served by the Parramatta Club's Ladies Branch.

'It's not much of a place but I'll meet you there about eight if you want to do some slumming,' James had said. The idea of them both in these surroundings obviously amused him.

James was an unconditional snob. But it satisfied him none the less whenever Violet displayed an interest in politics, which in effect meant Gareth. As she looked around the stuffy room a new thought entered her mind: sometimes it was as if James knew all about their affair and was secretly pleased by it.

On the stage a man in a fawn suit was announcing every result as it came in, bawling the figures through a battered tin loudhailer that must have seen a lot of service at sports days and agricultural shows. The atmosphere both repelled and excited Violet. Here was ordinary Sydney life, 'than which nothing is more ordinary', as her cousin-in-law Andrew had condescendingly written in the London *Gazette* in one of his run-up pieces on the election. This was the world she had first discovered on her arrival in Australia, and though she had deserted it for James's enclosed society 'at the big end of town', she was always glad to be back. Her pleasure in being reminded of the dear old Roxy was also a rebuke to her husband. Not that he, nor his parents, were to blame that he hated this world so much. It was an effect of his education, which had ensured he only respected people like Billy Sorrell whom he had known from the cricket fields of his expensive schools since he was six or seven.

Someone touched her arm, as if to make sure of a hearing. In Rex Pountney, Violet found herself accosted by a man whose appearance guaranteed that he had never been to school with the Franklins and Sorrells. She could not help flinching in revulsion and the reflex momentarily embarrassed her. Then she saw that Gareth's agent, 'the only man who can bring in Parramatta', was in no way offended by her gesture. It probably even excited him. His paw had left a sweaty mark on her long glove, and as he leant heavily towards her she caught a whiff of stale sweat and bottled beer.

'No Mr Franklin?' he said flirtatiously, as if being on their own was a situation he could turn to erotic advantage.

'James will be here later on,' Violet explained. 'I thought I'd have a look at the party.'

'Gar isn't going to be here till later, either.'

He said 'Gar' with an emphasis that made the sentence like a nudge in the ribs. Don't think I don't know all your little secrets, his thick voice seemed to say.

Violet looked at him without reaction. Inwardly she was appalled. Gareth had assured her that he had his own key to the political agent's house. But Pountney clearly suspected her involvement. Had Gareth betrayed her, prey to one of the camaraderies that existed between men?

'He's in the office – working on a speech,' Pountney was saying. Suddenly there was an announcement from the stage.

'And the count now stands as follows: 271 seats for the National Party; 190 for the United Australia Party; 70 for Labor. To win an absolute majority, the National Party only requires another 29 seats.' There was wild cheering around the hall, and a few of the men carried on whooping like maniacs.

'They're full,' Pountney said with a wink. His face was very red, as if he had had a few himself. 'They started a bit of a party when we got the Kullawalla result – who wins there is always a favourite to sweep the whole shooting match. And Kullawalla was the day before yesterday . . .' He gave a throaty chuckle.

Violet made to move on, and Pountney shouted across the room, 'Can I have a word, Father?' O'Fallen, whom Violet now saw for the first time, was talking to a group of ladies with cheap hats. After a characteristically whispered exchange with Pountney, the priest moved in on Violet.

Pountney volunteered to find drinks for them all.

'Where's the champagne?' asked O'Fallen.

'Later,' grinned Pountney. 'And only in private. We have to be careful about the wowsers.'

'Wowsers?' asked Violet.

'Fundamentalists,' said the priest, eager as always to teach. 'They're always prominent at elections, asking candidates to come out for the teetotal lobby, bringing pressure. They're puritans, that's all.'

'And Methodists, a lot of them,' Pountney said, sourly. 'We have to make sure all our people have blameless lives when it comes to election day. And before.'

He was looking straight at Violet and now she was sure that he knew.

She tried to look as if she were interested in the rest of the conversation. In fact she could not have said, afterwards, what she had uttered or to whom. All she could register was fear and dismay at the squalor of having Pountney as an accomplice in her affair with Gareth.

James eventually arrived, and after they had spent some time exchanging pleasantries with their various political acquaintances, it became apparent that something important was happening. Rex Pountney's voice, amplified by the bullhorn, bellowed from the stage for silence. He looked enormous up there, with his wide-shouldered suit and his red, swollen face. It was clear that 'the only man who could bring in Parramatta' had something momentous to announce.

Afterwards Violet remembered his thick voice announcing Gareth's victory, and the almost simultaneous arrival of the victor himself, as a moment when her life changed. The memory was always to be dominated by Gareth, standing above the crowd, his face transfigured, his eyes apparently searching every face in the hall. Almost everyone there was left with a conviction that he had searched them out personally, to accord them a moment of recognition. Violet was sure that he had seen her too, even though she was buried in the crowd. It was only afterwards she learned that he had searched in vain, and that like many others there who would never get closer to him than a seat in the back of the hall, she had been the victim of an illusion. 'The lights were too bright for me to make out anyone's face,' he told her later. 'I looked for you everywhere – I knew you must be out there.'

At the sight of him in the most triumphant hour of his life, Violet could not bring herself to acknowledge what resentment lurked in her heart. For the sake of a nudge and a wink with Pountney, that beer-sodden toady – for nothing more – he had let her down.

Damn you, Gareth.

19

'Is Mrs James Franklin going to be the Official Hostess for our new unmarried PM?'

Violet prickled with anxiety. Needlessly, though: the article merely pointed out the dozen social occasions she'd so far shared with Gareth, in addition to the 'memorable "Victory Barbecue at Killymoon" which Mrs Franklin single-handedly organised and hosted with her husband, owner of the *Gazette*, within forty-eight hours of the National Party's mandate from the electors'.

The parties had begun the morning after the election. By tradition George and Daisy had for twenty years given an annual party in the gardens of Killymoon. In the house address book, a solid calf-bound volume as thick as a bible, the initials 'GPO', laboriously pencilled in by Daisy, stood for 'Garden Party Only'. Now Violet, assisted by the old lady herself, summoned almost everyone with any claim to importance in Sydney for a victory celebration.

There was not only the Killymoon house list. Rex Pountney produced countless names and addresses of people who had helped the campaign – schoolmistresses who had held fund-raisings, suburban matrons who had organised bring-and-buys, and an infinity of ladies with daring hats and genteel voices, many of whom were to some degree infatuated by 'the PM'. Gareth too had checked through the guest list – he was anxious, he said, not to forget some of the 'little men and women' who had helped him on the way up.

'I only wish I was to be more than your official hostess,' Violet said as they walked round the Killymoon garden just before the party, examining the barbecue pits dug by a hastily assembled team of gardeners.

'You are, to me. This is only the beginning. I couldn't manage without you,' he said, taking her arm. And with that she had to be content.

The party was destined to be a success, thanks to its efficient organisation. Coloured lights had been hung between the trees, and sixteen sheep had been slaughtered. Several dozen barrels of beer had been set up, and an army of wine-waiters, cooks and other catering staff stood by in readiness for the first arrivals.

One of the Franklins' several house guests, in Sydney for the election, was Andrew. He had put on weight, Violet noticed, but it suited him, giving him a physical presence that he had once lacked.

'When is Gareth coming to London?' he asked her, as together they watched the grounds fill up.

Andrew was prefiguring a habit that later everyone fell into – that of using Violet as a conduit to Gareth. Contrary to the truth, they all assumed she was his confidante, an extension of James Franklin, the prime minister's closest friend and ally.

'I don't know,' Violet replied. 'You've spent more time talking to him than I have.'

'Yes, but he's necessarily vague in interviews. He's developed the politician's habit of imprecision very quickly.' They were standing on the terrace above the sloping lawns of the Killymoon gardens, whose neatly manicured lawns were beginning to be churned under hundreds of feet.

Violet was about to ask after various friends in England, when they were interrupted by Cissy, who appeared with the *Gazette* photographer. She briskly organised Violet into a line with Gareth and James, Rex Pountney and a number of other party officials and politicians, standing outside the main porch of Killymoon. The flash gun seemed weak in the fading light, and Violet knew that, by the time it appeared in print, the photograph would be shadowy and unflattering.

After their group had dispersed, Cissy had time to gossip, despite her official function at the party. She was about to take a long leave from the *Gazette*, having been seconded to the newly created press department in the Mayhew government. As they glimpsed the new prime minister at the centre of a distant group of revellers, Cissy said, 'Rex Pountney told me Gareth once had an affair with old Peg Bosworth. It's hard to credit, isn't it? Except her figure's not bad, considering her age. You remember what they say about stoking the fire . . . ?'

Cissy's lecherous grin, so Violet guessed, must help make her a favourite with the intense, driven men who spent their life reporting politics. She could see that Cissy would be far better equipped to deal with the press gallery in Canberra than any run-of-the-mill representative of government, however much better educated and more polished. Gareth was astute in his appointments, even the comparatively humble ones. He saw instantly what people could do – and, usually, what they could do for him.

'Oh Cissy!' she said. 'So young, and so coarsened by the world.'

'C'mon, Vi, don't come the grand English lady with me. What do you think? Did you ever hear anything about a love affair in the past?'

'All I know is that he used to practise his speeches on Miss Bosworth. I wouldn't believe anything Pountney said. He's repellent, that man. Even his fingernails make me shudder.'

But she knew there was more to it. If Pountney gossiped about Gareth's faithful old secretary, who had been with him ever since the early days in Phillip Street, might he not also be indiscreet about her?

She hoped that Gareth had stuck to his agreement never to tell Pountney of his plan to take an apartment in Double Bay under a false name. It was partly because of Pountney's knowing looks that she had insisted on their setting up the place. She would have done so anyway, but the thought of her private life in Pountney's head, in his awful leering imagination, had settled the matter.

'While I was on the campaign trail the boys all decided that Gar was a kind of political eunuch,' Cissy went on. Violet wondered whether she might be prying. Or was it only the itch of curiosity that all journalists seemed to have? 'And someone said your friend the Jesuit called him "the political priest".'

Violet smiled. For once she was grateful to Father O'Fallen. His grasp of human nature was feebler than she thought. Perhaps priests understood nothing about sex. Even now, married, with children of her own and a lover, she felt far from an expert herself.

'Some of the press boys thought he might be, you know, queer. But I know that's not right, either. No bloke has eyes like that without being interested in women.'

'Pountney always maintains that Gar's widower status pulls in the female vote. They like to mother him; that's the theory.'

'Possible. Still, he's got a lot more attractive since he was elected. He and James make quite a pair.' There was a wistful note in Cissy's voice. 'You're real lucky, Vi, being married to him. He's the handsomest man in Sydney – far better looking than Gareth, even.'

'My God, Cissy. You think happy marriages depend on how handsome the groom looks in morning dress?'

Violet realised from Cissy's disconcerted expression that it had never crossed her mind how things really were. Just as people failed to see the reality behind newspaper paragraphs about 'the fashionable Mr and

Mrs James Franklin' so, fortunately, they were equally blind when it came to Gareth and herself.

How long could it last?

'You mean you're not happy? You certainly hide it very well. Is James . . .' Cissy faltered.

'Is James having affairs, you mean? I don't know and I don't ask is the answer to that one. But don't worry. There isn't any crisis. All I'm saying is don't think catching Mr Right solves all the problems in the world. That's the idea I had when I came here and I sometimes wonder where I got it from. I am reasonably intelligent – or at least I'm not a complete fool. But it never crossed my mind that marriage and children weren't everything . . .'

Violet shook her head and glanced away, leaving the sentence to hang unfinished in the air. Cissy had looked suddenly like a child who had seen some cherished object removed from her grasp, and Violet was not about to make things worse.

'I'm not whingeing,' Violet went on brightly, 'or to be frank I am, but I shouldn't be. I know I've been lucky in a lot of ways.'

'You sure have, Vi,' Cissy said, her face clearer now. 'I don't think there's going to be anyone for me, let alone someone like James Franklin. It looks as if my destiny's to be a career lady.'

'It might have been mine, too,' Violet said. She was thinking of her part-time work at the Roxy, and also Gareth's promise of a job. 'But it's probably too late now.'

Gareth himself had been in a state of euphoria ever since the moment of his election victory. He was constructing the new cabinet, on the assumption that within 'a year at most', there would be a war in Europe, in which Australia would also have to fight. His government was loyal to the crown and the 'old country' – but so was almost everyone in Australia. Gareth's own passion with England was, if anything, even greater since his election. It was strange to Violet that both her men should be so bewitched by the country. James, who, ironically, had probably married her because she was English; and Gareth, whose background was so different to James's. She wished that it would be Gareth, not James, who was going to see her family during the visit both men were shortly due to make to London. James had been reluctant to undertake the delivery of letters and Christmas presents on her behalf, recalling the last time he had tried to visit her father, and the fiasco on the steps of the house.

'Your parents have never liked me. Your mother writes to you as if you weren't even married.'

'I know they're difficult. But you must go. They're going to be so disappointed not to see the children.'

Violet had already packed the presents – a silver hip flask, an ormolu snuffbox and an engraved cigarette case for her father; and for her mother an angora shawl, a string of perfectly matching and graded amber beads and a photograph of the children, set in a delicate silver frame. She had also bought a leather-covered photograph album and filled it with pictures, each carefully annotated in small, neat writing. 'The beach house at Palm Beach – under construction.' A later shot showed the finished house, with the family gathered on the terrace. There were photos of Killymoon, of Daisy, of James playing tennis with a desperate-looking Father O'Fallen, of Bunty and Dick on their yacht.

But mostly the book was filled with pictures of the children – reading, sleeping, playing, swimming. Violet had spent hours sticking them into place and writing careful captions, trying as best she could to explain in pictures what her life was like. She had sent odd photographs to her mother at intervals – but the album was an attempt to flesh out the letters and the one-off shots taken at birthday parties or on special occasions.

The party shifted gear and the first wave of guests departed. Violet found herself gratefully sitting down at one of the wrought-iron tables with her husband and Andrew. The stained table-cloths had been whisked away, and the caterers had generally cleaned up and cleared away. But despite their efforts, the overall setting looked as though a battle had just been fought. Flowers were trampled and the lawn was pockmarked with heel marks. On one of the flowering cherries a branch had snapped after an exuberant party worker had attempted a victory swing. It hung like a bird's broken wing, the leaves already starting to wilt.

'What's this I hear about your new lumber mills in Tasmania, James? I thought you'd bought up enough raw supplies to keep yourself in paper till the middle of the century.' Andrew was tapping a filtered cigarette on the back of a gold cigarette case.

'I have, but it's all going cheap right now. This way I can triple our capacity, and the accountants say we double the size of the *Gazette* while reducing our print costs.'

'What about the war?' Andrew asked, igniting a heavy gold lighter.

'There isn't going to be one this year, or next year either.'

'That's not your new prime minster's view,' said Andrew. 'I'm glad for Australia's sake that Gareth takes it more seriously than you do.'

'We only differ over time,' James said – so quickly that Violet almost missed the edge of irritation in her husband's voice. He added, 'I'll tell you one thing – if there is a war, people are going to want more news, not less. And if we don't have to go outside Tasmania for our supplies, we'll be sitting pretty.'

'And what if there's paper rationing?' Andrew asked.

'Gareth's in full agreement that there won't be.'

Only later, when the trouble started, did Violet realise there had been no agreement at all. James had been calmly lying. But that night, at the victory party in the grounds of his own house, he still thought the politician was a protégé of his own.

Whenever Violet looked back on that evening, she could see too that it was the high point of her own relationship with Gareth – for a brief moment everything had looked possible. It even seemed conceivable that one day she might be Gareth's acknowledged first lady, without all the subterfuge. That night, as she found herself accepting the guests' thanks and admiration, it didn't seem like a silly dream. Even James was a benign presence.

But it was all a honeymoon, a strange slice of time between a wedding and a reality; and the last moment when James and Gareth were truly in political accord. No one could see then that the son of the failed entrepreneur who'd come up the hard way through Phillip Street was no longer for sale – no longer, at least, in Australia. If anyone could buy Gareth's time it was only Neville Chamberlain and his fellow grandees in London. James's failure to understand was as though he too had loved Gareth. It was to be a final irony, that wife and husband alike had loved him and had helped to make him.

The party continued well beyond first light, as a hot December night was followed by the fierce sun of early morning. Daisy, still on her feet, noticed Violet's exhaustion. 'This weather's no good for anyone,' she said, as they trailed up to bed. 'It was like this in 1914 – George and I went up to the mountains for Christmas, but it wasn't any cooler there. And the fires – the whole land was like a bed of cinders.'

'Don't remind yourself,' Violet said. 'The weather will probably break this time. It can't go on like this.'

20

Gareth's first letter from London was addressed to Miss Harcourt, at the Double Bay apartment. The same diplomatic bag had brought another, from James to Mrs J. Franklin at Killymoon. Violet wondered if anyone had noticed the connection between the two letters. The idea was followed immediately by the silly thought that maybe James himself knew, and that both men had handed in their letters together, in collusion.

Gareth had become, she saw, a name-dropper – the Duke of Westminster, Lord Cranborne, 'Chips' Channon, the Coopers, and Churchill had all invited him – to Belgrave Square and Eaton Place, the Ritz and Claridges, and Chartwell and Belvoir and other ancestral homes of the British political establishment; not to mention Windsor Castle, where the new Queen Elizabeth, preoccupied with her own daughters, 'Lilibet' and Margaret Rose, had been surprised to discover that he had neither wife nor children. 'She sees me as a grieving widower,' he had written:

It wasn't possible to explain that as Kay died before I was thirty and the next ten years were mainly spent in court I haven't had a lot of experience of the nursery or of family life.

The more formal side of his visit was not going so well.

I spent another unproductive hour with Chamberlain this morning. It's obvious to half Britain (and all the readers of Northcliffe's *Daily Mail*!) that Herr Hitler isn't going to be satisfied until he has completely rewritten the treaty of Versailles and in all probability recreated a German empire on a scale even old Bismarck failed to imagine. Yet Chamberlain called him 'a sincere little man' and clings to the idea that his 'scrap of paper' at Munich will save Europe from war and provide adequate time for England to get her defences in order. I tried to ask him about the intelligence reports on the German air force – they have these new Messerschmitts which apparently outfly anything the English can put in the air, but he didn't seem impressed. 'I'm afraid you've been listening too much to Churchill' was all he said. Like so many others, he sees Churchill as a political failure who looks to the war to restore his fortunes. The same goes for Duff Cooper and anyone who opposes the Foreign Office policy of appeasement.

It's very disappointing. As far as I can see the great British Empire is going down the drain.

She could scarcely be bothered to read James's letter. But she wondered, indifferently, if he had planned to extend his stay because of an affair or because, like Gareth, he was fascinated at being close to the centres of power in Whitehall.

Folding Gareth's letter, Violet sighed, and carefully put it away in its hiding place. While she had been meeting him at Rex Pountney's home, she had concealed his letters under a floorboard at the beach house. After she had insisted that they lose no time in escaping this connection with Pountney, she had begun to hide them in the apartment at Double Bay.

She closed the drawer in which she stored all her mementoes of Gareth, and appraised the new apartment. Its main feature was a huge bed with crisp new linen sheets, facing an open verandah that overlooked the yacht basin. The apartment was functional and very masculine; the carpets were dark brown, the walls cream. For the drawing-room Violet had bought a Chippendale desk and a heavy chintz-covered sofa. An oak refectory table with Regency ladder-back chairs filled the dining-room. There were Victorian water-colours on the walls.

It was Violet's creation entirely, and considering it had all been done very quickly – and in secret – she was pleased with the result. Her inspiration had been memories of Peter Ironside's chambers in the Albany, near the Ritz in Piccadilly, and she was delighted to discover that she had guessed Gareth's tastes correctly.

Moreover, it was theirs alone. The thought gave her huge relief, as she shut the door behind her and squirrelled the key back into the compartment of her handbag containing a tortoiseshell mirror. Gareth had wanted to hire a manservant to live there permanently, but Violet had resisted the suggestion; it would have been just one more person who would have needed to know. It hadn't been like furnishing the beach house, so much as an efficient camping expedition. No longer was there time in Gareth's schedule for them to leave the city together. Nowadays, the house at Palm Beach was used only by women and children – almost as if war had already become a fact.

The pattern of Violet's life was changing in other ways – though she was doubtful if it had done so for the better. For Cissy had been right so far about the 'job'. The Women's Information Committee for New South Wales showed every promise of being a desultory, formalised body that no one would want to take seriously.

It was chaired by Connie Meldrum, the wife of Gareth's old rival for the party leadership. Connie was in her middle fifties, an ex-headmistress of a girls' boarding school. She was small and slightly overweight, with a tight determined mouth and a gift for annoying everyone.

The other members included the retired senior matron of a teaching hospital, a university lecturer in education, a dietician, the wife of the mayor of Sydney, and the publisher of the *Australian Women's Weekly*. Violet noticed that she was at least ten years younger than any of the others.

Connie had prepared a neatly typed agenda. She suggested that they all note it down, and Violet felt that she was taking dictation. Jerry Jerome, the magazine publisher, obviously thought so too. He sighed, and when their eyes met across the well-polished official table he looked down quickly as if to avoid being rebuked by teacher for not paying attention.

'In my experience there is almost nothing women cannot do when it comes to an emergency,' Connie said. 'Our job is to equip our women so that when the worst happens they will be able to free our fighting men for the job they are ready to do. You notice that, in common with the government, I prefer "when" and not "if". From the start we must assume that war is inevitable.' She's been listening to Gareth, Violet thought.

Jerome was drumming his manicured fingers on the table as if practising a silent scale. On the way out at the end of the morning he stood aside to let Violet step into the lift. He was too elegant for their mundane government premises, and could hardly wait to get back to what he regarded as civilisation. However, his commitments were not too pressing for him to invite Violet to luncheon at the Australia Hotel.

'Don't suppose your husband would mind,' he said after she refused. 'I expect he'd be pleased you were getting some relaxation. There won't be much of that if the Headmistress has her way.'

Violet could not help smiling. The morning had indeed been like a return to school.

'She'll probably have us working round the clock. I only hope it serves some purpose.'

'I haven't got time to find out, I'm afraid,' Jerome said, stepping into the street like a man who had been released from jail. 'But if you change your mind about luncheon any day give me a call.'

When Violet told Daisy about the committee that night the old lady was quite shocked to hear that they had met in an office.

'In the last war the ladies used to come here for tea. And we used the ballroom at Government House for packing the billies.'

'What were they?'

'We had hundreds of women knitting scarves and comforters and making parcels to send to the boys in France. We used to pack little presents, cigarettes, matches, lollies, and sometimes even a drop of spirits, in the billy-cans they had in the trenches. But all the committee work was done in ladies' homes – I was out to tea every day for two years.'

Violet thought such activities sounded very marginal to the real business of war. She only hoped her own work would not be as limited.

21

Christmas came and went. Violet thought longingly of the crisp cold of England, the snow, the bare trees and the burgeoning London shops. The weather in recent days had turned hotter than she could remember, and was set to break all records. After the New Year the temperature soared into the hundreds and stayed there, day after day. The heat was like a physical wall. On the road between the beach and Sydney, smoke could be seen curling off the distant yellow hills. There had been no rain since October; crops had wilted and livestock were dying. In the north, where the temperatures were the fiercest, farmers were shooting cattle and sheep, burying the carcasses in open graves before abandoning their arid properties.

In the city, dust clouds darkened the midday sun. The dirt sneaked in through windows and doors, getting into hair and mouths and under fingernails and making people short-tempered. For a number of elderly people the heat was fatal.

Gareth delayed his return from London, partly for negotiations about the sale of wheat, flour and wool. In his absence, Lynch Meldrum had set up a commission to deal with the worst effects of the drought. From Queensland to Tasmania bushfires now raged. The newspapers shunted stories of wool quotas on to inside pages, as the headlines announced the latest information on the weather.

Connie and Violet transferred their energies as well, and the Women's Information Committee, now known as WIC, joined forces with the Red Cross to bring relief to people who had been forced to abandon their homes. There was also a growing number of refugees from Europe, likewise living in temporary hostels following the loss of everything they had.

In the second week of January, news reached Sydney that the hills outside Adelaide had exploded into flames. Cars in the city were blowing up like bombs whenever sparks from the fires connected with petrol tanks. In the previous week it had been a joke that the cabbies in

Sydney were frying eggs on the bonnets of their Packards. Now it wasn't funny. Seventy people had died in Victoria, and babies were being sent to hospital suffering from dehydration. There were even food shortages. One paper blamed the government for committing itself too heavily to exports while there was an emergency 'in our own back yard'. Violet snorted with annoyance as she read it over breakfast, already irked by the heat. She had become almost as avid a newspaper reader as Ben, who had sent a card from Rangoon complaining about how long it took to get contracts signed in Burma. 'I hear your political buddy is all the rage in London,' he added. Certainly more so than in the pages of the *Sun*, she thought. The implied criticism of Gareth was the first she had seen since the election. She was to remember it later as a straw in the wind.

'I need a favour – can I borrow your car?' It was Cissy on the telephone. Breakfast was being laboriously cleared away by a new maid, who looked stupefied by the heat.

Cissy sounded worried.

'Yes – what's the matter?'

'You know my mum lives up in Katoomba – or just outside – and of course she's not on the phone. We've just had a report here that Katoomba's being evacuated, and there's no way to find out if she's gone too. She's getting very slow . . . I keep telling her she shouldn't be in such an isolated spot any more . . .'

'I'm sure she's all right.'

'So am I, of course; but you never know, especially when people are getting on . . .'

'I'll drive you,' Violet said. 'Even if it's for nothing, you'll feel better.'

'Yeah. I'm sure it's nothing. But all the same . . .' Violet could hear the relief in her voice.

They arranged to meet outside the *Gazette* offices in an hour's time. Violet quickly saw the children off to school and packed blocks of ice in the eski and some bandages and towels in a beach bag.

As they drove west towards the mountains the temperature steadily rose. The moment they left Springwood it was as if the weather had changed – instead of unblemished blue the sky turned a bilious yellowy grey. It became increasingly overcast the further they climbed. Soon there was grit turning the windscreen opaque, and even clouds of what might have been insects but that were in fact charred particles. Dust was seeping in through the closed windows. Cissy stuffed towels along the joins to try to keep it out; but that meant no air in the car, so they alternated between the two evils. The acrid smoke made their eyes water as they strained in second gear up a road that grew steeper and more winding.

They almost didn't get to Katoomba. About three miles outside, where a group of vehicles stood at the level-crossing gates, a Bush Fire Brigade chief advised them to turn back.

'No place for women up there,' he said, pointing with a huge blackened thumb. 'We're gettin' 'em all out.'

He spoke flatly, with a rebuke in his voice. Didn't these two unaccompanied women know any better? He lacked the conviction, however, to resist the power of the press. After a couple of minutes' resistance he let them pass, and even sneaked a smile of comfort at Violet. She saw that he had been reluctant to lose face with his bunch of unshaven, red-eyed fire-fighters, lying about smoking, or leaning against the gate with the exaggerated slowness and care of people who had been a long time without sleep.

Violet was grateful even for this guarded comfort. Although they had resolutely avoided anything but optimistic remarks about Mrs Greeley in her isolated cottage, each knew what the other was thinking. Cissy said, 'In winter she gets cut off sometimes, and in the summer they all forget about her except the postie. But someone will have been up, won't they, Vi?'

Violet tried not to share her look of panic. As they got closer, it seemed that Mrs Greeley ran a good chance of having been forgotten altogether in the chaos they saw unfolding.

Katoomba was like an Alpine village, perched on the edge of a mountain range and served by a spectacular railway. The road flattened out shortly before the first houses. Round a bend they saw several hundred people apparently parked by the roadside. Others were trudging along the road, some carrying bundles. They all had the same robotic, exhausted look and many had dirty clothes and faces. It was now unbearably hot, a throat-smarting gritty heat which drained energy and will. Many of the people seemed no more than half awake.

A stream of cars and emergency vehicles was heading east; but they were the only people travelling in the other direction. 'Turn round – they've banned all cars there,' a passing driver shouted.

'It's no good,' Cissy said. 'Even if we get there, we'll be too late.'

'Look, it's clearer here. Nobody's going to stop me now.'

'Did you read yesterday about those people in Victoria who were boiled alive while sheltering in a water tank?'

'*Cissy*! If you don't shut up . . . What's happening here?'

It was another check-point, close to the station. The road had been closed, with a row of boxes that looked as if they had been purloined from the corner store. There was another group of dispirited-looking fire-fighters taking a break. The woman in the shop had come out with bottles of soda and thick sandwiches. There was a picnic air about the people eating and drinking against a thorn hedge, until you caught the expressions on their faces. Some of the men lay as if they had collapsed on their feet. Violet was beginning to realise how frightened she was.

Cissy got out and waved her press card hysterically at a man in high boots and the fire-fighter's ashy working shirt. Violet watched him as a fire brigade truck pulled up. A man, walking so heavily his boots could have been made of lead, stepped out of the red-painted fire-wagon and moved the cartons, kicking them over into the side of the road. He climbed back in and started his vehicle again. Almost without thinking, Violet too started up and followed it. Cissy caught her at a run and jumped in after a few yards on the running-board.

'Go straight on,' Cissy directed excitedly. They were left alone on the smoky road as the fire-wagon turned off. Violet would have been grateful for anything to delay the prospect ahead. She could not see fifty yards and it looked denser further along the narrow road. 'Maybe she's already been rescued.'

'I know she's been left,' Cissy said. 'I've known it all along.' She was close to tears.

'It's obviously much worse down there.' Violet was saying anything that came into her head, to prevent Cissy collapsing with hysteria. She swerved to avoid a fireball, pretty and harmless-looking as it danced across the road. Then, with relief, she saw they had climbed level with the houses.

Cissy's mother lived beyond the Carrington, a grand colonial-style white hotel that lured people from Sydney for the weekends. It dominated one of the steepest main streets in Australia. The moment their road started to plunge, there was oily, sinister smoke. Violet almost missed a gear when a shed exploded somewhere on the side of the hill. Some way below, obscured by the murk, she thought she glimpsed dirty-looking flames.

'That's my mother's house.' On the outskirts of the town Cissy pointed to a shabby clapboard bungalow set on a hillock. There was smoke rising from the bush below, but the house itself had suffered no damage so far.

The track to the bungalow was deserted, except for two dogs who came up to them the moment they stopped. They scratched at the car, whining to get in.

'She probably left long ago,' Violet said. 'Heavens, it's terrifying!' she exclaimed involuntarily, opening the car door and wincing at the heat outside. She let the dogs jump into the back of the Tourer. They sat panting, their tongues hanging out.

They drove up to the house through the smoke. Cissy jumped out almost before they had stopped, and ran to open the front door. There was a roaring noise in the air, otherworldly and frightening, as the fire sucked up everything in its path, like a giant engine running out of control.

It was hard to breathe in the house. Violet remembered reading about people dying of suffocation when they were trapped in the centre of a fire, in the vortex where flames had devoured all the oxygen. She felt a gust of wind on her back and pulled the door closed behind her. The room was small and immaculately neat and tidy. A wireless standing in the corner startled her by crackling into life. She recalled that at a certain heat the airwaves were affected. As she crossed the room she heard Cissy cry out from the back of the bungalow.

Violet ran into the small bedroom. Cissy was crouched over her mother's body on the floor. The old lady was still breathing, but her face was pallid and her lips had a bluish tinge. On the walls were framed pictures of Cissy: at high-school graduation, at her first dance, holding a copy of the *Gazette*. She was an only child, a source of pride.

From below the house, they heard a loud boom. Violet looked out of the window. The fire was eating through the bush below the garden. As she watched, in sick fascination, the flames licked along the white wicket fence, consuming it like cardboard. The stripped and tortured gum trees were crackling; suddenly one large one exploded into flames and within seconds had toppled sideways, burning a path as it fell.

Fear made her move and, ripping the coverings off the bed, she ran to the bathroom. They covered Mrs Greeley with wet blankets and draped soaked towels over their heads. With Cissy holding her head and Violet her feet they struggled towards the front door. The old lady was still unconscious; they stumbled under the heavy weight and heard Mrs Greeley's knee bang sharply against the corner of a chair.

They opened the front door on to a solid wall of heat which threatened to slam them back into the relative cool of the house. A tree fell against the back wall of the wooden building, and panic gave them extra strength. The pathway to the car was still clear, though black smoke was billowing up the hill.

The paint on the bonnet was bubbling in the heat and the two stray dogs were whining loudly. Violet put Mrs Greeley down and then ran back to the house whilst Cissy shouted for her to stop. She grabbed a saucepan from the kitchen and filled it with water, then raced back to the car. She grasped the door-handle with a wet towel and between them they bundled the old lady on to the back seat before jumping in themselves. Flames were licking along the street, jumping through the dried grass like a million devils.

Clouds of smoke filled the road they had driven up. Violet threw the car into second gear and raced uphill, swerving to avoid fireballs and falling branches. Within minutes they had passed the town boundary. The air was clearer as they climbed higher. Violet wound down the window and breathed deeply. Her eyes were red, her eyelashes singed, and her hands were shaking so hard that she gripped the wheel till her knuckles shone white under her tan. Cissy was crouched on the back seat, her mother's head in her lap.

'I think she's dying – her breathing is getting fainter.'

'Where does this road go?' Violet asked urgently.

'Over the side of this mountain and back on to the plains. It's an awful road – hardly more than a track.'

'There's no choice – the wind is blowing the fire uphill.' Violet was taking the car as fast as she dared along the deeply rutted track. Several times she thought she had lost control, as it floundered in the deep hard ruts carved out over the years by passing carts. They were buffeted and jostled until every bone and muscle screamed in pain.

Below they could see the fires raging unchecked, leaving behind blackened tree stumps. The car skidded on a bend and slid helplessly into a tree, bouncing off it and back on to the track. Violet slowed right down and changed into first gear. They crawled on down the hill into Wallamba.

The town was in chaos. Families were piling furniture on to pickup trucks; children were running this way and that, clutching precious treasures in their arms, weeping in fright. In the centre of the town, a bush ranger was bellowing instructions through a megaphone.

'Which way to a hospital?'

The ranger looked at the burnt paint and the smouldering tyres. 'Two miles down – emergency unit. You'll get through.'

They joined a slow-moving line of traffic that was travelling down towards the plains. Beside the railway line, men were hacking down the bush, creating a natural divide to try to halt the flames.

Ten minutes later they were pulling up at a crossroads where a Red Cross tent was pitched and fire engines and relief units had congregated. Violet switched off the engine and sank her head down on the steering-wheel, barely aware that Mrs Greeley was being lifted out of the car and placed on a stretcher, or that the two dogs had leapt out of the car and were now running around, yapping hysterically. Later she reckoned she must have fainted for a few moments, because the next thing she knew was that someone was gently shaking her shoulder, and a male voice was asking if she was all right, if she wanted a drink.

She got out, her legs trembling so much she had to hold on to the orderly's arm to stop herself falling.

'You could do with a stretcher too.' He handed her a glass of water and helped her sit down on the grass.

'How's the old lady?' Violet asked.

'Bad – but she should pull through. Get some rest. You're all in.'

The Pathe Pictorial truck drove up just after the photographer from the Australian News Agency had finished with his flash camera.

A small energetic man wearing a trilby leapt out.

'Wait a mo, Mrs Franklin: we want to interview you for the newsreels.'

'Can't I go and get cleaned up first?'

'You're fine as you are – it's only going to take sixty seconds.' He was holding a stop-watch in one hand, like a time-keeper at a running track. The camera was set on a tripod in the back of an open truck, already revolving.

'What happened when you found the old lady, Mrs Franklin? Just tell us in your own words.'

22

Next day a different journalist rang Killymoon every minute. Violet must have seen a dozen reporters in the course of the morning, and there was even a posse of photographers following her when she left to visit Mrs Greeley, in hospital in Sydney. The story that eventually caused most controversy carried the headline WOMEN IN THE FRONT LINE.

Connie Meldrum's letter in the *Sydney Morning Herald* also cited Violet and Cissy's bushfire experience to telling effect. Here was a chance to do more good for the Women's Information Committee than they could have achieved in a month of meetings.

If they had obeyed the rules, devised and operated by men, there would have been yet another fatality. What these two heroic women have demonstrated is that society ignores the capacities of half of its members only at a great cost to itself.

'You shouldn't have called us heroines,' Violet said. 'We were scared half to death and it's sheer good luck that we weren't asphyxiated.' The memory still made her feel shivery.

'You have to take your chances when they come, my dear,' Connie answered. 'Even the press is on our side now. If the only way to get them to take us seriously is to make you and Cissy heroines, then I'm afraid you'll have to bite on the bullet. The papers need success stories in these awful times. And this is the first good Australian news for months.'

The story was also distributed world-wide by the agencies. An inside page of the London *Daily Express* described Violet as the wife of the proprietor of the *Sydney Gazette* and unofficial hostess for Australia's new prime minister. In the *Chicago Tribune* a photograph showed her with the two dogs, over a caption describing how she had rescued them as well as Mrs Greeley.

Gareth, seeing her in the Pathe-Pictorial newsreel, sent an exultant letter tinged with concern.

You can't imagine how wonderful it was to see you on the newsreels and in the papers. I wanted to tell everyone that I was in love with you, but all I could say was you were a friend. Every man watching could think of nothing but how he wanted to change places with your husband.

The worst ordeal was seeing herself in the newsreel. Aggie had called, to say that Jack wanted her to see it privately at the Roxy the night before they began a public showing. It had been impossible to disappoint her friends, and in any case she had been curious to see herself for the first time on the screen.

The report of 'Australia's Raging Inferno' came first, with pictures from all over the country. The section on New South Wales was horrifying; but it ended on an optimistic note, with a hospital scene of Mrs Greeley sitting up in bed and praising her rescuers. The interview with Violet came immediately before, filmed as she was standing beside the Rugby Tourer, which showed all the signs of its recent adventures in the pitted, bubbled paintwork, and the scrapes and dents in its wings.

Bill, who was operating the projector, stopped the film when the final interview was over.

'Don't turn up the lights,' Violet said. She turned to Aggie. 'I hardly looked like Joan Crawford, did I?'

In the gloom Aggie was studying her strangely. She had been as shocked as Violet was by the face that had looked out so directly from the screen. There were shadows under her eyes and a discernible droop in her stance. But it wasn't just that Violet had looked tired. There was something else that had caught Aggie's attention – and was to catch the notice of James and even of her father, later in London when they saw the newsreel. Not only had time further defined the classical elegance of her features. There was a knowing, guarded look in her eyes, a stubbornness in the set of her mouth. She hadn't grown less beautiful as she had grown older – even the dirty streaks on her face couldn't obscure that – but the innocence and gullibility had gone. Violet was more taken aback than she cared to admit. It was as though someone had handed her a mirror for the first time.

The newsreel rolled on again and the famous Pathe cock strutted on the screen.

Afterwards they had drinks in the office, which was nowadays smartly decorated and furnished with comfortable chairs.

'You must feel a bit shocked to be on the silver screen without all your war-paint,' Bill said. 'But you don't have to worry, Vi. I thought you looked beaut. Like one of those Bolshie women soldiers who've just been storming the palace in one of those Russian films.'

They laughed at the backhandedness of his compliment, and Aggie said, 'If things go on like this we'll probably all end up in uniform.'

The item about the bushfire had been followed by a piece of film about Gareth in London, inspecting aircraft and other military hardware. Violet had stiffened in her seat as she saw his larger than life figure striding along a row of fighter planes at a windswept, rainy aerodrome.

'Too right,' said Jack. 'I'll be signing up, for one.' He ignored Aggie, who looked as though she wanted to bite her tongue out. 'Your Mr Mayhew's a good bloke. He doesn't try to kid anyone about the future.'

The screen image of Violet, besmirched, shaky, but at bottom self-determined, was also to bring a response from Ben. He had seen the photographs in the *Chicago Tribune* and the *Express*, and also a story in the *South China Post*. Immediately he had written, enclosing the cuttings.

The pictures are blurred, but one can still see you've changed. You look tougher, as though you've been through an ordeal – and something more. I liked the dogs – a nice touch.

As you may have heard, Litzie and her parents got out of Vienna with the Nazis on their heels and are in New York. In the mean time she has kicked me out and is involved with some new bunch of fanatic lefties. I guess, all things considered, that the split is for the best.

Her cousin Joe wasn't so lucky. He and his family were arrested and badly beaten up. Joe lost all his money trying to bribe the guards – but his wife was shot anyway. I'd tell you more, but he's understandably reluctant to give details. He's *en route* now from Czechoslovakia to Australia, and has your address. Can you help look after him? He used to teach psychology at the university. I'd come myself, but there's one heck of a lot to do preparing for this European brawl.

Don't ask Joe too many questions, will you? The answers could be unspeakable.

I see they say that your new prime minister is wowing the London ladies and that you're described as his hostess in Sydney. What the hell does that mean?

Other people fleeing for their lives had already been passing through Violet's hands. The WIC had suspended much of its war work during the drought. What it couldn't put off, though, was the relocation of Jewish refugees. It made Violet feel like two people, one of them increasingly unreal, to move between Killymoon on the one hand, and her job, on the other, organising a stream of empty-handed families – or, more often now, fragments of families. Every day she grew more conscious of glimpsing things unknown even to James and his like in the world of newspapers.

She came home one evening from the WIC office to find him back, two days earlier than announced in his cable. James too had altered his view of Violet since seeing her in the Pathe newsreel. He greeted her with a look of pride that she, still impatient for Gareth's return from London, found unpleasantly disturbing.

Everyone was in the drawing-room, where Sam and Liz, surrounded by wrapping paper and empty boxes, had been opening their late Christmas presents. Daisy too had received presents from England; the shawls and scarves, and the toys and trinkets on the carpet made the room look as if James had bought up half of Bond Street. Daisy's cheeks were slightly flushed and there was an empty glass of port by her elbow. Violet too accepted a glass of wine.

Sam had a set of lead soldiers – 200 of them, packed in tissue paper in a wooden box. There were diagrams to show the battle order at Waterloo, and he was clearing the wrapping paper to make a space to set them out. There was also a model train from Gamages, the 'Royal Scot', record-holder for the fastest time between London and Glasgow. With it came 20 feet of tracks complete with points, and two stations, level-crossings with gates, and signals. Liz had been showered with clothes – a white mink muff, which everyone laughed at in view of the heat, a tweed coat from Harrods, a silk party dress from Fenwicks.

'Your mother gave me some suggestions . . .' James admitted. Violet held back an exclamation of surprise. It was almost impossible to imagine her mother and James exchanging ideas about shopping. He handed Violet a pile of neatly wrapped parcels, from several different people.

Many of them were apparently to do with Pathe-Pictorial. Already her father had sent a telegram: 'Congratulations – I'm proud to have a hero in the family.' It had also announced that he was sending a package containing Harry's medals from the Great War. Though Violet had been pleased with the telegram, she was angry that it had taken an action like that for her father to show approval.

'Your father insisted that I see the newsreel with him,' James had said. 'I think he went a dozen times. But then everyone saw it. The Duke of Westminster invited me shooting – he was amused when I told him that we had practically met on his wedding boat. He's married again, by the way.'

Even from a distance of 12,000 miles she had become an asset. James's passport to the aristocracy. She remembered that on a previous occasion Westminster had been uncommonly rude about Australians – he had made some fatuous comment about them walking on ceilings. Now James was mentioning him as if he were an old friend. Violet wondered what such people would have done if the newsreel had been about a divorce scandal.

She examined her presents before opening them. Among the familiar handwriting on the labels – her parents, Aunt Henrietta, Andrew and Petra – was a gift from Tony Quigley.

'How on earth? Where did you see him? How is the old monster?'

'Still monstrous – but he insisted I bring you this. I don't know what it is. I met him about a dozen times; he's everywhere.'

Violet laughed. James too was in an extraordinary mood. She tore the wrapping off Quigley's present. Inside was a copy of *When The Going Was Good*.

23

Joseph Sternberg heard the latest news of troubled Europe through the wireless officer of the SS *Port of Wellington*, as they were steaming into Sydney Harbour. After he had fled Vienna, Litzie's cousin had subsisted for some months in Prague. But in September 1938 Hitler had invaded Czechoslovakia, too, and he had been forced to flee again.

Joseph disembarked, thinking about the invaders marching over the cobbles of Wenceslas Square, while his first glimpses of Sydney seemed, as he later remarked, 'innocent and blithe in the way a child is, or should be'. In his collection of essays, *A Map for the Desert*, he was later to analyse his impressions of Australia, in a way that drew upon his European nightmares. In Prague he had been hungry, having spent all his money on what had proved a vain attempt to save his wife from the Nazis. There had been fear in the streets, and he had walked cautiously, afraid of being identified as Jewish by local 'people's vigilantes', a 'guttural, beer-swilling rabble of unemployed thugs', as he was to write, 'with armbands and cropped hair, eager to practise their bad German, more eager still to ape the brutalities they associated with their Nazi brethren across the border. Hourly they expected this Aryan army to arrive and help them cleanse the city of its "racially impure elements".' In Sydney, there had been rain at dawn, so everything smelled fresh under the alien sunlight. The people, he noted, seemed to have a national superiority complex. 'The English regard Australians as a cockney species marooned on the wrong side of the earth. To me they seemed aristocrats possessed of an effortless superiority conferred by climate. Even the most ordinary people had something sunny and languid about them, a lizard content.'

Violet couldn't forgive herself for arriving late to meet Joseph. Connie had said she mustn't miss that afternoon's committee meeting, and Violet had miscalculated the time it would take him to clear customs and immigration. When she found he had already dis-embarked she was shot through with guilt, imagining him confused at finding no one to welcome him.

She need not have worried. Joseph was sitting on his single suitcase, puffing a cheroot and reading the paper. He gave an impression not of a helpless fugitive but of a competent man in control of everything about him.

Killymoon delighted her guest, particularly the garden, which he toured with Daisy, sharing her enthusiasm for a shower of rain that promised to brighten everything, though without making much impression on the long-parched and unabsorbent earth. He also made instinctive friends with the children, though he was somehow taken aback by Liz and protested fiercely when Sam called him 'Uncle Joey'. With the adults, however, he was pleasant and yet unreachable.

'Ben sent this letter for you.' Violet had handed it to him the moment they entered, thinking he would be eager to find such a lifeline. Instead he put it aside to read later and gravitated towards the garden, where he refused to share Daisy's umbrella, but insisted on holding it for her while staying in the rain himself. When they came in his damp hair was slicked back off his face, accentuating his fine head.

She rang James at the office to remind him that he was due home for dinner. It took her a long time to get hold of him and when she did it sounded as if he was carrying on another conversation at the same time. No, there was no question of coming back for dinner. He would sleep at Macquarie Street, if he slept at all.

There was a new crisis coming in Europe, he explained. He would probably have to keep the political staff up half the night before they got it right. He was in a state of excitement; Violet remembered Cissy describing how his readiness to roll up his sleeves and join in endeared him to the staff.

'Ben's cousin has arrived,' she said.

'Oh God, I forgot. I'll be back for an hour, then.'

In the event he stayed only fifty minutes. He cross-questioned Joseph about Prague, but without receiving any more than vague answers. Only when he could speak in generalities was Joseph prepared to talk about his life back in Europe. Conversation briefly turned to the recent drought, and he remarked:

'Where I come from, disasters are not "natural", as they say, but of human construction. People give these catastrophes labels culled from politics and political leaders, not geography: fascism or communism, Hitler or Stalin . . . Australia, as I could see merely from the ease of the immigration formalities, has not fallen a prey to these human epidemics. On the other hand,' turning to Violet, 'I understand that your committee has been concerned for some months with preparing Australian women for their lives in wartime.

'It seems to me that even this place is vulnerable, since you too are aware that one day soon the sun might turn to blood.'

At Vienna University, Joseph had held a full professorship in psychology, despite still being in his middle thirties. James, discovering that their guest had written several books, suggested 'a quick piece' in the *Gazette*, describing his recent experiences.

Joseph took a long time to reply. Finally he said: 'It will take me a lifetime to write about it. If I ever do.'

James, to everyone's relief, forbore to make one of his harsh, sardonic comments, and concentrated instead on his *crème brûlée*.

Daisy gave James a reproachful look – don't you realise the poor man's suffering from a terrible bereavement? it implied. From then on her son did most of the talking. He gave his views on Czechoslovakia, so vividly that it seemed as though it was the host who had experienced the traumas of Europe first-hand, not the quiet man sitting next to Daisy. Violet saw that James was confused beneath his garrulity. He appreciated the reason for their guest's reluctance to talk, or so he thought, but was too much of a journalist to be patient with it. He made his excuses and, as soon as was decent, or a shade before, he returned to his office.

Joseph too retired early, being given a lift by Sean in the Delage to an address in Paddington where he said friends of his had already found him lodgings and work. Despite his reticence Violet had the feeling that Litzie's distinguished cousin would shortly have a great deal more to say for himself, in a way that she would not be able to ignore.

Gareth returned from London in February. Rex Pountney had mobilised a large crowd at the harbour to greet the Cooee, the flying-boat of Qantas-Imperial Airways, when it splashed down on to the waters of the bay. Violet was not amongst them. They cheered and waved banners as Gareth stepped ashore, jostling to shake his hand. Parents pushed their children forward to greet him or held them up for a better view.

Most of the publicity surrounding his homecoming was good. Photographs in the papers the following day showed him smiling and laughing. The picture in the *Gazette* captured him next to James, shaking hands.

But the enthusiasm of the press was short-lived. It had begun to be intimated that the prime minister should not be spending so much time in London, to the neglect of Australia. The only paper to carry an editorial of wholehearted support was the *Gazette*.

The outstanding feature of this year has been the growth of Mr Mayhew in political stature. He has proved his capacity to take a grip on affairs and to give a lead. No one has ever denied that he is one of the best public speakers in Australia. Nor has anyone questioned his ability as a debater of singular brilliance. Yet in spite of these great qualities, he has done and said things that made seasoned politicians shudder, shake their heads woefully, and murmur that a man like that would never make a successful politician.

Well, he has confounded these wiseacres . . .

Elsewhere, there was an undercurrent of feeling that he should have returned sooner to fight the effects of the drought. In his absence, Lynch Meldrum's political star had risen. Connie was surprisingly loyal to the party leader, but she was quick to see Gareth's support of Britain as a gift to the opposition.

'He was right to stay on until he'd got them to agree to what he wanted. And he was right anyway to insist that if it does come to war, Aussie soldiers will only be led by Aussie generals. But dinners at Windsor Castle, when half the country's blazing. That wasn't very clever politics.'

Once home, however, Gareth seemed to be everywhere at once. Violet's heart raced every time the phone rang at Killymoon. When eventually he telephoned, she could hear aides in the background, and their conversation was brief and unsatisfactory. It was clear that there would be no chance, for weeks, for Gareth to find the time or the opportunity to go to the Double Bay apartment. Violet felt strangely betrayed. She had arranged armfuls of flowers there on his return; days later she went over to empty the vases of their drooping blooms.

'You know the PM's going to Brisbane?' Connie asked Violet one day, across a desk piled high with files.

'No,' Violet replied truthfully. 'I heard he was planning some trips . . .'

'Well, I've heard he'll be in Brisbane on Friday for a few days and I think you ought to stick close to him. I'd go myself but there's too much to be done. Someone has to catch his ear.'

'Why?' Violet forced herself to sound casual.

'Because it's easy for him to forget us. Don't think I don't keep reminding Lynch about the woman's side of things. But he says it's Gar's committee, Gar's idea, difficult stuff politically, the usual flannel

223

we get. You're well known now, you can talk to the women there, you can find out whether they'll be able to work in the factories when the war starts.'

Violet knew that Connie would expect her to question this, and she had to fight hard to keep the excited smile from her face as she said, 'I thought our responsibilities were for New South Wales.'

'For the moment.' In Connie's hands the range of WIC's responsibilities had expanded almost daily. All her life, Violet realised admiringly, Connie had been confined to too small a canvas. As a headmistress, she had been in charge of 500 girls – now she was thinking on a bigger scale altogether.

'Call it a fact-finding mission,' she told Violet. 'We need to know if they're doing anything up there that we can do here. And remember, it's useful to us to keep your name in the papers.'

James's chauffeur, Sean, drove Violet to the railway station and carried her matching pigskin luggage on to the platform. Anxiously she scanned the crowd for Gareth. The first person she recognised was Rex Pountney, and her heart sank; a bad omen, she thought. Wearing a checkered suit and a pork-pie hat, Pountney was shouting at a railway official across several rows of suitcases.

Gareth was almost invisible, shaking hands amid a crowd of supporters who were waving placards saying GAR. She found herself wondering disloyally whether Pountney had been responsible for getting the crowd together. He was still arguing with the guard, who was gesticulating frantically towards the train. Three children, clutching autograph books, tried to get close to Gareth. But Pountney, spotting them, broke off and intercepted them, with a hint of former athleticism. He shooed them away, raising a fist in a gesture of surprising and inappropriate violence.

Cissy was waiting at the barrier to the platform. She waved to Violet, who said:

'Did you see that awful man threatening those children? He must be drunk. That's the worst press Gareth could have – Pountney ought to be sacked.'

'Take it easy, Vi, you're talking about the one and only king of Parramatta!'

'And that's where he should stay.'

An infuriating thought struck her. Her cheeks were flushed as she asked, 'I can't believe it. He's not down for the Brisbane trip, is he?'

'His name's down all right. "Mr R. Pountney / Constituency

Liaison". Whatever that means. Some lurk or other that he's invented for himself.' She showed Violet a list.

Reading the typewritten names Violet struggled to contain her anger. Revulsion and fear, she knew, were what caused it.

Five minutes before their departure, she finally managed to get a word with Gareth. Even so he was not on his own – there was still a secretary in the compartment, counting the briefcases. This was not how she had envisaged their reunion. Violet was forced to whisper, which added to her rage.

'Gareth, I refuse to go if Pountney is with us. You said you'd fired him.'

'I said I'd get him right out of your way. I can't fire the guy for no reason – he's my electoral agent, remember?'

'I know. He's the king of Parramatta. But you don't want him lording it over people in Brisbane, any more than I need him hanging around in Double Bay.'

Gareth threw a look in the direction of the secretary, but she gave no hint of eavesdropping. Violet used the moment to consult the list of names.

'You don't need him; I'm sure he's sneaked on somehow. You've already got Cissy for press relations, two stenographers, an official photographer, three secretaries, Miss Bosworth and your parliamentary aide, a private secretary, a telephone and wireless expert from Canberra, a baggage-man . . . What in God's name is Pountney supposed to do? Hold your beer for you?'

'What we don't need is a scene, especially with all those photographers around.'

'I'm perfectly ready to leave this train if that man's on board. I'll go when you say. Take your choice.'

Violet turned her back on him, trembling slightly with the force of her anger. Never before had she put an ultimatum to Gareth, and she was well aware that she had chosen a particularly difficult place and time to do so. She went into the corridor and concentrated on looking out at the bustle of Central Station.

The guards were trying to get the party in order. The famous Bosworth, a gaunt, commanding woman with her greying hair confined in a net, was standing by the entrance to the official carriages with a clipboard in her hand, marking off the late arrivals, and allocating sleeping-compartments. Steam drifted along the platform under the wrought-iron canopy. The place was alive with the groaning noises of shunting and the blowing of whistles. There was an ornate clock which showed the time on all four sides. They had just four minutes.

Gareth came out of the compartment behind her without speaking and walked down towards the dining-car. She turned her head and saw him talking to his parliamentary aide, gesticulating and shaking his head. Then he walked back towards her.

'Time for a drink, I think. Shall we join the press corps in the bar? We'll probably find Cissy there.' In a less public place he would have put his hand out, in a clumsy placating gesture meant as love.

As they walked along the corridor Violet saw Pountney on the other side of the window. At the same moment he saw her, from no more than ten feet away. He was holding a huge and brand-new suitcase, which he had evidently reclaimed from the train at the very last moment. The guard shouted something and a whistle blew. Instantly the train lurched – and Violet, to steady herself, put a hand on Gareth's shoulder.

She saw Pountney's face. In a second his expression had changed, from deepest chagrin to a concentrated malevolence. Violet recoiled, seeing a look meant to kill.

Although Violet had got what she wanted, her falling-out with Gareth was by no means over. At dawn, crossing the Queensland border near Coolangatta, they had to descend from the train, on account of a change of railway gauges. Though they had been travelling through a sub-tropical landscape of banana plantations and the occasional plot of sugar-cane, it was surprisingly cold. While the train shunted, the disconsolate party of officials waited by the track, with blankets over their shoulders. As usual Miss Bosworth stayed close to the prime minister. At one point his eyes met Violet's. But neither of them smiled.

It was, besides, impossible for Violet and Gareth to be alone together during the day. By night-time on the first day, they had been officially welcomed by the lord mayor of Brisbane in the town hall, and attended a dinner of Queensland businessmen. The next day there had been a visit to an aircraft factory outside Brisbane – with the press party unhappy because Cissy had placed an embargo on their story until the following weekend. Violet meanwhile had been offered a meeting with the local representative of WIC and a guided tour of the local facilities for children.

Her first stop, accompanied by the WIC representative for Queensland, was the Far East Children's Home, a large Gothic building like a seminary, gloomy and hot. It was overcrowded and understaffed, but the children looked cheerful. Some of them were wearing leg-irons to correct bone deformations caused by rickets; according to the home's governor, an agreeable woman of about forty, most would recover, after a few months on a proper diet.

Violet's brief was to establish a budget for a place almost twice as large, accommodating 500 children.

'We'd need an annexe,' Connie had told her. 'And we'd need more staff. That may be difficult if they want women to work in the munitions factories when the war starts.'

Walking along the home's dark corridors, Violet asked the local WIC representative, 'What about crèches, if the women have to go into war work?'

The man, seconded from the Civil Service, looked glum.

'There's not much been done. People keep wishing it won't happen; hoping, you know? And it's not as though Mr Mayhew came here on a sightseeing trip.'

Violet mentally noted down the details. Connie was much further ahead in her preparations for the female mobilisation of New South Wales. But then she would be.

When she got back to the pleasant, old-fashioned hotel there did not seem to be anyone about. Then she discovered that they were all crammed into Gareth's suite. He was giving the press corps a special briefing. To do it he'd taken off his coat and rolled up his sleeves: the informal, all-friends-together approach. Violet watched from the doorway. She deduced that he was trying to write their stories for them.

'That's a topic your boss's friend Lord Beaverbrook is keen about,' Gareth was saying with a smile, to a journalist from the *Gazette*'s rival, the *Sun*, who sat in the front row scribbling on a pad on his knee, a fag in the corner of his mouth. She recognised the technique – Gareth was always taking up a particular journalist, making little references to him in front of his colleagues, building him up. This man must have written something Gareth liked – or maybe he was hoping he would in the near future.

'Yes, I know Lord Beaverbrook's papers have been saying "There ain't gonna be no war." And – this is off the record, mind – I know why. He's trying to buy time for Britain, trying to buy another year or two's peace. Anyone who prints that sentence will be shot. Got it?'

The reporters laughed appreciatively. Cissy was moving round with a bottle of whisky, filling glasses.

'We have to organise our production along Yank lines, even if you don't like the word. Beaverbrook saw how Henry Ford does it and he says we can do anything he can. Why not? The first thing is to take factories that were built to manufacture small parts of aeroplanes, and reconstruct them so you can go from start to finish under one roof. A full production line it's called. Yes, Don?'

'Are they going to be converting existing aircraft into fighters, or building from scratch?'

'Both. In England I didn't spend all my time at Buckingham Palace.' Gareth paused for the laugh and it came as expected. 'In Cowley, where they build the cars, they've converted the Envoy into the Airspeed Oxford, and that's now the standard training plane used throughout the Commonwealth. There are numerous additions that can be added to aircraft to make them suitable for combat.'

'Can you give us an example, sir?'

'Yes, bomb racks and release gear, mountings for guns, detachable lavatory roofs that can be replaced by roofs carrying gun turrets.'

He knew every detail, because he had done his homework – he always did. Even on their stolen afternoons in Palm Beach he had brought files about aircraft, files about finance, letters to sign. He never stopped. And tonight, there would be yet another official reception, more toasts, yet another speech.

Violet suddenly found herself almost nauseated at the thought of having to listen to Gareth perform another variation on his speech about preparing for war. He was good, certainly; indeed, better all the time. Yet something in her reacted against watching him do his tricks – the pauses she knew so well, and the gesture when he looked up towards the lights, as if waiting for inspiration – when she knew that every word had been planned in advance, every inflexion rehearsed.

It was an art-form, as Cissy never tired of saying. But it no longer inspired Violet. She remembered the night at Hobart Town Hall, which now seemed long ago. It made her tired to think of all the speeches there had been since then. Politicians on the other hand never got tired. They never thought, if I shake another hand I'll throw up.

By the time she got to her room, having had two whiskies, she was feeling more relaxed. She was beginning to regret making a scene over Pountney. Perhaps she should somehow send Gareth a note.

For the first time since falling in love with Gareth, she wondered whether it was all worthwhile. Just as he never seemed to be spontaneous in his public life, so their private life was full of contrivances – disguises and hiding, and letters in different names, and flats rented for fictitious people. When she first met him he was a man filled with a sense of destiny, both his and the country's. Now she wasn't sure what he believed in, apart from himself. When they had first met she had known little about politics. She knew a lot now, and none of it seemed as important as rescuing one refugee child.

Violet put on her make-up slowly, dreading the thought of another official dinner. It was hot and humid and the slab of black mascara in her make-up box was soft and spongy.

In the end, she was almost late. Hurriedly she put on a tight-fitting black crêpe-de-Chine dress, and collected her evening bag and wrap. Just as she was opening the door, she noticed a small square of paper on the floor.

It was just two short lines, in Gareth's spidery handwriting, on the hotel notepaper.

I must see you tonight. Will you come to my room after midnight? I'll expect you if you wear that green dress I like so much.

Violet felt a grin pulling the corners of her mouth. She dropped her wrap and bag and quickly took the green silk dress out of her wardrobe.

At dinner she sat between the mayor and another senior local official. Gareth was at the head of the table, flanked by the mayor's wife and by the wife of the manufacturer who owned the aircraft factory. Although he was apparently giving each of them his full attention, Violet could tell he was bored. His eyes had lit up when he saw her arrive for pre-dinner cocktails wearing the green dress.

After the meal, he made a quick speech of thanks to their hosts in Queensland, which was rousingly received. Between retrieving their coats in the lobby and ordering their cars, he and Violet managed a few private words.

'One more briefing to the journalists, then two reports to dictate, and a final look at tomorrow's speech in Darwin, then I'll be there.'

'That could take all night,' Violet said. 'I'll come to your room – at 12.30. Be there. Make sure Bosworth's gone to bed!' She was by no means drunk, but she felt reckless. The war could start tomorrow – it could have started this second in Europe, and they wouldn't know till it was hours old. She remembered her last conversation with Emerald.

'Never forget, Vi darling, you have to run like hell to catch what happiness you can.'

By the time she was knocking on Gareth's door it was a quarter to one.

He opened the door immediately, as though he had been waiting on the other side. Holding her, he undid the row of silk-covered buttons down the back of her dress, his mouth buried in her neck. He pulled the dress down off her shoulders and stood back from her, holding her face in both his hands.

'God, I love you. You can't imagine how bad it is having to look at you from a distance all the time, unable to touch you, talk to you . . .'

'It's as bad for me . . .'

He pulled her to the bed, removing his clothes in a rushed frenzy, leaving them scattered on the floor. They made love quickly, climaxing together. Violet's skin gleamed in the darkness, shiny with perspiration. She was sober now, and more alert than at any time that day.

'I needed you,' he said.

'You make it sound as though I'm a stiff drink.'

'You are. Pure spirit. It's been so long.'

'I wish we could go somewhere alone – get away together for a few days. Even for one day . . .'

'What do you expect me to do? Take you to the pictures, wearing a false beard and long raincoat?'

He moved away from her for a moment; then apologised, when he saw her expression. 'There's nothing to be done at the moment. It's a problem of public life.'

'It's not going to change, is it?' she asked. 'It's always going to be pretence.' She rolled away from him. He looked at her shadowed profile.

For a long time he didn't say anything, and she half expected him to try to defend himself, to say that, yes, it would be all right, it would be better; so she was surprised when he finally answered.

'It'll be like this till the war's over. It won't last. Then we'll be able to survive a scandal. To be together.'

'That's a lot of "maybes" and "ifs".' Violet had turned back to him. She was lying with her head in the crook of his arm, one leg across his thigh, her hand tracing patterns through the light matting of hair on his chest.

'I know – but it is the truth. I love you; we wouldn't be here if I didn't, if you didn't love me.'

'I know.' She snuggled her head against him. 'I'm proud of you – even if your speeches bore me stiff sometimes.'

He laughed in the darkness and turned towards her again.

She left just as the first dawn light was visible behind the curtains. The green dress was creased as she pulled it back on, and she didn't bother to put on her stockings or shoes. Gareth was already awake, seated at the desk by the window, correcting and signing a batch of letters which Bosworth had deposited there the previous evening. His hair was rumpled and his chin was stubbly. Violet felt a mixture of tenderness and pride as she glanced back at him from the doorway, seeing his head already bent over his work. He had superhuman energy, more than anyone she had ever met. It was like a well which never dried.

She closed the door quietly behind her and padded down the corridor. Ahead, she heard a door opening. She flattened herself into the recess of room 209 – she was later surprised that she never forgot the number. But it didn't hide her. Cissy was walking towards her down the carpet, wearing a long dressing-gown and leather slippers. She looked pale.

'I must've eaten something last night. I've been up and down since three o'clock this morning. Violet, are you all right? You're on the wrong floor . . .' Her words drifted away as she noticed Violet's crumpled dress, mussed hair and bare feet.

Violet watched Cissy stare past her down the corridor. A look of comprehension flashed over Cissy's face. She turned back to Violet and hesitated before speaking.

'Oh God, I've got to go to the bathroom again. See you at breakfast.'

In vain she tried to sound casual. Violet knew that the secret she and Gareth had guarded, almost miraculously, for so long was now shared with yet another person.

24

One evening after her return from Brisbane, Violet went to call on Joseph Sternberg at the address he had given her, over a café in Paddington. She found Joseph in the empty café itself, sharing a quick stand-up snack with two other men. All had the appearance of preparing for work there before the place filled up – Violet had not realised that the former psychology professor was now employed as a waiter.

She undertook to call later, and when the café had finally been cleared for the night Joseph introduced her, over cooking brandy and strong coffee, to his workmates.

Avram was the former proprietor of a Viennese restaurant in Brussels. Yehuda, from Frankfurt, was a ruddy, ox-like figure whose Anglo-Saxon looks could have been those of a farmer from deep in New South Wales. He had been a fur salesman in his father's business until 1935, when it had closed down. Since then there had been many adventures, before he had managed to catch the same emigrant boat as Joseph.

Yehuda spent much of his time doing 'political work' – evidently they were all impassioned Zionists, enthusiasts for the establishment of a national home for the Jews in Palestine. Avram expressed particular indignation at the plight of the Jews still left in Hitler's Europe.

'I've been getting information from people I know in Switzerland and Palestine. Thousands of refugees could still get out of Europe; some are all set to go – but they're being stopped from entering Palestine for fear they'll offend the Arabs. The rest of the world seems ignorant of what will happen if something's not done very soon.'

'It's the British,' Joseph said. 'They could issue entry permits but they won't. They pretend it's a rational policy but it isn't. It's their own special anti-Semitism, the kind that sounds polite and reasonable. They're cold-blooded bastards, the British. My father used to say that, and now I know he was right.'

He paused. Violet was sorry to see his thin face blushing with embarrassment. She had come to admire this sensitive and polite man.

'I'm sorry, Violet,' he said. 'I forgot your origins.'

'Don't be silly. I'm not responsible for everything my fellow countrymen may do. And I'm half Australian now in any case. The children are completely so – you realise they've never seen England? I call it "the old country" now, like Daisy, and they give me funny looks.'

'With your various connections you probably have even better information on what's happening than Avram,' Joseph replied. They fell into exchanging what they knew or had heard. There were all kinds of rumours.

By the end of the night Violet was aware for the first time how perilous the situation was, despite the apparent stalemate in Europe. Avram seemed to know a lot about the Wehrmacht, Germany's army, which he said was the best in the world. He had less faith in the Luftwaffe, the vaunted air force led by Reichsmarschall Goering, a flying ace from the Great War who was now said to be too fat to climb into a cockpit. It was intimidating none the less to hear him talking about the Luftwaffe's new bomber, the Dornier, and the effect on civilians of modern techniques used on the big cities.

'Goering's only waiting for his moment to come. They practised saturation bombing in Spain, with the raid on Guernica. I'm surprised they've held back so long.'

Violet returned to Killymoon full of dread.

That night she dreamed of Emerald, an Emerald wearing khaki and a black Sam Browne belt. It was obviously during the Great War because her sister-in-law was driving a car with an official flag on it, at great speed, despite a heavy London fog of a kind that Violet had forgotten. Emerald drove faster and faster; and Violet realised that she had arrived at Victoria Station, and was meeting someone very important off the boat-train from the continent.

There were, in fact, two arrivals. Emerald saluted, before settling them in the back of her fine car, and covering them with a wonderful rug from Peru that had hung on the walls of her studio in the old days.

To her surprise, Violet saw that the passengers were both children, one a boy she thought she had seen before, the other a girl who looked like Liz. After a moment or so she remembered the boy: his photograph had been in a news magazine Yehuda had produced that evening, containing pictures of the invasion of Czechoslovakia. There had been one shot of a small boy Sam's age asleep by the roadside, his head pillowed on some army webbing. Ragged scissor marks had been visible at the back of his hair – someone had done an amateur but very short pudding-basin cut.

Emerald set off again at a terrifying pace. Her driving skill had been a byword among the military staff of Whitehall – she had always got them to their appointments on time, even in the worst winter weather. Even in her dream Violet knew the children would be safe with Emerald. She was hurrying the children off to somewhere secure, where they would never have to worry again.

Violet woke with a sense of relief, and wet cheeks. Slowly she realised that she had been crying, not in the dream, as she first supposed, but in the moments since she had woken. In reality the children were facing Hitler's armies and Hitler's bombs. It was only in the dream world that they were safe.

On the afternoon of 1 September 1939 Hitler invaded Poland. Two days later Neville Chamberlain declared war on the German Third Reich. The British prime minister's broadcast went out at 11.15 GMT, late at night in Australia. Immediately afterwards, Gareth's voice came on the air.

'. . . it is an evil thing we are fighting.' Gareth's words were an echo of Chamberlain's as he confirmed that Australia, like the other countries of the empire, was now at war.

Afterwards James said, 'He did that very well.'

Violet was not so convinced. Gareth's voice had been stronger than the British prime minister's, younger and without the upper-class exaggerations. But there was something contrived about his delivery. She was beginning to see how much in politics inevitably involved falsity. Yet she was still uneasy that Gareth's gifts as an actor, his instinct for presenting himself in the noblest possible light, should intrude into a matter of such gravity.

There would be no turning back now. She looked out on to the lawns of Killymoon, where the lights from the house were showing up long shadows. The spring night was bringing the enemy with it. And also, Violet thought, taking Gareth away, though as yet she was not sure how.

'We'll have to let the servants go,' was Daisy's insistent, querulous reaction. The old lady was wearing a pair of slippers and a padded silk dressing-gown, and even though the night was warm and still she was shivering. Violet poured her a small glass of brandy.

'They'll be needed in the factories . . .' Daisy was studying the backs of her hands, the brown blotches caused by the sun. Eventually she brightened. 'Still, we managed before.'

James got up to leave as if relieved the time had come to escape. He kissed the top of Daisy's head and she reached for his hand.

'Don't go tonight,' she said, as if Hitler's armies were poised to flood through Killymoon's wrought-iron gates. Violet thought that she had never seen her look so old.

James sighed. 'I have to, and you know we're not in any danger here. It's London where they'll be dropping the bombs, or Paris.'

It did not seem to have crossed his mind that the idea of London burning would scare his mother. His thoughts were evidently far from Killymoon and everyone in it. There was something strange in his voice, as if he were concealing a subterranean excitement.

'I need to be in the office,' he said, in the same voice.

Violet wondered if he had been imagining himself as a general, leading an army into battle.

Leaving, he felt obliged to justify his departure once again. How often Violet had seen him standing in the doorway, telling the room how heavy his responsibilities were.

'I can't hang around any more – there's eleven papers now. And they all need watching.'

How many nights had he spent at the office since they were married? Several hundred, probably. But never before had there been so perfect a justification. Tonight he could march out with a sense of history. All over the world women were getting ready to live their lives without their men.

Soon there were crowds waving flags on the streets as the first convoys of Australian troops set off to join the European campaign in North Africa and the Mediterranean. There were uniforms everywhere, an air of giddy expectancy. Jack Maguire and Bill South, having joined the reserve the previous autumn, were called up at once. After a fortnight at a camp in French's Forest they came home for 48 hours' embarkation leave. Aggie rang up Violet to tell her, and she arranged to see them all at Belle View.

'They're as happy as dogs with two tails,' Aggie said, when she opened the door. Jack and Bill were both wearing uniforms which were stiff in their newness. They looked fit and young, with very short hair and very pleased with themselves in an ill-concealed way. Aggie and Nona shared their pride, though in Nona's case there had been periodic fits of complaint.

'You didn't have to go, at your age. You fixed it through that mate of yours from Strathfield, the captain who had a collection of 200 pictures of Myrna Loy. They did, you know,' she told Violet. 'They only got in through a lurk.'

'Too right,' said Bill, with a wink. 'Without Captain Fletcher we'd have stood no chance. The over-35s aren't on the immediate list unless they had experience last time. We were specially picked. Right, Jack?'

'You mean you bought him drinks and gave him free seats until he put you down. Men of your age should have more sense. What about the business?'

'It'll tick over, no worries,' Jack said with cheerful earnestness. 'You'll probably do it all far better than us. Vi ought to come back too, that would be beaut; but she's got her war work. Never stops, our Vi.'

Conversation turned to people they knew who had been less fortunate than themselves. Violet was taken aback to hear the name of her bête noire, Pountney.

'That agent for Mr Mayhew – the bloke we used to see around here – he was trying to join up. They turned him down. Not his age in this case; I think he had flat feet.'

Bill laughed. 'And flat broke, too. You knew he was sacked? Hasn't stopped him going to the races, though.'

They considered his fate in silence for a few moments. 'Poor bastard,' Bill said, and then apologised for his language in front of the ladies. He was already comporting himself as if unused to female company.

Violet, with Sternberg, went to see them leave. To her surprise even Joseph was not immune to war fever. 'I wish I could go with them. Much easier than staying here and hearing about horrors you're powerless to change.'

He would have stayed on the quay until the ship disappeared over the horizon.

Joseph's memories of what he had left behind in Europe had made him reticent too about any current hardships. Violet, telephoning his workplace one day to invite him to supper, was dismayed to find that he was about to come down in the world even further. The effects of the war, in the form of recruitment and dwindling custom, meant that the café was to close. While Yehuda had found a similar job elsewhere, and Avram, trading on his experience in Brussels, had been offered an assistant managership in the same district, Joseph was about to become both homeless and out of work.

It mortified Violet to think that even in a place of safety like

Australia, anyone with Joseph's qualities should continue to be so put upon. Only a few minutes' worry, however, was enough for her to find a possible solution. Could Aggie help?

Violet had unwittingly set events in train already, when she had used her influence to get Aggie herself a different job. Now that the picture houses were open only half-time, Aggie had agreed to work in munitions.

'We're trying to recruit people as organisers,' Violet had told her. 'You'd be very good at it.'

Initially Aggie had been doubtful.

'Violet, I don't know one end of a gun from the other.'

'Neither does anyone else. Do you want a job?'

The same evening Aggie telephoned to say, using one of Jack's more Australian phrases, 'I'll give it a go.' And by the end of a few weeks, she was in charge of the factory floor, where cordite and explosives were packed into 25-pound bombs. At first she wore her flat black shoes and blue uniform with many complaints, but soon she was saying civilian clothes made her feel uncomfortable. The war had already changed Aggie.

So many absences, despite Jack's prediction, had left the Roxy short-staffed. Violet felt a glow of relief on Joseph's behalf as she telephoned Aggie to make a suggestion.

'What would you say if I offered to help solve both your problems?' With Jack and Bill away, Nona and Aggie had been wondering whether to take a lodger.

'That would be beaut, Vi – I mean, just fine – so long as your friend isn't used to somewhere grander than Belle View.'

'Aggie, when Joseph lived in Prague, he wasn't above eating out of the local restaurants' dustbins. And he could write the publicity material far better than I, as well as running the box-office.'

It was with a sense of *déjà vu* that Violet performed the introductions between Aggie and Nona, and Joseph, still with no more possessions than would fill one case. Seeing him occupy her old room at Belle View reminded her in several ways of her own arrival in Australia. She hoped his life here would be successful – in some ways more so than her own.

WIC was now a 24-hour a day job for whoever could be found. Organising the workforce for the munitions factories, sorting out crèche arrangements for children, issuing ration books and planning home propaganda programmes kept Violet in the office till ten every night.

At times it seemed that Australia was full of women and children; but Violet knew from Sybil's letters that it was the same in England. Everyone between the ages of sixteen and sixty had been forbidden to leave the country for the duration of the war; only the soldiers were free to travel. Sybil said they were living in a ghost city, where everyone carried gas masks. Rupert had had an air raid shelter built in the cellar and stocked it with tinned bully beef and claret.

The letters from London made Violet feel closer to her mother than she had ever been. They were full of the new words 'evacuee' and 'evacuation', and it amused her to learn that her mother now regarded her escape to Australia as providential. 'I don't have to worry about my grandchildren, and that's a great relief,' Sybil wrote. 'People here think of nothing else but how to evacuate their children to America and Australia.'

To Violet's surprise, Sybil also wrote that she had joined a committee concerned with evacuating children to America, 'so that I can do my bit'.

When she heard by chance from Cissy that an official delegation was leaving for London, she seized the chance to send her mother a reply which would arrive within the week. She also sent photos of Liz and Sam and, almost without thinking, added a postscript enquiring about 'war evacuees' coming to Australia. If she could help, she said, please let her know.

25

'I can drink and think as well as any of them. The only thing I refuse to do is listen to their schoolboy dirty jokes.'

'Perhaps you could learn a few yourself,' Violet suggested to Cissy. They had met for lunch in the Australia Hotel, to discuss a series of fund-raising events and for Cissy to discover how W I C was getting on.

Since being promoted deputy to Gareth's press director, a role she relished and which no woman had ever before held, Cissy had become an unrivalled source of political gossip, insider stories from Canberra. But although she and Violet had met a number of times since the dawn encounter in the Brisbane hotel, Cissy had never referred to what she had seen there. Violet alternated between thinking that Cissy suspected nothing and fearing that she did but was keeping quiet for some unknown reason.

'Gar doesn't like the war fashions,' Cissy said, breaking a bread roll in half and grimacing because the white bread was flaky and stale. 'I can't say I do either. You're lucky, Vi, anything looks good on you. You're a walking clothes-horse.'

Violet shook her head. 'No one looks good in these heavy-heeled shoes. I've even trimmed my nails since *Vogue* said long nails are telling evidence that you never work.'

If Cissy did suspect something then questions would only confirm it. The knowledge of what she had seen lay between them, a barrier to anything serious in their friendship.

Gareth himself had become reluctant to talk to her about his real worries. Nowadays he used her as a kind of geisha: someone to mop the resting warrior's weary brow. There had been a time when this role was attractive to her – she had loved to cook things for him, to delight him physically, to mother him. Now she was impatient for something more.

'They're sure to introduce smaller papers, and probably strict censorship as well,' Cissy was saying. 'It's the only way to run a war.'

Violet knew that her friend was quoting someone; Gareth, probably. 'But he's not going to cut the *Gazette* back at the same time as the new Norton paper comes out, surely?'

The relationship between James and Gareth, once so close, had recently been deteriorating apace. It had started with the government issuing a licence for the publication of a new evening paper belonging to Ezra Norton, a man James regarded with contempt as 'a gutter publisher'. All the great proprietors felt the same, and Violet wondered why Gareth had taken them all on when for years he had been careful to remain friends with the press. It was all the more surprising because the new paper would appear at a time when everyone had been asked to undergo a voluntary cut in their newsprint consumption.

At James's behest, the proprietors, in an act of unwonted solidarity, had together written to Gareth in protest. Gareth had sent a bland reply, and James had gone to a lot of trouble to get an hour with him in private. It was a meeting that Violet suspected had not gone well for her husband.

Cissy deliberately drank some wine and composed her features into a neutral look that Violet was sure she used when briefing journalists. She feared that in asking about paper rationing she might have gone too far.

'It's bound to come,' Cissy said finally. 'I'm not saying it will be next week.'

'I won't mention a word about this to James.'

'I should hope not.' Cissy looked severe and official.

Violet had always been careful to preserve the confidentiality of anything Cissy said about Canberra. It was one of the reasons Cissy spoke to her so freely. She knew that discretion would be observed, and once or twice Violet had even asked permission to pass on something to James.

On this occasion, though, she dreaded the idea of herself or anyone else breaking the news to James that his old friend was going to betray him.

Besides Cissy, the only person who might have suspected Violet and Gareth was Rex Pountney. Violet was happy that he seemed to have vanished. But she was shocked to find herself hoping that his efforts to enlist had been successful – and that he would be one of those never heard from again, one of the first casualties. Not that her evil thought was likely to be fulfilled in reality. Surely Pountney of all people would find a comfortable berth where there was plenty to eat and drink, not much work, and no danger at all.

One day she found herself asking Gareth what had happened to his former supporter.

His handsome face had taken on a closed look. 'I did what you wanted, and you ought to be satisfied. I never worry about decisions once they're made. And I don't let other people make them for me.' Seeing his own inflexibility in Violet's gaze, he quickly added, 'Except you, of course. You're the exception.'

They had met in Newcastle, repeating the Brisbane experiment only with extreme caution. It was a measure of how far her personal life had been taken over by larger events that Violet was to remember that stolen weekend most vividly because of a political confidence Gareth divulged. Late on the Saturday evening, they were rowing a dinghy across a lake stained rusty red with secretions from the clumps of tea-trees ringing the water's edge. It was there that Gareth first confided his suspicion that the British government would have to change.

'They'll have a new prime minister within the next few months,' he said, resting on the oars. 'I think it's going to be Winston.'

'*Churchill*? That's hard to believe.'

She remembered seeing him in London a few times, an over-weight, somewhat dissipated man of middle years, a political plotter and mischief-maker who had gone as far as he could in politics, people said. They also said he drank. Violet had thought of him as a sad comic, eager to do a turn everyone had already heard many times before.

'It doesn't sound at all right to me. I know he was an important figure in the last war; but surely . . .'

'His time is coming, I'm certain of it.'

'There was a story in the *Post* saying the war will be over by Christmas.'

Gareth gave one of his unexpectedly violent laughs. 'It may not have started properly by then. And pray God it hasn't. Because when it does it's going to be like nothing we've ever imagined.'

With so much in hand, nearly a month passed before Violet saw Joseph again. One Sunday he called on her – though she suspected he had really come to see the children. They gossiped about the fortunes of his growing number of refugee acquaintances, including his friends from the café, who had found lodgings with a recently arrived chemist from Brussels and an emigré cellist from Belgrade.

But Joseph's attention, as on previous occasions, was not entirely on their conversation.

'You look as though you want to paint her.' Violet was struck by the intensity of the gaze he fixed on Liz, working on an animal jigsaw puzzle.

'She reminds me of someone.'

'You never had any children, did you?' Violet risked. She felt she should give him an opening, if he wanted to take it.

'We wanted to make our way in the professions first. Or Irene did – she was a doctor, you know.'

'Ben said.'

There was a pause, which Violet felt she ought to fill. She did so by asking about the Roxy.

Joseph did not answer immediately. Violet was about to repeat herself, when he said, 'It's not altogether to my satisfaction.'

'Really?' Violet was dismayed. Her immediate thought was of a falling-out among people she loved.

'Oh – the job is basically fine; and so are the people with whom I work. I've no complaints there.'

'So –?'

'I suppose it's to do with the material you and your partners show.' Seeing her expression of incomprehension, he set himself to explain. 'You may think that because the great British Empire has declared war on the Germans it means Britain is on the side of all those people whom the Nazis persecute.'

He hesitated again. Violet started to say something, but he motioned her to silence.

'I know I've mentioned the British authorities' own brand of anti-Semitism. It distresses me to have to watch them advertise the fact. Since you ask.'

Violet knew better than to interrupt. She watched Joseph frown and search for words. Beyond the shadow of the verandah, where they sat, the garden was brilliant with spring foliage and fierce bird-song. Only the two of them, with Liz playing at their feet, were still, in the warm breeze.

'Of course one thing not mentioned in the newsreels is the quota system. For several reasons the restriction on the number of people let into Britain means that the routes of exit from Europe are even more limited than they might be. And even when people can get into Britain they're often beyond the protection of the law. Imprisonment there – of emigrés from all German-speaking sources – it's something the British government is boasting about! At least in Europe there were places, such as one's own home, where one might avoid mixing with the dregs of Nazism. But in the British prison camps it seems one must live like close kin with people who boast of what they'll do to us when Germany has won.'

Violet knew a little of what he described. The press and wireless reports had been jauntily righteous about the number of foreigners imprisoned in Britain on a suspicion of espionage. And the newsreels, edited to make queues of bewildered internees look caged and shifty, would be even more humiliating to watch.

Joseph paused, looking down on Liz's bent head as she busied herself with the puzzle. 'I daresay I don't exactly know what is disturbing me,' he said in an inconclusive tone. A few moments passed, and he added, 'One thing, though. It was just as well Irene and I didn't have any children. I say that because of the one thing I do regret; something I regret even more than Irene – because at least I did everything in my power to save her, before I failed. This other person, she was a child not much older than your Lizzie.' He nodded at Violet's daughter. 'I might have been able to do something for her.'

There were no tears in his eyes but his voice was throaty and there were lines of tension around his chin. Violet said nothing for a long time, frightened to interrupt his thoughts. Then she met his dark eyes and shuddered as she recognised the pain in his expression. But there was no self-pity; his feeling was far stronger and much more terrible. Something like self-hatred.

An instinct told Violet to force the story out of him. It was a breakthrough for Joseph, or so he later admitted. For the little girl who looked like Liz had haunted him and the guilt he felt was torturing him with thoughts of suicide.

He had been on the central station in Vienna with all the right papers (which had cost 'about three years' salary') for the journey to Prague. The train had been crowded with people, some of whom did not have the right papers and who would inevitably be detected at the border.

'This child came up to me so confidently I thought she must know me. She had the most beautiful eyes, and hair like hers –' his eyes went back to Liz '– like straw. All she asked was had I seen her parents anywhere? I said no, but don't worry, they'll soon be back. She said they had told her the same when they went off with the men – but that was a long time ago, after breakfast, and now it was seven o'clock in the evening. I took her to the café and bought her a snack. The man

243

behind the counter gave me a funny look. He said she'd been hanging around earlier and he had told her to leave.

'In the end I had to go and catch my train. If I'd missed it, well, I'd certainly not be here now. I bought her another hot chocolate before I went and left her drinking it. When I got to the door I waved goodbye, and so did she.'

Violet sought for something consoling to say. 'There was nothing you could have done. The parents might have come back.'

'People never came back, or almost never.' He paused and she was sure that he was thinking about his wife.

'The parents must have known that rule; everyone did by then. No, they never came back. They left like that so she would have a tiny chance of survival, instead of none.'

'If you'd taken her with you, wouldn't they have stopped her at the border?'

'Very likely. But there's always the human possibility, isn't there?'

'What do you mean?'

'The possibility that someone you don't expect anything of will surprise you. That someone who has no good reason to behave humanly will none the less do so. The possibility that someone will make a sacrifice, take a chance, risk his neck.'

The light was fading and she feared that he would stop, lost in his thoughts and unhappiness. But he managed to finish what he was saying.

'I know these incidents are rare. Statistically, they would be negligible. But even so, these unlikelinesses, these long odds, are all they have in Europe under Hitler. There might have been a human emigration officer, even a human policeman.' He paused and smiled at her. 'Such possibilities mustn't ever be ruled out. The moment they are, then we've lost our humanity, it's vanished from the race.'

The children's bedtime approached; and not long after, Joseph took his leave. From then on there hadn't been a night that Violet watched the children asleep without her mind producing the image of the little girl not much older than Liz.

What could have happened to her? Might she still be rescued? Violet began dreaming of her, playing in the garden at Killymoon, her 'straw' hair gradually turning as light and then lighter than Lizzie's in the sun. Joseph's story had changed her life as well as his. For Violet it marked the start of her war.

The envelope with a London postmark, a crest of some sort, and the initials CORB on the outside, looked very official. It had taken six weeks to arrive, none the less, having been posted from the Children's Overseas Reception Board on 11 March 1940.

'I hope you will forgive me writing on a matter of the most extreme humanitarian urgency, but we're at the end of our tether here,' the letter began. Violet smiled at the expression: it was so English.

As I think you know from your mother, the CORB committee is organising boats to evacuate children to America and the colonies in cooperation with the Foreign and Dominion Offices. You will get an idea of the extent of our work when I say that 30,000 children have already been signed up for evacuation and there are another 100,000 waiting to register!

We have written to Canberra requesting their assistance, but there has been no reply. We understood that arrangements had been made for the first 350 children who wish to go to Australia, but we need official confirmation *as a matter of urgency*. Your mother suggested that, through your husband's influence, you might be able to find out what is going on.

The letter was signed by someone called the Hon. Mrs Dorothy Fane. Violet remembered her vaguely, a bossy, horsy woman whom her mother had disliked.

Violet rang James at the office. He came to the telephone sounding rushed.

'What children? Violet, I've got serious things to worry about.'

Once she would have expressed her annoyance instantly; now she kept quiet. James had become manic recently. For the last few weeks it was as if he had given up sleep altogether. In earlier years she would have assumed that he was having an affair. Now she thought it unlikely that he was involved in anything of the kind. He frequently sat up very late, drinking port and moving flags on various maps of the war. In the old days he might have invited business cronies round for cards or drinks, but now he was often alone. The issue of newspaper rationing had led his relationship with Gareth to deteriorate so badly that the prime minister no longer visited the house 'to see James'. In a sense this was a relief to Violet – at least there was no need to pretend any more, or to worry that Gareth would try to kiss her on the landing when someone might see. But it upset her to hear James's relentless, angry criticism of his increasingly beleaguered old friend.

James had regrets of his own. Some of them arose from the fact that, unlike so many of their friends, he was not in uniform. When Billy Sorrell had been sent overseas, a month after Jack and Bill's grey troopship had departed, James had scarcely attempted to conceal his own boyish attraction to military life. Billy's destination had been a secret; but he had seemed to assume he would be seeing friends in London. He had looked mightily pleased with himself when he had arrived at Killymoon in his army lieutenant's uniform. With him was his wife Jeannie, a striking blonde girl whom he had married two years before. In contrast to Billy's previous string of fiancées, Violet had found her company a delight; and Jeannie, a fast friend, was to stay indefinitely at Killymoon. James had cancelled an important meeting to see Billy – though none the less he had kept being called to the telephone in George's old study. He had heard out Billy's war views with unusual patience and asked all kinds of questions, listening avidly. It had been clear to Violet that he would have given anything to go himself. The men were all the same, even Pountney.

There did not seem to be anyone in Canberra who knew about CORB or any similar organisation. Violet could not even get news of the *Batory*, the ship on which the children were supposed to be travelling. She got in touch with Cissy, who told her there must have been some mistake. Perhaps to change the subject, Cissy tried to interest her in a big government-sponsored scheme to send food parcels and clothing to England.

'I'm more interested in getting children out. The bombing might start again any time. It horrifies me, frankly. Sometimes I can't sleep for thinking about it.'

'You said that there were a number of private organisations arranging evacuations. Why not work through one of them? Can't you do something through Joe Sternberg? You know how extensive his contacts still are – and in Europe, not just Britain.' She went on to remind Violet of at least two international Jewish organisations with which Joseph had now established links, including one that gave priority to refugee children.

'What about government visa requirements, if more refugee ships arrive?'

'The government hasn't precisely waived immigration laws for the duration. But as far as Europe goes it's very flexible. You can work safely on the principle that no children or other refugees will be turned away.'

The next morning Violet suggested to Connie that WIC ought to take over the resettlement of refugee children. The organisation was in touch with women throughout the state, so it would fit in with their existing work.

'We're overstretched as it is,' Connie answered. 'You'll have to take it on as your baby, if you want to do it.' Connie was sifting through the long lists of names of women who had volunteered for work in the munitions factories in New South Wales. 'It's a big enough headache trying to organise crèches for the children we have got, without having to think of handling any more.'

Violet replied to Dorothy Fane's letter, offering to act as the CORB representative in Australia. She also went to see Joseph.

'It's absurd that I can't get information from the government more easily,' she told him in the Blue Cat, a cafe in King's Cross he now frequented. His friend Avram was assistant manager, and Joseph's bills were always lower than anyone else's.

'There are tens of thousands in Europe who need to be evacuated – children, Jews, all kinds of refugees,' Joseph said, frowning slightly. 'But there's no one to coordinate work done here with the efforts of refugee organisations back in Europe. I've been helped quite a bit – and so have contacts of mine – by Ben, though. Did you know he was due here, by the way?'

Violet was surprised. 'What makes you think he's coming? I haven't heard a word.'

Joseph looked smug and ordered two more coffees from Avram in a lordly way, for all the world as if he intended to pay for them and leave a tip as well. 'Even the poor Jews of Paddington have their ways of sending smoke signals to each other.'

Violet leaned forward and looked at him. 'What contacts? Tell me, Joseph, what I can do.'

A week passed, during which there was news from England which made Violet feel that Avram's frightening prophecies about Goering's air force were coming true. There had been a series of bombing raids in the south. She wondered how her mother was. Through one of the names supplied by Joseph, she had managed to forge a liaison between part of the WIC and a London-based organisation funded partly by the Home Office and partly by private individuals.

Within a matter of days, telegrams were arriving, with the name of a boat and its proposed plan for sailing. The SS *Batory* was due to embark on 15 May and was expected to reach Australia by the end of June. No one knew the exact date of arrival; because of wartime secrecy, cables were restricted and censored, and no one wanted to broadcast the position of any boats on the high seas, even those carrying children and thus officially 'neutral'. The *Batory*, under the auspices of CORB, would be bringing a number of evacuees. It was also booked to carry a party of Jewish children, mostly from Czecho-slovakia and Austria, and through the offices of the World Jewish Congress and other agencies it was due to pick up a pre-arranged number of refugees *en route*, at Le Havre and Lisbon.

Connie, studying the outline plan of where the children would be fostered, said one day, 'Is it true that your sister-in-law wants to adopt a child from England?'

'How on earth did you hear that?' Violet asked.

'I can't remember. But I see that she's put her name down for a brother and a sister. Are they orphans, do you know?'

'Yes, they are. I don't think Bunty wanted people to know just yet. She can't have children of her own, and,' Violet paused, 'well, it's been hard on her. She's helped a lot with this – everyone at the Rose Bay Golf Club has been cajoled into accepting a child.'

'Why, Violet? Why are you putting in all this effort?' Connie was suddenly serious.

'I don't know, exactly.' Yet really she knew very well. It was to prove to both James and Gareth that she could organise and effect an operation on this scale, almost single-handedly, in the face of their opposition. And then there was Joseph's girl in Vienna, the girl on the platform; and the thousands, perhaps tens of thousands, of others. Above all there was the burning imperative to do something significant, to be really part of the war, to have a mental uniform she could wear herself.

Violet now found herself working all hours of the day, organising billets and temporary housing, together with foster parents for children who had no relatives or friends in Australia. For the first time, she found herself saying to Gareth that she couldn't meet him at Double Bay because she was too busy. James even accused her of neglecting Sam and Liz in favour of these unknown children from abroad. She wasn't, as she knew; she also realised that she was good at what she had undertaken. Being capable gave her a distance, a confidence which she had never found before.

26

At the end of May she received a telegram marked DASH 25/5 – which meant that the *Batory* had set sail, though a fortnight late. The lists were prepared, homes had been found, and beyond the inevitable last-minute hitches, the arrangements were as good as they could be. As Violet said to Connie, the government might be in passive opposition to the programme, but the women in New South Wales had been immediately responsive. They could, she realised, have handled more children and she sat down to compose a telegram to the Central Refugee Committee in London.

It was late, and she was tired. Just as she was dialling the number at Killymoon to tell Sam to start working on the guest list for his belated eighth birthday party, she noticed something unusual happening in Connie's office. People were hurrying into the room, craning to see the responses of a small group already standing, with dazed looks and frowns of anxious attention, around the big wireless. The Germans had launched an invasion on their neighbours to the west: Belgium, the Netherlands and France.

It was hard, that week, to know what was going on. The first night, James talked confidently about the Maginot Line, the French army, and the British Expeditionary Force in Europe. He spent hours working on his map of continental Europe, which occupied a wall in George's study, and on which he had marked all the latest military positions – but within a couple of days even James had to admit that it was no longer very useful. The German army, the Wehrmacht, had proved itself as mobile as Avram had warned – their tanks were everywhere, apparently, and for the first time a new German word entered the Australian vocabulary. Even the *Gazette* used it in a headline: BLITZKRIEG!

Gareth was too busy to talk even on the phone. There was a grimness in the air whose full extent Violet took a few days to recognise. James and the priest sat up for almost a whole night discussing whether the

249

war was over or not. It looked as though the retreat from Dunkirk had destroyed most of the British army and it was only a question of time – a couple of weeks, the priest guessed – before Hitler finished off the job and invaded England.

'Billy's been killed.' Jeannie was standing in the middle of the drawing-room at Killymoon, the telegram still balled up in her fist. 'And this letter from him arrived in the same mail.'

Violet crossed the room and put her arm round her. 'Oh, Jeannie! Jeannie, I'm so sorry! How did it happen?'

'Dunkirk. He was drowned when the boat he was escaping in capsized. He wasn't even fighting. Just running, like everyone else.'

Jeannie's eyes were crimson from weeping. She sat down on a sofa. Violet brought her a glass of brandy, which she sipped, very slowly.

'I didn't know that Billy was even in France . . .' Violet said. 'Oh, God, poor Billy, and poor you! He was so excited about the war.' It was impossible to imagine someone as full of life as Billy ceasing to exist. 'What are you going to do?'

'I don't know right now.' Jeannie started to cry again. Violet sat down beside her and held her hand.

'It's bloody ironical, isn't it? Everyone thought I married Billy for his money; and now he's dead and I've got it all and that huge house and all I want is Billy and his baby.'

There was still no news of the *Batory*. She had apparently set sail with her cargo of children from Southampton while the battle was still raging in France. After that, nothing. Violet wondered whether the boat had even succeeded in getting out of the English Channel. Was it possible that she had been sunk in the chaotic aftermath of Dunkirk, and that the news had never been reported? Would the British government even have wanted to publicise the deaths of hundreds of children at a time like that?

'They were mad to let the boat sail at such a moment,' she said to Connie in the WIC office one morning. 'Can you imagine? There must have been German planes and submarines everywhere.'

'I expect they thought it best to get them away while they still could,' her unsentimental friend replied. 'Hitler won't be sending any kids off to the sun once he takes over in England, will he?'

'He'll never get to England.'

'Of course he won't. But Lynch says it's going to be a long war. Sometimes being so far away makes you feel worse.'

Later that week, the WIC office did receive, by an indirect official route, a small piece of news from CORB. Its implications were terrible, and when Violet first read the Reuters' message from London she felt as though she was going to faint.

The smudgy blue letters told how an evacuees' boat called the *Andora Star* had been attacked and sunk 'somewhere in the Atlantic' by German U-boats. There had been no less than 341 children aboard, all of whom had been successfully taken off in the lifeboats. An unidentified British warship later rescued 150 of them; and two merchantmen in the vicinity, the British *Basset Hound* and the Norwegian *Olaf Forstersen*, had accounted for the rest.

The message ended with a statement from the Admiralty in Whitehall about Germans attacking 'civilian vessels in flagrant breach of the 1929 international convention'.

In fact, Violet realised, it was a happy story, somehow the children had all survived.

'Thank God,' Connie said. 'It sounds like a miracle.'

Violet was still looking shaken. 'But can we expect a miracle a second time? A miracle for the *Batory*?'

'My God,' said James as they peered across the water, 'isn't she beautiful?' It was a long time since Violet had seen him so excited and full of life. She herself was filled with excitement at the prospect of seeing Ben after so long.

The flying-boat was white and enormous like some stately and eccentric bird. A vast single wing supported four great engines. She settled herself down on the harbour and came to a stop only a hundred yards away. They could see heads moving behind the row of windows like portholes. Then a stairway descended to allow the passengers down into a waiting tender.

Ben was the first, a dapper figure who paused in the doorway and waved to them like a visiting statesman. He greeted them warmly and was so bubbling with news that neither James nor Violet could have got a word in if they had tried.

He was also full of the plane, a China Clipper belonging to Pan-American which in some mysterious fashion had come under his personal control. They had flown from San Francisco to Manila, he said, in under sixty hours, and when the time came he was going to use it to fly on to Singapore.

To Violet's surprise James invited Ben to stay with them; and when Ben said that he was going to Canberra directly, James renewed the invitation for when he returned. After a quizzical glance at Violet, Ben accepted.

James's newspaper instincts made it impossible for him not to probe Ben about his trip. 'I wondered if it was some kind of official visit, when they got in touch with me from Foreign Affairs.'

Ben laughed. 'I guess that's their way of making it one hundred per cent clear it's officially unofficial, if you get it. If they'd rolled out the red carpet, or sent a naval cutter to row me ashore, they think I might end up getting too fancy a view of myself.' He waved expansively towards the Clipper. 'Having a thing like that at your command makes you feel like God anyway. No wonder politicians are so egotistical.'

James's enthusiasm was obvious. 'How did you get her? Have you bought the airline?'

'I have shares as it happens, but that's not how this thing works. The plane's a temporary perk of office, if you can call it that. I'm now a presidential adviser for south-east Asia, or one of them. I guess Roosevelt may have dozens. When I was in London he had about six different guys driving the embassy crazy by turning up on missions to do what the ambassador's supposed to be there for – to tell the president how the English are taking it. That's the way FDR likes to operate: hear a lot of opinions, take nothing on trust. He's the smartest fellow I ever met, except Dad.'

'How are things in London?' James wanted to know.

'A lot of people are quite enjoying themselves, I think, including Violet's mother.' He looked at Violet and smiled.'I guess you know about her war work. Petra's pretty happy too – she's a squadron leader in the WRAF, piloting tansport planes. The only thing she doesn't like is they won't let women fly Spitfires.'

'But the war?' Violet asked. 'We're so far away.'

'I was in London ten days ago and I tell you something. If Hitler doesn't get there in the next four weeks I don't think he ever will. And all the reports from France are that there's no sign of an invasion being mounted. It looks as if the guy's decided to take time to enjoy his new conquests, set up an administration to keep the French in line, that kind of stuff. He's not followed up. It's the craziest thing; but I guess it's six to four now the British will get through the summer, and if they do they'll naturally win the war.'

'I hope you're right about "naturally",' James said. 'But it hasn't been like that so far. The German troops, the German tanks, they've just rolled through.'

'The French didn't want to fight – they had too much of it last time round. Americans don't feel that way. They want in – or that's how they're coming to see it.'

'You mean Roosevelt will bring America in?'

'Sure he will,' Ben said. 'Maybe not next week: but he'll do it.'

'Our correspondent in Washington doesn't see it like you,' James said. 'He says there's a wave of isolationism.'

'It's true we're not ready yet,' Ben said, stroking the lapel of his beautiful grey suit and beaming at Violet as though they were living through the happiest moment in the history of the world. 'But we will be. You don't need to worry about that.'

Ben was eager to be off to Canberra. The following morning a bouquet of yellow roses arrived at Killymoon for Violet. With it was a note saying that in three days he would be back. Would she meet him then, for lunch?

'You're the only person I know who's been improved by the years,' Ben said, after they had taken coffee cups on to the verandah. On his return from the American ambassador's residence in Canberra, he had telephoned Violet to say he was staying at the Australia Hotel. 'The world's at war, your country's set to be invaded, and you look as though you're starring in a fashion show.' Certainly, wartime fashions, austere and ungirlish, favoured women who had reached what Ben thought of as the definitive version of their looks. Violet was wearing a short-sleeved dress in heavy white cotton. Its sparse lines went well with her good bones and easy carriage. He hadn't realised it at the time, but seeing her at nineteen he had only half perceived the potential of her looks or her character. Lighting a cigar he said, 'There was a time when you'd have been mixing a Martini about now. You were all set to be a lush, Violet. How did you escape that fate?'

'I got interested in other things. It's not much of a story.'

'Not when you put it like that. But I guess you really mean you found another man.' Seeing her look disconcerted, he said, 'No, don't jump down my throat. I'm not digging for information; far from it. You know I have too much goddam information in my life nowadays. The more you know, the more complicated problems become, and the harder it is to make the right decision.'

She could see that he was sad about something. 'What's the news of Litzie?'

'We're now divorced. I heard a story she's planning on marrying the guy she's with. Six months ago she was never going to marry again; it

253

was a bourgeois institution that inhibited all spontaneity or growth between the contracting parties, a reactionary plot to keep women in thrall, an abomination in the eyes of all progressive people . . . And now she's changed her mind.' He shrugged. 'I never understood her. We shouldn't have had anything to do with each other. But so, I was twenty-four, Litzie two years younger. Both the families were in favour.' He opened his hands in a droll little gesture of despair. 'The story of everyone's life.'

'It's certainly a variation on the story of mine,' Violet said. 'But don't let's tell those old tales now. There's a war on, as my friend Connie always says. I want to find out about a ship. She may be on the high seas anywhere between here and the south coast of England. She may be under the waves. There's been no wireless contact that I know of, for two months. It's a tall order, even for you. But since you know the ambassador, the admiral of the fleet, the president, probably . . .'

Ben's face was impassive. 'You shouldn't tease me, Vi, you know that? You only end up with egg on your face.'

'I'm sorry, Ben, but I'm desperate. And no one . . .'

'Listen,' he said. 'I had a cable last night. Hang on.'

She could see a smile of satisfaction on the edge of his mouth as he went back indoors to rummage in an attaché case open on the desk.

He found the papers he was looking for, and held them up with mock formality as though reading from a scroll. 'The *Batory* sailed from Singapore three days ago,' he summarised. 'And she'll be in Sydney in less than a week. That's the strength of it.'

Violet cried out for joy. 'I don't believe it. Oh, Ben! What a relief. After all my nightmares!'

It occurred to her to ask, 'How did you know about this in the first place? And if you knew last night, why didn't you call me?'

'The answer to the second question is I was too busy with your prime minister, and all I can say is he's a very difficult guy. The answer to the first you have to work out for yourself.'

'I thought I was well placed to find things out.' She was thinking of Gareth, wondering why he had withheld such information.

'Joseph told me about the *Batory* first, if you want to know. But I set out to check his sources before I told you. There's been another ship here from Europe in the last seventy-two hours.'

Violet looked surprised. 'A CORB boat?'

'No, the *Dun Ray* wasn't carrying children; far from it. It was filled with what the British call "enemy aliens" as defined under a wartime regulation called 18B. Joseph was interested because a lot of them are Jews. And let me assure you there are no Jewish Nazis.'

'There are Jewish communists, I suppose.'

'That's the problem. As long as the Russians and the Germans have an alliance, and as long as the British are so ignorant of everything to do with continental Europe, including even the languages, they're going to put all the wrong people behind barbed wire.'

'What's happened to the boatload that arrived?'

'They've been sent to a camp near Goulburn. Joseph tells me it's a place he wouldn't leave his dog.'

'But you're sure about the *Batory*?'

'Damn right. I'm sure. The Australians have known about it for weeks. If they told you otherwise, then they were lying through their teeth.'

Violet was momentarily too delighted to take in his words, and kissed him on both cheeks. As she did so, she suddenly noticed that he didn't want her to draw away again. They concealed the moment in talk, however, and she forgot all about it. Until the following night, when Ben came to dinner at Killymoon. After the meal was over, they were all a long time talking in the drawing-room. It was a smallish party, mostly family. Jeannie was no longer at Killymoon, having decided to return home to Hobart. But Dick and Bunty were there, as was O'Fallen. On his arrival, the priest delivered his usual urbane greeting, offering Violet compliments on her hair, her dress, her jewellery – he always noticed every detail. Now, sitting nearby, she caught a whiff of his unmistakable aroma. It was not dirt – far from it, because one element in O'Fallen's personal smell was carbolic soap, just as another was incense or guttered candles, and yet another alcohol. It was the smell of chastity, as unmistakable as the smell of sex.

'I was sorry to see you getting stick over the question of Australian defences,' Ben was saying to James over coffee. 'All the more as you've got it right. No one else has – or no one I got to see in Canberra.'

James's face had darkened at Ben's first mention of the subject, then grew pleased. Violet wondered whether Ben was being agreeable to her husband for her sake. James's displeasure at any mention of defences was straightforward enough. The German *blitzkrieg* had totally bypassed France's vaunted defensive enclave, the Maginot Line. With ill luck James, in writing about Australia's 'undefended north', had previously invoked the French fortifications as an example. A line of positions north of Brisbane, he said, would provide Australia with a sense of security, 'like the French have established with the Maginot defences'.

As the Maginot Line had become a joke, so had James. Someone in the Australia Club had christened him 'Maginot' Franklin, and a couple of newspapers started using the nickname in print. These included the new *Evening Post*, which Norton had been permitted to publish, in spite of James's furious opposition.

'They're jealous because the *Gazette* group's making such good profits; it's as simple as that,' Ben said. 'The rich are always vulnerable to jealousy in unexpected quarters. Never trust a poor boy who's made it in politics, my dad says. He's sure to be amply beholden to rich men. And he hasn't had the time yet to get rich himself, so he's going to bitch at everyone who's got a nice auto . . .'

'Not to mention a nice China Clipper flying-boat,' Violet interrupted.

'That boat belongs to Uncle Sam, and don't you forget it,' said Ben. 'But listen to what I'm saying: I kept thinking of my dad while I was talking to your friend Gareth. That guy hates the rich. That's why we couldn't do business. He couldn't bear the thought that some of my companies might make profits out of this war – out of making sane dispositions for the trouble we'll face once the Japanese war machine has rolled over the Chinese and gets around to us.'

James let out a snort of satisfaction – here was someone talking his language at last.

'But your companies' profits would be big ones, wouldn't they?' Violet asked. She did not like to hear Gareth attacked, all the more that she partly agreed with Ben. There had been no way to define it before; but it was true that Gareth owed a lot to the rich and powerful – James among them – and that these obligations had started to chafe him, almost from the moment he had won office. Nowadays he was always talking about 'war profiteers' – and making contrasts with England, where the entire economy was supposedly subjugated to 'the war effort'. If Violet knew her father and his friends it would be hard to believe that their profits would be reduced: just the reverse.

'Any of my companies still left ought to turn a buck,' Ben conceded. 'But the way things are going, it's only a couple of years before the Japs pocket the lot for their Empire of Greater Prosperity. It's a cert – as long as no one makes preparations to stop them. Or while anyone who has the horse sense to propose action, like James, finds himself the object of cheap jokes.'

'Isn't there any way of making a deal with the Japanese?' asked Dick McGrath.

'There's no way through that I can see,' said Ben. 'In the last three years I've spent six months in Tokyo. They don't want to do deals with Americans, or with anyone else who speaks English. Why should they? They're planning, just as James says, to become the dominant empire of south-east Asia. It's all going to fall into their hands anyway. Why should they pay for what they can steal?'

'So your finances and your patriotism are in alliance,' the priest said. 'Is that why the prime minister is suspicious?'

'He must think any damn fool can make money if he believes I'm as vulnerable to Japan as Australia is. I've moved two thirds of my operations to Texas, Mexico and South America. And if I'd been thinking about profits and nothing else I'd have moved one hundred per cent. Instead I'll be down here, to back up Uncle Sam. Our president, at least, understands that. But then, he wasn't born poor. Dad calls FDR "Houdini". He says the idea that this patrician is conspiring to destroy big business in the interests of the American wage-earner is the great political conjuring trick of the century. Did you know that a lot of American businessmen like to kid themselves the Roosevelts are Jews and communists? Dr Goebbels' propaganda machine keeps putting it out too. Incredible, isn't it? The Roosevelts probably have more money than my family.'

Several times, during dinner, she had caught Ben's eyes on her. There was something unmistakable in his glance. She had seen it, in other men, many times. Occasionally she had thought herself mistaken – only to have it proved, sometimes after a long delay, that she had been right in the first place. No man who ever looked at her like that had failed later on to make an advance. On the other hand her relationship with Ben had always been, not brotherly exactly, but something in which Ben was the grown-up and she wasn't quite, even after she had had children. Now it had changed; it was as though they had synchronised. They were the same age, or something like it, for the first time.

27

The 477 passengers of the SS *Batory* were unloaded at last on to the Sydney docks, the children forming a straggling, exuberant and sunburnt crocodile. So they had made it! Violet watched them with a thrill of delight, before going aboard to greet their accompanying officials and the captain.

Their voyage had taken almost three times as long as it would have done in peacetime. But once safely out of the Atlantic their great enemy had been boredom, rather than fear.

One of the escorts, a blonde Scots woman with a teacher's impatient face, was in haste to hand Violet a copy of a roughly assembled magazine, *The Albatross*.

'Shipboard literature,' said the woman, who introduced herself as Enid Temple. 'We spent a month doing that. They named it after the Ancient Mariner – "Water, water, everywhere, nor any drop to drink." That's how they've been feeling for the last few weeks. I don't suppose you'd believe it, but' – she dropped her eyes at mentioning something mildly indecent – 'we've not had enough fresh water to wash all our . . . *things* for a month now. There's no fresh water for laundry on board.' She paused to dart a look of female complicity at Violet.

'Do you know, in Panama they wanted £10 a ton for fresh water? *Ten*, and so insolent too. The way they look at you, up and down and all over. We were a month waiting to get through the canal – they treated us like dirt.'

She spoke in a prim, appalled voice, eager to share travellers' tales with another woman. Violet was amused at this native of Renfrew, unleashed on a world where values were so different from those at home.

'You could give a copy to your husband,' Miss Temple said. 'I hear he's in newspapers.'

He *was* newspapers nowadays, Violet thought, working twenty hours a day, many of them spent publicly fulminating about the impending newsprint rationing.

She herself spent that day working until nearly midnight, arranging for the children to be collected by their foster parents. When she got home James was there and, too tired to describe the day's events, she passed him the copy of their magazine.

To her surprise he read it from cover to cover with the closest attention. The following day he sent a photographer to the temporary home in Glebe where those children who were still waiting for foster families were staying.

In the *Gazette* there appeared a picture of four children holding *The Albatross* aloft. Beneath was an article by James himself discoursing on freedom and the necessity of printed information in wartime. There were also quotations from various patriotic poems by the children. The article concluded that at the *Gazette*'s behest a specially bound edition of *The Albatross*, including the signatures of every child on board, was being sent to the prime minister.

Violet doubted that Gareth would be much impressed by this delicate hint. Her husband was growing more eccentric, more manic and unpredictable, every day.

By the next weekend she found herself proved right. James, who had been playing golf with Dick, returned home in a frightening rage. In the clubhouse bar he had met 'Jerry' Jerome, the women's magazine publisher who was still devotedly trying to persuade Violet to join him for luncheon. Jerome was just back from Canberra, with a hot piece of inside news: within ninety days the government was ordering newsprint rationing.

Only days before, James had himself seen Gareth in Canberra. The prime minister had given not a hint of his plans for rationing.

The outside world was impinging further on Violet's relationship with Gareth. At the office next day she found Enid Temple waiting for her, determined to make a protest to the Australian government. For weeks during the voyage, so she had been told by one of the ship's officers, the *Batory* had been appealing to Australia for official confirmation that she was on a 'mercy voyage', and therefore Australia's responsibility.

There had been no response. 'They'd have left us to rot,' Enid exclaimed. 'The only thing your government cared about was a boatload of internees from England. They had priority over us, and arrived a fortnight ago.'

Violet was by now so accustomed to postponements that when, later that week in the Double Bay apartment, Gareth arrived and started to apologise she waved at him to be silent.

'I know,' she said. 'There's a war on, even though it's at the other end of the world.'

'Let's forget about it. We can pretend this is the world here.'

The late afternoon light was soft in the bedroom. He was eager to make love, and kissed her as he unbuttoned her cream shantung shirt. His mouth tasted of wine. His hands were gentle and familiar as they explored her body, arousing her instantly, making her forget any anger she might have felt for him. Her long fingernails moved over the hard ridges of his belly, and he groaned as she ran her fingers up the inside of his thigh.

She knelt astride him and gently eased him into her, leaning forward so that Gareth could kiss her breasts as she moved on top of him. When it seemed impossible that they were not both about to come, she leant back, changing the rhythm. She continued to move, very slowly, out of his reach, till they could no longer stand the waiting.

Afterwards they lay locked in each other's arms, grateful, familiar, accepting, equal in their possession and their surrender. The minutes after making love were the best times. It was too soon for Gareth to slip back into being a politician, and he still belonged completely to her.

Violet had been reluctant to ruin the meeting by introducing politics herself. But there was no choice. She had to seize the moment, before he was sucked back by his responsibilities.

As she expected, from the moment she began to tell him what she had learned from Edith Temple, his face began to warp with annoyance.

'She was sure they could have been here two months earlier. We're desperate for someone to cut through all this bureaucratic delay.'

He sighed heavily. 'Like me?'

'Who else?' she said. 'Only one boatload of children has arrived here. All the rest have been to America. It's a disgrace to Australia, you know that?'

To her annoyance he only smiled and said nothing. She felt a surge of anger.

'I gave you the benefit of the doubt, you know. I thought you were too busy with more important things to worry about the refugees. Now it sounds as if all along you were trying to kill off the whole thing.'

To her surprise, he did not make even a token denial. Instead he shook his head, and gave her a look which said how hopeless it was to expect someone like her to understand what things were like in the real world. Violet noticed for the first time that there was grey in his hair and that his hairline was creeping back from his temples. She lit a cigarette and went to sit on a chair away from him.

'You have to think of the propaganda effect, I'm afraid,' was all he said finally. 'And the problems with government funding, in London.

'Give me one of those cigarettes.' He inhaled deeply, looking at the cylinder of paper with dislike. 'Silly habit. To think, before the war I kept a packet for a month.'

In a measured voice, he began to explain. Violet realised that, finding them on the point of quarrelling, he had decided to try to make her understand, even though the process would be lengthy, and probably tedious to him.

'The day the Belgians surrendered, or maybe it was the day Italy declared war – I forget which, though there was a time when I'd have known to the minute – I happened to see a British cabinet document. It was called *A Certain Eventuality*.' Gareth paused, and laughed. 'Very British that, I thought,' he said in the musical comedy version of a British accent he employed sometimes. He was an excellent mimic, a natural actor. Violet wondered if he was trying to deceive her, feeling a certain stirring of doubt that nowadays she constantly felt in her dealings with him.

She realised that she was no longer sure she was in love with him. The realisation alarmed her. Being in love with him had become a fixed habit, as fixed as not being at all in love with James.

Gareth had paused, and she could now see how tired he was. The man was exhausted; it was cruel of her to bully him. Yet she knew it was important that she did so.

He said, 'This *Certain Eventuality* was one helluva document, I'll say that for it. It was about the kind of Britain you could expect with the Fuhrer in Buckingham Palace – oh, there were also some ideas about tropical islands where the royal family could find decent accommodation and the union jack would still be flying. The ex-king, poor old Windsor, has just taken up residence on one as a matter of fact; something not immaterial to the red tape your *Batory* had so much trouble with.'

'It seems entirely immaterial to me,' Violet said tartly. 'Nobody's threatening to bomb the Duke of Windsor and he's not short of money. These children could have been blown to smithereens overnight.'

'They sure could,' Gareth agreed. 'The document assumed that large central areas of the main cities would already be blown away through bombing and the effects of house-to-house fighting. But I tell you, the

British government is unlikely to help shift another 20,000 people, and you might as well accept the fact.'

'Churchill isn't a monster. It's inhuman when you can do something . . .' She tried to prevent her imagination moving ahead and picturing what London would be like after the bombs and the artillery.

'No, he isn't a monster; and he's certainly not a fool either,' Gareth said. 'He knows that the British can only get through on bluff; and he needs to make the world believe that Britain will fight to the last man. He has to convince America – and by that I don't mean Washington, or the president. Roosevelt's convinced already; that's one of the few things Mr Schiff and I agree about. It's a question of convincing the American public.'

Ben had left a few days earlier, after a farewell party at Killymoon attended by the American ambassador. It had been a muted occasion, and Violet knew that Ben had been sad to leave her.

'So?'

'So every boatload of children they unload on the east coast assuages their conscience. That's not what Churchill wants. He wants them to feel pangs so acute they can't stay out; I know it sounds bad put that way, but it's the case. The British government doesn't want to use its resources to help people escape. There's also a lot of people it badly needs to get rid of – all kinds of aliens who would form a fifth column the moment there was an invasion. They need the boats to get rid of Italian fascists – did you know there are 30,000 of them in London, paying subscriptions to an organisation whose honorary president is Benito Mussolini? God knows how many there are who do the Hitler salute; but Churchill wants them locked up somewhere safe and remote, and I'm giving him every support.'

'You always do, don't you?' Violet said. 'He has you on a string.'

Gareth smiled, as if to himself, a smile that said if you only knew.

'Australia has obligations,' he said. 'As to your committees, it's just that the tide of events, history if you prefer, is tipping in the other direction. You'd do best to accept it, my dear. Nobody's sadder than me, but there aren't going to be many more people leaving for here with the help of the British, if any at all.'

'Oh yes, there are,' she said. 'I'll go there myself if I have to.'

'You'll probably have to swim, then,' Gareth said. 'It's a very tight little island. Hard to get out, even harder to get in. I think it's become impossible now.'

Little did he know, she thought. The *Batory* had set off the day before on her return voyage, with a new addition to the crew – Joseph

262

Sternberg. He had taken Edith Temple's place after she had accepted an offer from Jeannie to go and help care for a group of children at Glendevon.

'Even for you?'

He laughed and waved the question away with a gesture.

'Don't let's talk about it any more,' he said. 'It makes you unhappy. And when you feel bad . . .'

He reached for her, but she moved away. It was the kind of dispute that they might once have settled by making love. But this time they did not.

Despite Violet's increasing lack of sympathy with what she thought of as 'all that Canberra stuff', there was no place of escape from politics – or from the increasing ambiguity of her position as Gareth's lover. That same night, at Killymoon, she found herself listening to a dinnertime conversation that made her long in vain to defend him. More frustrating yet, the men entirely ignored her presence, once they had delivered the required compliments on her appearance and the food, and made dutiful enquiries about the children. Even Jerome made little effort to flirt with her, having come for an evening of conversation serious enough to exclude all the women.

Newspaper rationing was the inevitable topic. It was probably the reason why James had invited Jerry Jerome in the first place. Violet saw it as just another example of James trying to get close to people he didn't particularly like but who he thought could help with information.

The priest too was there. 'The government is never going to make enemies of every newspaper in the country. You saw what Murdoch said about the freedom of speech in wartime?'

'He's mad as a snake at what's happening,' James replied. 'Gareth's gone off his head. It's pathetic. He won't listen to anyone.'

'He *is* the prime minister,' said Jerome. 'Not listening is something that probably goes with the office.'

'A lot of people would say it was the *Gazette* that got him there in the first place,' the priest remarked. 'And I think our friend James is one of them.'

'I was his first and most loyal supporter,' James agreed.

'*Was?*' Jerome asked, looking shrewd.

James selected a cigar. 'It's not reached that point yet. Not quite. But you *can* take it away from him, as a matter of fact. If every paper in Australia was against him, he wouldn't last six months.'

While the men talked on, Violet played dominoes with Daisy, keeping her dark thoughts to herself. She hadn't expected to feel so angry. The men, in excluding her from talk of business and politics, weren't treating her any differently than in the past. What had changed, she realised, was her own desire to participate.

'I'll change his mind, or I'll kill him.' James was pacing the room. The look of ferocity on his face made Violet wonder for a moment if he was going mad.

Jerry Jerome's information had swiftly proved accurate. The government was about to impose a limit of four pages on all national papers.

Violet decided to go out to Palm Beach. She couldn't stand the prospect of listening to her husband's attacks on Gareth.

As she left, James was arranging to go to Canberra. She was surprised, therefore, on her return to find him still at the house. He was on the phone, convening an emergency meeting of the newspaper owners' association, for breakfast the following morning.

'The man's stubborn; he won't change his mind at any price,' he remarked as if to himself, as he put down the receiver.

'Then what do you hope to achieve?' she asked him.

'It's an act of self-destruction to set the whole of the press against him. We're going to make sure he understands this.'

'And if he doesn't?'

'Then I'll have him out of office if it's the last thing I do. I've already got Hooker working on a series called "The Lost Leader". If the *Gazette* turned against him, the rest would follow overnight. I know how it works.'

'You wouldn't print scandal about Gareth?' She was seized with terror at where such a series might end.

James looked impatient. 'Scandal has nothing to do with it; the *Gazette* isn't the *Sun*. It's just that Gareth can't get anything right any more. All we have to do is point it out with a bit of passion. And Hooker will see to that, no worries.'

Always, during James's absences, Killymoon took on a pleasant domestic rhythm that Violet enjoyed. She would leave for the office very early, making sure there were two or three hours free in the middle of the day that she could spend with the children. Then she would come home in the evening with plenty of time to play with them before they went to bed. These domestic interludes were something to savour and construct the day around. She enjoyed the house with its smell of polish and cooking and liked to hear the children tell her about their adventures.

James was still in Canberra when, one overcast Monday morning before leaving for the office, Violet read a tiny item on the bottom of the *Gazette*'s front page that left her utterly taken aback. Without explanation, the *Gazette* had announced that the government's regulations on newsprint rationing, due to start on 1 September, had been suspended. She phoned James's secretary. James was expected from Canberra after lunch, she was told. Was there any message?

'No; except tell him how pleased I am.'

'It's a miracle, isn't it?' came the reply. 'No one knows how he did it.'

In the course of the morning Violet had a meeting with Connie and mentioned her astonishment at the item.

Connie laughed. 'You're not the only one. Lynch couldn't believe it. There wasn't even any cabinet discussion, apparently. It looks as though the PM had a rush of blood to the head, and simply changed his mind, just before he caught the plane. Lynch thought it must have been James who convinced him – they went to the aerodrome together, and it was all done at the very last moment. I don't think Lynch is at all pleased.'

At Connie's mention of a plane journey, Violet tried to hide her confusion. What was all this about? 'This is one of the secrets they didn't tell me,' she said as lightly as possible. 'Where's the PM gone?'

'You haven't heard?'

Violet shook her head.

On Connie's desk was a sign someone had brought back from London as a souvenir. It showed a man holding his hand conspiratorially over his mouth and bore the slogan: CARELESS TALK COSTS LIVES.

Connie solemnly walked across the office, and opened the door to check that no eavesdropper was crouched in the corridor. Despite herself, Violet smiled at the precautions.

'It's been kept quieter than most government secrets,' Connie confided. 'But the decision was only made during the weekend. He's gone to London again. But it won't be announced until he's landed safely.'

For a moment Violet could not think of an answer. 'It's brave of him,' she said finally. 'It sounds as though things in London are as bad as they've ever been.'

Connie hesitated, not wanting to be disloyal. 'Lynch says that he's not brave, but reckless. Gareth insisted on going, even though the cabinet was dead against it. Lynch was against it too, though of course he's in

265

charge now. He doesn't think it's the right moment. What use is Gareth going to be to us if Britain is invaded?'

'Perhaps he thinks at a time like this he should be –'

Connie interrupted. 'He wants adventure, the same as all of them. I wish men weren't so much like little boys. If you offered Lynch a general's uniform he'd be off tomorrow, responsibilities or not. They're hopeless.'

Violet was so stunned at Connie's news that she hardly heard the rest of what she was saying. She felt betrayed and desolate. Surely Gareth could have let her know he was leaving the country? He could have told her at least.

28

One lunchtime while the children were having a picnic at the zoo, Violet went to the apartment, ostensibly to write to Gareth. In reality, she was going there because it would make her feel closer to him. Since he had gone away so unexpectedly she missed him badly. Such feelings annoyed her, because in her heart she no longer believed in him. He had let her down too often.

There was a desolate feeling about the place; it seemed unlived-in and unloved. It was time to sort out her things – time perhaps to move everything out. It was hard to believe that she and Gareth would ever meet there again. It was surprising how much had accumulated: shirts, shoes, dresses, books, and writing paper. All the things that a home is filled with – yet this had never been a home. In a bottom drawer, layers of tissue paper separated half a dozen neatly folded silk shirts. It was here, under the shirts, that Violet kept Gareth's letters. The thought occurred to her that the time had come to burn them. She felt under the crinkly white paper for the familiar bundle, tied with a blue ribbon.

Then she stiffened. She started flinging everything out of the drawer – then the next drawer – then the next. An hour later there was nowhere in the apartment that she hadn't searched several times over. There could be no mistake. The letters had gone.

Who had taken them? For weeks Violet lived alone with the mystery of the letters. At first she had returned to the apartment again and again, pulling clothes out of closets, towels off shelves and china out of kitchen cupboards, until it looked as though there really had been a burglary. She had done the same in her room at Killymoon, and she had even sneaked through all of Sam's and Liz's things while they were at school, on the off-chance that they had somehow picked the letters up and decided to play hide and seek with them.

One morning she got up at dawn and drove down to Palm Beach to see if another batch she had preserved from the early days of their affair was still there, in its hidey hole under the floorboards.

They were, but might someone come looking for them? On the beach in the early morning she built a fire with driftwood, and watched as the well-thumbed envelopes were consumed by the flames. She left the beach hurriedly, and without her usual regrets.

Gareth must have taken them himself, she decided, driving back to town. If it had been the priest on the other hand . . . Of course it could not have been Father O'Fallen. How could he have got the key? Yet there was something cold and disdainful in him nowadays, just as there would be if he were to have something to do with the missing letters. Rationally, though, it made no sense that O'Fallen was involved. There must be some other explanation for the priest's veiled hostility. In his way he was getting to be almost as oppressive as her impatient, disparaging husband.

She could not shake her mind free of the letters. Pountney might easily have kept a spare key. But he had disappeared long before, presumably into the army. And if he had taken them, surely he would have been around looking for money. There, at least, one could trust Pountney.

'I'm shacked up at the embassy. And counting the minutes to seeing you.'

Hearing Ben's sanguine American voice, with its echoes of the great world outside, Violet realised how lonely she had become. 'I don't think I've ever been as pleased to hear anyone.'

To her disappointment this was to be only a brief visit. After a meeting with Lynch Meldrum he would be leaving for the United States, to join the election team of President Roosevelt, who was campaigning to be re-elected for a third term. Meanwhile he was also meeting James, at a luncheon of the Australian Newspapers Conference. Though there was no time on his schedule for a visit to Killymoon, he and Violet were able to see each other twice.

The first time, they went walking in Hyde Park. The whole of Sydney was bereft of men between the ages of eighteen and forty-five; and there was a shortage of young women too. The two of them, with Ben in his beautiful civilian clothes, attracted curious glances.

He was thinner, and there were lines in his face that had been absent six weeks before. He had brought Violet a present of some silk, and a beautifully produced book of poems by Madam Chiang Kai-shek, wife of the Chinese leader. Ben had been in Chungking with the Chinese forces.

There, he had met Slim Slessor, one of the *Gazette*'s long-serving foreign correspondents. Slessor had formerly been based in Tokyo, but had been withdrawn – partly because of Ben's warnings. The Japanese, so Ben now explained to Violet, would soon announce a treaty of friendship with Germany and Italy.

'I saw a story in the *Gazette* saying that today,' she said. 'I suppose you had it put there.'

Ben made no attempt to deny it. 'The story's true. And Australians might as well get used to knowing who their real enemy is.'

'We all talk like journalists now,' she said. 'Or politicians. In the old days we'd have started with lots of gossip. Now, everyone we know is somewhere else. At the other end of the world.'

'The country sure looks empty. Like it's anyone's.'

'People are frightened of the Japanese, but they don't talk about it.'

'Your husband does.'

Violet laughed. 'He doesn't talk about anything else. It's his current obsession.'

'It's safer than flying planes, anyway. You know, when I let him come aboard the Clipper, he seriously tried to persuade the pilot to authorise him landing the goddam thing in the harbour. The pilot thought he was some demented Australian general in civilian clothes, and nearly let him. We'd all have been dead.'

They walked for half an hour. Violet wished desperately that they could spend more time together. Only with Ben could she say what she thought, without hesitation or the need to weigh her words.

'Vi, tell me something. Who's Victor Trumper?'

'He's a famous cricketer. An equivalent of your Babe Ruth.'

'Is that so? I wondered if it might be a race-horse. Anyhow, I wasn't about to reveal my ignorance.'

'Tell the story properly; don't tease.'

'I heard James saying to Murdoch and some of the other big press fellows that your Gareth is like this Trumper. Any idea what he meant?'

Violet admitted that she did not. She found herself yearning to tell Ben the truth about herself and Gareth, so that she could have the benefit of his advice.

'What's Gareth's news from London?' he asked, almost as if he had guessed her thoughts.

'There isn't anything, except what you read in the papers.'

'Yeah, I saw that stuff. Sitting out the London blitz in a tin hat, in Downing Street with Winston Churchill. It's the kind of story no reporter could resist.'

'He's very popular,' Violet said absently.

'Are you sure? There are plenty of people in Canberra with knives out for him.'

'Including yourself?'

'I don't feel acrimonious,' Ben said. 'All I know is that I can't get anywhere with him. And there are plenty of other guys in government who are a goddam sight easier to deal with. They're not all in love with the British aristocracy, either.'

'What do you mean?'

He hesitated, then said, 'There are lots of Americans like that too – they can't resist the English upper classes. Why do you think he's always been so keen on you?'

Violet didn't reply. Was he inviting her to admit her relationship with Gareth? Had he somehow found out? She found herself lighting a cigarette, something she never did outdoors. She had a feeling that Ben was hiding something from her. But his face gave away nothing.

He looked at his oval Cartier watch, with its smooth snakeskin strap.

'It's a shame I have to go now.' They arranged a late supper the following night in his suite at the hotel.

'James won't be jealous,' he added. 'He'll still be in Canberra.'

'You know more about his movements than I do,' she said, pleased to recover her composure.

Again he seemed on the verge of saying something. In the end he just gave his crinkly smile, and remarked, 'I guess you aren't as close as you should be to the men in your life.'

The next night, at dinner with Ben, Violet had two gin and tonics, took a deep breath, and said, 'Are you in the mood for a confession?'

It was hard to tell anyone the truth after so long. On the way there she had even thought of trying to tell him the story with someone else, someone anonymous, cast in her own role. But from the moment she arrived she saw that this would be impossible. She could just see Ben's eyes wrinkling with laughter at any attempted deceit.

'I'm happy to listen to anything you want to say,' he replied. 'Feel free, make yourself comfortable.'

She told the story from beginning to end. When she had finished she asked, 'Do you disapprove of me?'

Ben leaned across and squeezed her hand. 'Never,' he said. 'But I kind of disapprove of your choice. The man's an asshole, if you'll forgive the expression. But it sounds as if you found that out for yourself.'

'What do I do now?' she asked. 'I suppose he must really have taken the letters. Out of fear, out of. . . ?'

Ben said drily, 'I guess he was taking prudent precautions. You don't get the top spot by taking unnecessary risks all over the goddam place. No hostages to fortune for me, FDR says, when it's a question of anything, well, indiscreet.'

'Gareth once told me he always destroyed the letters I wrote him. I was very hurt.'

'The guy's smart,' Ben said. 'But don't try to write to him in London. There's no such animal as an uncensored letter in wartime.'

'I've done it already,' she answered. 'Three times. And he hasn't even replied. Do you think they got through?'

'Who knows? It sounds like he's tied up, what with the bombs and the duchesses.'

'Supposing someone is trying to blackmail him?'

'Let's hope he's paid 'em off.'

'You really don't like him, do you?'

'We don't see eye to eye . . . In fact, I can only think of one major point of agreement.' The look that she had recognised at Killymoon was there again.

Ben paused, then added, 'You know what I reckon's the best part of all that? It's all over. The past historic. It's the same story when it comes to Gareth as well as James, isn't it? They're not in your life any more. You've grown out of them.'

'Or, put less flatteringly, they got bored with me.'

'Maybe a bit of that too. You've changed one helluva lot. So have we all, I guess, but you more than the rest. So the guys maybe don't like that, maybe they don't feel as comfortable with the new person.'

Her mind moved back to Gareth. She thought, yes, he's right, it *is* past historic. That was what made it so sad. They had been happy once – and what was there to show for it?

Violet realised she had gone into a reverie, her head bowed. Ben gave her a cigarette and lit it, watching her with a look of absorbed attention.

She sighed. 'I suppose I got what I deserved. I betrayed James, and Gareth betrayed me in turn. I feel so foolish.'

Ben looked thoughtful. 'He's betrayed you and Australia both, I wouldn't be surprised. It's as if he's become transparent suddenly: completely goddam insubstantial. You look at the guy and there's nothing much there. But Lynch – well, Lynch wouldn't let you down.'

'Lynch is pathetic. He's so scared of Connie, it's a joke.'

'That may be, but he has political courage, and he sticks to things. It's not exciting, maybe, but I think people have enough excitement in their lives right now; they're not looking to the politicians for adventure. I tell you something: Lynch knows how to call the bets. Your buddy Gareth's got drunk on this war. People want something reassuring in their leaders at times like this. They want an appearance of wisdom and solidity. They don't want Errol Flynn, except at the pictures. Gareth's going to screw himself.'

'And you're pleased?'

'It couldn't happen to a nicer guy. If I read another story about Gareth and his tin hat I'm gonna puke.'

She had to laugh. 'I don't think James likes the "heroic prime minister" stories, either.'

'Forget both of them,' Ben said. 'You're too good for them.'

The next morning he sent her roses. A day later, to her desolation, Ben and his Clipper flew north.

Gareth returned to Australia two days after the victorious capture of Tobruk, in north Africa. Thirty thousand Aussies were now fighting in the Seventh Army, and Gareth arrived at Mascot Airport carrying not only a London air-raid gas-mask, but an ANZAC helmet, a memento he had picked up during a visit to the command head-quarters in Cairo.

The photographers asked the prime minister to pose wearing the helmet. However, at the instant behest of Cissy, who on his return had regained her glory as his chief press adviser, the mask was kept out of camera range.

'People will think you're worried about air-raids in Australia if they see that,' she insisted. Gareth accepted her ruling with easy charm, dumping the paraphernalia behind a convenient chair. But he posed patiently with the helmet – set at a slightly rakish angle – and the resulting pictures, published around the world, were the most famous ever taken of him. However, to the surprise of all except those who had recently spoken to James, they were not printed in the *Gazette*. Instead, there appeared a not very becoming, single column photograph of Gareth wearing his black 'Anthony Eden', the semi-formal hat popularised by the British foreign secretary. It was accompanied by an idiosyncratic report by 'A Political Spectator', the byline James usually employed for his own increasingly frequent political articles.

The article calculated the number of days Mayhew had spent out of the country since the war started, and floated the idea that the prime minister's return might only be the prelude to yet another departure for London, where he might remain for the duration of the conflict.

'He sees his role as in the eye of the hurricane,' the article continued, 'and feels that Australia is too far from the centre of events to make Australia's voice adequately heeded from Canberra.'

The story concluded by describing the close links forged between Mayhew and the British cabinet during the blitz, and mentioned that the hat in his photograph had been a gift from Anthony Eden himself.

Within twenty-four hours Gareth was addressing the nation over the airwaves. In a speech obviously modelled on Winston Churchill's 'blood, sweat, toil and tears' oration after the Dunkirk disaster, he appealed for 'total sacrifice for total war'.

Gathering to hear Gareth speak was by now a ritual occasion at Killymoon, with everyone staring fixedly at the huge oak wireless in George's former study. To Violet's relief James was absent. The speech disturbed her none the less. There was a falsity about it, with the hint of an English intonation apparent despite the distortions of the crackling airwaves. Daisy, too, was upset by the sound of Gareth's voice. 'He never comes here any more,' she lamented. 'Nobody does. When George was alive we often sat down thirty-six for dinner.'

Violet listened to the practised modulations of her lover's public voice, and wondered how soon she would see him again – and why not one of her recent letters had had a reply. Was their affair over? If it was, she wanted to be told face to face.

'In these dire days the government has not only the right but the duty to commandeer, requisition or regiment all national resources and industries that it sees fit, in order to intensify the total war effort.'

Gareth's speech announced yet more wartime measures: wider conscription, petrol rationing, a government directorate of exports, a new minister of munitions, and increased taxes. Every one was fated to be unpopular – and, in the Franklin household, one in particular.

For the regulations rationing newspapers, which had been so unexpectedly suspended on the day the prime minister left for England, were now abruptly reintroduced.

'A Political Spectator' wrote:

Now the Empire faces the gravest crisis in its history, doubts are expressed by political observers about the prime minister's capacity to provide leadership of the kind the country demands. Since his (some say reluctant) return from London, Mr Mayhew is a lacklustre figure, sadly lacking vigour and inspiration.

The article concluded:

Gareth Mayhew has become the Victor Trumper of politics, with almost all talents – except captaincy.

Violet shrugged and put it in an envelope, to send it with a note to the United States embassy in Canberra. One day with any luck Ben would receive it and have his curiosity satisfied.

But the article made her uneasy. The extent of James's chagrin could be judged by something she had heard him say to Bunty. 'Last year our profits were nearly a million, or ten times what they were in 1939. The *Gazette* alone made £300,000. We'll be lucky to make £30,000 next year.'

'Isn't there anything you can do?' Bunty had said, more upset by her brother's rage than by the collapse in the family fortunes.

'Not as long as this government is in power.'

That night before dinner Violet took the opportunity to raise the question of his article with James. Hearing him in his dressing-room, she knocked at once, a rare gesture. She was keen to catch him before he finished changing for dinner.

'I read your Victor Trumper piece. It doesn't make sense. You were the person who got Gareth in.' She tried to sound lighthearted, but she knew she wasn't succeeding.

'More fool me. He's certainly repaid his supporters with ingratitude.'

It sounded like a phrase he was trying out for another article. James was sitting on a cane armchair by the window, untying his shoelaces. Violet couldn't help noticing how he had lost all trace of his youthful looks. His face had set now in a mask of authority and will – it wasn't surprising the children were always a bit frightened of him.

He seemed indifferent to her presence, taking off his newest pair of black leather shoes, which he had had made in London, by Lobb's of St James's. She remembered how excited Gareth had been, returning from his first visit to the famous shop, delighted that his personal 'lasts' were now stored in their cellar for his lifetime.

She said, 'But why are you writing like this? And why doesn't he ever come here now?'

274

'I wondered if you'd noticed. No, he doesn't choose to come. And if you want to see him it's like interviewing the Pope.' He started to rub eau-de-cologne into his dark jowls. 'I got a confirmation today from Chiang Kai-shek in thirty-six hours flat – and *he's* a Generalissimo.' James had already hinted that he might accompany Slessor, his old Tokyo correspondent, and one of their guests that evening, on a visit to China.

In defence of Gareth, Violet said, 'I expect he's working twenty hours a day – he used to put in eighteen in peacetime.'

'I'm not saying he's idle. But he's let the English ruin him. Especially Churchill – that fat old drunk who wants to keep the empire where it was in the year 1890 and will sacrifice the last drop of other people's blood to do so. Australian blood, Canadian blood, American . . . it's all the same to him.'

He had obviously been drinking, probably at the Australian Club, on the way home. There was a burr to his voice that was absent when he was sober, and a reckless anger just below the surface. Under normal circumstances Violet would have avoided discussion when he was at this stage.

'You believe that the English are so omnipotent they turn him into a puppet?'

'They're damn hard to resist, I'll say that. I can understand how it's done – even though, unlike Gareth, I didn't precisely come from nowhere.'

James was constructing the knot in his black tie with bad-tempered skill. He gave a sudden disconcerting laugh and she saw his face flush in the mirror.

'You remember how they do it – all that urbane chat and the assumption that you're one of them, until, oops, "but you're from down under, aren't you?" they say. "I quite forgot for a moment." Then there's some crack about cricket or convicts or kangaroos.'

He paused, challenging her, pleased with himself.

'And when they finally take you up, and ask you to shoot their bloody birds, it's like being ushered into the garden of Eden. No wonder Mayhew likes London so much, bombs or no bombs. They're all over him, especially the women – and no kangaroo jokes nowadays, you can bet on it. It'll be "the sturdy digger and his cold steel" and all that bull. Why? Because they want something. They want to save their bloody skins.'

'What women?'

James gave her the triumphant grin of a small boy who had won a

275

prize. She remembered Bunty talking about James's bullying – and also about his protectiveness, when they had been children. Now he had made his victim rise like a fish.

'I thought you might have heard. There's supposed to be one in particular. She's called Lady Rowena Campbell, and if you think that sounds like croquet and Hurlingham you don't know our Rowena. She looks like Dorothy Lamour – jet black hair and a bare midriff.'

'She sounds just your type,' Violet said. 'You probably wish she was.'

'Unlike Mayhew, I've had quite enough English women,' James said unpleasantly. 'This one has money too – he probably thinks she'll make him the perfect wife and political hostess. Poor bastard, he doesn't know the half of it.'

'I expect you're jealous.'

James laughed again, louder than before. 'I'm not vain any more; those days are past. I don't care what Mayhew does with women. He can have anyone he likes. What I care about is the effect on the company. The fact that he betrayed me. That I'll never forgive.'

He looked straight at her. With a sense of release she thought, this is it; he knows. Unable to speak, she waited for him to continue.

Almost to her disappointment, he went to the door and opened it for her. 'We'd better get on down,' he said. 'I want a good talk with Slessor.'

At dinner Violet kept up her share of small talk with her usual vivacity. She was careful not to drink more than half a glass of wine, divining a deep sadness within herself that might overwhelm her if encouraged.

Towards the other end of the table sat Slim Slessor, the old Asia hand, grey, disillusioned, always expecting the worst, with a face wrinkled like that of a platypus. Violet would have liked to talk to him more, but he was monopolised by James, their conversation filled with Chinese names she only dimly recognised. Slessor was shortly going to Chungking, the increasingly beleaguered temporary capital where Chiang Kai-shek had his headquarters. All James's bloodthirsty warnings now seemed to be coming true. He had been talking for days about Slessor's belief that the Japanese were withdrawing troops from the Chinese front in order to launch an invasion south – and, ultimately, of Australia.

Slessor, Violet noted, put away drink like a camel. Seafood mousse was followed by saddle of lamb, roasted very well as they preferred in Australia and flavoured with the sweetness of rosemary. Among their half-dozen guests, O'Fallen and Jerry Jerome were mainly content to listen and observe. Like me, Violet thought, they are having a night off. No need to shine when there's a new star present.

By the time dessert was served, the men were engrossed in their own conversation and palpably eager for the port to start circulating. When the time came for Violet to escort Daisy up to bed, she made her excuses for not returning herself. No one, except Jerome, who expressed exaggerated disappointment, paid more attention than courtesy demanded.

From her room she heard them on the verandah, talking and laughing late into the night. She sat for a long time beside her window. After going in to look at the children, she was surprised to notice that there were tears on her cheeks.

A wave of deep sadness overcame her as she contemplated her love affair with Gareth, and her marriage. Surely the best days were gone, long gone, even, and the pain she suffered now was part of a chain and would continue until the end of her life. Defeated by regrets, she lay on her bed and wept and wept, for how long she did not know. At length, she got up and went to her dressing-table. Staring at her inflamed eyes in the mirror as she removed what was left of her make-up, she recovered just enough sense of purpose to get undressed.

Just before falling asleep, she became aware of a chorus of raucous male laughter from the garden. A thick voice was shouting something combative. A challenge, perhaps; or a curse.

Next morning, breakfasting surrounded by newspapers, James confirmed that in May he would be going to Chungking to interview the Chinese leader. He made the announcement absently, without looking up at Violet from his reading. He might have been informing the housekeeper.

But after draining his coffee cup and getting up from the table he could not resist a postscript. 'You don't have to worry about me getting up to anything in Chungking,' he said with a broad grin. 'From what Slessor tells me I don't think Madam Chiang is one to go for the Dorothy Lamour look. *She* won't be showing anyone her belly-button.'

Later that day, when James had left for Tasmania with an accountant to close down a wood-pulp factory, Violet heard a disquieting rumour about that rowdy evening on the Killymoon verandah.

She wondered how to verify it. Jerome would be no help – he would treat any enquiry as an invitation. In the end, she telephoned the priest. Once she would have invented some social pretext for the call. Now she asked straight away.

'. . . is it true, then, what Connie said?' According to Connie, James had asserted that, by the time he left for China, Gareth Mayhew would no longer be prime minister. '*Did* he bet on it? And was the stake as large as I've been told?'

Violet's lack of niceties produced an edge of irritation in O'Fallen's suave voice, as, reluctantly, he confirmed that it was true.

'I suppose you were all drunk,' she said.

She could hear him sigh. 'That would be an exaggeration, Violet. They – we – can all take our drink.'

Violet pictured the scene on the verandah. James would have been flushed, vehement and as fearless as a bull charging a horse. Jerry, in contrast, would have been entirely cool, laconic and yet sarcastic – it would certainly not have been he who had shouted so loudly.

'You should have stopped it,' she said.

'It's a common fallacy to think priests are miracle-workers,' O'Fallen replied. 'Even James falls into this confusion sometimes. And he's known me longer than any of them. Last night, nobody on earth could have stopped him. It was *in vino veritas*.'

Violet could not bear to give him a civil response. She put the receiver back on the hook, as a substitute for having the last word.

She really would have to talk to Gareth now; she must see him.

In the WIC office the word 'Canberra' was usually spoken with weary derision. For practical reasons, everyone abhorred the inconvenient and fatiguing journey. And then there were all the Sydneysiders' ingrained grievances about the new federal capital. It was both a joke and an insult that this artificial enclave, on what had previously been virgin New South Wales territory, should have ousted so much of the dominance of an established city. For Violet, arranging an assignation with Gareth in Canberra would have been far too risky. It was too intensely concentrated a community for clandestine activities to stay secret for long. As she set off she felt she was making an incursion into alien, probably hostile territory.

The first day was spent on WIC business. Meanwhile the prime minister's residence responded to Violet's telephone calls with nothing more than polite rejection. Finally she called Cissy. Would she please use her influence, to arrange a brief meeting with Gareth on a private matter? Once, Violet would rather have died than resort to such a humiliating course. But now she had stopped caring. She was staying at an undistinguished hotel, the Glenella View. At another time she might have stayed with Cissy, or at least been her guest in a tour of the press gallery: but they were no longer close enough. She spent the late afternoon sitting in the hotel's nostalgically English garden, which was filled with irises about twice the size of their English counterparts, together with sweet peas, gladioli, and roses the size of cabbages. Closing her eyes, she could feel herself drowning in the smells of England, only more pungent, against the background sounds of birds whose cries were harsh and tropical. Beyond the garden was an unbroken perspective that might have been Scotland, a series of blue lakes like Scottish lochs and hills of a fainter blue on the limit of the horizon. Nowhere was there a tree or a fence or any other human intrusion.

It was beautiful but scarcely alive – 'a one-horse town', as Gareth had once remarked, 'where somebody shot the horse.' The whole place was pretty, but with a makeshift, unfinished atmosphere. Its inhabitants were pleasant, with a serenity bordering on indifference that Violet suspected was part of belonging to a professional government bureaucracy. They had the look of people awaiting pensions.

Cissy had nothing at all in common with them.

'Come in, Vi; we don't stand on ceremony here.'

She greeted Violet with a hearty handshake, as if they were about to fight a championship, and offered a chair. Next to her piled, utilitarian desk a shorthand typist was sitting with a big reporter's pad. 'This is Mary, Mrs Franklin.'

The manner was very assured. Cissy was pale, though, as if the office were underground and she hadn't seen the sun for weeks. She had lost weight, but it did not suit her. She looked older and her face had developed a pinched look. She was also noticeably more dominating here. Violet remembered her first visit to Killymoon, as a country girl looking for a career step via the boss's wife.

'I'll just finish what I'm doing . . .'

Cissy was dictating a letter to the parliamentary press gallery specifying embargoes, and a background briefing on a forthcoming speech by the prime minister on the subject 'Women and the War Effort'.

There was a lack of spontaneity about her gestures, and Violet wondered whether she had delayed the dictation session deliberately, so that she could be seen at the helm of state.

The office was painted grey, with official steel furniture and a wastepaper basket to match, an identifying room number stencilled on its side. There was a brace of modern Remingtons on a side-table, a calendar from the Sydney Show, and a poster from London asking IS YOUR JOURNEY REALLY NECESSARY? The room could seat six or eight people, squeezed in tight, and a number of folded chairs against the wall suggested meetings often took place there. In comparison, the WIC's nineteenth-century chambers in Sydney were almost extravagant. This place smelled of stale cigarette smoke and carbon paper, and long hours of grinding administrative toil.

Violet picked up a copy of London *Vogue* that was lying on the desk. December 1940. She was surprised Cissy was so up to date, and wondered how she had got such a magazine. Her own subscription had ceased to arrive after the outbreak of war. She flicked through the pages, which were filled with the wartime styles – a strange marriage between fashions and uniforms, made out of air-force-blue tweeds and khaki-coloured cottons. The suits were boxy, the shoes built up. Every haircut was either a sensible bob, or plaits pinned up close to the head. Cissy's own hair was styled in a neat collar-length bob and she too was wearing a military-style suit, with narrow epaulettes and buttoned pockets.

On the society pages, one name caught Violet's full attention. Lady Rowena Campbell. She was photographed standing next to a miniature submarine; the text referred to her father's shipbuilding company. Violet looked carefully at the grainy photograph. Lady Rowena was very pretty, with wide laughing eyes and a generous mouth. She was wearing a hat that looked like a Nazi helmet, with a white feather on one side.

'That'll do for now, Mary.' Cissy might have been dismissing the parlour maid.

When the typist had slipped demurely away, Cissy lit a Craven A. Briskly she passed some sheets of paper across the desk to Violet.

'This ought to interest you – Gareth, on Woman at War.'

'Cissy, you know I wanted to ask . . .'

'Go on; read it first.'

Violet did as she was asked, reading aloud.

'In this, the first total war in history, women fit in wherever they can. They have replaced men in some of the toughest jobs in our country – cane-cutting, cattle- and pig-farming in isolated areas, sheep-shearing. As I see it, the factor of women in war work of all kinds is the great unknown of the conflict we are in. Women are going to swing the balance of this war.'

'That's the main thrust of the speech. Sounds like Christabel Pankhurst, doesn't he?' said Cissy.

Violet smiled politely. 'We should send copies to WIC – we could do with some support from this quarter.'

She spoke truthfully enough. But this was not what she was here for.

'You know why I've come. Did you have any luck?'

'With the PM? No luck at all.'

There could have been no flatter rejection. For a moment they were both silent.

'Damn him, he's so bloody rude,' Violet said at last. 'It's something important. He's supposed to be a friend. What the hell is going on?'

Cissy sighed and made a helpless gesture – not very convincingly. Impotence was not at all her style. 'If you knew how many times I've had this conversation. It's made me a lot of enemies. But not you, thank God.'

'No, it's not personal between us.'

'I just wish I could help, Vi, but it's NBG: no bloody good at all. When Gareth wants to be unavailable, he's like a ghost.'

'James says it's like interviewing the Pope,' Violet answered as lightly as she could.

But she was thinking, does she mean with other women? Were half the matrons of Australia trying to spend ten minutes with him, to be ravished on the floor, as Mussolini was said to ravish the ladies he received? It sounded more like political life in nineteenth-century Paris: grey-whiskered presidents in top hats smuggling their mistresses in and out.

'I never thought it would come to this,' was all she could say. 'Incidentally, do you know who Rowena Campbell is?' The copy of *Vogue* had been open on her lap throughout their conversation.

'Campbell? No, never heard of her. Is she English?' Without waiting for an answer, Cissy went on. 'The trouble is these articles. The *Gazette* went to war with Gareth from the moment he was back on Australian soil. And he's, well, aggrieved.'

Violet could hear Gareth's voice saying 'Australian soil', with a metallic twang that made the words poignant. Cissy was quoting him indirectly, as no doubt she always did when briefing political correspondents on a non-attributable basis.

'The *Gazette*'s first article hinted that his major concern was not with Australia, but how soon he could get back to England. Then it got worse. It talks as if he thinks that the only way to draw attention to Australian interests is to go to Britain and sit on their doorstep. It's an insult to the country as well as to the prime minister. Especially at a time like this.'

'James would say that the government had declared war on the press.'

'So I see from the *Gazette*'s leaders. But what do they expect? In wartime a 24-page paper is a luxury item. It will still make thousands a month for the shareholders; I've seen the statistics – while the cost in paying for imports is borne by the government. Rationing's a fact of wartime, whether it's newspapers or silk stockings. In London, for eighteen months now the papers have been down to four pages.'

'I don't see why I should be defending James's arguments – but the *Gazette*'s newsprint comes from Tasmania, not anywhere involving foreign currency payments.'

'That was the only reason why rationing was delayed,' Cissy said. 'I'll tell you privately, Vi. When Gareth was responsible for that decision, it astonished everyone in government. In any case it was only putting off the inevitable. The delay has given James six months' leeway, and his profits over that period ought to tide him over several years.'

'If you're saying this because you think I'm here on James's behalf, that's not so. My business with Gareth is personal. Important, but still personal. I can't believe after all these years . . .'

'Sorry, Vi, but he won't see you. Better accept it.'

'If I write a letter, will you see he gets it?'

'Of course. But I don't think it will make any difference. And about those *Gazette* articles: you know what hurt him most? That piece about that cricketer.'

'Victor Trumper?'

Cissy looked impressed. 'I didn't know you followed cricket,' she said. 'Yes, that one. Gareth saw him play as a boy, and you know what these things mean to men.'

'To Australian men.' Violet sighed.

'Don't be so sure,' Cissy said. 'I'm no expert on men, heaven knows, but if you want my opinion, they're all the same. That's what Ma always says.'

On another occasion they might have shared a joke together; but not now. Getting up to go, Violet hesitated, then said, 'Do you remember one particular night – I think we were having dinner with Joseph in Paddington – and you said you believed in Gareth and that you *had* to believe in him as a man of principle, or else you couldn't work for him?'

Cissy nodded.

'Is it still true?'

'I'm still working for him, aren't I?' Cissy replied, opening the door. They were both relieved that the interview was over.

There was no time to lick her wounds after the fiasco in Canberra. Under Connie's ardent chairmanship WIC's responsibilities were becoming wider-ranging all the time. Her staff had more than tripled since the early days and the busy sound of Remingtons clattering and phone bells ringing across two floors of offices did much to assuage her hungry, industrious spirit. Violet had come to think of her with affection, and to hear the sounds of work as appreciatively as a music-lover listening to a cantata.

A fortnight after Violet's return to Sydney there was pressure on her to go to Hobart for some weeks. Thus, with the children installed at Glendevon and Violet commuting, she spent the first part of the autumn in Tasmania.

At Glendevon the season was magnificent. It put her in mind of the fall in New England as Ben had described it. After the war, if there was an after the war, she would travel.

'Don't even talk about "after the war",' said Jeannie, as Violet confided her thoughts one night after all the Glendevon children were in bed. 'My only ambition is to get to this stage of the day, where I can have a glass of sherry and a cigarette with my feet up. It may not sound like a great life for a girl, but it gets me through. And God knows how I'll cope if it ever stops.'

For nearly a year now she had been using the old Sorrell property as a cross between farm-house and temporary orphanage. The children included a dozen of the *Batory*'s arrivals who for one reason or another had been best housed there as a group.

Violet had found formerly pinched, urban children transformed, by sun and work in the fields. They were helping with the harvest, bringing in apples and pears and damsons from the orchards, and collecting hedgerow blackberries to make jam in huge steaming pans. Sam had a pig to feed, and spent hours collecting acorns in pails beneath the great Glendevon oaks, since Jeannie had told him that acorns were the pig's favourite breakfast.

The war was far away and, except for the absence of men, and the sight of women in rows doing the harvesting, its existence was forgotten. With this kind of natural bounty all about them, rationing did not apply. They ate giant marrows stuffed with wild rice, and the children set out in parties after first light to collect mushrooms before the cows trampled them down on their way in to milking.

Every night they were fourteen to dinner, which they ate together around the huge dining-room table. In the evenings, when the children were in bed, Billy's rotund old gramophone, veteran of a thousand rowdy parties, served as their source of music; and the women would pass the time by dancing quicksteps with each other.

Jeannie's main source of help was Edith Temple, the escort from the *Batory*, who had decided to stay in Australia. Edith had fallen in love with Glendevon, which made her feel at home.

'It's such a beautiful place,' she said one day to Violet. 'I almost think I could be happy living like this for ever.'

'Yes,' Violet had said. 'If only the world outside didn't exist.'

But the hostile world intruded daily. Aggie had written, distraught at having had no news of Jack, in Tobruk, for over two months. Every post brought the dread of some loss. One evening Violet had gone for a ride. She cantered her horse past the duck-pond on the home farm, across a gold carpet of fallen beech leaves. Her way took her over the same fields through which she and Gareth had ridden during that weekend just before he had been elected. Coming home she was walking her horse, cooling the sweat on his shoulders and flanks. Then too it had been autumn. The air had been full of the same sweet smell of ripe apples and freshly cut corn. How crazily they had been in love, back then.

Along the road she saw their venerable local postman pedalling his way home. He waved at Violet to stop.

From habit now, the sight of him troubled her. There were so many kinds of bad news he might bring. She reined in, and he laboriously dismounted from the heavy old Royal Enfield. Whatever his news, it was too important to be delivered while still in the saddle.

'Have you heard?'

Unable to say anything, Violet shook her head.

'The government has fallen. There's going to be a coalition under Mr Meldrum. This afternoon, Gareth Mayhew resigned.'

29

Back in Sydney, James was jubilant. Already he had spent time in conclave with two of Lynch's new economic ministers, and emerged with a hefty print contract for 6 million ration books. He was also hoping to follow this coup with other contracts, for military identification documents. Much of the print capacity created by newspaper rationing could now be employed again. It was also a reprieve for the Tasmanian mill.

Violet could not bear his high spirits. They reminded her so acutely of Gareth's defeat and her own helplessness. She and Gareth had been so close, or so she thought. Now, at probably the worst moment of his life, she might as well have been on Mars.

Angry and frustrated, she confronted James. 'I heard about your bet and I thought it was disgusting. Imagine wagering on something like that happening to an old friend – and then setting up a campaign to bring it about.'

'You did notice how he dropped us, I suppose? Once he'd got what he wanted.' James's good humour was indestructible. In addition to his part in the fall of the government, he was shortly due to leave for the Sino-Japanese front in northern China. The conflict he foresaw with Japan had become one of his leading preoccupations.

All the same she wanted the last word.

'It was a shameful thing to do, however you try and justify it.'

'You don't like what I did? You find it caddish and loutish, the kind of larrikin behaviour that Australia is so full of? You know, I agree with you in a way. It's probably morally indefensible. A proper English gentleman, a proper Christian, I suppose, would turn the other cheek when he's betrayed. But we don't react like that here, or I don't. As a matter of fact they don't react like that in England either. It's just that they're more hypocritical. In Australia there's a long tradition of political abuse; politicians call each other rude words like "mongrel" and "dingo"; and worse. I don't suppose it would be the thing at all in the House of Commons. Anyway, Jerry challenged me. Of course I had to accept the bet.'

He smiled. 'Mayhew turned out a disappointment to us all. He had plenty of warnings. He just got too big for his boots. I'm not going to waste any more time on him.'

And neither, his look implied, should she.

The new thing in James's life was Lynch Meldrum's coalition, which had no ministerial post for Gareth. James planned to be four weeks in China, and Violet was to make arrangements for a party to honour Lynch to be held the day after James returned.

'It's not as if he won an election, exactly,' Violet demurred. 'And it will seem a bit late in the day.'

'It's a good enough excuse for a party. I know all about war and the need for austerity. But it doesn't mean that if you offer people champagne they'll flush it down the dunny. Lynch should have one smart occasion. Your speciality, my dear.'

It was his way of 'duchessing' Lynch, the natural thing for a press man to do.

Yet there was more to it. James wouldn't admit it, but he really wanted a big party so that he could celebrate Gareth's defeat. Her husband wanted publicly to savour the changes in which he had played so big a part.

Violet declined to waste her time arguing with him. But she did nothing about the invitations before he left; and she planned to do nothing afterwards. I won't have anything to do with this, she thought. Whatever he says, I won't budge.

James had gone to elaborate lengths meanwhile to have himself kitted out by Sydney's leading military tailor. The Sino-Japanese combat area involved no Australian troops, and he was chagrined to find that consequently he could not wear a captain's three pips, the automatic rank for accredited war correspondents. His own dress had been one of many topics he never discussed with Violet. Now, however, he asked her opinion: did the shoulders of his tailored tropical shirts look naked, or even silly?

She reassured him politely, having no view on the subject. Everyone nowadays was accustomed to uniforms and badges of rank. To Violet, other than the gaudy flash of a red-tabbed General Officer, they all looked much the same.

On the day of his departure with Slessor her husband looked impressively military, even without the pips. He could have been a high-ranking officer travelling incognito to a conference. Certainly he was far too smart, as Slessor tactlessly remarked, to look as if he had come from a battle-front.

James was not about to forget the party. On the tarmac at Mascot Airport he told Violet, 'Get the invitations out by the end of the week, will you?'

'We ought to have a marquee,' he added, as he kissed the children goodbye. 'Don't forget.'

The children were used to their father going away, but they had never before been brought to the aerodrome to see his plane take off. Sam cried inconsolably, and got a playful cuff on the ear from his father. James gave Violet a hurried but warm kiss and set off briskly across the tarmac. She could see that he felt a free man at last, a soldier even, and was mighty proud of himself. His pace was brisk enough to leave Slessor, who was carrying both cases, like a batman, flagging behind. A *Gazette* photographer flashed some bulbs. From inside the aircraft, James was visible through the cockpit window, talking to the pilot. He was probably explaining that he was qualified to fly the plane himself.

In her years in Australia, Violet had heard a great deal about Gallipoli. The word was one, like cancer, that you could not safely say without choosing the time and company, in case your audience had lost someone twenty years before – they almost always had. Now Crete had become the new Gallipoli. The day it was announced that the airport there had fallen, another piece of news came that boded ill. Aggie had heard that Jack's name had come through on the lists from Tobruk: 'missing in action'.

'That's just the same as dead, they all say.' Aggie's voice on the telephone was harsh with grief. 'Thank goodness, Vi, that you don't know what it is to lose your man.'

Amid the gloom a letter came from Ben. Working through one of the London-based refugee organisations, he had located a boat, a Dutch cruise liner called the *Wilhelmina*. 'I thought it would be impossible to get a boat to sail across the world at the time of the biggest blockade in naval history. Not for love nor money. But, as usual, money has worked. For $20,000 we can sail her almost anywhere. We have a fine Dutch captain, a crew from Liverpool, a steward from Glasgow – even an entertainment officer.

'Joseph has interviewed every Jewish refugee in London . . . The ship will be calling at Lisbon and Marseilles. Also, I've got him to swear an oath that he won't leave a single member of my South China payroll anywhere within range of the Japs, because they've put my name on a

287

death list. That will mean stopping in Singapore, probably in the New Year. They say Singapore's defended like the Rock of Gibraltar. I hope it's true. But I've kind of lost faith in the British army – they're having a worse run just now than my favourite baseball team, and *they're* in bad shape.'

On the way back from the WIC offices, ten days after James had left for China, Violet made a detour through Double Bay. As if the car was driving her, she found herself stopping in front of the old apartment building. On impulse she entered and went upstairs. To her horror, the key grated in the lock and refused to turn. After a few seconds' struggling she managed to pull it out. The locks had been changed. She fled, appalled that Gareth might have been inside with someone else, and that he would realise that she was the would-be intruder.

Back at Killymoon, Don Hooker, a political reporter from the *Gazette*, was waiting in the hall. Hooker was a tall, inordinately thin man, with a receding forehead and sparse dark hair that made him look like a kangaroo. He was sweating in his serge suit and looked profoundly uncomfortable.

'Can I get you a drink?' Violet asked, showing him into the drawing-room.

Nervously he accepted. He had the look of a man who wished he was almost anywhere else.

The telephone rang, and Violet went into the hall to answer it.

'Oh, Vi, he's alive, he's alive!' Aggie sounded as though she were dancing. Violet could picture her in the hallway at Belle View with the yellow telegram still in her hand.

'They made a mistake. It's always happening in wartime. But he's coming home – invalided out, but alive and coming home.'

'That's wonderful, Aggie. I'm so happy.'

They exchanged news of other people now abroad, including Bill who was on an entertainment tour for ENSA with Vera Lynn. Aggie could barely stop talking; her relief and joy were inexhaustible: 'I feel as though nothing could make me unhappy again.'

Violet went back into the drawing-room with the reflection of Aggie's cheerfulness still lingering on her face. Don Hooker looked haggard as she finished pouring his drink.

'I think you should have one yourself,' he said, 'and sit down.'

She knew before he could continue.

'I have very bad news, I'm afraid, Mrs Franklin.'

'Yes?'

'The worst.'

'Go on.'

Violet was to be grateful for his directness. He said, 'Mr Franklin has been killed.'

'How did it happen?'

'We've only had garbled reports from Chungking. But it appears he was flying a plane, a fighter belonging to Chiang Kai-shek. It crashed. Everyone was killed.'

'Poor old Slessor.'

'Oh no, not old Slim. He stayed on the ground. It was Slessor who sent the cable.'

'He's a nice man,' Violet said absently, thinking of Slessor's old legs buckling under the weight of James's suitcase.

Hooker misheard her.

'You're right, Mrs Franklin. He was a lovely man. A real journo, and one of the best, even if he did have his moods. We won't see his like again.'

To her surprise there were tears in Don Hooker's eyes. The man had probably not cried since he was nine years old.

The trouble was that Violet herself found it impossible to cry.

Don Hooker's coverage of the funeral occupied an entire page of the meagre wartime *Gazette*. There was a black border and the caption:

James George Franklin

1896–1941

A Great Newspaperman

The page was divided into sections: James's career, and the development of the *Gazette* under his ownership; his position in Australian politics and society; and, finally, his status as a family man. The history of the paper's initial support for Gareth Mayhew, followed by the *volte-face* which had proved instrumental to his losing office, was not dwelt on. The rift had been no rift, the feud no feud, only – in Hooker's words – 'a disagreement over the need to apply restrictions on the scope of the press in wartime'.

There was also a long extract from a speech James had made on the role of the press. It had been delivered to an audience of newspaper dignitaries at a Melbourne conference in 1937, and declared, 'The *Gazette* believes certain ideals and values are indispensable to Australian society . . . and is not afraid to say so. A newspaper needs a soul as well as a heart.'

Daisy read every word as though it were a prayer book. But Violet could only skim through with a heavy heart. The section devoted to James's private life – to their life together – was illustrated by an old photograph from Killymoon taken not long after Liz's birth. It showed George and Daisy and the two of them by the tennis court, with James holding his racket jocularly, as if shooting at the photographer. They had all been dappled with sun and shade – an idyllic group. As Ben remarked later, 'It's the kind of thing they'd print in the *Saturday Evening Post* to illustrate a piece about the joys of family life.'

The picture disturbed Violet, largely because she could remember neither the precise occasion, nor the photographer. Eventually it emerged that it was the creation not of a professional, but of an enthusiastic amateur. The priest had been holding the camera that day. A second photo was of James and Slessor at Mascot Airport, under the caption, 'Duty Calls: Off To War In China.'

Among the many things the newspaper failed to specify were the peculiar terms of James's will. There was merely a short item, under the headline THE FUTURE OF THE GAZETTE, saying that to ensure the paper's continuity, James had created a family trust.

It was some time before Violet could take in the full implications of James's will. In the meantime Ben made one of his unannounced, and flying visits. He had already sent a telegram of condolence. Then one day a note arrived at Killymoon, offering his company for 'an afternoon off the day after tomorrow, something we can steal from this bloody war'.

Violet drove him to the beach, where he established himself on the verandah, reading a pile of Australian papers – including the *Gazette*'s special edition announcing the sudden death of its owner. It provoked the American to splutters of mirth.

He looked sideways at Violet to see if she was annoyed. 'I can speak frankly, I guess?'

She shrugged. 'I don't see the point of speaking any other way.'

'Hooker's one loyal guy.' Ben jabbed at a paragraph with his finger. 'This is all very sincerely written.'

'Why shouldn't it be?' Violet knew that Don Hooker had formerly worked for a rival paper. She also knew that such a fact usually counted for little.

'Because it's all bullshit. You must know that, Vi.'

He drank his tea and continued musing over the paper. Finally he said, 'I guess it often happens if you hire someone from the opposition. They really go down the line to show you they'd have been on your team from the start, if only they'd seen the light earlier . . .'

It was months since she had been down to Palm Beach. It seemed months, too, since she had been alone with another adult with whom there was no need for caution or pretence. Their sudden trip – a hiatus between meetings for him, a day of rest for her – should have brought with it a sense of youthful escape from responsibilities. But she still felt leaden.

Thank God for Ben, though. He was the ideal companion; the only one probably, who could help her exorcise the ghosts of this beautiful place. All the memories of breakfast under the flame tree, of fragmented voices half drowned by the surf long ago and now vanished for ever.

Now they both were there she felt almost nothing. As if the past had never happened.

'I don't know what's wrong with me. It's as if I've gone numb.' She got up from the deck chair. 'Would you like some more tea?'

'I couldn't swallow another drop – it's too damn English for me, if you want to know. And sitting next to that . . .' he gestured towards the long surf-line, 'it makes me feel silly, as if I'm really in the Savoy watching the rain on the Thames.'

'There's Australian beer, if you'd find that more appropriate.'

'The only appropriate drink is palm toddy. But, as it happens, I've got some champagne in the car.'

'It sounds like a seduction,' she said, and was instantly annoyed with herself.

Ben shrugged – he was not about to be disturbed by anything. 'More a celebration,' he said. 'The seduction will come of its own accord later –'

'If ever,' she interrupted, and wondered again why she was being so unforthcoming.

'Let me open it.'

'I thought you were against me drinking in the afternoons?'

'This could be the right afternoon,' he said serenely; and the first bottle was opened.

He returned to his steady devouring of the old papers.

'They've done James well,' he said, with an appreciative chuckle. 'Five thousand words, and almost everything important left out. It's as if he'd dictated it himself from the other side.'

'I haven't really read it properly. I pretended to Hooker I had, because he was proud of it. But in the end I couldn't do it.'

'I guess the fact you didn't love him doesn't make it any better.'

'Oh yes, it does,' Violet said. 'I *am* very sorry he's dead, especially for the children. It leaves a terrible empty space for them, and there wasn't much of their father there when he was alive. But it would have been much worse if I loved him. Then I'd have been in agony. As it is I just felt left over. What the girls in the office call "at a loose end".'

'What's this about "the future of the *Gazette*"?' he asked.

'It's complicated.'

Ben laughed. 'I guess it would have to be.'

'A family trust has been set up for Sam and Liz. It means I don't get any capital, only some income; and even Killymoon is in trust. If I marry again, the income stops. The lawyer was quite embarrassed, and talked a lot about income tax provisions and continuity down the generations. But it still seems a bit – well – exclusive.'

'It excludes you from the family's wealth, that's what,' Ben said. 'And if you remarry, you lose even that.'

'It may be fair, given the state of our marriage. If he'd lived I'd have tried to get a divorce sooner or later. The will recognises that.'

'Bullshit,' Ben said. 'Did the lawyers say that?'

'They hinted.'

'Cheeky bastards,' Ben grunted to himself. 'It's pure James, that's all. Trying to possess you beyond the grave, trying to keep you in line. You know, in his way he sure did love you. You were of great value in his eyes. I guess that's something.'

'No, no, he didn't. He was mad; he didn't love anyone but himself. At one time he liked a certain kind of woman for sex, young women who wore *Vie Parisienne* underwear, that kind of thing. But I think that deep down he really hated them, too.'

Ben refilled their glasses. 'He was a very solitary guy, except for that suave Father. I had sympathy for James.'

'Because you agreed about the war?'

'No; we shared more than that.'

She knew what he was trying to say. But for the moment she could find no response. At least it was easy to talk to Ben on other subjects, and, bit by bit, she managed to say what she felt.

It took a long time, and the trouble was that by then she had drunk most of a bottle of champagne. The next morning, when they drove back, she could hardly remember what she had said, merely that at one point she had been weeping while Ben stroked her hair. She had slept alone, in the big bed that reminded her of Gareth, and when she came down early for a swim she had found Ben stretched out on a sofa with his boots on.

'Jeez, I was drunk last night,' he said, opening one eye and holding his forehead.

'So was I. It's been a long time since I got like that.'

'Just what you needed.' Ben got up and went towards the kitchen in search of coffee. 'You cried for the bastard once and now you'll never have to do it again.'

'Which bastard?' Violet found herself saying.

Ben laughed through his hangover. 'Both of them. The phoney newspaper boss and the phoney politician. You don't have any more skeletons in your closet, do you?'

He had to be in Sydney by eleven, and they scarcely mentioned the subject again.

Violet was staying as close as possible to the children. Sam had reacted by becoming overly protective of Liz, reading her stories at night, and going to check that she was asleep after her light had been turned out. Yet, the fact that his dad had died as a result of the war, if not exactly in action, turned out to be a help. There were other boys at Sam's school who had been similarly bereaved, and once, when Violet had gone to collect him at the end of the day, she had seen him standing aside with a small group of his friends, all of them wearing the same grim expressions, like a military detachment. The master who was in charge by the gate told her that all four had lost their fathers.

'They've been sticking together,' he said. 'They've got something the others haven't, poor little sods.'

She realised sadly that Sam, with his stoical expression, had learned there was kudos in having lost a father who had been, supposedly anyway, a hero. He had learned how to play the bereavement card. She was alarmed at this evidence of his growing up. She knew that it meant he was also growing away from her.

The *Wilhelmina* finally set sail from Tilbury docks in the first week of October, nearly seven weeks behind schedule.

Almost half the passengers it was due to carry were orphans, and Violet faced a heavy task when it came to their resettlement in Australia. For them it wasn't just for the duration of the war, but for ever. The workload was demanding, but she absorbed it easily, taking Sam and Liz with her wherever she could, using her children's eyes to help her vet prospective families.

293

Sam had become noticeably less timid since the death of his father. He was very determined, and when one morning Violet overheard him talking to a Mrs Dunnit, who was planning to take two children, she realised that he had learned how to turn his bereavement into a strength.

'Is Mr Dunnit away at the war?' Violet heard him ask.

'Too right he is,' the future foster mother replied. 'He couldn't wait to be off. Tom was one of the first to go.'

'My dad was killed in China,' Sam announced, only approximately following the conversation's path. 'It was in a plane crash. He was flying.'

'You poor little pet. Let me see if I can find you a biscuit. Or would you prefer a piece of my seed cake?'

'I think I'd like cake,' Sam replied judiciously.

Violet came into the neat little kitchen, leading Liz and trying to hide her smile. Her son, like his father, knew how to get what he wanted.

Gareth had failed to attend the funeral. Instead he sent a formal note excusing himself. Opening the letter, with its familiar florid handwriting, had been for Violet a major ordeal. But the contents, save for the last sentence, were bland and conventional – too much so. The letter ended: 'This is not the right time, but one day it will come – and then, I pray, we will comprehend each other better.' It was signed 'Love, Gareth.'

His absence was unavoidable, he said, 'because of a foreign commitment'. She thought it sounded like a statement to the press; but, of course, nowadays all overseas destinations had become a secret. Later she noticed a brief mention in the *Gazette* of his undertaking an Asian tour on a fact-finding mission to do with defence. It sounded like small beer, a self-created task.

There had been no role for him in the coalition, but he was still in parliament, speaking periodically but attracting little interest. His force was apparently so spent that some political commentators wrote about the phenomenon. Gareth Mayhew, they agreed, was the latest victim of the country's passion for turning on former idols and hacking its heroes down to size.

When Connie Lynch moved to Canberra, Violet took over her job; at first because there was no one else to do it and she was obliged to fill the gap herself. By the time she was officially appointed, with increased powers and responsibilities, she found that she was using work as a drug. Connie had once remarked that she could have spent a hundred hours on WIC affairs every week and would still need more time. Now Violet was discovering the truth of her words.

The people she worked with were sympathetic about her bereavement. But once she had thanked them for their condolences and then turned their attention firmly to the matter in hand they were grateful to take the hint. They saw that she needed to carry on with 'business as normal', one of the year's wry catch-phrases.

Meanwhile there were people outside WIC, particularly business friends of James, who made a nuisance of themselves in their desire to help or protect her in some unspecified way. There was another factor: they were all people she had known slightly for years, directors of the *Gazette* or other companies, prominent people in Sydney. But the last thing she wanted was to have dinner with them or borrow their houses in the Blue Mountains. The assumption that she would be lost without James was insulting, a kind of condescension.

They had not generally been any closer to her husband, she suspected, than to her. And in due course she came to see how isolated a man James had been, even though he had never seemed to be alone. Billy Sorrell apart, there was no one he had been really close to over a long time.

Admittedly, 'Jerry' Jerome had been a crony of two or three years' standing, thanks to having taken the same side at a meeting of newspaper proprietors. 'James liked people who agreed with him. And it happened that we were on the same side,' was how he explained the relationship one day when, out of politeness, Violet agreed to meet him for lunch.

To mark the occasion, he had supplied the restaurant with a bottle of Veuve Clicquot '27; Violet knew at once that the meeting was going to be fun. To her surprise he was as flirtatious as usual – when she had accepted his invitation she had been thinking of herself as in purdah. But Jerry clearly didn't see it this way.

'You're looking very beautiful,' he said. 'Even though you work too bloody much. Do you ever think of the *Gazette* – you used to write things for them, didn't you?'

'A long time ago, as it seems. When Cissy Greeley was still a *Gazette* reporter. But I'm far too busy for that now.'

'I see she's working for Meldrum.'

'So I hear. I can't see her getting on with Connie: but maybe that doesn't matter.'

For three quarters of the meal they gossiped about everything, from a forthcoming charity party which was to begin with a cricket match, to the latest films, none of which she had found time to see.

Then Jerry, ordering a brandy, poked his fine nose into the balloon glass, in a gesture of appreciation, and told her he wanted to make a proposition.

'You've done nothing else since the day we first met.'

Jerry laughed into his brandy. 'I know. I went for you the moment I saw you – though nothing like as much as I do now. But that's not what I want to talk about.'

So even Jerry conformed to the convention of widows being sacrosanct. He was wearing an expression of seriousness, one she had noticed very occasionally at meetings. Strangely, it did not add any weight to his personality; rather it suggested the intentness of a greedy child.

'You know I'm on the board of the *Gazette* now?' he said.

'I noticed you had shares. That's a recent development, isn't it?'

'I bought them a year ago. It was part of a plan. Now listen, Violet; I want to make you a proposal.'

She raised an eyebrow. 'A serious one,' he added hastily. 'Nothing romantic.'

In this vein he had actually lost some of his assurance. It was evidently hard for him to find the right level, when discussing serious matters with a member of the opposite sex. He was used only to the Don Juan/Errol Flynn approach.

Still, for half an hour he talked persuasively, and with a bluntness she found attractive. But not irresistible, she realised, as she heard herself saying, 'No, Jerry; thanks but no. I want to do something else.'

The next day she realised that if he had just asked her to go to bed with him she would probably have said yes. He was a very attractive man, and she was beginning to feel oppressed by her celibacy. It was like the mist around an iceberg, a damp emanation that chilled the rest of the world. She had recognised the quality in Father O'Fallen years ago, and hated it.

But what Jerome had proposed was not merely an affair, but a partnership; and she was not ready for anything like that. Her excuse of being too busy had been perfectly true. The question of the refugees was more absorbing than anything else in her life; besides, she felt revulsion against spending the war in trying to make more money.

Jerome gloried in money, she saw – his brown hands had patted the old champagne bottle like a pet, some pedigree animal he kept expensively in the kennels. He would like to have owned her like that, or possessed her. But he had missed his chance.

At least twice a week Violet made time to take the children out

296

somewhere. One bright afternoon they all set off for a charity match at the Sydney Cricket Ground. It had been organised by the War Service League, a group campaigning for what they called 'complete mobilisation' of all resources in Australia and the rest of the British Commonwealth. Violet was due to make a short speech – something that happened often nowadays, though not often enough for her to have conquered her fluttering nerves.

The children, detecting her unease, seized the chance to tease her. 'Aren't you nervous, Mum?' Liz had kept asking. 'I'd be so frightened, I'd . . . turn into a bird and fly right out of the tent.'

'You'd get caught in the ropes, silly,' said Sam, who had turned up for the occasion wearing white flannels and carrying his own small bat. Violet knew he secretly hoped that somehow they would invite him to play.

They concluded their inspection of the official marquee and, dragging her behind them, led the way to a children's fair which was operating behind the pavilion. It was here, twenty minutes later, that she saw Gareth going past the Punch and Judy stand. He was wearing a light grey suit, beautifully cut – spoils from London, probably – and a dashing panama hat with some kind of club ribbon round it.

Gareth was looking straight ahead, and no one paid him any attention. He must have felt like the invisible man – once upon a time there would have been someone greeting him every few feet and within seconds a crowd would have started to form. It would have needed a Pountney to clear the way and hold them back.

She would have gone over, but she was waiting for the children to finish a ride. By the time they were back he had vanished. Then she was due to be back in the marquee, making her speech. In it, she was to thank the organisers for their cooperation on the question of mobilising women and thus freeing more men for the military.

Once she had started, she spoke the conventional words with apparent assurance. As Connie had taught her, she concentrated on aiming her voice at the centre of the back row of the audience.

'Whatever rot you're talking, it's only polite to make sure that the poor people hear it,' Connie had said. 'So speak up – and learn your lines word perfect.'

Now, carrying out her lesson conscientiously, Violet had fortunately almost finished before she saw Gareth again. He was sitting in the third row, near the end, an obscure and anonymous spot which she had ignored. Once, he would have been in the middle of the row – or, more likely, on the stage itself.

The physical change in Gareth was not apparent. But, as he came towards her outside the marquee afterwards, there was something different about his walk. He was holding himself cautiously, as if he had a sore back and was anxious not to strain it.

At close quarters she saw that he had lost some weight, and that it made him look older. In his dandified hat, he looked like an elder statesman. He gave her a little bow. Then, as if aware that the gesture had been too formal, he closed one hand round her wrist.

He started to apologise for not being at the funeral. But she stopped him.

'I knew you'd have been there if you could.'

'Why?'

'Because you were so fond of James. What a pity you had to quarrel about the rationing.'

He looked at her as if he couldn't believe what he was hearing.

'Fond?' He gave a little laugh. 'I assure you there was no love lost. He kept you in the dark about everything, didn't he?'

'Coming from you, that's good. I've been wondering where you went, for about the last year. It was as though I'd died, long before James.'

'What could I do?' he said, despairingly.

'It's fine to say that now. You were a bastard to treat me that way, that's all. I suppose you always do that to women.'

There was a ripple of applause from the spectators watching the match.

Gareth was looking pale under his tan, as if he had been ill.

When he spoke there was pain in his voice. 'You mean you didn't understand? You didn't know I hadn't any choice?'

'Of course you had a choice. All you had to do was pick up the phone.'

'James really didn't tell you,' he said, wonderingly.

'Tell me what?'

He smiled and let out a long, low whistle, as if surprised by something that had happened on the field.

'My God,' he said, 'you don't know, do you?'

'I must go and get the children,' she said.

Gareth put up his hand to prevent her leaving. He seemed unexpectedly buoyant, as if he had received good news.

'You may not understand it, but what you've said makes it all the more important we have a proper talk, and very soon. It may make you think differently of me.'

She hesitated. There was a roar of excitement from the crowd. The ball had been struck prodigiously high and seemed to be heading directly for them.

'Watch it,' said Gareth, and touched her arm.

In fact they were perfectly safe. After reaching its maximum height, a blob of perfect red against the blue, the ball fell sharply, and almost straight into the hands of a fielder down below them on the very limit of the pitch.

Violet heard the smacking sound as it struck his open palms. Then there was another roar from the crowd, as it rebounded and bounced full toss into the first row of seats, only yards from where they stood.

Gareth looked at the disconsolate fielder with amusement. 'It's the sun,' he said. 'He was scared of being dazzled, so he took his eye off the ball. That's what happened to me – with you.'

'I don't know what you mean,' Vi said. 'I really must get the children now.'

She agreed all the same to meet him later in the week.

It was hard to put her emotions at risk again. In the end she delayed for nearly a fortnight before seeing Gareth. He had aroused her curiosity – it was clear that something had been going on with James that she knew nothing about. When she had used the word 'fond' it had suddenly come to her that Gareth hated her dead husband more than anyone in the world.

All the same, she was so repelled at being involved again in his affairs that when he finally appeared at the house, she almost regretted having agreed to see him at all.

He accepted a drink and sat down, looking at her expectantly. His demeanour was far brighter than it had been at the cricket match, and this time he did not look much older than his years. He was dressed so perfectly, in a double-breasted blazer and beautifully cut flannels, that at first she did not notice his clothes at all. His tie had the faintest blue stripe – he had lost the taste for garish neckwear that had first attracted Quigley's attention on the Harbour Bridge. Perhaps someone in London was buying his ties.

Within seconds he was talking about his newly announced job. His animation was just as Violet remembered from the first day at the beach, when she had found him rehearsing his speech before a mirror with the surf booming at his back.

'It's a new position, roving envoy abroad. But it will mainly be

London and Washington – I'm actually moving into the ambassador's residence in Georgetown.'

Violet offered her congratulations.

He smiled deprecatingly.

'I'm not deceiving myself. It suits Lynch to have me out of the way. So do you know what I'm going to do?'

She shook her head.

'I'm going to enjoy it – the position, the people, the freedom to go where I want. That, above all. We're too far away here. In wartime it makes you feel vulnerable – caged and at the mercy of decisions people take far away.'

'So you're going to change that?'

'A bit, perhaps. There are things a man with the right prestige can do over there which would be impossible for a career diplomat. But I won't pretend it's as good as being defence minister, let alone . . .'

'Do you miss it very much?'

'At first I did. I missed not knowing things any more. But now I'm used to it, and I'm going to turn what's happened into an advantage.' He paused. 'And so are you.'

'I don't see where I come in.'

'That's what I want to talk about. How much did James really keep you in the dark? That's what I need to know.'

'In the dark about what? All I know is that you and James quarrelled about the newsprint rationing. And that you disappeared out of my life, and from then on you treated me as if I were a leper.'

'Yes, that bloody newsprint. God, I hate businessmen. Their greed, their hypocrisy. So you think it was all to do with rationing. What about *us*?'

'There was no "us", once you'd taken back your letters and given orders not to be disturbed. If you knew the humiliation I went through in Canberra –'

'What do you mean, I took them back? After I sent them I never saw the bloody things again – until James arrived in my office with them under his arm, that is.'

Violet wondered for a moment whether he was lying. *James* had the letters under his arm. How had James got them? She felt unsure of everything – she didn't know what to trust any more. Certainly not Gareth.

He had not stopped talking – about how James had blackmailed him, how he had also insisted there be no contact between them, and how he had threatened to bring down the government.

'I always assumed you'd taken the letters because you didn't love me any more.'

'Damn it, no. Why would I steal my own letters?'

'To remove the evidence . . .'

'I wish to God I had,' he said. 'I find it hard to believe you never knew. Why do you think James attacked me so mercilessly in the *Gazette*?'

Violet side-stepped the question by asking another.

'Is that why you cancelled the newsprint rationing at the last minute?'

He nodded. 'And it's why I didn't see you when I returned from London. James exacted that as part of the price.'

Now she understood why James had been so triumphant when he had told her about Gareth's London girlfriend.

'I thought you'd left me for somebody else.'

'There was never anyone else who mattered enough for me to risk more important things. It never crossed my mind. But you were different. You dazzled me. Because of you, I took my eye off the ball. And, crash, James had me by the throat.'

'So that's what you meant the other day.'

Gareth nodded. 'I fell in love with you,' he said heavily. 'And it ruined me.'

'You wrote the letters, Gareth. It wasn't all my fault.' Violet hesitated. 'If you knew what was at stake, why did you impose rationing?'

'I had to. For the country. For the war. For the same reasons I thought James wouldn't go ahead with his crazy scheme, provided I didn't see you. My God, but that man must have loved you.'

She had an image of James with Gareth's letters, facing him across the desk. They had fought over her as though she was a pedigree bitch. Matters of principle or politics or economics had not even come into it – let alone the war. There was something very primitive about it. She loathed them both.

'I'm still trying to take it in that you would allow James to influence government policy like that. It must be illegal. That's the kind of thing they send people to prison for.'

'Oh, James would have gone to prison if I'd had my way. But what was I supposed to do? I wasn't going to resign to please him. All I could do was make a deal – and then the bastard turned and betrayed me all the same.'

Gareth got up and poured himself a whisky and soda from the

sideboard. He emptied most of his heavy glass tumbler in one swallow.

'I didn't come here to argue,' he said, standing with his back to the window. 'It's all a misunderstanding. I want you to come with me – to Washington. Think of the children, think of the opportunity for them. America will be safe during the war, for all of you. Then when the war is over we can come back here. With the newspaper behind me, I can get back into office. Lloyd George managed it.'

'Even if you wanted to marry me, you know you'd be marrying a poor woman. James left me an income on condition that I never marry again – and now I understand why.'

'Why don't we make a virtue of not taking the money? We'll be Australia's representatives at Buckingham Palace and the White House, and fight the will together. There are no trust arrangements that can't be broken. And we'll have the government money in the mean time. We'll have a wonderful life together – we'll be the perfect couple.'

She had a vision of herself wearing white gloves and standing in endless reception lines, the perfect political hostess.

'It doesn't make any difference,' she heard herself saying. 'I don't love you. Can't you understand that? If I did love you, then I wouldn't mind about the money. But I don't. What I want to do is carry on the work that you – inadvertently – started for me.'

'You owe it to me, Violet,' he said, with anger in his voice. 'I gave up too much for you.'

Violet interrupted him. 'I'm not in love with you any more, Gareth,' she said quietly; and for the first time she realised it was true.

'Don't you see what I sacrificed for you? My job? The country?'

'And what about me? What about what I sacrificed?'

'You don't understand the constraints of political life.' The anger in his voice had been replaced by a wheedling note, which she remembered from political speeches. It sounded offensive in Killymoon.

'They're invented by politicians – and anyway, even if they weren't, I don't want to understand them. I'm bringing more children to this country, and you can't help me with that, can you?'

'Violet, darling Violet, listen to me. I loved you; I still love you. Why do you think it all happened – for love of you, that's why.' He had come across the room, and put his hands on her shoulders.

'No, Gareth,' she said, moving away from him. 'It's all far too late.'

For love, yes, she thought, as she sat alone in the growing darkness after he had left. But also for pride and power and bloody-mindedness.

302

'You'll be stuck here,' Gareth had said, as he collected his hat. 'One day you'll want to get married again . . .'

'Maybe, but not now. Now, I want to be my own person.'

Gareth's story asked more questions than it answered, and Violet wondered if she would ever find out the truth. It was somehow inconceivable to her that James had gone to Double Bay and stolen the letters himself. But if not him, then who?

The only question it had solved was the issue of the will. How James must have hated him, she thought. Hated him with a hatred that can only be inspired by a love betrayed.

30

There was a spray of purple frangipani on the desk at Raffles Hotel, the only living thing, as far as Violet could see, that wasn't wilting in the oppressive Singapore heat.

The Malay clerk smiled encouragingly at her, as he held out a pen for her to sign the register. She understood the reason for his smile: her room was reserved. She was not another desperate refugee from up country trying to bribe or badger accommodation.

'It's a very nice suite,' he said, as he gave the room key to the luggage boy, 'Mr Maugham's favourite.'

The flight from Sydney to Singapore had taken five days. Violet had made the journey harnessed inside a grey Hercules bomber, with two RAAF advisers from Canberra. After their first overnight stop she had changed from a skirt into dark blue trousers; the parachute straps had hitched her skirt up well above her knees. Even so, she had quite liked her brief period in the forces; there was a relief in not having to think, in merely doing what she was told. The RAAF had simply shifted her like the parcels of top secret despatches for the Singapore garrison.

They had put down at Gladstone, and at Townsville, where Violet had spent a sleepless night listening to the carousing of drunken sailors in the bar below her room. Then, via Karumba and Darwin for refuelling, and on to Timor, Kunpang and Mokodo, names out of fairy-tales, where the plane flew low over the endless, deep-green jungle, which after so many hypnotic hours seemed no different from the dark-blue sea.

She asked the desk clerk for a telegram form, and he directed her to a poky office behind the porter's lodge. Perched on a stool beside the teak counter of the Long Bar, she wrote: 'Arrived safely. Thank you for all your help. Will inform you when I have made contact with Joseph.' She added the date, 9 February 1942, and addressed it to Connie at the WIC offices in Sydney.

There was only one working telephone, and a long, argumentative queue had formed beside it. She joined the group, which was dominated by a florid, ugly man vehemently protesting his right to use the phone first. For a while she expected that one of the men would have the good manners to invite her to go first. But none did; instead they all looked away. No 'ladies first' in wartime, she thought. She was anxious to go to the lavatory, so she finally gave up her place in the queue.

While she waited for the phone, she ordered a cup of coffee and sipped the scalding liquid slowly. The hotel hadn't changed much. Outside the terrace, the huge green leaves of the banana palms continued to shut out the light. It was hard to believe it was only a week since she had first seen the top secret cable from Colonel Norton, Military Police, Singapore, sent when the *Wilhelmina* docked in Singapore, which was to have been her final stop before reaching Sydney. Eleven families who had worked for Ben's South China Oil were waiting there to embark. The cable had said, 'Sternberg, Joseph Julius, answers the description a communist agitator. Under the "emergency act" he is being held indefinitely, pending positive identification to the contrary.'

In Australia, Violet had been unable to find out further details, beyond the fact that written authorisation wasn't sufficient to secure his release. His identification had to be made personally, by someone who knew him. She didn't want to ask Lynch to intervene, much less on behalf of someone he had never met, because of the *Wilhelmina*. The CORB programme had been unpopular in government circles, and she was worried that the *Wilhelmina* might arouse similar hostile reactions. So when Cissy urged her to go, and Connie said that someone she knew in the RAAF could get her a seat on a garrison transport, Violet had eagerly accepted.

She would have liked to consult Ben before leaving, but he was incommunicado, 'somewhere in the Pacific'. She had heard that he had become an official consultant to General MacArthur, with the temporary rank of colonel.

Two days later Violet had found herself climbing into a camouflaged bomber at Mascot Airport, equipped by Connie's good services with a letter to a Colonel Grogan in the Australian military mission in Singapore. She had been assured that, as long as she could identify the prisoner, Joseph's release should be certain. She only realised how lightheartedly she had undertaken the adventure when Sam had wept and demanded to come to the airport. Now that she was in Singapore, she realised how right her boy had been to worry.

305

'If it's dangerous, then I ought to protect you, Mummy. If it's not, then why can't I come?'

'There's no danger,' she had said.

Coming in from the military airport, the main road from Johore had been a chaos of people fleeing south. They were stuck behind an ancient Austin tourer piled high with domestic possessions including a parrot cage and two bags of golf clubs. A grander Humber had a brown and white Welsh spaniel tied to the bumper with string. These were respectable people travelling like gypsies. It was as if the whole world was fleeing south. For the first time she smelt the fear.

My God, she thought, this is what a defeat looks like. Singapore was like a city under siege. Sam, aged nine, had known more than all the military minds in Australia. It had not occurred to her that once she had carried out the identification there would be any trouble getting Joseph out. Now she wondered whether either of them could make it.

As they drew up outside Raffles, she thought at first that demolition work must be in progress on the row of shops opposite the hotel. Then she realised that the jagged gap, like a missing tooth in an old man's head, was the result of bombs. She felt simultaneously frightened and annoyed. What the hell was going on? Why didn't anyone know just how bad things were? Astonishingly, the headline in that day's *Straits Times* read: SINGAPORE NOT IN PERIL — GOVERNOR MAIN-TAINS. James, with his devotion to Japanese scare stories, would have found the headline infuriating. But it would have upset him even more to see that the paper was reduced to a single sheet.

Violet wiped the sweat from her forehead. The heat was almost frightening. It was like being locked in a car on a midsummer's day with all the windows tightly shut, and it made her feel weak. The ceiling fans had broken in the hotel and the black telephone receiver, when she finally got to use it, was damp with sweat.

Grogan, to her surprise, was abrupt to the point of rudeness.

'Lady, I'm dealing with several hundred real Australians who want to get themselves home. I don't have any time to worry about Jews or communists.' And the colonel rang off.

'It's the end of civilisation,' someone was saying next to her in the Long Bar. She recognised the speaker as the ugly man from the telephone queue. 'We can't even buy drinks on chits any more. They insist on cash. Up country in Malaya, we smashed all our whisky cases to stop the bloody Japs getting pissed.'

The fear leaked out of him like blood from a wound, but he was looking at her hungrily all the same.

'You'd better get out of here. You must have heard the stories about what Japs do to women they capture. Are you waiting for your husband?'

'He's dead,' she replied without thinking. The man immediately started shouting for more drinks.

'Hey, Lee, Lee, a drink for the lady. All these bloody Chinese are called Lee. A damned cheek. It's my name.'

As if she might not otherwise believe him, he slid a visiting card from his shirt pocket. It was a practised gesture. She saw English on one side and Chinese calligraphy on the other.

'I must go,' she said.

'Stay, stay,' Mr Lee called. 'You can have a good time anywhere if you're in the right mood. I know every inch of this town.'

As she walked across the lobby towards the wide staircase, purposely not looking round in case Mr Lee was following, there was a noise like a train crashing into a wall, a terrifying, clattering, thundering roar. Instinctively, she flung herself to the ground, feeling the wooden floor tremble beneath her.

The crashing pounded at her eardrums and the floor seemed to move upwards, as the windows of the Long Bar shattered into a million pieces, drowning everyone in small shards of glass. Lights stuttered and went dead. Just before they went out, Violet saw the barman topple sideways and disappear. Then there was a stillness, punctuated by the sound of falling bricks and roofs and trees. Then the screams.

She didn't move until she was sure that the floor had stopped shaking. Then she lifted her head, trying to see in the darkness. Someone had lit a candle and was busy lighting others. She got to her feet, gingerly testing the floor, expecting it to collapse under her.

'The Mostyn-Owen offices,' a voice said. 'Missed us by about a hundred feet.'

Violet's legs were shaking and the muscles of her jaw were clenched, nervously rigid. From a distance, she could hear glass tinkling on to concrete. A car horn was blasting into the night, like an unearthly siren. Someone took her arm and steered her towards a bar stool, and a moment later someone put a tumbler of brandy into her hand.

'Is anyone hurt?' The voice was remarkably controlled. By now, most people were standing, looking around them in the flickering candle light like newborn babies. If the pilot had touched the button half a second earlier – or later – she found herself thinking, the bomb would have landed on us and I would be lying in my own blood on the floor of a bar in an Asian hotel. She shivered violently, as though she had been submerged suddenly in icy water, and took a long drink of the brandy. No one in this room would be alive; the woman in the corner who had been nursing a baby only seconds earlier would be a bloody mess, the clock above the bar would have stopped and this brandy would be mingling with the still-warm blood of the dead. She shook herself to stop this train of thought. War, like the rest of life, was full of such accidents, these moments when only chance kept one person alive while another died. She became aware that people around were crying and talking, and that someone was actually laughing in the crowded confusion.

She spent a miserable night in her suite, which overlooked the magnificent tropical garden in the centre of the hotel. It was very different from the room she and Aggie had stayed in all those years ago. In addition to a large bedroom featuring a mahogany fourposter bed with lion's-claw feet, there was a drawing-room opening on to a spacious private verandah, and a bathroom that would have been big enough to dance a highland reel in it. In another place and time, it would have been romantic to sit on the verandah and sip champagne, knowing that the deep, comfortable bed was only feet away.

Violet didn't bother to unpack all her clothes. The world felt too temporary for such a gesture. Instead, she took her pigskin suitcase, with pound notes, and twenty gold sovereigns, sewn into its lining, and put it straight into the wardrobe. The fans had broken and there was no hot water in the tiled bathroom.

She slept erratically, waking in sweaty dread as she remembered the noise of the bombs falling and the breaking glass, and then remembering the last time she had been in Singapore, and seeing as though it was yesterday, the faces of the men who had raped her. There was no lock on the door, and she found herself imagining the sound of the doorhandle turning. I could have been in Washington now, she found herself thinking. She wondered what life with Gareth would actually have been like, if they had lived together openly. It seemed absurd now, to be here, in this terrifying place. At the time, when she had volunteered to help Joseph, it had seemed like the sensible thing to do. She remembered that she had also been delighted with the excuse to miss tea and cucumber sandwiches with the lady mayoress of Manly – there was to have been a fund-raising garden party. Washington with Gareth, of course, would only have been a more sophisticated version of the same. He was lost now in any case. The war had already claimed James and Billy. She was going to have to fight to ensure it didn't claim her.

As dawn broke, she got up, and dressed in her sand-coloured Chanel suit with a matching close turban. It was probably far too chic, but what the hell. Time was clearly running out – might indeed have run out already. In the hours after the bomb blast, when the inhabitants of the hotel had huddled together, assuaging their fear with drinks and loud, jocular conversation, she had learned for the first time just how desperate the situation was. The Japanese armies were pouring down the peninsula towards Singapore, the Lion City: the one city in the Orient which everyone believed would always prove invincible. Among the people at the bar there had been a combination of lies and bravado. Violet had heard one frightened woman saying, with apparent sincerity, 'Singapore will hold, won't it?'

She was sure that there would not be enough boats to get all the city's refugees away. At one point she had been foolish enough to mention the *Wilhelmina*. Within seconds everyone was crowding round, requesting a passage, offering fabulous sums of money. She had wanted to say yes to them all, but how many would the boat take? More to the point, would the boat still be there? The Japanese were bombing the harbour, trying to sink any potential escape vessels. If Van Steenwyjk had had any sense, he would have turned and run, orders or not. However, she was sure that Ben would never have employed a quitter. It all depended on their captain. She was as much a prisoner on the island as anyone else, and her only way out was the boat.

In the lobby, there were people asleep, bundles of homeless humanity, lying with their heads pillowed on suitcases and coats. The temperature had dropped; Violet shivered, wishing she had bought her coat from her room. She must find Joseph today. The hall porter was asleep in a cubicle beside the front door. Without hesitation she woke him.

'I need a car.'

'There aren't any. They've all been requisitioned by the army.'

Violet went outside. There were four cars parked on the circular driveway, around the once immaculate green lawns and trimmed flowerbeds. They were already looking battered and neglected. She selected the grandest car, with a fine staff flag flying on the bonnet. A soldier was asleep at the wheel. Violet tapped him on the shoulder.

'Government House,' she said imperiously, not waiting for him to get out to open the door for her.

'Sorry, madam,' the soldier replied, yawning. 'I'm under orders to Colonel Tennant.'

'I know that,' she said impatiently. 'He told me to take his car.'

The man shrugged. But the tone of Violet's voice had convinced him. 'OK, madam.' The car eased out of the driveway, moving slowly to avoid piles of rubble and broken glass.

In the *Straits Times* she had read the name of the man she needed to see. It was also familiar to her from home: she had seen it on one of Daisy's famous guest lists, for Killymoon parties in George's days. Now, Sir Shenton Thomas was governor of Singapore. If I ever get out of here, she said to herself, I won't be so cynical about George's social register.

Government House was set in vast formal gardens that were separated from a solid-looking wall of jungle by delicate casuarina trees whose lacy leaves in the early morning light seemed to belie the horror of the night. Pandanus and traveller's palm lined the driveway, and around the white steps were borders of orange and red canna lilies.

The uniformed guard took her card. She waited in a vast hallway, with a black-and-white marble-tiled floor. Large pieces of oriental furniture stood against the walls. On an oval table of ebony inlaid with an intricate design of birds and flowers in mother-of-pearl and ivory, there lay a leather-bound visitors' book. Above the table was a signed portrait of King George and Queen Elizabeth, standing behind their two young daughters.

As Violet finished signing her name, Sir Shenton Thomas came to greet her.

'Mrs Franklin; what a surprise. I apologise for not receiving you more formally, but there haven't been many visitors at Government House lately. Won't you join me for breakfast?'

She followed him into the dining-room. A table had been laid with silver and a starched white cloth. There was marmalade in a silver pot, and on the sideboard covered silver dishes contained kedgeree, sausages, bacon, kidneys and a choice of fried or poached eggs. A liveried footman drew back a chair for her.

As she sat down, Sir Shenton said, 'I met your late husband, of course. And I well remember being entertained by your father-in-law at his wonderful house in Bellevue Hill. That would have been while Lady Thomas and I were in Australia, in the twenties . . . But I don't think I've had the pleasure of meeting you before. What brings you to Singapore?'

Violet was spreading butter on crisp white toast and helping herself to Cooper's Oxford Marmalade, Coarse Cut. Having missed dinner last night, she was ravenously hungry. Without pausing, she said, 'I'm

310

here to identify a man wrongly charged with being a communist agent. But I'm having trouble finding out where he is. I thought you would be able to help.'

A servant refilled her coffee cup. Another offered her a tray bearing a silver dish of brown sugar crystals, and a silver jug of cream. Stirring her coffee, Violet waited for Sir Shenton's response. This is absurd, she thought. Last night I was lying on the floor of a bar while bombs exploded only feet away, and somewhere on this island Joseph is in gaol – and here I am, stirring coffee in a porcelain cup with a silver apostle spoon and sitting opposite someone who looks as though he's dressed for a military tattoo.

It's the way the world works: it's all a façade, like the falsehoods told about James in the newspapers. And the lies people like Sir Shenton Thomas habitually tell in the misguided notion that if people don't know the truth, they're better off.

'I'm afraid that in wartime there does tend to be the odd case of mistaken identity. However, I am sure we can clear up this problem with your friend.' He placed a questioning emphasis on the last word. 'Now if you'll give me the relevant papers I will get someone to help. In the mean time, would you like another piece of toast? Alternatively, have you tried pomelo? It's like grapefruit, but far sweeter.'

As Violet stood up to go, one of the splendidly liveried servants showed in a tall, thin Englishman. The new arrival wore a lightweight tropical suit, a panama hat, and open-toed leather sandals over white-stockinged feet.

'Peter! What are you doing here?'

'Violet – Violet!' It was Peter Ironside. Seeing him there, Violet found herself absurdly pleased. She clasped his hands, while the governor coughed quietly in the background.

'We're old friends, sir,' Peter explained. 'In fact we used to be engaged.'

'In that case, Peter, this one's got your name on it,' Sir Shenton said blandly. 'Can I ask you to give Mrs Franklin the assistance she requests?'

Although Peter had addressed the governor as 'sir', Violet guessed it was in recognition of age, not authority.

'How long have you been here?' she asked.

'Just six months – I'm running a political mission. Look here, later on we must meet. I'd suggest you came to the residence, but we're short-staffed there, what with all this going on. Where are you staying?'

He walked outside with her to where the unknown Colonel Tennant's car was waiting.

'The first thing you need is a car and a driver: it's indispensable. I'll organise that. Ah, I see you already have a car; you must have found a friend.'

'Not at all; I just took it over.'

'You're coming along very nicely. I always knew I married the wrong woman. Sorry to hear about your husband.'

'You needn't be. I married the wrong man.'

There was a plane overhead and she flinched.

'One of ours,' Peter said. 'You don't see many of them.'

Even with Peter's mandate, getting to Joseph was no easy matter. No one trusted anyone's documents, everyone was tired and disorganised. Joseph, it turned out, had been moved to another gaol, after the previous one had been bombed. Locating him took till the late afternoon – by which time Violet had argued with numerous po-faced officials, waited around for promised transport to appear, and endlessly held on to the telephone while her calls were connected.

At four o'clock she finally found herself outside the iron gates of a large barracks, a collection of Nissen huts laid out in a two-acre compound surrounded by jungle and lallang, the coarse grass that grew everywhere in Singapore. In the centre of the compound was a long two-storey building. There were people rushing in and out of its main door, carrying piles of papers and boxes of documents, which they were burning on a bonfire. She forced her way in, looking for an office marked 'Intelligence' and the elusive Colonel Norton who had sent the original cable to Australia.

The desk sergeant barred her way. 'No civilians allowed in here, miss.'

'It's *Mrs* Franklin,' she said. 'And Colonel Norton is expecting me.' The sergeant jerked a thumb at a Malayan messenger boy, whose turbaned figure Violet followed down the bustling corridor to an unmarked door.

Colonel Norton greeted her perfunctorily. But after checking her identification he showed her into another small room. Joseph was sitting there at a bare table, under a single naked light.

'Is this the man?'

Violet nodded. She walked over to where Joseph sat and put her arm round his shoulder.

Outside in Norton's office she sat down quickly, not wanting him to see that she was shaking. Joseph looked pale, and as though his resources of character had been stretched in some terrible way.

Norton asked again, 'Is he the man you know?' He was fingering the official government letter showing Sternberg's authorised immigration into Australia.

'There's a picture of him attached to that,' Violet said. 'Wasn't that enough? You didn't need to keep him locked up like a criminal. That man has been largely responsible for bringing over four hundred children and other refugees out of Europe.'

Norton smiled for the first time. 'Sorry. It must seem pretty wretched behaviour. But we're looking for a communist agitator from Europe. He was supposed to be coming on a boat. We've been checking them all. Your friend fitted the bill – or at least so we thought. Now we're no better off.'

'I thought you were fighting the Japanese, not the communists.' Violet was still angry.

'We are, but in Malaya the two things are hand in hand. The Malayan communists want independence – they reckon the Japs will get rid of us and that they can then get rid of the Japs.'

'One master for another,' Violet murmured.

Norton looked at her sharply. He had pale reptilian eyes. The sort of person you wouldn't trust with your dog, Violet thought. She almost pitied the communists.

'That's right. Everyone else is worrying about today. But we – I mean the authorities – are more concerned about Malaya and Singapore after the war.'

'So the city is going to fall?'

'I didn't say that.'

Outside, Joseph was sitting on a bench, his hands folded across his chest. He was so tense that Violet thought he might be about to shout at her. Taking him by the arm, she led him to where her driver had parked under the shade of a cedar tree. He refused to talk about what had happened since his arrest. It was only when Violet asked about the *Wilhelmina* that some of the life came back into him.

'She's a wonderful boat,' he said. 'But there are some strange vessels out there in the shipping lanes – cargo steamers from Bangkok, pirate junks with big Ford motors who've fled here from Hong Kong and now have to flee again. And in the middle, there's the *Wilhelmina*, with Captain Van Steenwyjk.'

'What's he like?'

313

'Van Steenwyjk? He's a cat lover from Amsterdam who likes playing Lehar on his gramophone. Ben's promised him enough money for a lifetime – provided he brings his cargo safely home.'

Joseph lapsed into silence as they were driven away from the barracks. His dark eyes moved fitfully, taking in the bomb craters, the rubble, the endless signs of war.

'Joseph, I think you ought to go out to the ship immediately. I'll radio when we get back to Raffles – they could send in a boat to fetch you.'

Violet had expected him to resist. She was surprised – and relieved – when he agreed with alacrity.

'I don't know how anyone stands this weather,' Joseph said dispiritedly. 'I'll feel better when I get to the boat. Van Steenwyjk must be desperate to leave.'

The *Wilhelmina* was moored a mile out into the shipping roads. There would be a boat waiting for Joseph in an hour's time. Tomorrow the *Wilhelmina* would come right into port, to pick up the main party.

The families of Ben's employees were billeted at St Catherine's Orphanage, in the Tanglin Road. Violet had had no chance to visit the orphanage, and by now it was almost six o'clock in the evening and she was soon due for a promised appointment with Peter. She would have to go there in the morning instead. She wrote a note to her contact at the orphanage, explaining that the ship was now ready to embark, and paid a native driver way over the odds to deliver it.

Peter arrived late, but within minutes there was a chilled bottle of Bollinger on their table. Yet another luxury in this collapsing world.

'Cheers,' he said, raising his glass. 'Now, tell me what on earth you are doing in Singapore – apart from rescuing your communist friend, in which I assume you've succeeded.'

'He's not a communist, but he is my friend. And yes, he's safe. But he wasn't the only reason I came. I'm sorting out a refugee and evacuee boat from Europe – that's the boat my friend was on when your inefficient secret service arrested him. We're taking on some families here. It's a private enterprise.'

'Quite right,' Peter replied. 'You don't want to be at the mercy of governments when it comes to looking after your own children. Portia and I got into trouble because we sent Caspar and Rupert to Canada after the war started. Winston didn't take it at all well. Said that as I was in the government, I shouldn't be panicking like an old woman. So he sent us here – where I'll probably die in some wretched camp.'

'And your wife?'

314

'Oh, Churchill sent a telegram a month ago. He clearly couldn't stand the idea of darling Portia at the mercy of the Japanese.' Peter gave a short laugh. 'She couldn't cope without her wardrobe.

'Funnily enough, the trouble really started because that wretched journalist – the one who used to be so keen on you – wrote a story about English upper-class kids going off to Hollywood for the war to live with Douglas Fairbanks Junior. He used me as an example, so you can imagine I wasn't too pleased when he showed up in my office here, wanting a story on the last diplomats in the empire. He's worse than a vampire.'

'It's not true! Tony Quigley, here?'

'Yes, that's the fellow.'

'Where is he?'

'Well, he's certainly not at this address, and I've given orders at the mission that they should boot him in the arse if he tries to get through the door. I can't believe you want to see him.'

'He's not that bad.' Violet was thinking that somehow Quigley's presence was a good omen. He had a knack of turning up at momentous occasions.

'If you want to find him he'll be in a bar, a brothel or some wireless office. I can find out, if you want. Either way, you needn't worry; your Quigley isn't the kind of person you have to look for. He's probably hiding under your bed.'

Peter bore no grudges on account of the past, and next morning he lent Violet a car and a driver. The journey to the orphanage – like everything in Singapore – took ten times longer than usual. It was four miles from Raffles Place to Tamin Serasi Road, down Orchard Road, and past the Presbyterian Church, the constant reminder of this European foothold in Asia.

Three times their way was blocked, by craters in the roads or by fallen masonry and rubble. The army driver cursed as he was forced to sidetrack down small urban streets.

The orphanage was an ugly Victorian brick building, with the date 1902 etched on a concrete plaque above the door. Only the lush foliage of the banana palms on each side of the front steps differentiated it from an English building of the same period. Inside, the floors were covered with linoleum. There was a rank, sour smell of too many people crowded into too small a space for too long. In the main living-room, children, some with their mothers, were seated in rows on the floor, clutching toys and meagre belongings. A nun was playing 'De Campdown Race Track', on the piano, and most of the company was singing.

315

'I'm Sister Eugenie.' A tall nun wearing a stained robe and cowl held out her hand. Violet returned her firm handshake, thinking that the nun's hand felt like a man's. 'Thank heavens you've arrived. We've been waiting for ten days.'

'Is everybody going? I thought there were only about twenty people.'

Sister Eugenie raised her hands in an expression of helplessness. 'Ever since the Japanese first landed in Malaya they have been coming. Not everyone has an employer like Mr Schiff. They're arriving every day. Sixty-two of them now – mothers and babies and children. We can't turn them away; we're their last hope.'

'Are they all ready to leave – now?'

'They need exit visas. Sister Catherine has been queuing for two days to get them.'

'Surely the government doesn't need to know how they leave?'

'They won't get through the guards at the docks without visas. Have you any idea how many people want to leave Singapore?'

Violet nodded, keeping her face expressionless. Just then the room shook as a bomb exploded in the main street. The window-panes rattled and cups fell off a shelf. Overhead, the whine of the passing aircraft drowned the children's screams.

As Violet, returning, alighted under the traveller's palm in the forecourt of Raffles Hotel, she found the lobby a scene of confusion. Suitcases were piled outside on the white marble steps. A handful of harassed soldiers were attempting to keep order.

'Violet.' Peter put his hand under her arm and steered her towards the terrace restaurant. With him was his aide, a sombre, prematurely aged man in a white duck suit and an Old Etonian tie. 'I have to speak to you. Now.'

Violet was tired, and the closeness of the bomb at the orphanage had frightened her. She didn't trust Sister Eugenie to get the exit visas. And she knew there was only a little time before the Japanese would be over the causeway from Johor.

'I have to speak to you too. Peter, you have to help. I need exit visas for sixty-two people. *Sixty-two*. Tonight. They can't get off the island without them, and we have to leave tomorrow.'

'Nothing could be easier. Except that you don't want sixty-two. It's actually sixty-three.'

'I don't understand.'

'You soon will, my precious. But we need to take a little something. I wonder how Nigel's face is today with the manager.' He turned to his aide. 'Do you think a magnum would be excessive, Nigel? Tell the manager we need somewhere private.'

'His own suite might do,' Nigel said pleasantly.

'And perhaps some caviare for Mrs Franklin as an *amuse-gueule* – he might even think of something more inventive. Oysters? A little rhino horn to lift the spirits?'

'I'll see he gets the picture,' Nigel said.

'For God's sake, Peter. This isn't a gastronomists' convention.'

She found his languid ways suddenly irritating. It could have been the heat. Or the fact, as she confessed to herself, that she was getting very frightened.

He touched her hand in a gesture that was meant to placate – but then, as if finding her touch magnetic, he held it.

'Don't think I'm not being serious,' he said. 'I can't remember ever having been more so. But I can't bear to think of those unpleasant yellow men who bayonet babies and rape women sloshing through the Raffles cellar.' He sighed. 'Not to mention my own at the residence. Ah, here's Nigel.'

The aide led them into what turned out to be the manager's personal drawing-room. As he did so there was an astonished exclamation.

'I don't believe it. No, I absolutely bloody refuse to believe . . . '

'Jesus Christ,' said Peter, his voice filled with dislike.

'*Tony!*' said Violet. 'I don't believe it either. My dear!'

They embraced warmly; so warmly indeed that they might have been old lovers. Quigley looked grubby. His suit had not been laundered in an age and there was a wild, frightened look in his eyes. Beneath a tan so dark it would have stood out in Sydney, he looked haggard. In his hand he carried a pile of wireless forms covered with type.

'I was just thinking I'd filed my last fucking story,' he said, 'and, God save us, here's another one. There was a time when I'd have got a William Hickey lead out of you two. "Recently widowed Violet Franklin, reputed to be Australia's most beautiful woman, has been seeing a lot of her former fiancé, the Hon. Peter Ironside, minister of state for far eastern affairs. The two have been wining and dining in war-torn Singapore's romantic Raffles Hotel. Lady Portia Ironside, daughter of the Duke of Perth, is presently –" ' He paused with a horrible leer. 'Exactly where *is* Portia at the moment, Peter?'

There was no way of keeping Quigley out of their commandeered parlour, even though Peter insisted angrily that they were about to have a private conversation. 'You'll have to call in the army to get rid of me,' Quigley said cheerfully. He sat down on an imitation Louis XV commode. 'Not exactly chinoiserie, is it?' he commented. 'Isn't the manager a chink?'

'He's Swiss as a matter of fact,' said Peter tightly. 'Rather an amiable man, with nice manners. Unlike yours, Quigley. You know, I've never liked you. In fact, you nauseate me.'

'That's very healthy,' Quigley replied, brightening as a waiter appeared carrying an ice bucket. 'It's only in corrupt societies that politicians like journalists. Though it's fair to say this is also a corrupt society – as much so as you can get, in fact. When are you two going to name the day by the way? If you stick around another twenty-four hours you can probably get old Hirohito to do it for you in person.'

Before they could answer a servant arrived to say that the journalist was wanted on the phone. Quigley left reluctantly, glass in hand, assuring Peter that he would shortly be back.

'God damn it, that's all I need.' Peter took a deep breath. 'Listen, Violet, I'll have to tell you now, but don't tell that wretched man. There's a girl I have to get off the island. I thought she could get away in the plane with the governor's luggage – but there wasn't any room. She's a native. You can probably imagine what the Japs will do to someone they think has been, let us say, cohabiting with an Englishman. Particularly me.'

'And you want me to take her on the *Wilhelmina*?'

'You have to. There's no other way. The few boats left are practically sinking, they're so full. But for Christ's sake don't let Quigley hear a hint of this.'

'My exit visas . . .' Violet left the question hanging in the air. 'By tomorrow?'

Peter nodded and gulped down the remainder of his drink.

'The war has changed you, Violet. You've become tough.'

'It's changed us all.'

'That's true. When I last saw your mother, in the CORB offices when I was arranging the twins' passage to Canada, I hardly recognised her. And you – you're much more beautiful than you used to be. If only there'd been more time.'

He brushed the tip of his fingers across her throat.

'Finish the champagne,' he said. 'You're sweating.'

Her shirt was damp and she suspected that the outline of her breasts was emphasised as a result.

'You like the dusky eastern lovelies?' she said.

'All men do. They're erotic professionals,' Peter said. 'Wait till you see Haya.'

'Is she beautiful?'

'She's like a star in the sky,' Peter said with a reverence that surprised Violet. 'You look at her and your heart lightens. All truly beautiful women have the same effect.' He sighed. 'Your boat should sail the moment you're safe aboard. I don't suppose I'll ever see either of you again.'

She was about to offer some word of consolation when Quigley reappeared waving a sheaf of flimsies in his hand. Peter prepared to leave, kissing Violet's cheek, and telling her to come to the residence as soon as she could.

'My last story bites the dust,' Quigley said, filling his glass, draining it, and filling it again. 'The censor's killed the whole bloody lot. So I end up with a Nip bayonet up my arse, and all for bugger all.'

Sinking another glass, he turned his attention to the champagne again. 'One for the road?' he asked Peter. 'Before the Greater Prosperity Zone arrives to get its little yellow snout in the trough? I always think magnums make a good impression on a girl. Were you hoping to get your leg over, Peter?'

Ironside turned his back and Violet marvelled at how quick Quigley was. Peter had been thinking of trying to seduce her, she realised, or moving towards it, even though he was about to say farewell to his mistress. She supposed it was a compliment.

'In Tobruk I thought it was going to a German bayonet,' Quigley remarked. 'But it looks as though there's a Jap one with my name on it. How are you getting out, Vi, or has the door closed on you too? You realise the bastards will probably be here in seventy-two hours, whatever the censor says. They've been cutting through the Essex like a knife through butter. And the intrepid Diggers I saw looked as though they'd been through a chip-slicer. They're peculiarly skilled at warfare, these yellow blokes, and damnably persistent. They also don't seem to object to dying, unlike some of us.'

'You'd better not be heard saying that in public,' warned Peter. 'We could have you in chokey for spreading defeatist rumours. Some of the soldiers might even put you against a wall. And you needn't come whining to me –'

'I know,' Quigley said. 'You'd be waiting with your black cap.'

'I was right never to like you,' Peter said.

'I should hope not,' said Quigley. 'It would be an insult to my professional reputation.'

319

'Is it that bad?' Violet asked Quigley when Peter had left.

'Yes – and worse. The Nips have crossed the causeway at Johor. They'll be drinking sake here not many hours hence, and there's no rip-cord. You can't bail out of Singapore.'

The moonlight lay in bars across the bedroom floor. Peter undressed silently and lifted the white sheet away from her.

His skin was pale and Violet could see his sandy eyelashes shadowed on his cheeks. He crouched between her legs, his penis hard, upright against his stomach, his breathing quick. His hands rested on the inside of her thighs for a moment, then his fingers were inside her, and her legs spread open.

In the distance, a bomb exploded. Glass was breaking, and she could hear someone screaming in the tropical night. His fingers were tossing her into the centre of the hurricane, into its vortex, and the storm overtook her. Its long funnel of twisting power engorged her, held her in its grip, contracted round her. She felt herself start to moan, and her hips arched towards him.

It broke in showers of wild spray, crashing through her. He became a nameless source of release, an earthy reality against all the pain and fear in the world. Violet heard herself groan, a sound that seemed unreal, disembodied, the cry of a ghost struggling to return.

It was almost too hard, too fast; then he was inside her, moving with stabbing motions, as the juices flowed from her. She felt him pound into her, as though he was trying to make love to the world, to leave himself behind, and tears were running down her cheeks, and damp behind her ears.

31

The following morning there was smoke drifting across the city from the north. Japanese planes screeched across the sky. The golf club was hit, and there was a rumour, quickly scotched by the authorities, that the airport too was under attack. Was the smoke coming from the airport? Or from the oil supply depots near Johor and the causeway?

Such were the topics discussed by those civilians left in Raffles Hotel. The smoke had accelerated panic to the point where it was impossible to walk into the lobby without someone rushing up to ask how you were leaving. Violet now refused to talk about the *Wilhelmina*. Hearing the sound of gunfire, which grew louder as the morning wore on, she was beginning to envy the other women who had been evacuated the day before. The hotel was full of soldiers and civilian husbands; they looked grim, but probably felt relieved that their wives and children now had a chance. Quigley was flitting back and forth, hearing rumours, testing them, passing a few on, and satisfying himself that there was no chance of getting any stories past the military black-out. Some time around nine o'clock he started to quiz Violet on the subject of escape routes.

'I've concluded it's my duty to get out of here, just as it's poor Peter's to stay. And there are no more planes, I hear. I don't like the look of that airport anyway.'

Violet refused to be drawn. She was preoccupied with worries about transport, and drinking water. Worst of all was the bombing. So far it had been sporadic. But Peter had told her the night before that the Japs might decide to experiment and subject Singapore to saturation bombing.

For reasons of geology, Singapore was not a place where large-scale excavations could be made. So there were almost no air-raid shelters.

'Quite honestly,' Quigley said broodingly, 'I can't believe it's all *that* safe on the high seas. Not since they bombed the *Repulse* to kingdom come. And the *Hood*. And there's no guarantee your old

321

Wilhelmina's stayed offshore. Even if she has, she may have been bombed.'

'Shut up,' Violet said.

'Or torpedoed. Or run into a British mine – the way we've organised the defence of this place, it's perfectly possible we'd torpedo our own ships. Did you know, by the way, that all the artillery positions are dug in the wrong way round? It apparently never crossed anyone's mind that the Nips might take to their bikes and come this way. The empire deserves to end, I've decided. Like those damn fool Romans.'

In the end he advocated abandoning the children altogether. 'He travels fastest who doesn't have sixty-two bloody orphans and nuns in his knapsack. You're not the Pied bloody Piper, after all. Have a heart. Think of me instead – we go back a long way.'

Violet could not help rising to this.

'Yes, and you got me into trouble from the first moment I even spoke to you.'

Quigley looked philosophic.

'We always used to say to people on the phone: "We have two kinds of news, good or bad. Which kind do you want?" Publicity amounts to the same thing in the end. Just publicity.'

'I wouldn't help get you out of hell,' Violet said sweetly. She was remembering something that Peter had told her.

'Where are the trucks?' Violet asked, side-stepping a teddy bear and narrowly missing a battered satchel, as she made her way along the crowded hallway at the orphanage.

Sister Eugenie's stride didn't falter. 'There are no trucks. The driver sold them to pay for an air passage out of here. You mustn't blame him.' She said it without rancour, which annoyed Violet even more.

It was five o'clock. Two hours ago Nigel, Peter's aide, had dropped her at the gates of the orphanage. He had given Violet the exit visas, with instructions to fill them in and hand them to the sentry at the entrance to the docks. Peter was to meet her there and deliver his girlfriend into her keeping.

She felt suddenly very lonely and scared. Quigley had gone off earlier on some personal mission and he still hadn't returned when Nigel had arrived. Violet had intended to take Quigley along. It was surprising how much she missed him, and how much she depended on him to keep her spirits up.

The *Wilhelmina* had been instructed to move into the harbour and have landing craft ready for the party to embark. They were already late, even though Eugenie had assembled the children very quickly, lining them up in front of a makeshift desk in single file and filling in their names on the forms.

'How are we going to get to the docks?' Violet asked, as she followed Eugenie into a courtyard. On its far side an archway led into a lane.

'Like this,' the nun replied.

Violet stopped short. Eugenie's solution was staring at her – bicycles and rickshaws, maybe fifty of them altogether, leaning against the walls and each other.

'We have to get everyone there by bicycle?' Violet turned to Eugenie in alarm. 'It's five miles – maybe six.'

'Only four, to the Keppel Road entrance. They've all been told what to do – who's to ride and who's to go in the rickshaws. And I've made them leave most of their luggage behind.' She added the last bit with a touch of pride. Violet could well imagine how hard that had been. What would she take, she wondered, if she had to reduce all her worldly possessions to the contents of a single suitcase.

As though reading her thoughts, Eugenie murmured, 'It's quite amazing what people pin their hopes on. One woman said I could leave the Malayan children behind, to make room for her Royal Worcester dinner service.'

Astride the first bicycle, her robes fluttering, Eugenie led the way out of the courtyard. The curious procession started off down the Tanglin Road, and passed the long lawns of the old colonial houses, and all the other outward signs of a once great and prosperous city. They crossed Orchard Road, where the long line had to halt while a convoy of army vehicles made its way southwards, and then turned into the River Valley Road.

Violet pushed downwards on the pedals, easing the heavy load along. There were two children sitting behind her on a striped canvas seat with straw coming out where it had been worn into holes. The paint on the rickshaw was peeling and the rubber tyres on the wooden wheels were so worn that every bump jarred her arms and neck. She wondered how on earth anyone managed to do this for a living. Within minutes she felt her legs tremble – the only way to stop them was to keep pedalling. It was all right when you were moving; it was just starting up that was so hard. Thank heavens the gradient was either flat or slightly downhill. She risked a glance over her shoulder. The children were wide-eyed and silent, each clutching a small parcel. Eugenie said that no one knew where their parents were – they had

323

arrived in Singapore in a group of children who had all been separated from their families in the confusion following the Japanese invasion. Violet wondered if their mothers were still alive. And if she were killed or captured, who would look after Sam and Liz? She should never have come; she shouldn't have taken the risk. If she died they'd never understand. A bomb exploded somewhere to the west of them. No one said anything, but they all started pedalling a little faster.

'What are your names?'

'Tom and Jessica,' the boy answered.

'Are you brother and sister?'

'Yes.'

It was too exhausting to talk. Violet could feel the beginnings of blisters on the palms of her hands. Then they were in an area where the bomb damage was especially bad. It needed all her strength to steer the rickshaw between yawning holes in the road, and piles of rubbish and broken glass. Partially destroyed buildings stood with their insides exposed: broken staircases, and all the signs of family life – bathrooms, and gay wallpapers, even tables and chairs still somehow standing on ledges. It was obscene, a violation of privacy, as though someone had come by with a can opener, ripping off roofs and walls.

Further down the River Valley Road they passed a group of soldiers stumbling towards the docks. All pretence of saving Singapore had now gone – people were fleeing any way they could. The men's eyes were vacant, and their clothes hung on bodies crippled with fatigue. Violet saw Eugenie slow down, and she shouted at her angrily to keep going. They couldn't stop now, they couldn't take on more people. As it was, she still wasn't sure there would be room for everyone.

Eugenie's right arm went out, and they turned off sharply, down a steep narrow road through the bazaar. Violet wrestled with the rickshaw, which was now bouncing along with determined speed. The bicycle wheels bumped over two shallow steps and she felt her legs trembling with tiredness. She was drenched in sweat. There were signs of looting – bags of flour had burst open on the pavements, rolls of silk were unravelling, ornate teapots, painted with splendid gold dragons, were smashed on the ground. The bicycle hit a rock and they lurched to one side, almost toppling over.

'Stop, please stop!' Jessica sounded tearful. Violet pulled up, waving the bikes behind her onward.

'It's Jemima,' the little girl said. 'She fell off.' Violet looked back up the street and spotted the yellow felt duck lying in the gutter. She ran quickly back to get it and remounted, pedalling as fast as she could to catch up. The straggling convoy was now out of sight. She was alone in the street.

As she turned into the next street, a man loomed out of a shop doorway. He was wearing greasy mechanic's overalls. His few remaining teeth were filled with gold.

'Money.' He hissed the word in her ear, while one hand seized her wrist and the other aimed a glancing blow at the side of her head. She raised her foot, aiming a hard kick directly at his groin, hearing the thud as her leather shoe banged against his flesh. His eyes widened in pain and surprise, as he let go of her. She righted the bike and stamped down on the pedals.

A minute of agonised effort, and then she was close enough to Sister Josephine at the rear of their convoy to know she had survived.

Violet felt tears prick her eyelids. The whole incident had taken just seconds; but they had been vital seconds in which you either froze and were lost, or ran and escaped. The last time, when she had been raped, she hadn't known that she must run or fight. Now she did. There was nothing that could stop her now.

She felt an upsurge of triumph. Here, in the crumbling city, at this perilous moment, she felt an overwhelming sense of joy.

The bike scuttered over the cobbles, bouncing like a circus ride. They took several more bends, and went through an alley so narrow the children could have touched the walls. Then suddenly in front of them were the chainlink gates leading into the docks.

A writhing, cursing crowd was forcing its way towards the narrow entrance. The doors of the shipping offices, long since abandoned, swung on their hinges. Pacific and Orient, Cunard, Union Castle, White Star, Olau Line, evidence of the strings that once had linked Singapore to the world. Violet could feel the burning heat from the ground through her shoes, as she pushed her way through to where she could see Peter.

For once he was taking on a job himself instead of deputising his aide. He stood by the gate, checking off the children as they filed silently through on to the dockside, and helping to hold back the angry, frightened crowd who were attempting to break through. Overhead two Japanese planes flew low across the harbour, their machine-guns rattling as they strafed the few craft in the water. In an uprush of panic the crowd surged forward – Malays, Chinese, Europeans. Someone lunged for Peter, but with surprising agility he side-stepped the man, who blundered on into the fence. Two British soldiers armed with tommy-guns were trying to enforce order.

'Only people booked on the *Wilhelmina*,' Peter shouted. He elbowed someone backwards, so that Violet could stand beside him.

'You've cut it fine, sweetheart.' Sheltering behind him stood a slender Malayan girl, with eyes like pools of ink and the most perfect skin Violet had ever seen.

'This is Haya. She doesn't speak any English. I've told her to stick close to you. Now you must go. Now.'

He opened the small entrance gate and shoved them through it, using his arms to prevent an hysterical Englishwoman from forcing her way past him. 'Don't leave me here!' she was crying. 'Don't leave me here to die!'

Violet looked back at him and bit her lip. Then she was running, holding the weeping Haya with one hand, ushering the children ahead of her towards the gangway of the *Wilhelmina*. She was shaking with exhaustion and her fingers were cramped from gripping the handle-bars so tightly. The gangway swayed; beneath it in the oily black water a dead dog, bloated and horrific, bumped against the wooden pilings of the quay. Violet looked quickly behind her. At the gate, people were begging for the chance to come through and board the ship. She saw Peter's head in the crowd, moving away, back to the city. Why him and not me? She had no idea why providence had placed the exit visa in her hand, and she knew she would go to her grave with the English-woman's accusing face stamped on her memory.

The light was fading when her feet first touched the wooden deck, day changing to night with familiar tropical sharpness. She felt the engines start to rumble, and heard the sloshing of water far below, together with the sound of the gangway being lifted.

'Stop!'

Violet turned back to the deck rail. It couldn't be!

But there he was, his suit jacket ripped, his typewriter in a battered blue case clutched under one arm, an old fawn briefcase under the other. He took a running jump at the gangway, which was slowly ascending, and, with an agility born of fear, hauled himself up. The next second he was beside her on the deck.

'Not very sporting of you to leave without me. I've had a hell of a time.'

'How on earth did you get a visa for the boat? We're full.'

'No aeroplane, boat or newspaper is ever full,' Quigley said happily. 'At least, not for me.'

326

The boat slipped anchor, and they started moving slowly away from the docks, already shrouded in dusk. Across the harbour, the dying sun made rainbow colours on the oil slicks.

'Mrs Franklin. I'm more than pleased to have you on board at last.'

'It's an understatement to say that it was good of you to wait,' Violet replied, greeting the legendary Captain Van Steenwyjk for the first time. She found herself charmed by the vivid blue of his seafaring eyes.

'Mr Schiff didn't give us much choice: there was a matter of pensions and money.' He smiled. Through the growing darkness, Violet could just make out the people still waiting by the gate. Their anger seemed to have faded: now they were standing in resigned groups, waiting for whatever was going to happen. She knew they would have paid anything to have changed places.

The government of Singapore had failed them at this last desperate hour. Whereas Ben, wonderful Ben, had somehow managed to bribe the right man to wait.

Violet's jaw ached. She rubbed it, feeling the bruise, and remembering the moment when the man had hit her. Around the harbour were impenetrable blocks of shadow, but behind them Singapore looked like London on the fifth of November. Flames leapt upwards and tracer bullets scorched through the dense tropical night. The *Wilhelmina* was picking up speed. Violet felt the lurch of the boat in the water and put out a hand to steady herself.

Heavy steel shutters covered the windows of the main saloons and sandbags were piled against the doors leading off the promenade deck. Once in the light of the ship's interior Violet blinked. Her beige flannel trousers were ripped across the knee, and her dark blue cotton shirt was smeared with grease. She was almost too weary to introduce herself to the waiting escorts and take in the emergency instructions that Lieutenant Carmody, the ship's second officer, recited to all the newly joined passengers.

Joseph was also below, sitting on a red velvet bench under an enormous painting of a tranquil Amsterdam canal. He was cuddling a sleeping child in his arms, crooning to her. He smiled at Violet, and raised a finger to his lips, indicating for her to be quiet. He looked better than when she had last seen him, but he still seemed fragile and somehow breakable. She kissed the top of his head, and gently smoothed the little girl's hair.

Violet's cabin was on B-deck: teak walls and brass fittings, floor carpeted in pale grey pile, a chintz spread on the single bed, chintz covers on the small armchair. It was designed to look both English and maritime; the result was luxurious but ugly. A drawer still held brochures advertising the *Wilhelmina*'s cruises for the year 1939. THE WORLD'S MOST DELIGHTFUL CRUISING LINER: the slogan ran above details of the Mediterranean ports where the ship would be stopping – Capri and Cannes, Beirut and Alexandria. Kicking off her shoes, Violet found herself absorbed by the gentle rocking motion of the ship. Within seconds she was fast asleep.

Throughout the hours of darkness, the *Wilhelmina* headed southwards towards the Sumatran island chain, throwing up dancing phosphorescence in its wake. They were escaping to the uneven string of islands that lie along the equator. Their vessel was not alone. Every boat fleeing Singapore had had the same idea: to disappear among the millions of outcroppings of land, some so small they were uninhabitable, others supporting full-sized towns. In the complex waterways that threaded the islands, enemy planes and ships might not find them. The common plan was to put as much water as possible between them and the Japanese Zeros before first light. Van Steenwyjk himself was making for the Bangka Straits, the narrow strip of water dividing Sumatra from Bangka Island.

In the chart room the captain was explaining this to Quigley. Van Steenwyjk was evidently torn between his natural distrust of the journalist's appearance and manner and the need to be affable with someone who had introduced himself as 'one of old Ben Schiff's closest business associates'. He jabbed a spatulate finger at the chart to indicate their position. He knew these waters well; every shoal was photographed in his head.

'Once we get through to here, the Karimata Straits, we can probably lose them in the Java Sea. If we can survive until darkness tomorrow . . .' The captain paused.

'You'll get your bonus?' Quigley said.

'I'll probably get a medal. Of course, if we don't . . .'

'You took a helluva risk waiting so long in Singapore. I'd have legged it off days ago.'

'You don't work for Mr Schiff or his father,' Van Steenwyjk replied, with distaste.

'I'm going to bed with a bottle of rum,' Quigley said. 'With luck I'll wake up tomorrow night and we'll be through your straits of whatsit and ready for a hero's welcome.'

Violet awoke at sunrise, to the sound of running feet in the passageway outside her cabin. Then bells started clanging, a cacophony of alarm that had her sitting up in the bunk, every nerve end responding with terror. She was trying to find her shoes before she remembered where she was.

'Action stations!' came over the tannoy. With her lifebelt round her shoulders Violet tried to make for the boat station the steward had pointed out to her the night before.

She ran up one gangway, then another, before emerging aft on deck. At the stern a crowd of merchant seamen were looking anxiously across the *Wilhelmina*'s foaming wake. Violet took in at a glance the double decks, the two tall stacks painted dull grey, and the bridge, where she could see Van Steenwyjk looking through a telescope. There were piles of rattan chairs stacked against the bulwarks, echoes of the days of sybaritic cruising through calm waters.

At first she could see nothing but the heat haze, a solid shimmering bank of colour that obscured the line between sea and air. Then, suddenly, she caught sight of a black shape, like a fly, motionless on the horizon.

Sternberg was beside her, a hand on her arm.

No one moved as the dot grew in size, transforming itself from a dark speck into a Japanese fighter. A lot of time seemed to pass before someone shouted, 'There's three of them!'

From the shelter of a row of sandbags, Violet craned her neck to look up. The planes were circling the ship, banking left and right, sizing them up. She thought she could almost make out the expression on the leading pilot's face, even though his features were partially obscured by goggles and a flying cap with earflaps. It was obvious that he hadn't missed anything. She watched the tiny machine curve sharply away from the ship, heading back out to sea. The noise of the aero engine was infinitely threatening, far more terrifying than the sound of the planes that had droned across Singapore.

'You should go down to the lower deck and help distract the children,' Joseph said. 'Try to make them think it's a game.'

'I don't think they're that suggestible,' Violet said. She hurried back the way she had come.

She was on the stairs leading to B-deck when the first stick of bombs hit the *Wilhelmina*'s deck. The boat shuddered and began listing to port. Violet lost her footing and fell down the last few steps into the broad passage towards the stern. Children were crying; then the lights flickered and went out, plunging the corridor into darkness. Someone started to scream. There was a pair of violent explosions, followed by the rattling vibrating noise she knew was a heavy machine-gun. At length, dimmer than before, the lights came back on.

The children were huddled together in the B-deck dining-room, which had been converted to a play area. In the intermittent light, Violet could make out children's paintings on the walls. There was even a line drawing of a donkey – minus its tail.

She put her hands over her ears to shut out the roar of the planes. The teeth-chattering vibrations of the exploding bombs made her bones shake and her nerves scream. The boat was still listing heavily, though she was showing no signs of sinking. Violet felt someone reach for her hand. She opened her eyes, to see Haya's frightened face only inches from her own. They were both under a table, their arms linked round its central support. Violet wondered where Sternberg and Quigley were, amid the chaos. The noises seemed to go on for ever, getting more intense and harder to bear. They seemed to be coming from inside her head. Violet thought, this is impossible to endure. I'll go mad unless it stops.

And then quite suddenly, it did.

She clambered to her feet. No one, at least no one in the B-deck dining-room, had been hurt. There are so many of them, Violet thought, seeing for the first time the reality of the shipping manifests, the long lists of names of the children from Malaya and the refugees from Europe. It hadn't seemed that many when she had last looked at the neatly typed four-page list that the WIC secretary had prepared.

'Mrs Franklin?' Carmody, Van Steenwyjk's second-in-command, was standing in the swing doorway leading to the companionway. 'Could I see you for a moment?'

Violet followed him up the steep stairs, holding on to the brass handrail. The *Wilhelmina* no longer seemed to be listing, and the engines sounded normal.

'Mr Sternberg was hit. He wants to see you.'

Numbly she broke into a run down the thickly carpeted first-class passageway, past the ornate doors leading into the state cabins. Someone had carried Joseph inside and he was lying on a palliasse on the floor of the ballroom. There was glass everywhere from the shattered chandeliers and the windows, some of which had blown out despite the steel shields.

Joseph's eyes were closed. His face was as white as the petals of an arum lily. The colour was bleeding out of him, soaking into the crimson carpet in a black, sticky mess.

'Joseph? Joseph? Can you hear me?' She took his limp hand. After a few moments she felt him return the pressure. His eyes flickered open and he tried to smile.

'Thank you for getting us all this far.' His voice was little more than a whisper. 'I wanted to tell you. I deceived you – all that time ago, when I told you about the girl on the railway station in Vienna.' His eyes closed again and Violet looked around her desperately. She started to get up, but he opened his eyes again and his grip on her hand tightened.

'Don't go. It was my child. She was taken away by the Nazis, in front of my eyes. There was a warrant for my arrest, for being a Jewish agitator in the ghetto, and they tracked us as far as the station. Someone recognised her. There was a train going to Krakow and they made her get on it. I had to watch as they put my baby on the train. She was all alone. I've never slept without seeing her face since then.' Tears rolled down his cheeks. 'I've never been able to tell anyone. Here I am alive and safe, while she . . .'

Violet stroked his dark hair back from his forehead.

'Joseph, there was nothing you could have done. You couldn't take on the whole German army.'

He nodded and tried to speak. But instead of words he made a hoarse, gravelly sound, like a cough. Flecks of blood bubbled between his lips, dribbling down his dark unshaven cheek, and dripping on to the collar of his shirt.

'Don't try to talk. The doctor'll be here in a moment. Joseph, it wasn't your fault. And look what you've done now – you've brought all these children out of Europe.'

He coughed again, an unearthly gurgling sound that seemed to come from deep inside him. The flecks of blood became a steady flow from his mouth, draining even his lips of colour. He opened his eyes once more, but they were heavily glazed, and though he seemed to be looking straight at her, Violet was sure he no longer saw her. The pressure on her hand lessened, his eyes closed, and then he was still.

'He's gone,' said Carmody, who had been standing beside them.

The Japanese aircraft would come back. 'You'll be pleased to know we're approaching the straits of Karimata and it ought to be dark in an hour,' Quigley told her. 'Admittedly, they're supposed to like attacking at sunset. But if you ask me they like attacking round the clock. You know that steward? He's a wonderful fellow. For cash he can produce fresh orange juice, ice and overproof rum, and I think you ought to join me for a cocktail. I've found a secluded spot to colonise and now it's getting cooler . . .' He grinned and touched her on the shoulder. 'Come on, Vi. Let's seize the moment. We don't know how many more there are going to be.'

There were plenty of people to look after the children – Joseph had recruited escorts in a ratio of one to twelve, and Sister Eugenie's nuns had been added to the strength. As they walked, Quigley gave her the latest news. A middle-aged escort called Larkin was the other civilian casualty besides Joseph. The crew had suffered three deaths and a dozen wounded, most of the injured suffering from burns.

The fires had been put out and there was no serious damage. 'I helped with the fire on the fo'c'sle,' said Quigley. 'It's thirsty work being a hero.'

He had found a small dining-saloon which was now unused; no one except Quigley would go near such a vulnerable target.

'The construction's of wood and apparently it's open to something called fore and aft strafing,' he explained. 'But it got me through today. I hid there, under the long table. Ugh, I can still hear that machine-gun throbbing in my head. Now, rum and orange is what you need. Rum and orange and a yarn. Look, it's almost dark. Three minutes and we'll be safe. Until tomorrow, anyway.'

He sat down on a velvet-covered circular seat and pulled Violet down beside him. The red glow of the setting sun made the mahogany of the bulkheads give off a roseate hue. Despite her sadness over Joseph she felt her spirits lifting. Everything looked very beautiful to her and she was immensely happy to be alive.

'To the future,' Quigley said, raising his glass.

'We should drink to poor Joseph,' she said.

'Why not?' Quigley agreed, and raised his glass with a perfunctory gesture. 'But also it's a matter of let the dead bury their dead. I know it sounds callous, but since Tobruk I've become a fatalist. It concentrates the mind wonderfully, I find. Once the dead are dead then you write the obit, respectfully and accurately if possible, and, if not, making sure you get in one thumping lie. And then . . .' He made a gesture of a soul flying away to heaven, or something like it.

'And then it's time for another drink. No delay – all that is past. That's what I like best about war. No point in drinking less, no point in saving money for your old age, or cutting down on smoking or desserts, or being polite to people you despise, or pretending that the working class is going to rise spontaneously one day and turn the world into a school run on progressive lines with Bertie Russell on the board of governors to deliver speeches in praise of the League of Nations and sexual hygiene. Talking of which . . .'

'Yes,' Violet said, 'you viper, talking very much of which. What was this nonsense you told Peter Ironside about me?'

'Nonsense?'

Quigley threw her a quick glance like a card-player assessing an opponent's bet. 'Nonsense? It was a statement on oath made by a dying man.'

'Which dying man and what did he say?'

'Well,' Quigley admitted with a grin, 'not exactly dying. Not even dead, to be truthful, which is a helluva unusual thing when a journalist's sources are under scrutiny. Have you noticed how often they turn out to be conveniently dead?'

'Who was it?'

'He was someone who had been through an experience like ours today. He'd felt the Grim Reaper breathe down his collar and then for some reason decide to pass on.'

Quigley drew the curtains meticulously and lit a candle in a bottle. 'The electricity's still not back in here,' he said. 'But I like this light, don't you? We had candlelight in Tobruk.'

Violet drank some more rum and orange. She was beginning to think he had made the whole thing up. In any case, she didn't much care. The alcohol, unless she was running a fever, had made her light-headed. 'I don't believe in your story; it doesn't sound any good,' she said.

'No good?' Quigley was indignant. 'It's terrific. Hollywood couldn't do better but this is real life. You begin with a simple country boy, the honest Abe Lincoln/George Washington kind of fella, who rises to power while still young (though tragically widowed), on a wave of populist sentiment. He falls in love with the most beautiful woman in the land, and writes her the sort of love-letters you should engrave on jewels – the best since Dante was knocking off his nightly stanzas to Beatrice in the quattrocento. Of course there's a snag. The lovely lady is married to someone else; a millionaire newspaper proprietor, to be exact. He's the villain of the story, because he shatters the idyll and resorts to blackmail. Our hero is forced to resign his high office and . . .'

'Told like this it sounds unreal.'

'These letters were real enough. Tied in blue ribbon, I expect. It's surprising how often this happens to politicians. It even happened to the Duke of Wellington, you remember. He said, publish and be damned. But he could afford to, because he had already retired from politics and anyway he was a duke. Most unlike our hero. According to my source . . .'

'Who was it, Quigley? I'm tired of your joking around.'

'Ah, but, Violet, you know his name very well. A quartermaster sergeant, no less, in the A E F. A very distinguished gentleman. Presently domiciled in a prison camp in Tobruk or a grave in Crete or a raft in the Mediterranean . . . Whatever your imagination prefers.'

'He's more likely in a bar somewhere.'

'That sounds like a well-informed guess,' Quigley said with a twinkle.

'How many hundreds of people have you told this to?'

'Only Peter, of course. He's the only person I've met since Tobruk who could appreciate it properly. That's the trouble with gossip. To really appreciate it you have to know the people – and the true story, which is always far better than the one in the paper. That's why I'm such a famous journalist. I always put in a line more of the real truth than anyone else.'

'I suppose by that you mean there's one accurate fact in every story you write.'

He laughed. 'One or two. But I had to tell Ironside. Since I couldn't actually print it . . .'

'You'd never dare.'

'Oh, I'd dare all right, never you fear. I'm not the one who pays libel costs, or even goes to gaol. That's the privilege of the owner and the editor respectively. Peter may seem a dry stick, but he has the odd human quality, one of which is he's a randy bastard. The inspiring tale of a buxom woman he had himself deflowered in the jump-seat of a Hispano-Suiza, aged fourteen, later locked in the heights of erotic passion with a man of power and destiny . . .'

'For God's sake shut up. I'm not just a name in one of your wretched stories. I don't think you can tell the difference between life and a good headline.'

Quigley bowed his head like a fencer indicating his opponent had scored a point. He was grotesquely unkempt now, his beard an unbecoming pepper-and-salt after three days' unrestrained growth. Long ago, a year before he had written his first story about her and the car accident in Hyde Park, she had been horrified, when in Paris with Emerald, to see vagabonds – people whom he now resembled – sleeping in lines along the grilles of the Metro subway at the Porte de la Chapelle.

'You look like a clochard,' she said. 'The only difference is that wretched people like them have higher principles than you. You're beyond words, Quigley. And I wasn't deflowered by Peter aged fourteen, just for the record.'

And a good thing too, she added mentally, never allowing her gaze to leave Quigley's mocking face. If it had happened then, I'd never have been able to enjoy it, and neither would Peter. She was sure that Peter owed his erotic education to Heya, and that it was newly acquired. As for his capacity to abandon himself completely, that she surmised was a strange gift of war, which had released her too. Something you'll never know about, Quigley: one small secret I'll save for myself.

'That reminds me,' he said pleasantly. 'Why don't we go to bed while we can? You've given everyone else a run round the block; and remember, we may be dead tomorrow.'

'We may be dead tonight,' she said. 'But it's not going to do you any good.'

His face creased with laughter in the candlelight. 'There's my girl, Vi. I think you're very sexy when you're angry. Still, I suppose it might spoil our relationship. It's my destiny to be the chronicler of your wonderful career, and there's nothing to suggest that Boswell ever went to bed with Dr Johnson.'

'Now you've given me the Hollywood version of what happened, you might tell me the poor man's version. How did you come up with a story like this, when you were supposed to be a war correspondent?'

'I was where all the best war correspondents finish up, in the sergeants' mess, buying a bottle of Scotch off the Australian who was running the black market. He had a very cushy billet, I must say that, or as cushy as you could get there. They were in a big cellar deep down, and reckoned that there wasn't an Italian bomb invented that could touch them. So naturally we got pissed.'

Violet sighed. It was impossible to get Quigley to tell a short tale. He enjoyed the process of disclosure too much.

'When we heard the news of Mayhew's resignation on the wireless my friend, the quartermaster sergeant, cursed and swore and put down a dram that would've killed a camel. Then he said, "I could tell you a few stories about him", and I said, "Go on then", and he said, "What I know's worth a lot of money." They all say that. Well, we haggled away, I said I couldn't pay till I knew what it was about, he said he wouldn't talk without some guarantee. You know how it goes.'

'I can imagine,' Violet said. 'Go on.'

Quigley sipped his drink. 'In the end he decided that he might just as well tell me anyway.' He paused. 'They always do that too. The unusual thing was that once he started you were the heroine.'

'Why didn't you make the obvious assumption – that the man was a drunken weaver of fantasies? Imagine all this in a court of law.'

'I see you've benefited from long exposure to a legal mind. Mayhew began as a lawyer, didn't he? And my bloke claimed he'd once worked for the PM. In fact, to hear him speak he was largely responsible for Mayhew's early political successes. He was the man behind the scenes who mopped up the damages, kept the ladies off – where was it? Some aboriginal name like that brand of tea with the old lady on it. Could it be Mazzawattee?'

'Parramatta,' Violet said quietly.

'That's the very one. He said he kept the ladies happy and convinced of the myth of this blue-eyed widower. And he was glad to do it. Mayhew had political magic, he kept on saying, like Churchill.' Quigley looked reflective. 'I had to agree with him. Even though I only met Mayhew once.

'Then he fell in love. Nothing wrong with that; but the future prime minister's choice was a married lady. And not just any married lady, but the wife of his best friend, the owner of Australia's most powerful newspaper chain.

'My informant got pretty maudlin at this point. He also saw the danger ahead. He knew it would somehow be the end for Mayhew, and he spent hours covering up for him, explaining his absences, fabricating stories of other girls. Safe girls. Then the lady turned against my informant and got Mayhew to boot him out on his arse with never a thank you. She had him thrown off a train, if my memory serves.'

Violet was back on Central Station, hearing the whistle blow for the Brisbane departure. The man on the platform with the brand new suitcase. It had been pathetic. But she had been so angry with Gareth, letting that man pry into her life.

'So one day he had his revenge?'

'You bet. They had a secret hide-away, where he came across a bunch of incriminating letters while he was dusting the drawers in the bedroom.'

'That's very good,' Violet said. 'I like that.'

'So did I,' Quigley said. 'He didn't say how much he got from your lamented husband, but it wasn't enough to keep him away from Tobruk, so he was probably rooked. I guess they were actually worth a few bob.'

'He didn't say what happened to them?'

'Oh yes, he did mention that. The husband tore most of them up on the spot. He didn't enjoy the style at all. Sounds as if he was the jealous type. Still in love with the faithless wife. You know the kind of thing.'

'And then. . . ?' Violet asked.

'That's about it. Except I've forgotten the chap's name. You know how it is when you have a few.' He paused. 'I suppose you couldn't jog my poor old alcoholic memory?'

'Rex Pountney,' she said. 'And I only hope Rommel gets his hands on the rat.'

'Don't you worry, he will,' the journalist said happily. 'Unless he's got him already.'

He got up to refill their drinks. It was dark now but the night showed no sign of growing cool. There were sounds of children playing, a welcome return to normality. Violet lit a cigarette.

Later, she went down to the children's room, where the adults had managed to organise a series of rowdy games. The children were playing musical bumps, to a loud cheerful tune coming from the gramophone. Violet leant her head against the dining-room's fake mahogany panels. By the light of the ornate carriage lamps set into the walls, she watched Haya cuddling a tear-stained child who was even now starting to laugh at the faces she was pulling. Violet wondered what Portia Ironside would think if she knew that Peter had bribed his old girlfriend to save the life of his current mistress.

As the danger receded, the voyage became more monotonous, and more exhausting. There was no point in quarrelling with Quigley over his revelations, and each evening they met for drinks in his personal saloon. It was like being isolated in a floating palace, a ritual they came to savour. Even Quigley became silent at sunset. They strained their eyes watching the western horizon, the sun turning blood red and slipping downwards as if someone out of sight below the horizon was hauling it down on a line. Towards the east, the rim of the sea was already blurred by darkness as the night rapidly covered up the glass-smooth water, smoothing out the great gashes of colour left by the sinking sun.

It was several days, though, before she told Quigley her side of the story. He must have said a dozen times, 'C'mon, Vi, there's no point any more in denying it.'

'No,' she said finally, 'I don't suppose there is. In fact there are parts that make me proud.'

'That's the spirit, Cleopatra,' Quigley said, reaching for the bottle.

32

ॐ

'It seems like a hundred years ago, thank God, especially now I've got rid of Quigley.'

Cissy winced at the name, but forebore to make any comment. She didn't want to interrupt Violet's story. Nowadays Cissy was an adept interviewer, a far cry from all those years ago when she had blundered into Killymoon to interview the boss's wife.

Violet conjured up a memory of an embroidered peasant blouse emphasising the young Cissy's rural shoulders and – or was this an invention? – a Tyrolean hat with a feather.

They were in the fish restaurant in Watson's Bay, a place they had frequented off and on over the years, though never before with Cissy as hostess. She had issued the invitation and told Vi of her grand new job at the same time. Cissy had become a director as well as editor-in-chief of Jerry Jerome's magazine group, APP. She had said that they were considering running a feature about the Singapore rescue and why didn't Violet come down for the nearest thing to a slap-up lunch left in the city?

Success suited Cissy, and so did being back in Sydney. In Canberra she had taken on the protective colouring and even some of the smugness of government service. It had never really been Cissy. Now she had regained her old exuberance, the raciness that people affected here. She must have started swimming again and had lost weight. She was dressed in a beautifully cut dark suit and lace blouse and wore her formal outfit with panache.

It had been more painful than she expected to talk about events she had wanted to put behind her. Amazing how her mind had performed the desired trick. Only six weeks and a couple of days had gone by since the *Wilhelmina* had falteringly put into Port Darwin on the north-west coast, and already the Singapore nightmare seemed like ancient history, a page the war had turned.

All the same, some part of her acknowledged that the experience would be with her until she died, and that in later years images of Singapore would dominate her dreams.

'One day someone's going to take one of Quigley's jokes the wrong way and shoot the little bastard,' Cissy said, making Violet smile.

'He wasn't an asset in Darwin. He came ashore expecting a hero's welcome and they were more concerned with digging air-raid shelters along the esplanade.' She was making it sound funnier that it had really been, less of an anti-climax.

While still ten miles out they had seen the smoke rising from the coastline and assumed there must be freak bush-fires. As they limped in it became apparent their dangers were still not over for the fuel dumps were still burning and the ship lanes even in this mighty harbour were strewn with wrecks. Once ashore, they learned that there had been two heavy raids in 48 hours, the first involving 70 Japanese bombers with a heavy fighter escort. That helped explain why they hadn't bothered to finish off the battle-scarred *Wilhelmina*. There were more important targets.

Quigley had scrambled out of the launch, with the last bottle of rum in his gladstone bag, and straight into another story, the first attack on the Australian mainland.

It had left the garrison trigger-happy and the civilian population, who had borne the brunt of the attack, traumatised and forlorn. They had thought themselves a protected backwater, a community so notoriously inaccessible that it attracted men on the run, and here they were in a war zone. There were no defences to speak of, because they had always relied on geography. Now there was barbed wire being unrolled along the shore and people cast anxious looks north as if expecting an invasion force to appear over the rim of the South China Sea.

In this front line atmosphere Violet knew at once that it would be hard to circumvent 'red tape' and bureaucratic hostility to those unusual, ill-documented refugees.

'I don't care what you say, lady, they all look like bloody Nips to me,' one immigration officer had said. This was no moment to make unnecessary enemies but Quigley contrived to provoke everyone they met. Finally, bored to distraction by the interminable delays, he went some way to convincing a young customs officer that Sister Joseph, the Mother Superior's horn-rimmed Goanese deputy, was Tojo, the Japanese prime minister, in disguise.

It was not an easy time to establish new lives for a party of oriental-looking children and without Con Lynch's discreet intervention they might have spent the rest of the war in an internment camp. As it was, within a month all but three children, who had gone to live with Jeannie in Glendevon, had found foster homes.

'So, it came out all right in the end?' Cissy said, closing her book. She had been taking notes from time to time but without any effort to get it down verbatim. Violet sensed a slacking of interest.

'Are you going to print this?'

'To be honest I doubt it.'

'Why's that?'

'This will be a decision for Jerry but my guess is the words Singapore and refugees kill it dead. Nobody wants to hear about Singapore any more than the British want to dwell on Dunkirk. And refugees aren't an issue now. Nobody can get through from Europe. People here are wondering whether they're going to become refugees themselves.'

'Why did you ask me then?'

'I wanted to hear for myself how bad it had been. Remember, I encouraged you to go.'

'For all the good I did poor Joseph I might as well have stayed in the CORB office.' She sighed. One day she'd tell Cissy the whole story about Joseph, but not now.

'I adored Joseph,' Cissy said finally, 'but I'm not surprised about what happened. It was inevitable, somehow. He either half wanted to die, or something in him had died already before he came here. It wasn't like James. That shook me, because James didn't want to die at all.'

She looked as though she was on the verge of saying something else, but evidently she changed her mind. Delicately, she removed a bone from her filletted sole. 'At least we can still get good fish,' she said, draining her glass of wine. 'Although the price of lobster's gone through the roof. Isn't this like old times?'

'In some ways it is.'

'And others?' Cissy prompted.

'Well, look around here. There's not a man under fifty, and so many women eating together. And waitresses instead of waiters.' She stopped herself. 'I sound just like my mother writing about the horrors of London in 1939. Waitresses in the Savoy Grill.'

And also like Bunty who so loathed the war, which she saw as a plot against herself and the British Empire, in that order. Its only consolation had been the two 'reffo' children off the *Batory*, already tanned Australian children in the magenta and grey uniforms of the city's most exclusive convent. Dick had been absent for over a year serving as a lieutenant on board HMAS *Shropshire*. As Bunty never tired of saying, the cruiser was a gift from Britain to the royal Australian navy.

'Can you take a break and come down to Jeannie's with me?' Violet suggested to Cissy on impulse. 'Like old times.'

'Far too busy, Vi,' Cissy said. 'I've got to do my bit for the war effort here, and also for me. Do you know that 80 percent of Australian women rely on one of our magazines for everything from knitting patterns to assurances that the Japs won't ever get here. As for the war, I wish it would go on forever. How long do you think it would have taken me to become a director of APP in peacetime? I could have waited a thousand years. And once the men come home with their medals I'll be fighting for my life because they'll want every woman to become shorthand-stenographers and call them "Sir". That's not going to happen, by the way. I've made sure.'

'Doesn't the war scare you? With Australia so unprotected?'

'Not me, Vi. The Yanks are supposed to be getting here any day – and anyway it's the peace that scares me. Remember, I was brought up in the last one. They'll all come home, or most of them, and find there's nothing here. Like my dad after the last war – they gave him thirty acres of bush no one could cultivate in a hundred years and finally it killed him.'

Violet was wondering whether Ben might be with the Americans. She had heard nothing since first sending her report via the embassy in Canberra and she was terrified to make enquiries in case it turned out that he was a casualty. The more she thought about it, the more she realised how lucky she had been. Maybe another sacrifice would be demanded. It wasn't a track she could follow without starting to feel giddy.

She hoped that Ben had read the exhaustive document she and Captain van Steenwyjk had prepared from the logs. They had used very sober language but they were both proud of the story. The only other person who really knew what had happened was Quigley. To his despair (and her private relief), the epic account of their escape which had kept him feverishly occupied for most of their last 72 hours at sea had first been blue-pencilled into gibberish and finally confiscated altogether by the Military Censor.

To add insult to injury he had also been forbidden to cable a word about the raids on Darwin, or about the recent attack on the railway junction at Katherine, 200 miles south.

They passed through Katherine themselves a day later on a very slow train. The children were happy singing their new songs, 'Waltzing Mathilda' and 'Roll Out The Barrel'. You could already hear the beginnings of an Australian intonation. Meanwhile, Quigley drank rum and looked out of the windows in horror at the desert spreading to infinity on both sides of the track. His chagrin at the loss of his story would have been comical if he hadn't looked so ill. He had even lost interest in Violet since they arrived on Australian soil.

'Do you miss James?' Cissy said suddenly, breaking in on her thoughts.

Violet looked at her friend with surprise.

'Miss him? When he went away we were on bad terms, I don't know if you knew. It was like a war. We'd been bombarding each other for years.'

'I thought it might be like that,' Cissy answered in a thoughtful voice, and then continued with another questioning look.

'I heard on the news that Gareth had dinner at the White House and, did you hear, Mae West was among the guests also present?'

'He ought to marry her,' Violet said, laughing. 'She's the kind of hostess he needs to keep his career going.'

'Did he ask you to marry him on that basis?'

Violet gave Cissy a surprised look. 'What makes you think that?'

'Oh, I've known about you and Gareth for a long time, but I was just guessing about him proposing marriage. But it makes sense. He was always jealous of everything James had.'

'That's not flattering to me, even if it's true,' Violet said. 'But you could be right, unfortunately. How long have you known?'

'Since Brisbane.'

'That awful hotel.'

'Of course. Even though I'd suspected, I hadn't known for sure. I felt I'd been very naive, but then of course so I was.'

'No more than I was. Why didn't you ever say anything?'

'I couldn't talk to you. I was jealous, you see.'

'What do you mean?'

'I had an affair with him too – oh, not like yours, I don't suppose, more a night here and there. It started in Melbourne during the campaign while I was still on the *Gazette*. It was after that, Gar gave me the job. God, I wanted that job, Vi. Do you understand that?'

Violet nodded. She had wanted the WIC job and CORB, so much that she didn't much question how they came to her.

'And I wanted him too. He seemed like a genius, a god almost. And he was free. It wasn't such a crazy idea until I found out about you, and that really put me in my place. You were beautiful, rich, I obviously hadn't a chance. But then he couldn't marry you. I soon found out he wasn't going to marry anyone, me least of all, and it was humiliating. But I wanted the prestige and power, and I wanted to be near him, even when I'd taken over from Pountney and was doing his covering up for him.'

'I knew there had to be worse to come,' Violet said flatly. 'And Rowena Campbell?'

Cissy shrugged.

'All right, I lied to you. It was the only direct lie I ever told you. Gar did know her in London.'

'And he wanted to marry her?'

'Yes, yes, he did. When he came back from London he was set on it.'

'So she was to be his ticket out?'

'I expect so, but ex-prime ministers didn't appeal to her in the same way. Not long after he resigned, she announced her engagement to someone else.'

'Poor Gareth.'

They had finished the bottle of wine and Cissy signalled to the waitress for two more glasses.

'What's happened to the priest?' Cissy asked, 'I hear you banned him from Killymoon.'

'It was tempting – but Daisy would miss him of course. What I did was ban him from me.'

'Somebody said that he was James's only friend,' Cissy said and then asked, 'Could the Father be a bit – you know. . . ?'

'God knows, but I'm sure he's a bit mad. He wanted me unhappy. It suited him.'

As they were waiting for the bill, Violet said, 'I used to envy you your freedom. Your job.'

'Every woman in Australia envied you.'

'Was it all my fault? Would Gar still be prime minister today if it hadn't been for me?'

'I don't see anyone else to blame,' Cissy replied. She was laughing as she said it, but Violet knew that she was speaking the truth.

'So we're going to forget the interview?' Violet said, as they walked to their cars.

'I'm a bit surprised to be honest. I'd have thought Jerry would be keen . . .'

'To have something in about you?' Cissy added.

'Yes,' Violet replied. 'That's how he used to be.'

'Well, you're wrong,' Cissy said with an edge that was entirely unexpected. 'Those days are gone – he's going to marry me.'

'You?' There was no point trying to conceal her surprise.

'Yes, he's asked me to marry him. The last bachelor in Sydney. I think he wants a wife to help him run the business.' She was so delighted with her news she could hardly stop grinning.

'I know you're wondering why. I know. The poor old sod can't get over not being in the war. You know he's got gall-stones? Pathetic, isn't it? And flat feet. And he's one of the richest men in Australia. You'd think he'd bless his luck, wouldn't you?'

Cissy was certainly blessing hers.

Driving home, Violet thought again of her own luck. She was glad she had been to Singapore, to a place where she had been tested to the limits and survived. The incident on the rickshaw had liberated her and also brought back memories. She knew now that she couldn't have prevented the rape, couldn't have changed the course of things. She knew, too, that now she was better equipped to deal with the world – and at last she was free of the guilt.

A week later, wearing an old pair of gardening boots and a light raincoat, she was in the garden cutting roses. They were too big really, caricatures as Quigley called them. They had been exceptional this year, she thought, flowering late into the autumn as if to thwart all the destruction in the world. The huge yellow blooms were heavy, rich with scent. She could hear Sam and Liz arguing on the tennis court about whether a ball had been in or out and for a moment debated whether to go over and adjudicate. In the end she left them to it.

Haya was living at Killymoon, standing in for Maeve, the children's nanny, who was now working as a machinist producing naval uniforms. Sam and Liz had evolved a form of pidgin with her – unintelligible to anyone else – and Violet liked having her there. She was endlessly kind to Daisy, and though they couldn't communicate, Haya spent many hours walking her round the garden, helping her up and down the steps. Since James's death she had become very feeble.

Violet had closed off a part of the house, and the family of women and children were living between George's study and the kitchen. The previous weekend Bunty had come over for lunch with her two well-behaved children. Maeve and her younger sister were there too, visiting Sam and Liz. They had sat down to lunch in the servants' kitchen, round the long refectory table. It had been like eating in a girls' boarding school – or perhaps a nunnery.

Maeve had been wearing overalls, and Violet was in her oldest clothes. She'd given up dressing to please men, but it went further than that. She'd given up trying to please men at all. It was the first time in her life that she wasn't obliged to be a clothes horse, or modify her behaviour to ensure a man's approval.

Apart from the priest's discreet arrivals and departures there hadn't been any men in the house until Tony Quigley had demanded refuge. Before that he had been trying to move heaven and earth so that his epic escape story could be sent to London. The authorities had refused point blank, and remained indifferent to his arguments that there could be no breach of military security as Singapore had long fallen. In the end he had even had an interview with Lynch.

Violet had known Quigley's story was doomed from the start. The refugee programme for children was well and truly over. Churchill had always considered it a sign of cowardice – and now the doors of Europe were closed altogether to civilians.

Sam and Liz had taken to Quigley. They had found him singing in the garden and mistakenly assumed he was doing it to entertain them. From then on, they never left him alone. They had inveigled him into agreeing to try to repair their tree house – sadly dilapidated since Sean's departure to the navy. It was a task far beyond him, so Violet had ended up repairing the roof, balanced precariously on the knotted branches of the mulberry trees. Once she had replaced the carpet inside the little wooden hut, Quigley had come sauntering across the garden, a gin and tonic in his hand, and ascended the wooden ladder. He said it was a place where a man could lick his wounds. Later on, she had been alarmed when he tried to get Haya up with him.

He had earnestly tried to persuade Hooker to employ him on the *Gazette* as a gossip columnist, but Hooker was wary of the crazed English journalist and so Quigley had gone to Hawaii, cadging a lift with the airforce. Once in Honolulu he was sure he could find his way back to civilisation.

'Come with me, Vi,' he had said, standing in the hall in Killymoon, his battered suitcase and typewriter on the marble floor beside him. 'You'll rot here. You're turning into a bloody maroon.'

'I'll be fine, Quigley. I like it here.'

'If you ask me, it's like being on a very large south sea island, only without the dancing-girls. Doesn't it make you feel lonely?'

'Not any more. I lost that years ago.'

War meant that you couldn't make a decision. There had been more news about Gareth's diplomatic success in the newspapers and though Quigley was right that the war had marooned her from the world, she was glad she hadn't gone with him. It was a breathing space in which to

345

decide: whether to go back to England or stay in Australia. She was aware that she was mentally preparing herself for departure and the prospect saddened and excited her simultaneously. She couldn't express what Australia meant to her – but both a sweetness in the place, and its emptiness, had entered her spirit. For Gareth, she knew, life in the 'old country' seemed more real, as it did to Bunty: it fulfilled their childhood dreams. Her own memories of London, revived by Quigley, were like a charade. Sydney was where her life had begun.

It wasn't an easy place but in its oblique way it had been good to her.

She heard the car turning into the driveway. A black Packard, a car she didn't know, but a very new car, surprising to see in wartime. Then she was running across the lawn which so needed cutting.

'Ben, Ben, you're back,' she skidded to a halt in front of him. He kissed her on the cheek, then held her at arm's length. 'I could look at you for ever,' he said.

He was wearing a full colonel's uniform and when he saw the questioning look in her eyes said:

'I've joined up – advance guard for MacArthur and his brass. They're coming to save you from the Yellow Peril next week.'

Sam and Liz came loping across the lawn, tennis rackets under their arms. Ben shook Sam's hand and lifted Liz up to kiss her on both cheeks. Opening the boot, he took out a brown cardboard box, marked Hershey, and handed it to the wide-eyed children who squealed with delight.

'They'll want you to come every day,' Violet said as the children disappeared towards the tree house.

Ben was producing bounty like a pirate. The fabled nylon stockings, Chanel No. 5. There was no end to what they had in Hawaii.

Violet brought drinks from the house and they sat on the terrace.

'I have a present for you.' He handed her a wrapped parcel.

Inside was a copy of Evelyn Waugh's *Vile Bodies*.

'Where on earth did you see Quigley?' she said.

'In Honolulu. He said the States were the safest place for the rest of the war. You know he claims to be writing your life story?'

'God forbid.'

'It's amazing stuff,' Ben said, reflectively. 'Of course, if I hadn't had my own sources of information, I wouldn't have believed a word of it.'

She poured him another drink and tucked her legs up under her on the bench. In the twilight, her eyes were huge.

'He has a mission to communicate the latest story, the more scurrilous the better. They wouldn't let him do it here, and it made him ill.'

'He thinks the world of you. He said, you're the nearest thing to Cleopatra that he was ever likely to see. And he reckoned he'd met every interesting woman in five continents.'

'Did he really say "met"?'

Ben laughed. 'You know the guy too well. The truth is he used another short word.'

'He thinks you're going to waste here and ought to get married again.'

She looked at Ben's finely lined, shrewd face. She couldn't remember being so happy, so content.

'I haven't got a very good record as far as marriage is concerned. It didn't work out as it was supposed to.'

'Yeah, and you really believed in it. Like Litzie believed in Uncle Joe Stalin and the inevitable revolution.'

'You must have been laughing at me . . .'

'You were just young. And were you determined? I'd never seen anything to match it. You were going to get the guy. If it meant climbing the Great Wall of China or crossing the Kalahari to do it, then that's what you'd have done.'

'I knew what I wanted. The trouble is, I wanted the wrong thing.'

'You should have stuck to hunting money and power. Those don't let you down. Now, the human heart . . .' he said, folding his arm round her shoulder.

'You're getting philosophical, like Quigley when he's had a few Tigers. What was the Sage's last word on my future? How does he see my book ending?'

'Modesty forbids me to name names,' Ben said laughing, 'but he seemed to think your destiny was a temporary colonel in the American army.'

'What a nerve the man has,' she said, taking his hand.

'Maybe so,' Ben replied easily, 'but he always gets it right in the end.'

347